Russell Andrews is the pseudonym of Peter Gethers, author of 'The Cat Who Travelled . . .' books and roving editor with Random House New York.

Also by Russell Andrews

Hades
Gideon
Aphrodite
Midas

ICARUS

Russell Andrews

SPHERE

First published in the United States in 2001 by Doubleday,
a division of Random House, Inc.
First published in Great Britain in 2001 by Little, Brown and Company
This edition reissued by Sphere in 2017

13 5 7 9 10 8 6 4 2

A CIP catalogue record for this book
is available from the British Library.

ISBN 978-0-7515-6985-8

Printed and bound in Great Britain by
Clays Ltd, St Ives plc

Papers used by Sphere are from well-managed forests
and other responsible sources.

MIX
Paper from
responsible sources
FSC® C104740

Sphere
An imprint of
Little, Brown Book Group
Carmelite House
50 Victoria Embankment
London EC4Y 0DZ

An Hachette UK Company
www.hachette.co.uk

www.littlebrown.co.uk

To Janis
who has long deserved her very own, separate
dedication page and now has it.
Way to go, S.P.

ACKNOWLEDGMENTS

First and foremost, William Goldman, who deserves more than a mere acknowledgment for his extraordinary generosity, but it's the best I can do at the moment. This is for the idea, the inspiration, the wisdom, the *many* readings and conversations, the dinners, the wine, the basketball tickets, the e-mails, and the friendship. To make it official: he's one of the main reasons I became a writer and one of the main reasons I'm able to remain a writer.

And not too far behind, thanks to: Steve Eckler, Richard Coriane, Kerry Heffernan, and everyone at Eleven Madison Park for their info, expertise, and amazing willingness to share as well as let me get underfoot; Rocco Musacchia for his technical advice; Kathleen Moloney and Lynn Waggoner for their long-distance help; Dr. Roy Riddick for his expertise as a coroner; Doc Feldman for explaining all things medical so even I could understand them; Bruce Hanson for his extensive knowledge of physical therapy and personal training; Susan Burden for being the first "normal" reader to like the book; Wanda, Giovanna, and Paolo Tornabene for being the greatest of friends as well as the greatest of cooks and for, literally, sustaining me for the crucial two hundred pages; Ming Chew for the Team; Steve Rubin for his professionalism, graciousness, willingness to gamble, and enthusiasm from the very first *Gideon* conversation at the Halcyon; Bill Thomas for his superb editing as well as his calm and support during the storm; Hilary Hale for absolutely everything, past, present, and now future; Jack Dytman for many things but especially for working and calling me back even when I'm not making him a dime; and, as always, Esther Newberg, for her selling, her confidence, her friendship, and even for making me write her goddamn speeches.

Finally, a special acknowledgment to Linda Grey. I wish I could tell you in person, but thank you for this book, for giving me a new career, and for being nothing but honorable and straight in a business all too often not up to your standards.

. . . o my chevalier!
No wonder of it: sheer plod makes plough down sillion
Shine, and blue-bleak embers, ah my dear,
Fall, gall themselves, and gash gold-vermillion.

—Gerard Manley Hopkins, *The Windhover*

"Each betrayal begins with trust."

—Phish, *Farmhouse*

BOOK ONE

THE

FIRST

FALL

1969

The day started out beautifully for ten-year-old Jack Keller.

First, Miss Roebuck, his fifth-grade teacher, was out sick, which meant he had a substitute teacher, which meant he didn't really have to do much work, which meant he could do some serious daydreaming about the Knicks, particularly Willis Reed, whom he pretty much worshiped. Second: Dom was taking him to a game that night, just the two of them, and there was nothing he liked more than going to a Knicks game with Dom. Ever since he'd been four years old, which was when they first met, man and boy had connected. There was just something about the crusty old man—he kept telling Jack he was only forty-four but Jack insisted on calling him "old man"—that made Jack feel safe and protected. He was never afraid of Dom's temper, which could be terrible, or put off by his curmudgeonly nature, which could drive almost everyone else crazy. People seemed to shrink back from Dom as if they were frightened of him, but Jack never understood what it was that frightened them. Dom was thin and wiry and he used to be a boxer, so he looked tough, but a lot of guys looked tough without scaring people. They couldn't possibly *know* about Dom. Not the thing that Jack knew, anyway. That was a secret. A *big* secret. If they knew, Jack thought, they'd *really* be frightened. But sometimes, especially when they were together in public, he thought that maybe Dom's secret was the kind of thing you didn't really have to *know*. Maybe it was the kind of thing you could understand simply by looking.

Then again, it could have been the old man's arm that made everyone uneasy; people never knew how to deal with stuff like that. Jack had never thought there was anything much to deal with. Dom was just Dom, arm and all, and when they were at the Garden, he would let Jack eat as many hot dogs as he wanted—his record was four—and drink Coke, which his mom hardly ever let him do.

Third: As if all that wasn't enough, the Celtics were in town that night, so he'd actually get to see, in person, the despised John Havlicek and Bill Russell, whom Jack knew he was supposed to hate, being a Knicks fanatic and all, but whom he had to admit, although never out loud, he really kind of liked.

When he got home from school, his day stayed just about perfect, too. Billy Kruse's mom walked him home, with Billy, because they lived a couple of buildings away. Jack's mom wasn't home from work yet, which was fine with Jack because he liked being alone. He could do his homework and sneak in some TV and daydream some more. Sometimes he daydreamed about his father, whom he hardly remembered. His mom had told him that his dad was dead, that he'd died when Jack was just a baby, but lately he'd begun to suspect otherwise. He wasn't exactly sure why he didn't believe her, except it just didn't ring true. He'd heard about men who'd deserted their families or who'd gone to prison—that wasn't so uncommon in Hell's Kitchen; Billy Kruse's dad was in for three years for armed robbery—and something about the way his mom told her story made him think his dad hadn't really died, that he'd just run away. Or been taken away. Jack asked Dom about it once because Dom had known Jack's dad, had been his friend—Bill Keller had worked at Dom's meatpacking plant—and Dom said, "He's gone, Jackie. That's all that matters." When Jack had said, "Yeah, but is he *dead*?" all Dom said back was "Gone is gone."

At about five o'clock, his mom called and said Dom was going to pick him up in about half an hour. "Isn't it kind of early?" he asked, and she said, "He's bringing you up here to my office before the game. I want to talk to you."

"Did I do somethin' wrong?" Jack asked and his mother laughed. "No, sweetie," she told him. "I just want to see you. I have something to tell you. Something good."

"Cool," he said, and he meant it because he liked his mom, even more than he liked Willis Reed, and he liked going to her office. She was a paralegal at a law firm. The office was in a midtown skyscraper, on the seventeenth floor, and it had a great view of the East River and Queens through its oversized windows. Jack liked to go right up to the window and put his nose flat up against the glass. He'd stretch his arms out, as high as he could get them, spread his legs just as wide, pressing as hard as he could against the pane, and pretend that he was flying. Earlier that year, Miss Roebuck had taught the class about Greek mythology. Jack's favorite story was the one about Daedalus and Icarus. He even went to the library and checked out several books, reading everything he could about the boy who dared to fly too close to the sun. Jack loved the idea of making wings, then soaring higher and higher up toward the heavens. He thought about it almost every day, imagining that he was Icarus, leaving the earth behind, going higher than anyone had ever gone. Mostly he thought only of the glory, and he could see himself so clearly that it became real to him. He could feel the air rushing over his body; he could immerse himself in the silence of flight and thrill in the extraordinary freedom. But sometimes he dared to think about the fall. Like Icarus, he, too, would climb too high and his wings would melt, and then Jack could feel, in the pit of his stomach, the sensation of plummeting, of falling straight down, and the fear that overcame him would jar him out of his fantasy and he'd find himself in his room or in class, his hands shaking, his mouth dry, and his fingers clenched tightly around whatever he could grasp as if that thing were a lifeline safely tethering him to the ground.

But up in his mother's office, arms raised, there was never any fear. Just outstretched arms and cool window glass against his body. And he could be the triumphant Icarus, flying out over the river, above the whole city. Looking down at the world, climbing toward the sun . . .

Jack quickly finished up his homework, nothing too hard, mostly math, and changed into a pair of jeans, sneakers, his gray Knicks T-shirt, and his blue and orange Knicks jacket. Then he went outside on the stoop to wait for Dom to pick him up. Sitting there on the rough cement, he wondered what his mom was going to tell him and if the Knicks would win that night. He wondered a little bit more about his dad, too. But mostly he wondered how many hot dogs he was going to be able to eat. He decided that tonight he was going to go for a new record.

JOANIE KELLER WAS nervous.

She didn't understand it exactly. She knew what she was nervous *about* but she didn't really know *why*.

Possibly it was because, more than anything else in her life, Joan Keller wanted her son to be happy and she didn't know if what she was going to tell him would *make* him happy. If it didn't, she wasn't quite sure what she would do. Go ahead with the plans anyway? She didn't know if she could do that. *Don't* go ahead with the plans? She didn't know if she could do that either. Oh, God. When she thought about it like that, she guessed she did know why she was nervous.

She didn't want to think about it right now, she'd thought about nothing else for days, so she decided she'd keep herself busy and get some tiresome filing out of the way. But it didn't take her long before her brow was furrowed and her lips were moving and she was practicing exactly what she was going to say. This is nuts, she realized. He's ten years old and he's a great kid, so why *wouldn't* he be happy with the news? There was no reason that she could think of. No reason at all. So just tell him and hug him and kiss him and hope that he hugged and kissed her back. And, of course, he would. That's *exactly* what he'd do. So why be nervous? Pretty soon they'd be hugging and kissing and laughing all over the place.

She checked her watch. It was five-fourteen. Any second now Gerald Aarons, one of her three bosses—the most important of the three, he really ran the place—would come out of his office, glance at her, mumble something nearly incoherent, and head toward the elevator. He did it every day, unless he had an important meeting, leaving right at a quarter after five so he could make the five forty-five train to Westport. The minute hand on Joanie's watch moved and . . . Yup. Right on time. Gerald's door was opening, he was stepping into the outer office, and there it was—the glance, something that sounded vaguely like "gnightseeya," and then he was down the hall and gone. It didn't take long for the rest of the office doors to open and shut. Soon the hallway was filled with three-piece suits rushing by. Most of the lawyers were gone by five-thirty since almost all of them had commutes and families waiting for them, too. The ones who didn't left just as early. They had martinis or stewardesses or poker games waiting for *them*.

Okay, enough worrying about Jack, Joanie thought. It was ridiculous. There was nothing to worry about. Nothing at all. He'd come, she'd tell him, he'd be thrilled. No problem. So just get back to work, she told herself. How often does this happen? You've got half an hour, free and clear, to really clean up your desk. No one's going to bother you now. There's no one left *to* bother you.

With a little shake of her head, Joanie realized it paid to be a lawyer instead of a paralegal. It was five thirty-one and the place was already deserted.

Unbelievable, she thought. One minute after quitting time.

Empty.

Just one meager minute and she was all alone in the office.

REGGIE IVERS WAS certain that people were staring at him and he hated that. Really hated that. It made him crazy.

Walking quickly down Forty-second Street—no one was walking as fast as he was, he was passing them by like they weren't even moving—Reggie giggled. So what if they were looking? It couldn't really make him *crazy*. He *wasn't* crazy. That's what the doctors had told him. Maybe he'd *been* crazy. But not anymore.

He'd never *felt* crazy, Reggie thought. But he must have been. At least, if he'd really done what everyone said he'd done. You'd have to be crazy to do that. To go up to a complete stranger on the street and hurt her like that. When he heard the details, he actually got sick. Look, he said to the lawyers, I *couldn't* have done it. It made me sick to my stomach just hearing about it. But the lawyers insisted he *did* do it and everyone else seemed to agree.

Christ.

He could never have done such a thing. Pick up an empty beer bottle on the street? That alone, with all the germs, was disgusting enough. Really. He would never do *that*, much less the other stuff. Much less hold the bottle in his hand and break it, smash it so it was all jagged and sharp and deadly. And then go up to a stranger in the street, a total stranger, and . . . and . . .

He couldn't even think about it. It was too awful. Too sick.

Too crazy.

She needed three hundred stitches, they said in court. And she lost an eye.

How could he have done such a thing?

He couldn't, that's how.

It was all the lawyers' fault. They made everyone believe he was guilty. No, not that, worse than guilty. Crazy. His own lawyer! Telling the whole world he was as cuckoo as a loon! And then smiling afterward, telling him how happy he should be because they weren't putting him in prison, they were putting him in a place for loons. A special hospital for nut jobs.

God, he hated fucking lawyers. Hated them the whole time he was in the loony bin. Seven years of hate. And getting out hadn't changed anything. It had been thirty days since they told him he wasn't crazy anymore. Thirty days since he'd been back on the streets. He'd hated them every one of those days, too. Every single minute of every single day for thirty days . . .

Reggie Ivers realized he'd stopped walking.

He must have walked really fast because it was pretty chilly and even though he wasn't wearing a jacket he was sweating. But why did he stop? Where was he?

Reggie looked up at the numbers over the front of the tall building on the corner: 527 East Forty-second Street. Why did that sound familiar? Why did he know that address?

He heard the sound of paper rustling and he looked down, realized there was paper in his hand. Yellow paper. He smoothed it out, saw it was from a phone book. Oh, yeah. He'd been looking in a phone book, he remembered that now. But why? What was he looking for?

Now he remembered that, too.

He was looking for lawyers. Lying, cheating, cocksucking lawyers.

Reggie stared at the ripped-out yellow page, saw that he'd circled the name of a lawyer at the top of the page. The first lawyer in the phone book. It was the name of a firm.

Aarons, Reuss and Seaver.

And look at this. Look at their address: 527 East Forty-second Street. Right where he was.

Son of a bitch, Reggie Ivers thought. What a coincidence.

And you'd have to be crazy not to believe in coincidences.

DOM BERTOLINI WALKED with Jack into the lobby of the building on First Avenue and Forty-second Street.

"You know what floor she's on, right?"

"Seventeen. Aren't you comin' up?"

"No," Dom said. As usual, he spoke in a raspy growl and he knew it sounded harsher than he wanted it to. "I think she wants to talk to you herself. I'll be up in a little while."

"What's goin' on?" Jack asked. "What's the big secret?"

"You'll just have to ask her," Dom said. And then, with his good hand, he brushed Jack's hair back off his forehead. "We can talk about it at the game, Jackie, just you and me. But now I'm gonna take a little stroll around the block. And then I'll come up and see how you guys are doin'."

"Do you have to call me Jackie?"

Dom nodded. "It's what I've always called you."

"Grown-ups are weird," Jack said.

"You have no idea," Dom told him. "I'll see ya on seventeen."

He waited as Jack went up to the security guard, signed himself in, then stepped into the elevator. Dom watched the elevator door close before releasing the breath he'd been holding inside. Then he went back to the revolving door, pushed and stepped through, back to the sidewalk. He noticed the tall, skinny guy in the T-shirt coming across the street, heading right toward him, but he didn't really pay attention. He watched the guy go through the revolving door and into the building but all Dom thought was "Geez, he's walkin' fast." Then he shrugged and went for his stroll around the block.

REGGIE WISHED HE wasn't sweating so much when he went up to the guard at the front desk.

"What floor are the lawyers on?" he asked.

The guard smiled at him, not a friendly smile, more like you're-a-dumbshit smile, and said, "We got a lot of lawyers in this building. Which ones you want?"

Reggie held the yellow paper up so the guard could see it.

"Aarons, huh?" the guard said. "They're on seventeen but I think everyone's pretty much gone. You got a name? I can call up and see if he's still there."

When Reggie didn't answer, the guard repeated, "You got a name, pal? Or are you just droppin' somethin' off?"

"Droppin' off," Reggie said. "Droppin' somethin' off."

"Why don't you just leave it with me?" the guard told him. "I'll give it to 'em in the morning."

"Okay," Reggie said.

The guard waited but Reggie didn't move. "I don't see no package," he said. "You got somethin' or don't you?"

"I got somethin'," Reggie told him.

"Well, where is it?"

"Right here," Reggie said. And he pulled out the knife he'd been carrying in his back pocket, the one that folded, that he'd bought on the street a few days ago, and without another word he stabbed the guard in the heart, three, four, five, six, seven times, until he stopped moaning or moving or breathing. Reggie dragged the guard's body behind the lobby desk so no one would see it. Then he went to the elevator and pressed the up button.

It took him a second to remember what the guard had said, where he was going. Then he remembered.

He stepped into the elevator and headed up to the seventeenth floor.

JACK SAW HIS mom across the room, her back to him, busy filing. She didn't hear the elevator so she didn't know he was there. Half the lights were off and it looked like hardly anyone else was around. It was a little after six and the whole floor was in shadows; it was pretty spooky, and Jack knew he shouldn't do it, but he couldn't resist. He crept up until he was right behind her, she never heard a thing, and then he grabbed her around the waist and went "Boo!"

His mom jumped about three feet in the air and spun around. But when she landed she wasn't angry. She said, "Oh, my God, you scared me to death!" Then she hugged him, held him tight, and kissed him. She didn't usually hug him for so long, so when she let him go he ran across the room, right for one of the big windows. He pressed himself spread-eagle against the glass. Peering out over the city, he said, "Look, I'm flying, Mom, I'm flying!"

She was smiling at him, but he thought she looked a little . . . what was the word she liked to use sometimes? . . . edgy. Kind of like she had something to do and wanted to get it over with as quickly as possible. She looked like he imagined *he* looked in the doctor's office right before he had to get a shot. Like something not so great was coming but then afterward you know you'll feel better.

"What is it, Mom?" he asked. He put his arms down and slid his feet together and took one step away from the window toward her. "Whatever it is . . ."

What he was going to say was ". . . it'll be all right," but he didn't get to finish the sentence because she wasn't watching him now, she was frowning and looking to her left, toward the elevators. Some guy had just stepped out and was walking up to her. He looked kind of weird, Jack thought, and he smelled bad. The man was sopping wet, too, almost like he'd been swimming, but he couldn't have been, so it had to be sweat. Jack had never *seen* anybody sweat so much. And the guy's clothes were filthy. He'd spilled something all over himself. On his shirt and arms, all over his neck, too. A Coke, maybe. No, maybe not. It wasn't quite the color of Coke.

The man got closer, was just a few feet away from his mother now. Jack saw that whatever the sticky-looking stuff was that he'd spilled, it was definitely not the color of Coke. But it was all *over* the guy. Even on his face and on his shoes.

And whatever it was, it was awfully red . . .

"ARE YOU ALL right?" Joanie asked. "You're bleeding."

As soon as the man stepped off the elevator, Joan understood that something terrible was happening. This man should not have been allowed up to their floor. There was an emptiness in his eyes, a disturbing lack of humanity. And he was covered in blood, it was soaking through his clothes. At first she thought he was hurt, but he wasn't walking like he was hurt, he seemed fine, and that's when Joanie understood: it's someone *else's* blood.

That's when she knew that whatever was happening was *beyond* terrible.

"Can I help you?" She kept her voice as calm as she could. But the man didn't answer. Instead, he swiveled his head, taking in the entire office. She saw confusion on his face, then anger. She didn't know why the anger had appeared but it was definitely there and it was scary. He still didn't say anything, or even look directly at her, just kept turning his head, as if searching the empty office and bare cubicles.

Joanie felt a surge of relief because maybe the anger wasn't directed at her, maybe it was for someone who'd already left. Maybe this wasn't as bad as she'd thought . . .

"Is there someone you're looking for?" Even as she spoke the question she knew she wasn't going to get an answer. Because it *was* as bad as she'd thought. As soon as he turned back to look at her, she could feel it. The man's smell, so pungent now it swept through the office, was not just sweat and filth; he gave off the odor of violence, and all Joan could think about now was: *Get Jack out of here. Make sure nothing happens to my son.*

She tried to catch Jack's eye, he'd understand her signal, but it was already too late to signal, it was already out of her control, because the man had picked up a chair, a heavy swivel chair on rollers, swooped it up as if it weighed nothing, and hurled it through the air, straight at the window where Jack was standing. Joan watched in disbelief as the chair slammed into the glass, shattering it, the most frightening noise she had ever heard, and then crashed through. It sailed out of the building, followed by a waterfall of thousands of tiny, glistening shards, then disappeared, plummeting to the street below.

She started to run to Jack, yelling at him now to get out, to run, to just get the hell away, but then she couldn't move, something was holding her back. She felt herself rising, being lifted into the air, and she heard her son screaming, "Mom! Mommy! Mommyyyyy . . ."

At first she didn't understand, then she knew what was happening, what this lunatic was doing, and she didn't want to, but she couldn't help herself: she had to scream, too, right back at her son. And she knew she was hysterical now, but she didn't care, she didn't care about anything other than the fact that she didn't want to die, not like this, so she screamed, "Help me! Help me, Jack! For God's sake, help me!"

JACK WATCHED AS the man picked his mother up and carried her toward the shattered window. The hole that the chair had made looked like a raw wound in the glass. He saw his mom kick and punch and even try to bite, but the man didn't seem to feel any of it. Jack heard her screaming, begging him to help her. He was two feet from the window, he could feel the air being sucked in and out, could hear the horns honking down below and the people yelling as they looked up. It was hard to breathe, his stomach hurt so much now; all he wanted to do was run but he knew he couldn't. His mother was screaming, he couldn't leave her, he had to do something and he had to do it now because they were closer, the man was almost to the window, Jack could reach out and touch him . . .

Help me, Jack! You've got to help me.

He didn't know what would happen, it was the first time he'd ever tried this, but it was all he could think of, so Jack hurled himself in the air, low, shoulders down and tucked in, just like he'd seen Hornung do on TV when blocking for Taylor, and he hit the man right at the knees, exactly as he wanted to do. . . .

Jack, help me!

The man was looking down at him, surprised that he was there, as if he hadn't even felt Jack's attempt to bring him down and cut his legs out from under him. Jack tried again, grunted when he hit the man's bony shins, but it didn't do a thing. He was too light and too young and too weak and . . .

The man was raising his arms now. Jack could see his mother's eyes go wide, he could see inside her, right down into her soul and feel her total, absolute terror.

He wanted to hit the man again, to run at him and topple him, but now he was paralyzed because he knew it was helpless. *He* was helpless.

She was writhing in the man's grip, hitting him, scratching him wildly with her nails, but the man didn't so much as change expression. He just reached the window, and Jack wanted to close his eyes, but he couldn't do that either, he could only watch as the man held his mother in front of the large, jagged hole. She turned to stare at Jack, pleading, her mouth open, saliva dripping in long, messy gobs down to the floor, and she wasn't screaming anymore, she was silent now. Silent and staring and pleading with him to save her.

He wanted to answer her stare. To say, *I want to! I want to save you! But I can't! I tried, I swear to God I tried, only I can't!* But he didn't open his mouth. He was silent, too. He understood that words were of no use. Nothing was of any use . . .

His mother never said another word. She just stared at Jack, who could see the love and forgiveness, the desperation and then, finally, the sadness on her face as the man swung his arms forward and threw Joan Keller out the shattered window on the seventeenth floor.

REGGIE IVERS WONDERED where he was. He couldn't figure out why he was standing in front of this broken window and why there was this small, terrified boy cowering next to him. He knew he would never do anything to scare such a small boy, so what was going on?

His confusion deepened when he took a step toward the boy and the kid tried to run. The boy was fast but Reggie was faster and he grabbed him, held him by the wrist so he couldn't move. Reggie shook his head so the boy could see there was nothing to be frightened of but the boy wouldn't stop shivering. And now he was crying. And not just regular crying, long, choking sobs. It sounded like the noise an animal would make. An animal in the woods, in a trap, crying to be let out. Crying because it knew it was dying.

Reggie tried to will the boy to stop. The noise was horrible. Going on and on, cutting into Reggie's brain until he couldn't stand it anymore. Until he had to make it stop. It was driving him crazy. So he had no choice but to stop it.

He wondered what had happened to the woman. He remembered seeing her when he stepped out of the elevator. As he'd gotten closer, he was sure he recognized her. He knew it couldn't be, it was impossible, but he was seeing it with his own eyes so it had to be true because he wasn't crazy anymore. He was certain she was the woman on the street, the one they said he hurt. But it *couldn't* be her. That one had blonde hair and this one's hair was black. And how did she get her eye back? The one on the street only had one eye now and this one had two. Two big round brown eyes that were staring straight at him.

It was then that he realized: the lawyers, they lied again. She never lost her eye! She probably never even got hurt! It was a story they made up, the same as they made up the story that he was nutzoid. They made it all up so they could punish him and put him in the loony bin. He knew it! It was all one big lie!

And now it was too good to be true. Here he was and here she was. At the lying-liar lawyers!

Well, there was only one thing to do, wasn't there?

She'd tried to hurt him. She *had* hurt him.

So he had to hurt her right back.

Except he *couldn't* hurt her because now she was gone.

There was just the boy. The terrified, crying boy.

Maybe he should hug him, Reggie thought. Hug him and tell him he could stop crying because everything was going to be fine.

Unless, of course, he didn't stop crying. Then things wouldn't be so fine. Then he'd *make* him be quiet.

He'd *have* to, wouldn't he? What other choice did he have?

JACK WAS HORRIFIED to find himself crying. But he couldn't stop. His mother was gone and he hadn't helped her, and the man was reaching for him, was trying to pick him up, just like he'd picked up his mother, and Jack didn't want to cry, not now, but tears were all he was capable of.

He felt the man's fingers wrap around his wrist and then his shoulders. The touch of flesh against flesh repulsed him.

The man's hands seared him like an iron pressed against his skin, and without even thinking about what he was doing, Jack flung himself at the man's leg, clutching it with all his might, not trying to knock him over this time, simply refusing to let go. He could feel the man trying to shake him free, but it couldn't be done, Jack was holding on for dear life, would hold on forever if he had to because if he didn't the man would throw him out the window, too. Up close, the man's smell was even worse, it filled Jack's nostrils and made him nauseous, and the man was shaking even harder now, and pulling Jack's hair, yanking his head back, but Jack knew he'd never let go. There was nothing this man could do that would make him let go.

Then the shaking stopped, and Jack thought somehow maybe he'd won, but then he realized, no, there's no winning here, and suddenly Jack felt his insides explode. The man was beating him on the back with his fists. Slow, brutal blows hammering away at him. He felt like he might break in two, but still he wouldn't let go. *Couldn't* let go. Five minutes earlier he was pressed against the window, wanting to fly. Now he was crying and holding on to a madman's leg because he knew that flying was impossible. It was a fantasy, a dream, and not the dream of a little boy having fun with his mother or of some make-believe superhero saving the earth. It was a nightmare that had no happy ending. It was not the glorious Icarus but the Icarus with wings melting, high above the earth on a flight that ended only with an excruciating fall. With failure. With the sadness and fear he saw on his mother's face. And with death.

The man dragged his leg over to the window and Jack thought, *What's he doing, what now?* Then he could feel the man's leg kick forward and Jack's eyes widened as he realized what was happening. He tucked his chin into his chest as his shoulder and then his back and then the side of his head slammed against the thick glass. Jack remembered hitting a baseball once, shattering a window in a first-floor apartment; that's what he felt like, that baseball, because he was being skewered by new pieces of broken glass. Jack felt sharp stings in his arms and neck, he watched more glass tumble and fall, then the man gave one more kick. Again Jack was flung against the glass, only now he felt wind rushing by his face and . . .

No, no, please, no, he thought. Please, this can't be true.

But it was true. He heard screams from down below, and the heat, he could feel it soaking into him.

He was outside the building.

He was dangling, hundreds of feet above the ground, and the man was trying again to shake him loose. The man's leg was twisting back and forth, and up and down; it was like riding a bucking bronco, and Jack knew it was the wrong thing to do, to look down, but he couldn't help it. He saw new shards of glass tumble by. Then he saw a flash of the crowd, and even though he turned away it was too late. The street seemed to rush up at him, he felt as if he were already falling. He nearly let go, thought for a horrible moment that he had, was sure he was somersaulting through the air; he was the boy with the useless wings tumbling from the warm sun to the cold, hard earth, but, no, he was still holding on, his body was still banging against the window and the steel casing, his arms were still wrapped tightly around the man's leg and the man was still shaking him. Staring at him and hating him and shaking him . . .

And then the man was still. No movement at all. Jack couldn't understand it and he looked up. The man's head was twisted back toward the elevator, looking at something behind him. No, not something.

Some*one.*

The man turned back to the window now. Looked down at Jack, still dangling outside the building, unreachable, inches away from the ledge. The man laughed then. A laugh like Jack had never heard before. A wild, savage, and mad laugh that might have come from some inhuman creature, something that had risen up from hell.

And Jack knew what he had to do. Didn't know if he could do it but he knew he had to, had to if he wanted to live.

Had to so he wouldn't fall and disappear.

So he wouldn't be gone . . .

DOM LISTENED TO the lunatic laugh and he ran forward, ran as fast as he could because he understood what was going to happen. But he was too late. He couldn't stop it.

The madman at the window laughed again and, with Jack clutching the man's leg, Dom watched helplessly as the sweating man leapt out the window, a powerful jump, far away from the building, and Dom, grabbing at him, touched only air. He saw Jack's face the instant before the man jumped, saw what Jack was trying to do, and Dom said, "Yes," and then again, "Yes!" and the little boy let go . . .

JACK COULD FEEL the strength gathering in the man's legs, could feel it as surely as if they were of the same body, and a split second before the man jumped, so did Jack, but in the opposite direction, toward the building, reaching up and out with both hands for the frame of the broken window. His fingers grasped at it, and he felt a hot, slicing burn, saw blood flowing, *his* blood, as the shards in the frame sliced into his small hands, but he didn't let go. He felt the man freefall past him, saw him disappear, and now Jack was slipping. He couldn't help it. The pain and the blood made it impossible for him to hold on. He didn't have the strength to pull himself up and one hand slid away from the building and now the other hand was sliding too, it was going, he couldn't stop it, he was falling, he was gone . . .

Except he wasn't.

Someone was holding him, had him by the wrist. Was holding him steady, pulling him up with one hand, and then it was a miracle because he was back inside. He wasn't dangling over the street, he was on solid ground, and a familiar raspy voice was telling him that it was all right, that he was safe. That there was nothing to be afraid of anymore. That it was all over.

Jack grabbed Dom around the neck and cried and hugged him and listened as the old man told him that it was over. He felt Dom pick him up and begin running. He heard Dom say, *You're going to be fine, it's all over, we're going to get you to a doctor and you're going to be fine,* and Jack believed him. He closed his eyes because suddenly he couldn't keep them open anymore, and somehow he knew they were back in the elevator. As he felt the whoosh of the elevator going down, Jack did not know what was going to happen now. He understood that his mother was dead and so was the bad man. He was with Dom, he understood that, too, and somehow that felt right, Dom would keep him safe. He remembered how this day had started out so special, and he didn't understand, didn't know if he'd ever understand, how it had all gone so wrong. And before the elevator doors opened, before the policemen and the media and the emergency medical crew and the crowds that had gathered on the street began talking and yelling and taking pictures and wrapping him in a blanket and carrying him away, Jack understood one thing above all else: for the rest of his life, for as long as he lived, forever and ever, this would be the worst thing that ever happened to him.

Ten-year-old Jack Keller knew this beyond a shadow of a doubt, with absolute certainty, and it was his only comfort. He could never again be hurt like this. Never again would he feel this kind of suffering. This kind of pain or loss or paralyzing terror.

He knew it.

But he was wrong.

And many years later, when the terror came back, when the pain was worse and the suffering unimaginable, Jack understood just how wrong he'd been.

BOOK TWO

THE

SECOND

FALL

1979 – 2000

Jack Keller was twenty years old when he first thought he might be falling in love.

He'd been infatuated with Caroline Hale since he'd first seen her, sitting in a psych class, seven seats to the left and three rows behind him. Of course, in the late 1970s, just about every male on the Columbia University campus was in love with Caroline from afar. He was not the only one, by any stretch of the imagination, to keep turning and staring during that lecture. She was worth staring at.

And it wasn't just her physical beauty, although that was reason enough. It was certainly reason to crane his neck almost every day in class so he could glance furtively as often as he could. Her face was angular, yet soft and lovely. High cheekbones and lips were perfect, not too thin, not too full. Serious eyes that seemed to change with her surroundings, sometimes a piercing blue, then at times a melancholy gray, even a turbulent violet. Her hair was dark brown and straight, long enough to reach her shoulders, sometimes tied back in a ponytail that made her look seven years old. Her legs were long and muscular and tan and quite visible, usually extending from the bottom of a short black skirt, and she had a way of crossing them—particularly when she became absorbed in her extensive note taking—that was so casually provocative it made Jack's heart pound. Jack couldn't understand how her legs stayed so tan, even in the New York winters. Later, when he got to know her, found out that she came from money, it was the first thing he noted to himself about rich people: they seemed to always be tan, as if their money awarded them more sunlight than was allowed to shine down on poor people.

Jack was never tan. He was one of the poor people, there on scholarship, working at night to pay the rest of his way. He had never even thought much about having money. Not until he saw Caroline. And even then it wasn't the money he was thinking about. It was those legs that were always so brown and elegant. He wondered what he'd have to do to be allowed near them, to caress them with his rough and callused and very white hands.

He watched her for almost a whole year. Never following her, just noticing her when she was near. And not pining, either; she didn't dominate his thoughts—he had girlfriends, his life was busy and full—but never quite removing her from his consciousness. Whenever he'd see her, in a class, across a campus, at a bar or party, he'd study her, marveling at her ease. It was inconceivable to him how anyone could be so sure of herself, so relaxed and confident in any situation. Men and boys flocked to her adoringly. Women seemed not to mind, liking her despite her astonishing popularity, reveling in her friendship. Jack, from across rooms and from skewed angles, watched as she was able to let anything and anyone come to her and wash over her—and be gracious and respectful in return, all the while maintaining her distance.

The first time he heard her voice, it surprised him. It did not match up with the rest of her. He had not expected the Southern accent, which was not strong but still had a lilt that permeated every phrase. Her voice was playful rather than serious or elegant. It was ever-so-slightly hoarse, not smooth and perfect. And it was not soft and unobtrusive and gentle, as he'd imagined, but strong and commanding and barbed.

They were in a club on the Upper West Side, not far from Columbia, called Mikell's. A jazz joint, dark and not at all fancy, with good burgers and cheap beer. They weren't there together; as usual, they were on opposite ends of the room. Caroline was with a group of friends, all well dressed, all laughing and talking through the music, all egotistical enough to believe they were far more interesting than the sweet, doleful sounds emanating from the stage. Jack was alone, not particularly well dressed, and not laughing. He was a junior and in a constant state of shock at the way his horizons were expanding so rapidly. One of those expansions was his appreciation for music: rock and roll, sometimes classical, mostly jazz. In the right club on the right night with the right musicians and the right number of beers inside him, jazz could speak to him. Sweep him away into its sensual and mysterious world. This was one of those nights. He was lost in the music, which was why he didn't notice when someone sat down in the extra chair at his table. And why, when the set ended, he was stunned to discover that that someone was Caroline Hale.

"I know you," she said.

He nodded, his tongue frozen.

"From Goldman's class."

He nodded again. Since his voice had clearly deserted him, he hoped that his eyes showed pleasure.

"And from campus," she added. "I always see you looking at me."

Another nod. This one embarrassed. He knew his eyes did not show pleasure now.

"You're usually behind a tree or a statue or something. Kind of lurking."

A nod. Misery in his eyes, definitely misery.

"Can you speak?" she asked.

He nodded again and she laughed. "Do all girls make you this nervous?"

This time he shook his head.

"Only me?"

Nod.

"Good," she said, and smiled, and the smile practically knocked him backward it was so wonderful. "Would you like to join me and my friends?"

He shook his head again. Just barely.

"It's hard to keep asking yes-or-no questions." When he shrugged, she said, "Because you're a snob and you think they're assholes? My friends, I mean. Is that why you don't want to sit with us?"

He nodded. The unhappiest nod of his life.

"Hmmm. Well, I kind of agree. So do you mind if I join *you?*"

He shook his head. The happiest shake of his life.

After she signaled the waiter for a drink, a dark beer, Caroline said, "Don't you want to know why I'm sitting with you?"

He nodded.

"Because I love this music. And my friends don't get it. And I could tell you do, just by watching you. So I wanted to sit with someone who got it. Do you believe that?"

Another nod.

"Good. As long as you know that's the only reason. Because otherwise I don't think you're at all interesting or different, you're clearly just like everyone else I know, and on top of that you're not at *all* handsome."

"Do you like Italian food?" he asked. The first words he ever said to her.

She looked at him, as if surprised that he really could speak, then she nodded.

"You want to have dinner with me tomorrow night?"

She looked at him again, this time not surprised, but it was a long look, searching for something. And whatever it was she was searching for, she found, because she nodded again. A firm and decisive nod.

"What's the matter," he said, "can't you speak?"

This time she smiled another one of her smiles and shook her head, a long, slow, gentle, lovely, absolutely perfect shake.

They were together almost every minute after that. But it took four more months before he would know that he was truly in love with her, that he would have to marry her.

It was the day she met Dominick Bertolini.

AFTER JACK'S MOTHER died, Jack moved into Dom's two-bedroom Hell's Kitchen apartment. It was the most natural thing for both of them. They were good company for each other and they each provided a necessary and comforting tie to the past without ever having to talk about it.

In his early teens, Jack went to work in Dom's meatpacking plant on Gansevoort Street, spending most of his afternoons and evenings in the meat district. It wasn't a strange environment for Jack, just the opposite—it was where he felt most comfortable, where he felt grown-up. Dom paid him good money and young Jack had an affinity for the work. He was strong enough to lift and carry whole sides of beef, strong enough even to hack through just about anything. The blood didn't bother him. It was simply part of the job, something to deal with. The fact is, he liked the cold rooms, the sawdust on the floors, the stark walls, the carcasses hanging from hooks, surrounding him. He loved being around Dom, listening to his stories of the old days in New York, the saloons, the personalities, the infamy that had followed him around when he was young. It was most definitely a man's world and Jack was comfortable living in it. And he stayed there quite happily until he was old enough to move eighty blocks uptown and go to college.

But it took Jack quite a while before he could bring Caroline downtown to meet Dom that first time, to see the other side of his life, which she knew nothing about. Even after several months of dating, he was nervous about it. It was an alien world to her, as alien as her world, as she described it, would be to him. If hers was a world of privilege and refinement, his was dominated by sweat and hard work and the need to survive. He was afraid to bring her there, he told her. And the fear was not that she wouldn't like his world—that would not make him happy but he could deal with it—it was that she would cause him to dislike it also.

She didn't say anything when he told her this. Just said that she understood. Then, after a few months, they were having lunch—his treat, a Coke and a souvlaki in Central Park—and she turned to him and said, "Are you ready?" He knew immediately what she meant and he thought for a moment, then nodded and said, surprised, "Yeah, okay, I'm ready." But he prepared her first.

He couldn't do this to her without preparing her. So first he told her about his own past, told her more about himself than he'd ever told anyone.

Jack explained to Caroline that he had come to terms with the tragedy that cast such a long shadow over his youth. He'd *had* to come to terms with it—because he'd lived *through* it and because he knew he had to keep on living *with* it. It was what had happened, the way Little League or broken arms or divorce had happened to other children. But when she began to ask questions, tentative and careful but never embarrassed or awkward, and then to touch his arm gently and probe, as if it were her right to know everything there was to know about him, he admitted that sometimes he still awoke in the middle of the night, horrified at the images that flitted before his eyes: standing there frozen with fear, unable to help his mother; the lunatic dangling him from the shattered window; Dom pulling him up to safety. When he couldn't sleep it was often because the guilt overcame him. He had lived and she hadn't. She had moved to save him; he knew that's why she was running to him before the madman had stopped her. But he had not had her strength or will. He had not saved her. He had let her die and he would have to live with that forever.

That night, after they had made love on the single bed in his cramped dorm room on 115th Street and Amsterdam, he could see she'd been thinking about what he'd told her, and he thought she was going to say something sappy, try to make him feel better by saying *It wasn't your fault* or *You can't save other people* or *You were only a boy* or one of the other meaningless phrases that so many people had thrown out to him, trying to be kind, over the years. But she didn't say anything like that. Instead she murmured: "You said that your mother had something she wanted to tell you that day. Did you ever find out what it was?" Jack nodded and said, "Dom had proposed. She was going to tell me they were getting married." Caroline rubbed his shoulder with the heel of her palm and kissed the side of his neck, then she buried her head in his chest and told him that this is what she knew: when wounds healed, it wasn't as if they'd never existed. They left scars and those scars lasted a lifetime. She told him that he would never be the same person he was before his mother died, he was somebody different, somebody new. She also told him that she loved this new person. Then she closed her eyes and went to sleep.

The next day, Jack called Dom and told him he was bringing someone over to meet him.

"Oh, Christ, is it a girl?" Dom asked.

"Oh, Christ, of course," Jack responded.

"You don't wanna do this, Jackie. This ain't my best thing. What am I gonna talk to her about—hanger steaks?"

"Just charm her with your natural wit," Jack said. "But try not to use the words 'fuckin' and 'asshole' in the same sentence too often, okay?"

"Nothin' but trouble," Dom told him. "You know that? You give me nothin' but trouble."

Jack and Caroline went downtown straight from Goldman's psych class. They took the Broadway line to Fourteenth Street, walked the two blocks west from Seventh Avenue.

"What I'm going to tell you," he said, holding her hand, "Dom told me when I was eight. It's something I've known and lived with my whole life. He was a nervous wreck, told me it was a big secret he was sharing with me, and I'm still not sure why he told me when he did, but I remember he really wanted me to say something afterward, so I looked at him and said, 'Thanks.' He was kind of thrown and he said, 'That's all you got to say?' and I said, 'What else is there to say?' I never saw anyone look so relieved. He just told me, 'Yeah, I guess that's right.' "

"So are you ever going to tell me?" she asked as they got closer to the meat district. "Or are you just going to keep telling me stories about whatever it is without ever telling me what it is?"

He took a deep breath and nodded. There was no point in putting it off any longer, so he just started right in.

In 1948, when Dominick Bertolini was twenty-two years old, he was two fights away from getting into the ring with the lightweight champion of the world. Dom's record was 34 and 0, with twenty-eight of those wins by knockout. Of those twenty-eight, nineteen came within the first five rounds. Three of the men he fought never stepped into a ring again. One of them lost his hearing in one ear, so ferociously was he pummeled. The other two escaped whole, but their spirits were as broken as their ruptured spleen or lacerated kidney. Dominick was a brutal club fighter, not an elegant one, a favorite of bloodthirsty fans and cynical newspaper columnists for his clumsy and unadulterated savagery.

Dom did not like hearing himself referred to as a savage, although he did nothing to correct the image, at least publicly; his managers said it put people in the seats, which also put money in Dom's pocket. And since Dom hated very few things in life more than fighting and was doing this for one reason and one reason only—money—he had no desire to see those seats empty. If he had to use a word to describe himself, it would have been "unrelenting." That indeed is what he was and what he had been since a small boy.

He was certainly no stranger to violence or even to savagery. Fear and brutality were fairly common neighbors on the west side of mid-Manhattan, the neighborhood known as Hell's Kitchen, in the 1930s. They often invaded the walls of Dom's own apartment, in the form of his father. As near as young Dominick could figure out, Anthony Bertolini had absolutely no redeeming qualities. He was crude and loud and mean and he always smelled like an unpleasant combination of sweat, alcohol, and whatever harsh odors clung to him from the street. Tobacco. Dirt. Garbage. Sometimes even blood.

Sometimes it was Dom's blood.

Mostly it was his mother's.

On his eleventh birthday, after a particularly painful beating administered to both mother and son, Dominick realized he had to make a choice. It was clear to him that there were only two possibilities. He could remain quiet, stay frozen in his painful, silent world and keep on taking his father's punishment. Or, when he was ready, when he was able, he could fight back and win and put a stop to the misery.

By the time he was fourteen years old, he had become a fearfully tough child. There was no boy in his school, no matter how old, he could not take in a battle. It wasn't just that he was so strong or even so unrelenting, although he was both. It was that he didn't mind getting hit. He didn't fear the pain. He was used to it.

Three days before his fifteenth birthday, his father erupted at the dinner table. With almost no provocation— his mother had coughed nervously and Anthony took it as a deliberate slight—he lashed out with the back of his hand and knocked Rosemary Bertolini off her chair. He then began to slowly roll up his sleeves, got up from the table, and with a twisted sneer announced that he was going to beat his wife within an inch of her life. That's when Dominick decided the time had come. He stood up from his chair and without raising his voice said, "No, you're not."

His father looked at him incredulously. "Say that again?" he asked. "I must be goin' deaf."

"You're going to leave her alone."

"Fine." The word was stretched out into several syllables. Anthony finished rolling up his sleeves, then looked down at his wife, who was still on the floor but was now pleading for him to leave their son alone. He smiled at her, the first time Dominick had ever seen him smile at her, then he stepped around the dining table and moved toward Dom.

Dominick Bertolini was ready. He wasn't nervous. His voice hadn't quivered. His hands weren't shaking. He'd been preparing for this in his mind since he was a small boy. He wanted it, wanted it now, and as he took his first step toward his father, he knew that he would cherish this moment for the rest of his life.

Cower and die. Or fight and live. He'd made his choice. From now on, things would be different. Things would be better. It was time to win for the first time in his life. Not just win a fight but win a war. Win forever.

Unfortunately, Dominick was too young to have realized there were choices beyond the ones he'd envisioned. Yes, stay silent and suffer was one choice. And fight and win was another.

But so was fight and lose.

Which is what happened that night.

Anthony Bertolini moved slowly and deliberately at first, until he was two short steps away from Dominick. Then he attacked quickly. And viciously. He had palmed his drinking glass, which he now slammed into the side of his son's head. A deep gash opened up over Dominick's eye and blood poured out of the wound as if it were thick paint being dumped out of a can. Without giving him a chance to retaliate, Anthony picked up a chair and brought it down over Dominick's head. The wood splintered and the noise was like that of the sweet spot of a baseball bat meeting a fastball and sending it four hundred feet. Then Anthony's right leg swung back and the hard point of his shoe cracked into Dom's throat. The boy made a sad, gurgling noise, which only seemed to motivate the enraged father. The leg swung back several times and the shoe found the neck again, and then the ribs. The punching and the kicking went on long after Dominick lost consciousness. And then Anthony turned back to his wife.

This time he did not, as promised, beat her to within an inch of her life. He beat her to death.

When Dominick woke up, nearly two days later, he was in the hospital, his mother was buried, and his father was in prison. Anthony spent four years there for murdering his wife. When he got out, he never tried to find or contact his son. Even he understood that he would not survive the next meeting.

It didn't take long for the teenage Dom to find his calling. Within a year he'd had six amateur fights, winning them all easily. He turned pro. Over the next few years, he fought regularly, touring the clubs up and down the East Coast, and won always. At twenty-two, he was ranked number twelve. He would have been higher but no one in the top ten wanted to get in the ring with him. Until his manager came to him and said they'd gotten a fight with the number six contender, Sweet Lenny Sweets. If Dominick won that, he'd get the number one or two. And if he won that, he'd get a chance to fight for the title. He had no doubt that soon he would be champ.

Then, several days before his fight with Sweets, Dom got the word. He was supposed to lose. He wasn't naive and he hadn't been so protected that he didn't understand the ways of the fight game in those days. But he was arrogant and sure of his own toughness and, when he climbed into the ring, he knew one thing and one thing only: he was not going to lose.

He didn't. He knocked Lenny Sweets out in the seventh round.

A week later he was in his apartment in Hell's Kitchen. Not the one in which he'd grown up; after he'd gotten out of the hospital he never set foot in that apartment again, leaving everything he owned behind, even his clothes. There was a knock at the door; he got up from the kitchen table, opened the door. After that, it all happened very fast.

There were three guys. Fat, strong, slow, but slow didn't matter, the apartment was small, there was no room to move. Two of them held him down. One of them had a butcher's knife. Huge and gleaming.

"You got a good fuckin' right, don't you?" one of them said. "You're pretty proud of that fuckin' right."

Dom didn't say anything. Even when the cleaver came slashing down and cut through the bone of his right arm, severing it at the forearm.

The only thing he heard after that, right before he passed out, was "You two-bit piece of shit. Don't think you'll be usin' your fuckin' right much anymore."

CAROLINE HAD STOPPED walking for the last part of the story. She was leaning against a lamppost, one hand clenched around it, gripping it so tightly her fingers were white and blotchy.

"Oh my God," she said. She said it several times.

"I told you."

"You told me it was a different world."

"It *is* a different world."

"It's a different *universe*."

"Do you want me to stop?"

"There's more? That's not the end?"

Jack shook his head.

Her eyes closed for a moment. Then opened. "Tell me the rest," she said.

So he did. He told her how Dom recovered over the next few months, his ring career over. When he was strong enough, he got a job as a butcher. It was a deliberate choice—the career somehow seemed fitting to him after what had happened. He worked at a butcher shop for a couple of years, learned the ropes, started saving to open up his own place. During that time, he asked questions, kept his eyes and ears open. A little over three years after that night in his apartment, he finally found the three men who had paid him a visit. Now he paid *them* a visit. Two of them were together and he picked them up when they came out of a bar not long after midnight. Dom came up close behind, never identified himself, shot them while they were walking down the street. It took him ten more days to find the third man. But he did. Waited in the hallway of the guy's apartment building. This time he was going to identify himself but he didn't have the opportunity. The moment the guy saw Dom's arm he turned and ran. But he didn't get far. Before he could take two steps, Dominick Bertolini put a bullet through the back of the man's head.

Caroline was pale now and looked a little unsteady on her feet. "Did he go to jail?" she asked.

Jack shook his head. "No proof. And no one looked too hard to find any. The victims were not exactly what you'd call model citizens."

"But if everyone knew that Dom—"

"No one knew. Maybe some people suspected, but he didn't broadcast it. That's not what it was about. He only told the people he trusted. Even now, I don't think there are more than five people who know what happened."

"How . . . how is he going to feel about the fact that . . . that . . ."

"That I told you? I told him yesterday I was going to tell you."

"What did he say?"

"He didn't say anything. He trusts me."

Caroline exhaled a long, deep breath. "This man . . . he raised you?"

"I'm here because of him. And whatever it is I am, I mostly am because of him." He waited but she didn't seem to have any more questions. "Do you still want to meet him?" he finally said.

She nodded.

"What's the matter," he smiled, "can't talk?"

And when she shook her head, she was, for the first time since he'd met her, not smiling back.

He led her into the meat market, watched her eyes take in the carcasses and the blood on the floor and the men with their big bellies and greasy hair lugging meat. He watched, too, as she zeroed in on Dom. When he glanced up, noticed that they were there, Dom didn't move. He looked at Caroline as if waiting to see what she'd do. She went straight over to him, didn't wait for an introduction. She took his good hand in hers, leaned over, and kissed him gently on the cheek. As she did, she whispered something in his ear. Dom turned red, as if embarrassed, but he didn't pull his hand away. Letting her hold it, he stood there, remarkably at ease, asked her a few questions. *Where you from? How'd you get to New York? What are you doin' with*—a jerk of the head toward Jack—*a lug like him?* Then he said, apologetically, *I gotta get back to work.*

He gently pulled his hand away, turned, and headed toward the huge walk-in refrigerator. But before he got there, he stopped, twisted his head toward Jack, and nodded his approval.

When Jack tried to get out of her what she'd whispered to him, Caroline wouldn't say. It wasn't until later, when he called Dom, that he found out.

"What's the matter?" Dom said. "She won't tell ya?"

"No," Jack admitted. "All she'll say is that it's up to you."

"Ain't that somethin'," Dom said.

"So are you going to tell me?"

"You want her exact words?"

"Yes. Her exact words."

"Her exact words," Dom said with something approaching wonder in his voice, "were 'Thank you for Jack. You did a good job.'"

That night, he and Caroline made particularly fervent love in his room. When they were done, she shuddered with pleasure and when he tried to move she stopped him. She wouldn't let him escape from inside her and wrapped her arms around him, holding him tight. That's when he told her his plans. After graduation, he said, he wanted to open a restaurant. He could take what he'd learned studying business at school and combine it with everything he'd picked up living with and working for Dom. He knew exactly what the restaurant would be like, too. Comfortable and real, with good, simple food. The kind of food he knew about. And great service. Maybe it would be in a brownstone, he said, something that felt like home.

She waited to see if there was more and, yes, there was.

I want you to be my partner, he told her. I'll run the back, do the kitchen and the food and the business. You run the front. Make it look the way you want. Make it classy.

She waited and, yes, there was still more.

"I love you," he said. "And I want you to be my wife."

"Those are good plans," Caroline said. "I like those plans."

And after they kissed, a long and luxurious and enveloping kiss, and then made love again, she said, "Yes, I like those plans very much. I like the idea of living happily ever after."

The wedding was your basic nightmare. Caroline's parents wanted a fancy affair, several hundred people, held down in Virginia on the family grounds. Dom thought it should be upstairs at the Old Homestead Restaurant, the venerable steak joint on Fifteenth Street. It was near enough so the boys in the meat markets could easily get there, and they had good, icy-cold beer on tap.

They compromised. Jack and Caroline got married in the late morning in a judge's chamber down at City Hall. Her parents came up for the ceremony, as did her two sisters, Llewellyn and Susanna Rae. Llewellyn was the perfect Southern belle, gracious and friendly toward all. Susanna Rae was distant and seemed resentful of Caroline's happiness. She stayed separate from the group, barely acknowledged Jack's existence, and looked as if the short and simple vows were for no other purpose than to inflict upon her a painful and permanent wound.

Caroline's family did not attend the party that followed the wedding. It was their way of showing disapproval without having a confrontation. They waited back at their midtown hotel. Dom threw a bash at his market—it was Caroline's choice of locations. Jack stood in a tuxedo, the first one he'd ever worn, and Caroline was radiant in a white silk blouse and short, white silk skirt. The beer, scotch, and bourbon—and even a bit of champagne—flowed while a band played raucous rock and roll all afternoon. They danced among the hanging slabs of beef, kicking up sawdust, and everyone from Jack's and Dom's past lined up to kiss and hug the glowing bride. At six o'clock, Jack and Caroline hopped in a taxi, rode out to the airport, and met the Hale family. They all took the shuttle to Washington, D.C., then drove from there to the farm in Virginia, just outside Charlottesville. The next day was an all-day party. Tents were set up on the property, an orchestra played sonorous chamber music, hundreds of elegant friends pressed checks into Jack's or Caroline's hands and wished them well. Jack, for the most part, stayed silent, not wanting to say the wrong thing or reveal just how uncomfortable he truly felt stepping up in class. References were made to events he hadn't heard of. People laughed at jokes he didn't understand. There were toasts singing Caroline's praises from scores of people she'd never mentioned to him, including several obvious ex-suitors. Caroline's father spoke about what a fine young man Jack was, greatly exaggerating his background and accomplishments. Her mother kissed Jack on the cheek, the barest graze of a kiss, whispering to him that he had a real handful to take care of.

But he knew that wasn't true. Caroline was no handful. She was easy. And it would always be easy between them because they were in love.

They left the next morning for the honeymoon, a week in a small hotel on the Caribbean island of Virgin Gorda. They had their own one-bedroom cabin, with a thatched roof and an outdoor shower, which was all they needed since it never went below eighty degrees.

On the plane ride down, they were holding hands, sitting in a comfortable silence; he was thinking about the party in Virginia and he knew she was too. He squeezed her hand tighter and said to her, "Why did you marry me?"

"You mean seeing where I come from, seeing my friends, seeing the bucolic life I'm leaving behind to go live the pauper's life in the evil city with a nobody like you?"

He shrugged, then nodded and said, "Something like that, yeah."

She turned her head, just an inch, so her eyes could search his. When they were done searching, she smiled gently, then she, too, squeezed harder and said, "I don't want you to become like those people, you know."

"I won't," he told her. "I don't think I can."

"That's good," she said. "That's why I married you."

Their week in Virgin Gorda was a lot like being in heaven. They sat on the beach and read, took long walks, spent hours out on the water, motoring around in a little putt-putt that came with the room. They snorkeled and ate grilled lobster and drank rich, foamy piña coladas that were dappled with nutmeg. They talked long into the night, confiding their fears about and their confidence in their future and revealing what little they hadn't yet revealed about their pasts.

Day and night they lay in their king-size bed under the ceiling fan, the slats in the windows letting in a faint sea breeze, holding each other. She would stretch out, naked, and let him stroke her. He would kiss the tops of her thighs, staring down the seemingly endless length of her magically bronzed legs toward her slender bare feet. She would guide him into her and moan with pleasure. He was always surprised that someone so elegant and in control could be so sensual and sexually uninhibited. Sometimes she screamed so loudly they would start laughing. She told him it was a good thing their room was so close to the water, that the roar of the waves better drown her out or hotel security would come and drag him away.

When they returned to New York—there was never any question that they would live there—they began the daunting task of becoming not just life partners but business partners. They found themselves strategizing long into the night. They would go out for a pizza or some Chinese food, planning on a movie afterward, but they would get so excited discussing the details of their planned restaurant that the movie never materialized. They would stay in the pizza place, jabbering at each other, throwing out questions, tossing back just-thought-of answers, until they'd be asked to leave because the table was needed, then they'd move on to a coffee shop or a bar and plan away until they'd realize it was two in the morning and time to go home.

They searched for the right location. There were all sorts of variables and rules, they knew, but "right" meant "affordable," so they wound up breaking the rules. They found the perfect setup: a small brownstone with the first floor licensed for a commercial business. It was easily convertible into a restaurant space; there was even a garden out back with a patio. The only problem was that it was on a side street in Chelsea. Hardly any foot traffic. Not a very desirable area, not back then. Too far west, too far downtown. Too downscale, too rough a neighborhood. But they could afford it. Their first investment, before they bought a can of paint or a single piece of silverware, was a small blue-and-white awning. On it, it said "Jack's T-Bone" in small, scripted letters. The awning stood at the front of the building for a full year before the restaurant opened. Every time he saw it, it gave Jack the confidence to succeed and made him understand that his dream was about to become a reality.

Caroline was the one who insisted they buy, not rent. It made him nervous—Jack had never owned anything more expensive than a leather jacket. But she said they had to look into the future. If they owned the property, they could do what they wanted with it. They would be the ones in control. And, besides, they could live above the restaurant. Not only would they have a beautiful home, they could serve the last customer, lock the door of their business, and be in bed two minutes later.

"That'll save us an hour in travel time a day," she said. And then with a deviously innocent look, "We're going to have kids, Jack. I figure four or five of them. That means an hour more we can stay in bed and work on that."

She put up her trust fund as collateral, which the bank instantly accepted, and the town house was theirs.

It seemed like the world was theirs, too.

The restaurant was an immediate success. It started out as an old-fashioned chophouse, serving the best cuts of carefully aged meat, the perfect Caesar salad, and their signature dish, Jack's Potatoes, a circular sculpture of thinly sliced potatoes fried in a cast-iron skillet with shallots and onions. Jack learned about other kinds of food, too. He absorbed the details that, for him, made what he did an art, not just a business. From the fish vendors at the South Street Seaport, he learned that line-caught was better than net-caught— water got in a fish's mouth when it was net-caught; that bloated it and made it less tasty. He learned about baking. Jean-Guy, the white-haired Parisian who was the master baker at the Van Dam Street Bakery, taught him that hard wheat is best for bread, soft wheat is most proper for pastries, and it didn't take Jack long before he could, by taste, pick out the breads that were naturally leavened from sourdough starters. From the farmers who sold him fruits and vegetables at the Union Square Farmers' market, he began to understand the subtle tastes of the best tomatoes and onions and herbs. Gradually, as Jack became more sophisticated, gently guided by Caroline, so, too, did the restaurant. They traveled to Italy, rented a small house in Tuscany, and stumbled into a wonderful trattoria outside of Lucca called Prago. They asked questions, observed every little detail, and, most of all, made friends with the owner, Piero, who finally sent them on their way with the secrets to three of his special pasta sauces, all of which were added to the New York menu. And, suddenly, aromatic truffles began appearing, for special customers, in Jack's Potatoes. When

California cuisine came in, they resisted the extreme and faddish combination of tastes, but accepted that American cooking had changed and changed for the better. The restaurant reflected those changes. They were soon serving sliced onions and blood oranges on a bed of arugula, and their chicken and fish began to be influenced by everyone from Wolfgang Puck to Paul Prudhomme. The key to their success, though, was always simplicity; both Jack and Caroline recognized that and never strayed from it. Soon, even the name was simplified. Jack's T-Bone was shortened to Jack's. Within two years of opening, they were a New York institution. Reservations had to be made weeks in advance. But the menu stayed small, the atmosphere homely, the service impeccable. Jack knew, as good as his food was, people did not come to his restaurant for the food. They came because he and Caroline—and everyone who worked there—made each and every customer feel important. They made a point of only hiring nice people, smart people, people who cared. They paid well and treated the staff as if they were family and it paid off big-time because customers left the restaurant with a sense of intimacy and loyalty.

It did not take long before Jack's had made them successful and confident and, in an era where restaurateurs were often bigger stars than the celebrities they served, even somewhat famous. They were profiled in the *New York Times Magazine* and Caroline revealed her current reading list in *Vanity Fair*'s "Night-Table Reading" page. Periodically, one of the tabloids or TV shows would dig into Jack's past.

Sometimes a magazine would even reprint the infamous *Post* headline about his mother's death: HEIGHT OF INSANITY. But for the most part they were both able to focus on the present and the future. And, of course, the restaurant. They published *Jack's Cookbook* with Knopf, and in *Zagat*, almost every year, someone wrote a variation of: "And, yes, Jack himself came to our table to make sure everything was all right." But Jack's had never been about the money or the fame. From the very beginning, Jack's was always about doing what they loved more than anything in life.

Four years after the first restaurant opened, they expanded. First to Chicago, then to L.A. and Miami, finally overseas to Paris, where the idea of an American steakhouse became the rage. Jack and Caroline opened all of them, were involved in everything from the bottom up: they worked with architects and decorators on the design, consulted with chefs about the food, shared the risks with various financial partners, spent the time to make sure the quality and the ambience were up to their standards.

Seven years after the first Jack's had opened, business was booming and they began to plan a London opening. The restaurant in New York had become too small for their needs. They sold the town house—the yuppification of Manhattan was in full bloom and Caroline's prediction had proved correct: the property was sold for many times what they had paid for it—and moved the restaurant uptown to the heart of the theater district, on Forty-seventh Street between Broadway and Eighth Avenue. They needed a new apartment now, too, and Jack found a perfect one. He wouldn't tell Caroline anything about it, just led her up to Madison and Seventy-seventh Street, nodded to the doormen, who were expecting them, and took her upstairs in the elevator to show her what he hoped would be their new home.

It was quite spectacular: three bedrooms and a formal dining room, a wonderful kitchen, and a living room that was dominated by an ornate, hand-carved mantel over a huge working fireplace. But what made it truly special was something that made Caroline stop dead in her tracks. Something that stunned her and caused her to stare at her husband in wonder.

The apartment had a spectacular wraparound terrace. From different vantage points, it overlooked most of Manhattan. It was, without doubt, one of the great views in New York.

It was also the penthouse of the building.

On the eighteenth floor.

Caroline let Jack lead her through the sliding glass door and onto the terrace. She watched him step gingerly outside and walk to the large round cast-iron table and chairs that the current owners had left behind, set up in the center of the space, the only furniture left in the entire apartment. She walked past him, to the protective waist-high brick wall that went all around the balcony. Unthinkingly, she touched the wall, put her palm flat against it, and suddenly realized what she'd done. She watched Jack, saw his face go pale and his knees start to buckle. She immediately took her hand off the cool brick wall but it was too late. She saw him sit heavily in one of the chairs around the table, his chest heaving as he struggled to breathe. Caroline shook her head, furious at herself for her inadvertent cruelty, but she wondered what the hell he was thinking to want this apartment, because if she knew anything about her husband, it was that he was absolutely, insanely, phobically afraid of heights.

He had been ever since the day his mother was killed.

Since then, he had not, if it could possibly be avoided, gone above the sixteenth floor of any building. He didn't like to fly. He wouldn't sit in the upper tier of a sports stadium or a theater. She knew there were specific things that triggered the most painful of his memories and certain moments when the fear would overcome and even paralyze him. She had been with him long enough to know he could never go as close as she had to the wall. She also understood that he did not like seeing other people standing so close to a precipice. Especially women. And especially his wife.

She watched as Jack sank deeper into the chair, then took the six steps she needed to stand next to him and hold his hand. He looked up at her, the color beginning to come back in his face now, his breathing slowing, becoming easier.

"Do you like it?" he gasped and she had to burst out laughing.

"Yes," she said. "I love it. It's my dream apartment. But it might be a little tough living here if you're going to pass out once or twice a day."

"No," he said, his voice still low and hoarse and his breathing still heavy. "I want it."

"Jack, it's crazy. Let's just find our beautiful dream apartment that's on the third floor of some other building."

But he insisted. It was time to get over his fear, he said. Time to get rid of the ghosts that had been haunting him. She argued, told him there were other ways, but she stopped arguing when he said, "It's a good apartment for kids."

She didn't respond to that at first, let a long silence linger in the air. She spent those silent moments staring at him, squinting her eyes, and then nodding, finally, when she decided she'd come up with the answer. "Do you think," Caroline said, "that when we have kids, they'll grow up and not be frightened by things because they grew up here, above the seventeenth floor?"

"Yes," he said, not at all surprised that she had understood. "That's exactly what I think."

She nodded. Then said, "That's an ugly carpet in the living room, isn't it?"

"Hideous," he agreed.

"On the other hand, it looks kind of comfortable."

"Extremely."

"Comfortable enough to try to make a baby on?" she asked.

"There's only one way to find out," he answered.

And he let her lead him out of his chair and into the living room, where they began to make love on the hideous living room carpet of their new apartment.

RIGHT AFTER THEY moved in, Caroline got pregnant for the first time. Three weeks before the due date, they finished converting one bedroom into the baby's room—a room for a baby boy, as the tests had revealed—and filled it with toys and clothes and even painted stars on the ceiling above the crib. A week before she was due, Caroline doubled over with pain and Jack rushed her to the hospital. The baby was delivered by Cesarean and was stillborn. They grieved for months but they dealt with their loss by loving each other all the more and then Caroline was pregnant again. This time, two months into the pregnancy she began hemorrhaging and the baby had to be aborted.

A few days before their ninth anniversary, she announced to Jack that she was pregnant yet again. They took every possible precaution. She stayed away from the restaurant, didn't exercise the way she usually did at the gym, drank not a drop of alcohol, and went on a vegetarian diet. They had put off the opening of the Jack's in London because of the first two pregnancies, but they decided they couldn't delay any longer. The doctor suggested that flying was not in her or the baby's best interest, so for the first time she let Jack do most of the work and all of the traveling. He spent at least a week a month in England for several months, making sure it all went right while she rested and ate well and didn't drink in New York, making certain that all went right *there*. Since their very first date, they had spent nearly every minute together and Jack, to his surprise, found himself guiltily enjoying the separation. They spoke constantly and he filled her in on every business detail, but for the first time he understood that they now had secrets from each other. He could not possibly tell her everything he did and thought and he realized it was the same for her. Women flirted with him and came on to him and he enjoyed it. He went out with his male friends, too, at pubs and private gambling casinos in Mayfair, and he enjoyed that, too. He began to horde his little secrets and he wondered how that would affect his life with Caroline when he returned home. They were harmless, he decided, and would not affect it at all.

But Caroline's secrets were not as trivial. Right after the London opening, Jack came home and she told him that, once again, there would be no baby. She had gone into the hospital and now it was all over. She hadn't called him over there, hadn't wanted to tell him on the phone, not while he was overseeing everything. But this time was different. There were new complications: the doctor told her she could no longer have children.

She cried and they hugged and, as before, their wounds gradually healed. And, as before, as Caroline had said, the scars left them different people. Not better, not worse, just different.

ONE OF THE biggest differences was that they let Kid Demeter come into their lives.

It began the night of their tenth anniversary. They were home, just the two of them. Jack was going to cook and they were going to have a romantic evening, going to make love and try, as they often did now, not to think about the fact that they would never have a child. They were listening to *Chet Baker in Paris*. Jack would always remember that "My Funny Valentine" was playing because it was Caroline's favorite song, and they were touching their champagne glasses in a toast when the phone rang. It was Dom, and as soon as Jack heard his voice he said, "We're drinking champagne and whispering sweet nothings. When can you be here?" But when Dom was silent, Jack knew something was wrong, so then he just said, "What is it?"

"It's Sal," Dom said.

Jack put his champagne glass down and said, "Shit."

Sal Demeter worked for Dom, and had worked alongside Jack for years at the plant. When Jack was a teenager, Sal had always treated him like a man instead of a boy; he was the first one ever to take Jack out drinking and once let Jack, when he was fourteen, drive Sal's station wagon down an empty West Side Highway in the middle of the night. Sal was a hell of a guy. Huge, three hundred pounds, easy. An enormous belly that jutted way out in front of him. Hands that looked like ham hocks and arms that looked as if they could lift anything. That *could* lift anything. Not the brightest guy who ever lived, but kind and surprisingly gentle for such a giant of a man.

Dom told Jack that Sal had just finished work. He was walking across the floor, fiddling with the string on his apron, getting ready to yank it off, when he began staggering. The big man took three or four quick steps and fell to his knees. Remained there for another second or two, just long enough for people to start running over to him, then he toppled forward, twisting slightly to his side, and was dead. Sal wasn't quite forty-five and he'd left a wife and fourteen-year-old son and, Jack was certain, not much insurance money. The fourteen-year-old was George, but no one had called him that since, well, probably since he was three months old. Right from the start it was Kid. Kid Demeter.

It began with Dom and Jack helping him out. Jack, especially, and later Caroline, talked to the boy, eased him through the crisis of losing a father, and the bond formed easily and naturally. At first it was based on need—Jack's and Caroline's as well as Kid's—but it lasted because of genuine affection and, ultimately, love. They gave the boy money when he needed it. Gave him advice when he needed it, too, and he usually needed that more often than the money. Kid was a wise guy, a tough kid. Stubborn as hell, always in and out of trouble. But there was something about him that was more than just an iron-willed street kid. Kid wanted to make something of himself. Jack saw it in his eyes, recognized it because he knew he'd had that same look when he was young. Kid wanted out and up. Out of the life that had molded him and up to a new and different level. Jack and Caroline's level.

Jack took him to Knicks games, as Dom had taken Jack years before. Kid grew into a talented athlete, so Caroline went to Staten Island and talked to Kid's mother, explaining that they were willing to send him to a suburban prep school so he could play football. LuAnn Demeter agreed, saying she wanted whatever was best for her son, so off Kid went to Bay Shore, Long Island, and to Webster's Academy. Jack also arranged for Kid's best friend, Bryan Bishop, to get a scholarship there. Bryan was enormous; he didn't just look like an offensive lineman, he looked like an entire offensive line. He was also devoted to Kid; they seemed joined at the hip and had been since they were little boys. It had been Caroline's suggestion to try to keep them together. She thought it would make Kid's transition a little easier as he began his new life.

Jack and Dom would drive up to watch their football games—Kid used his toughness to quickly become a star quarterback; Bryan rapidly became one of the best blocking fullbacks in the state—and afterward they'd take both boys out for pizza or, if it was a weekend, into the city to Jack's for a steak. In his free time, Kid was always hanging out at their apartment or at the restaurant. Caroline brought out his soft side and to her he would confide his fears and his problems. These were the only times Kid let down his guard. It was as if he sensed that his presence seemed to salve the wounds that still pained her over her failed pregnancies. With Jack, he was always cocky and confident because that's the way he wanted Jack to see him. He worshiped them both. When Kid reached college age, he went to St. John's in Queens, Jack happily paying the tuition. It's not a loan, he told Kid, it's an investment. He meant an investment in Kid's future but he also meant more than that. When Kid was going on twenty-one and a junior—still a quarterback, still friends with Bryan, who was still blocking for him—Jack took Kid out to dinner after a game, just the two of them, and said that he and Caroline had begun talking about it and, if Kid was interested, they'd like him to think about coming into the business with them. Kid was overwhelmed by the offer but only said, cockily, yeah, he just might be interested at that. Jack had wanted more of a response but he knew the boy well, knew how pleased he was. A couple of weeks later, after another game, it was dinner as usual with Dom and Kid and Bryan, and Bryan got Jack off to the side, told him that Kid had mentioned what Jack had said. Kid's friend said that he'd never seen Kid so excited or happy about anything in his whole life.

But Kid didn't come into the restaurant business.

And he didn't grow into the son that Jack and Caroline had not been able to conceive.

Instead, he disappeared.

He had been devastated by something that had happened near the end of his junior year. A teammate, Harvey Wiggins, someone Kid had been close to, had been seriously injured on the football field during a team practice. Harvey had come in hard on defense, trying for a sack on Kid, and he got blocked at the wrong angle. Kid heard the snap when Harvey's neck broke and he saw him flop to the ground, a quadriplegic now and forever. Caroline had spent many hours talking to Kid about the accident; for some reason Kid had assumed a strong sense of guilt and shame and she assured him that he was not to blame. "People take risks," she told him, over and over again. "You can't protect everyone from what's nothing more than normal life."

But Kid changed after that incident. He became more withdrawn, spoke mostly in monotones and seemed to have little energy. Jack sat him down, asked him if he'd started taking drugs, but Kid denied that. There was no denying that a wall had come up between them, though, and then he came to Jack and Caroline at the end of his junior year, told them he was dropping out of school. Kid was very evasive, almost seemed angry, and reverted to his younger, sullen ways.

"Kid," Jack said, "I don't think this is something you can just decide on your own. Why don't you stay here a few days and we can discuss—"

"No!" It was the first time Kid had ever raised his voice to them. But he didn't back down. His words were forceful and full of fire. "There's nothing to discuss," he said. "I'm outta here."

"Is it anything *we* did?" Caroline asked. Her voice was soft and tentative, as if she were soothing a wounded puppy. "Because if it is, maybe we can fix it."

Kid responded to the softness. He looked, for a moment, as if he might collapse or burst into tears. But then his face turned grim. He wouldn't meet her eyes, just shook his head and clammed up again.

"I think you owe us more of an explanation," Jack said, and again Kid's anger seemed to surge through him.

"I don't owe you anything," he said, "except to get the hell away from you."

He refused to take any money, wouldn't give any further explanation. He said he'd get in touch as soon as he knew where he was going, but he never did. No call, no e-mail, no postcard with a phone number or address.

Not a thing.

One day he was there. The next day he was not.

Jack and Caroline were devastated. They discussed it endlessly. What had they done wrong? What had happened? Were drugs involved? Was he in trouble? They tried several times to find him through various friends and connections at St. John's. Bryan couldn't help them; he was devastated because Kid had cut all ties with him, too. Even Kid's mother had to admit that while she got postcards and letters from her son, she did not know how to get in touch with him. For many months, Kid's disappearance dominated their lives until Caroline said, "No more. We have to let it go," and when Jack said, "I don't know if I can," she shook her head firmly and insisted, "We have to. It's just as if we've lost another child."

Jack knew she was right. They *had* lost another child.

Gone is gone, Dom had said.

And Kid Demeter was gone.

ack Keller woke up, as always, one minute before his clock radio sounded. And, as always, as he'd done for nearly twenty years now, the moment he flicked it off he instantly reached over to lightly pat Caroline, to reassure her that he was up, that he was all right, and she didn't have to rise with him. That it was 4:30 in the morning and there was no reason on God's earth why she couldn't stay tucked under their pastel-blue down-filled comforter and sleep for five or six more hours while he went to the meat district and then the fish market and then, unless their new baby chef, whom they'd recently stolen from Danny Meyer and his Eleven Madison Park restaurant, had decided to go, to the Union Square farmers' market.

"Sleep," he would whisper in her ear almost every morning, then kiss her lightly, his lips barely grazing her soft cheek.

"Mmmmm," she would breathe her contented response, because even though she had no intention of doing anything *but* sleep, this was their ritual. She needed to feel his presence in the morning. However brief that presence was. She didn't like to wake up to find him gone. It frightened her. Caroline did not like either empty beds or surprises.

But this morning his fingers didn't find the silk nightgown clinging to the small of her delicate back or her firm and familiar lightly tanned shoulder. His hand instead groped the cool texture of their antique off-white linen sheet and, for a moment, his eyes widened, disoriented, before he remembered.

Virginia.

They had decided to expand again, one more time, and she was down in Charlottesville, Virginia, preparing for the opening of the new restaurant. The new Jack's.

He lingered in bed for a few moments, smiling at the fact—amazed, really, after all these years—that he still missed her when they were separated. They spoke every day, of course. Three or four times a day, in fact. Even when it was just the minutest details of business, he still got a kick out of talking to her. Even when she was brusquely discussing square footage and the number of tables and the impossibility of finding a quality "anchor" to work the front of the restaurant, he was soothed by the cool huskiness of her voice and the affection that seemed linked to her crisp pronunciation and firm lilt.

Lately they'd been discussing a lot of minute details and Jack thought—realized with a start—that, for the first time in quite a long time, Caroline seemed genuinely happy again.

Maybe for the first time since Kid had disappeared.

It was a wound that, for both of them, had not quickly healed.

Jack saw the effect on Caroline for several years. No one else could possibly have detected it but he thought she seemed lonely and just slightly less joyful. He did not sense her full recovery until they decided to open up this new Jack's.

This was her baby. He'd wanted to throw himself full force into the planning and opening in Charlottesville and, at the beginning, he had. But it soon became clear that Caroline had developed a special attachment to this one. And that attachment had added an extra weight, an importance and sense of urgency she'd never shown before. She was becoming possessive about it; it had become personal with her.

"I watch you sometimes, in New York," she said. "The way you look around the restaurant. Not at the staff, not at the customers, at the *place*. The bar, the tables, the scuff marks on the floor. It's a living, breathing thing to you."

"It's a part of me," he said.

"Sometimes, my darling husband, I wish you looked at me the way you look at that goddamn swinging door you bought for the kitchen."

"It's an awfully beautiful door." He grinned, and she shook her head in mock dismay.

But then she took his hand, held it lightly, ran her fingers over the calluses on his right palm. "That's the way I feel down in Virginia," she told him, and he was surprised at the seriousness of her tone. "I have something down there that's beautiful. That's mine."

She never said that she wanted to go it alone, to have her head this time, but he knew her too well to miss the signals. And he understood, too, that it was a way for her to do what he'd done in London—to be alone for a while, to develop her own secrets. This restaurant was her idea to begin with. The town was only thirty miles or so from the family farm where she'd grown up; it was still in the family, although rarely used these days. Caroline's father was dead, nearly nine years now. Her mother couldn't bear to sell the property, but couldn't bring herself to live there, either. She basically stopped going to the farm right after the funeral. Too many memories, she said. It was where she'd been young; she didn't want it to see her sink into old age. So the farm had become a kind of elegant retreat, a stately—if ghostly—second home. Caroline's two sisters used it on the occasional weekend. The eldest, Llewellyn, had too many children with too many soccer matches and a husband with too many golf games to make it a permanent retreat. The other sister, Susanna Rae—never married, never particularly connected to the rest of the family, and always resentful, somehow, of Caroline's success and happiness—just seemed to stay away. So, for the most part, the wonderful estate was left to the care and goodwill of the Trottys, the black couple who'd worked for the family for too many years to count.

Even though she had run away as quickly as she'd been able, Caroline had always felt a special attachment to Virginia. It irked her somewhat that she was still bound to it, but she cared deeply for its beauty, its tie to the old South that was rapidly being eaten away by the encroaching anonymity of Starbucks coffee bars, Gap stores, and Blockbuster monstrosities. She loved the politeness of Virginia and its gentility. Above all, she loved the farm, where she could foxhunt and skeet-shoot and, on the spur of the moment, still pull on a pair of slick, shiny riding boots, leap onto her favorite mare, and go racing across the rolling hills.

They'd been there together many times during the course of their marriage, but Jack had firmly remained a city boy. He believed that if man were intended to get around on horseback, he would never have invented the BMW. He was always ecstatic to see the Manhattan skyline upon their return and it never failed to thrill him when he stepped back into their apartment and onto the terrace overlooking Central Park. Now, *there* was the perfect melding of man and nature. Good, competitive touch football games in the autumn followed by a cold beer made a hell of a lot more sense to him than spending hours in tight pants and silly little hard hats chasing some poor, terrified fox for miles and miles through the Virginia mud.

At the beginning, when she'd said she'd been thinking about Charlottesville as a location, he'd thought it was a strange choice. But she reminded him that fortunes had been made on such strange choices. No one thought Vegas was a food city before Puck and Emeril opened up there. No one thought rich New Yorkers would venture downtown to Union Square until Danny Meyer decided to open his Cafe there. And their research and marketing people assured him it was the right move. The D.C. intelligentsia and media folk had discovered the town over the past decade. They now had country retreats in the area. Even Hollywood had been coming in droves. A lot of the actors, producers, and directors who kept people's heads swiveling at the Jack's in L.A. and New York were now taking over the culture of the Virginia countryside. As the townspeople became more and more sophisticated, so too did the shops and the local theater. The only thing lagging behind was the food. All food explosions, he knew, followed two trends: coffee and bread. When serious coffee shops opened in a city, followed by upscale bakeries, the market was ready for top-of-the-line chefs. It happened in Seattle exactly that way. And Portland. San Francisco had not only followed that pattern, it had created it. And Charlottesville was filling up with wonderful quirky coffee bars and equally wonderful pastry and bread spots. Had been for a year now. The city was a bonanza waiting to happen for the right restaurant—the right name, the right combination of tastes, the right prices, and the right atmosphere—and Jack's was the perfect fit. Added to all of that, Charlottesville was also a huge tourist center, so close to Monticello, that testimony to the genius of man— or at least *one* man, Thomas Jefferson.

What pushed Jack into his final decision—although deep down, he'd known as soon as she suggested it that it was as good as done, as soon as he saw the pleasure in her eyes— was that he visited some of the Virginia vineyards and tasted some of the local wine. Not there yet, but *getting* there. The Alan Kinne Chardonnay was absolutely first-rate, satisfyingly oaky. The Dashiell Pinot Noir was fine, not far behind some of the midrange Washington and Oregon vineyards. And the Barboursville Cabernet was both delicious and a smooth fit with Jack's menu. In another few years, he could have a perfectly nice Virginia section on his wine list. He liked that idea. After all, it was Thomas Jefferson who'd introduced wine to the New World. The local reds would eventually go very nicely with some of the Southern adaptations of the restaurant's classic recipes.

So they agreed it was a go.

"Is it still fun for you?" she'd asked.

He'd thought a bit, surprised he had to think, then he nodded and said, "It's still fun with *you*."

She smiled—the answer had pleased and touched her—and she leaned over, kissed him on the top of the forehead, let her lips linger long enough that he could feel her breath rustling his hair.

They got a good deal on a location, in the middle of the brick-lined Downtown Mall, near enough to the glorious university so it felt as if they were hovering in Jefferson's overwhelming shadow, yet far enough away so as not to be lumped with the raggedy barbecue and burger joints or the more staid places with their fake Colonial decorations and wild mélange of would-be sophisticated ingredients. Their staff came together easily, too, and would come easier in the future; Jack talked to the university and they agreed to start a small master's program in restaurant management. Not only would Jack and Caroline give several lectures a year, the students could apprentice in the new kitchen and on the floor. In the meantime, they brought several people up from Miami, including the manager, a wonderful woman named Bella who worked twenty-four hours a day, was scrupulously honest, and was in the midst of a not-very-friendly divorce, so that she was anxious to get out of town for a while. The sous chef in Chicago was definitely ready to take over his own place and staff, so when he willingly made the move, everything was set.

Now they were in the home stretch. One day to go before the opening.

Caroline had been down in Charlottesville quite a bit lately, two or three days a week for several months, making sure that this newest venture would run with the only two things that she demanded of everyone and everything around her: precision and elegance. He'd gone with her several times, of course, as often as he could, but there was much work to be done at home.

An overwhelming amount of work, really.

There was a lot more pressure being the president of the United States, Jack always said, but even the president didn't put in the kind of hours a topnotch restaurateur in New York did.

Now Jack glanced at the alarm clock: 4:45. He was fifteen minutes behind schedule.

I must be getting lazy, he thought. And then he went through, in his mind, what he had to do that day, and he laughed out loud. Lazy. Yeah, right.

With that, Jack started to swing his feet out of bed. But before they could touch the floor, he was startled to hear the phone ring. Then he was smiling, not so startled, as he picked up the receiver and, without asking who it was, said with mock sternness, "Why are you up so early?"

"An annoying habit," Caroline said on the other end.

"I've never been referred to quite that way," he told her, "but I guess it's better than nothing."

"You're running behind schedule."

"How do you know I'm not on my way out the door?"

"You sound too cozy. My guess is you're still in bed thinking about how much work you have to do."

"Lucky guess," he said.

Her response was a confident "Mmmmm."

Then she filled him in on what her day was going to be like, said that she was going back to sleep for a few hours, that she'd just felt like speaking to him before he headed out.

"You're talking so quietly," he said. "Everything okay?"

"Everything's perfect. It's just so quiet and peaceful here right now. It doesn't seem right to spoil it."

"You, my sweet, are incapable of spoiling anything."

"And you, my sweet, are going soft in the head. When are you coming down?"

"Tonight. I'll have an early dinner with Dom and then I think I'll drive. Probably leave around eight, get there around midnight. Should I come to the house or the restaurant?"

"Restaurant. I'll still be there. And you know you have a meeting with the Beauferme vineyard guy at five-thirty tonight," she said. "He wants to sell you a new Rhône."

"Oh, Christ. I forgot."

"Write it down."

"He's going to want me to drink with him and I'm going to have to argue with him—"

"Write it down, please."

"You know I don't taste wine that way. I don't drink with the salesmen. I drink it with dinner, the way you're *supposed* to drink it."

"Write it down and stop whining. Or wining . . ."

"Very funny."

". . . as the case may be."

"Even funnier."

"Write it down." And during the pause, as he made a face at the phone and waved his hand in the air, pretending to write down the information, she said, "Jack, don't just make faces and humor me. Write it down."

"I'll never understand how you do that," he said. "But it kind of steams me."

"Oh," she said. "Will you bring the hunting rifle? I want to go shooting tomorrow."

"It's here?"

"In the foyer closet. I brought it back to be realigned."

"This ain't what I thought romance would be—'Yes, darling, I'll bring your rifle.' "

"Don't forget," she said.

"I'm writing it down," he said, and again he moved his fingers in the air.

"Go to work."

"Sleep well," he told her and then they hung up.

The next few minutes were as always: a trip to the kitchen to put the coffee on, a quick shower, a few moments to throw on a pair of jeans and a comfortable sweater-shirt, back to the kitchen to pour a large mug of coffee, then a few steps over to the enormous wraparound balcony to sit—not too close to the rail, never too close to the rail—and sip the hot liquid, looking out, from on high, at the lights of the city caught in the fading night and rising dawn.

Jack took a deep breath, a satisfied breath, then left the terrace and walked into the elevator that opened up straight into his apartment foyer and took him down to the garage in the basement of his building. He slid into the driver's seat of his four-door, gleaming black Beamer, maneuvered out of the tight parking space, drove up the steep incline that led to the middle of East Seventy-seventh Street, then headed south on Fifth Avenue.

Manhattan was still asleep and there was a faint, predawn chill to the air as Jack's day began. He loved that chill, never failed to appreciate it when it hit him each morn. It made him shiver and come alive and thrill to the edge of the city. It reminded him, every single day, how much he liked that life, despite the ghosts that still haunted its edges. The life that he and Caroline had fought for, and worked for, and carved out for each other.

The life that, in one more day, when the Virginia restaurant opened, would shatter and change forever.

There it was.

Touch it. Hold it. Make sure it was real.

Yes. Oh, yes. Very, very real.

It was the key to everything, this little card. To the future. To the good life. To love and money and respect. To everything the two of them had always wanted.

To everything they were in danger of losing.

But now they didn't have to lose it. Any of it. Here it was and she had done it for them. Arranged it all.

Did she even know what she was doing? Maybe. Hard to know. Hard to know anything.

Except there was nothing else to know. They had what they needed.

THE GOVERNOR OF VIRGINIA

THE MAYOR OF CHARLOTTESVILLE

THE STAFF OF JACK'S

Invite you to the biggest off-Broadway opening of the year

OPENING NIGHT OF

JACK'S—CHARLOTTESVILLE

ADDRESS: CORNER OF DIVISION ST. & EAST ST.

DATE: APRIL 1

TIME: 7 P.M. UNTIL CLOSING

DRESS: CASUAL ELEGANT

We're thanking you for welcoming us . . .

The invitation seemed to get larger, growing all by itself, and it took on a surreal glow. It was indeed a magical thing. It was a solution to all their problems. A ticket to a beautiful new world.

And in this world . . . well . . . it knew the truth there, too. It most certainly did.

We're thanking you for welcoming us . . .

They would be welcomed, all right.

They were thieves, both of them, the very worst kind of thieves. Had been right from the start. Stealing dreams. Stealing love.

Stealing the future.

We're thanking you for welcoming us . . .

Oh, yes, they surely would be welcomed.

And they just might be dead, too.

If they were lucky.

t took Jack less than fifteen minutes to drive down to the Fourteenth Street meat market area. At five o'clock in the morning, it took less than fifteen minutes to drive almost anywhere in Manhattan.

His destination was two blocks south of Fourteenth, Gansevoort Street, where he turned right off Ninth Avenue. As always, over the past year or so, he was surprised by the almost daily change in the neighborhood. Much of it was as it had always been, at least for a long stretch of the twentieth century. The streets were old cobblestone, half the buildings were still warehouses—meat lockers and butchers—with generations represented by the words "And Sons" on almost every sign. Most could just as easily have read "And Grandson and Great-Grandson." The neighborhood was also still a haven—a graveyard, Caroline always said—for all the hot dog vendors in the city; these were the buildings where every street cart was stored. Watching the vendors roll out or roll in at the beginning and end of each day gave Jack the eerie feeling of being in a time long past, before fast food chains and department stores and Internet shopping. But the twenty-first century was rapidly encroaching on this last bastion of blue-collar Manhattan. Many of the butchers had succumbed to the high rents and disappeared, replaced by art galleries and chic women's clothing stores. Warehouses were being converted into precious co-ops. And upscale restaurants were springing up on every corner, luring models and actors and rappers with their posses. Briefly, Jack and Caroline had thought about opening up another place in what was being dubbed the Lower West Side but Jack had spent much of his adult life escaping from there. He loved taking quick dips back into this part of his past but, no matter how hip and trendy the area was becoming, he didn't want to retreat there on a full-time basis.

He eased the car over to the right side of Gansevoort and parked directly in front of Dominick Bertolini's Meat Mart. A burly guy, his back to Jack, his overalls and white T-shirt streaked with blood, was lugging a huge side of beef out toward a truck. He glanced at Jack's car, a hostile glance, started to yell that he couldn't park there, then as Jack stepped out the hostility turned to recognition. He turned back toward his heavy load and, as Jack walked past him, nodded a professional hello.

Jack stepped over a streak of light-red liquid—blood mixed with water—that was slowly streaming out of the warehouse. As he hopped up onto the metal-grating platform and toward the heavy sliding door that led to the enormous warehouse, he could hear, even from outside, the thudding and slamming of cleavers slicing through meat and striking into a butcher block.

He stepped inside and could see Dom, writing at a small desk. His right arm—what was left of it—was holding down a piece of paper. His left hand was busy scribbling. As usual, he was muttering to himself as he wrote. Jack waited; he didn't say anything, just watched the old man concentrate on his figures. His back was ramrod straight. And even under his butcher's whites it was easy to see that his stomach was still flat as a board and his good arm was still hard and muscular. The old man was astonishing. He hadn't aged a day since they'd first met, Jack thought. Still as feisty, still as hardworking. Still as strong and arrogant as ever. He was certain that Dom didn't know he was there and Jack was content to watch and admire, to let his friend work, but then he heard the familiar cigarette-and-whiskey–stained voice say, "What, you got the hots for me, you're just standin' there starin' at my ass?"

Dom turned now to look at Jack. His head was bobbing up and down—a sign of his usual nervous energy as well as his seventy-five years—and he growled, "Whaddya want?"

"Why do you ask me what I want every day when you know damn well you're gonna *tell* me what I want?"

"I don't want you to feel like you don't matter."

"So what do I want?" Jack asked.

"Baby lamb. Beautiful. All organic, four, five months old, twenty-four, twenty-five pounds. And before you ask, since I know you got weird notions of fair play and like to support the area, yeah, they come from around here, New Jersey, from Burden Farm."

"Okay, I'll take—"

"Jackie, gimme some credit, will ya? You'll take two hundred and seventy pounds, that'll cover you for three days. I already broke it down—shoulder, loin, chops, neck, and thighs for braising, no brain, no head. Although why you don't hire yourself a chef who knows how to cook brains . . ."

"You try selling brains to my customers, okay, Dom?"

"Your customers could use some brains, Jackie boy. That's a damn fact." He cackled, then walked over to one of the four-month-old lambs, not yet broken down, hanging from a ceiling hook. Dom slapped it and the thick sound reverberated for a moment in the warehouse. "Look at this baby. She's a poem is what she is, Jackie. You know how many people I give somethin' like this to? You. And you alone. And you know why?"

"I pay you more than anybody."

"Because *you* know the difference."

Dom walked back over to the desk, reached into an already open drawer, and pulled out a bottle of scotch. Nothing fancy. Plain old Johnnie Walker Black. Jack had tried to buy him aged and expensive bottles of single-malt but Dom would have nothing to do with them. A shot glass was already sitting on top of the desk and Dom filled it to the brim. "Care to join me?" he asked.

"It's five-thirty in the morning."

"Is that too early or too late?" When Jack didn't answer, Dom said, "Besides, I'm celebratin'."

"What are you celebrating?"

"The fact that it's five-thirty in the morning. Always happy to see another one roll around."

He downed the shot, licked his lips happily, and put the glass back on the desktop. Then he stepped over to Jack, the sleeve of his apron covering the stump that was his right arm. With his left, he wound up as if to throw a punch. The fist moved toward Jack's cheek, a perfectly thrown hook, even now, even at his age, then the hand opened and curled around Jack's neck. Dom pulled Jack closer and smacked a kiss on his cheek.

"What was *that* for?"

"She's away, ain't she?"

Dom adored Caroline. And rarely called her by name. It was as if to name her was to insult her. She was, under most circumstances, "she." Jack always told her it was the royal version, with a capital *S*.

"Yes. She's away."

"Well, I figured you'd take a little smoochin' wherever you could get it then, Jackie."

With that, the old man cackled his raspy laugh again, gave Jack a hard slap on the back of the neck, turned and headed across the market. Jack knew he was supposed to follow so he did. He smiled, thinking of Dom's relationship with Caroline. A more unlikely pair never existed. Yet she was one of the few people Dom trusted. And it was the same for Caroline. She loved the old man. Could make herself vulnerable with him, which she couldn't do with many people. Jack wondered if Dom had had a similar relationship with his mother. Had Joanie Keller loved and trusted him, too? Whenever Jack allowed himself to think about it, the answer always came up yes.

"Do you have to keep calling me Jackie?" he said to Dom as he followed.

"Yeah, 'cause it's what I always called you. And always will call you. Now, you wanna do some business? 'Cause I got some other good stuff for you."

Jack sighed. "Okay, lay it on me, old man."

"Do you have to keep calling me old man?"

"It's what I've always called you."

Dom shook his head and grumbled to himself but soon was all business as he led Jack through the room to show him the merchandise. "I got you eighty pounds of organic chicken, should be good for two days, I got plenty more comin' in, no need to overstock. Your chef asked for three days' worth of veal, a hundred and sixty pounds. Three days of rib eye, four hundred pounds; another four hundred of sirloin; fifty pounds of hanger steak; thirty pounds of duck, cut up – you guys can take the meat off the legs and breasts yourself. What are you doin' tonight?"

"Jesus, you really are getting old. I'm having dinner with you, then I'm driving to Virginia."

"Drivin'?"

"Yeah. After we open I thought Caroline and I would drive back, take a couple of days off. Stop off at a bed-and-breakfast or two. Kind of like a hundred and thirty-seventh honeymoon."

"You know where I was gonna take your mom on the honeymoon?" Dom asked suddenly.

"Yes," Jack said. "Italy."

"I guess I told you that, huh?"

"I guess you did."

"Never been there," Dom said. "Never been to Italy."

"You'll go."

"Nah," Dom said, not a trace of self-pity in his voice, just stating fact. "I never been anywhere. I'll never go anywhere."

"My mom would have liked Italy, I bet. She would have liked going there with you."

Dom stared at Jack, his leathery mouth and chin moving in a kind of smile, then once again he threw a perfect roundhouse left. And again, he wound up grabbing Jack by the scruff of his neck. His grip was hard and firm and felt good. The old man's calluses scraped against Jack's skin and sent pleasurable shivers up and down his spine.

"You're a good boy, Jackie. You're a good boy."

"Forty-one in a couple of weeks. Some boy."

"Forty-one . . . Jesus . . . that makes me—"

"A hundred and eight."

Dom shook his head as mournfully as he could manage. "You never gave me nothin' but a hard time."

"'Cause you never liked nothin' but a hard time." Jack leaned over to him, gave him a quick hug and kissed him on top of the forehead. "Don't work too hard."

Jack heard a mumbled "Yeah, yeah, that'll be the day," on his way out, and when he turned back to wave good-bye, Dom was already busy lugging a 150-pound side of pork under his arm.

"See you at six," Jack said to nobody in particular. And for the first time in years, he found himself staring at the warehouse floor, at the spot where he knew Sal Demeter had fallen, and he was thinking about Sal and his sudden death, about Kid and his disappearance. *No*, he said to himself. *Don't do this. No more ghosts.*

Think about Caroline, his inner voice told him.

Think about tomorrow. And the restaurant. And Charlottesville.

Turning his back on the market, walking slowly out to his car, he even moved his lips, just slightly, and whispered to himself, *"No more ghosts."* And to be on the safe side, he did it one more time.

"No more ghosts."

She stared into the mirror.

As always these days, she was surprised at what stared back at her.

She remembered an old joke; the girls in school used to mutter it after a date and giggle, "It looks like a penis, only smaller."

Peering into the mirror, she thought: *It looks like me, only older.*

Caroline Hale Keller flicked the switch on her small makeup mirror and recoiled ever so slightly when the dozen tiny bulbs exploded into a circle of bright light. She forced herself to examine the distorted, close-up image that seemed painted onto the glass. She looked past the elegant cheek-bones and perfect features. All she could see were the lines streaming from the corners of her eyes, the slight down-ward turn at the corners of her lips, the small pockets under the eyes.

She raised her right hand to remove her earrings. Slipping them out of the lobes, her hand loomed in the mirror, and she froze it, kept it hanging in the air, unmoving. Her hands, too, were lined. Those elegant hands of hers were no longer smooth and soft-looking. And her nails, long and un-painted, somehow now looked grotesque to her.

She thought of Jack, driving down later that night. She smiled because she knew he'd time it so he could listen to the Knicks game on the car radio. He loved his Knicks, he really did. Had had season tickets, second row, right under the basket, for years now. He always said that if he had one place he could be anywhere in the world, it would be at the Garden for a Knicks play-off game. He knew some of the players, a lot of the sportswriters, all of the ushers. The restaurant had long been a sports hangout, at least for those athletes and writers and executives who actually knew their food. She couldn't find fault with this passion of his. He worked so hard. So all-consumingly. He needed to relax. The boy in him needed to root for Spree to score his twenty-five points and for Houston to hit his outside jumper. She understood perfectly. And yet . . .

And yet she wanted him in her bed tonight. And tonight she wanted the man. Not the boy.

She turned her attention back to the mirror. Patted her neck and chin. Pulled the skin on her face back, smoothing it out.

God, men were so lucky. They looked better with age, so many of them, anyway. Salt-and-pepper hair was distinguished, not matronly. Their bodies could remain firm and flat, not turn menopausal. Craggy skin looked *good* on them. Young women were attracted to them. More than that, would marry them. No wonder so many of them discarded their longtime mates. What did compatibility matter, who cared about a personal history if you could move on to firm skin and upright breasts? It wasn't fair. It wasn't goddamn fair.

She released the skin around her eyes, felt the tautness grow lax. She closed her eyes and took a deep breath. Then another . . .

She had never thought of herself as vain before.

Of course, she had never thought of herself as many things. As secretive. Duplicitous. Unsure. Frightened.

Dangerous.

But she was all of those things, wasn't she? Maybe she hadn't been. But she was now.

Time was an amazing thing, she decided. It didn't just change the way a thing looked. It changed the very thing itself.

Caroline exhaled in front of the makeup mirror, her breath creating a tiny patch of fog on the glass. She flicked the switch, turning the ring of lights off. She rose, slowly took all her clothes off, and stood naked before the full-length mirror in the bathroom. Her body was good. It was. She weighed exactly what she'd weighed when she first met Jack. Her posture was perfect, erect and strong. Her breasts were small, they'd always been small, and, yes, they were not what they'd once been but they were still fine. She knew she looked damn good for a forty-one-year-old woman with a string of restaurants to run and the pressure of opening a new one.

She just didn't look young.

Stepping into her blue robe, Caroline did not want to go back into the bedroom, instead padded into the den, searched the bookshelves until she found an old mystery, one she thought she'd read before but wasn't absolutely sure.

She thought she could flip the pages, without having to think too much, until the sun was up and the new day began.

There were choices she had to make. Decisions she could no longer postpone. She knew that. She'd made some already. Hoped they were the right ones. For the rest, she didn't know how she would choose or what she would decide. She just knew that she had secrets now. Secrets she could never share with anyone. Secrets that, however they developed, would change her life and the lives of those she loved.

Whoever said that with age came wisdom was totally full of shit, she decided. What came with age was doubt. And fear.

Caroline wondered what was going to happen tomorrow.

But it was not tomorrow she was afraid of.

It was the tomorrow after that and the one after that and then all the tomorrows into the future.

Okay, stay calm. No need to be nervous. Nothing has changed.

The Plan was in place and it was a good one.

The Man had come down for the opening. Drove the whole way. He couldn't stay away but that was to be expected. The Plan allowed for that. There were still no surprises.

There were three stages. Just keep remembering that. The three crucial stages. Before, During, and After. Each stage was easy. Just stay calm.

That's all that was needed. Stay calm and keep to the Plan.

Before: It couldn't be better. No one suspected a thing. Not the real thing, anyway. And everything was set. The phone call this afternoon confirmed all that. Easy as pie.

During: What could go wrong? Nothing, that's what. Be quick, that was crucial. Quick but no rushing. Rushing meant mistakes. Quick but slow? Was that possible? No. Quick but relaxed? Yes, that was possible. That was the goal. Quick, quick, quick but nice and relaxed. Get in, wait for the right moment, do it, get out.

Quick quick quick.

Relaxxxxeddddd.

And then there was After. That would be the trickiest. Loose ends to take care of. And no way to practice what was going to *happen. Too bad. Practice was usually the key. Practice made perfect, didn't it?*

Well, at least it made it easier to be quick quick quick.

And easy and relaxed.

Still, After would be fine.

And then: Over.

All over.

Soon now. One more day.

Before, During, After, Over.

Very, very soon.

April 1, 4 P.M.

Jack and Caroline were surveying every tiny detail of the
new restaurant.

To Jack, every night he was at work was a little bit
like being in a Broadway show. The preparation, the pre-
curtain tension, the beginning of the performance, the
exhaustion that came after the final bow. Today, even this
early in the day in Charlottesville, it felt like an opening
night on the Great White Way.

They'd taken over an old soda fountain/restaurant/gen-
eral store in the Downtown Mall as well as the pizza parlor
next door. The location was perfect, right next to the
Piedmont Council of the Arts, the Thomas Jefferson
Planning District Commission, and the Virginia Economic
Development Corporation. Everyone who worked for those
influential organizations had been sent invitations to the
opening-night party and they, as well as all office workers
within a five-block stretch of the mall, had received a
voucher saying that Jack's would stock their favorite wine or
brand of liquor and keep individual bottles for private use
when they dined there. After knocking down walls and
redesigning the space, the restaurant sat 125 inside. They

had also negotiated for the use of outdoor seating on the long red-brick patio in front of the restaurant. So right outside were cast-iron tables and thirty chairs, along with clay planters overflowing with rosebushes.

The restaurant looked gorgeous. Jack didn't even bother to concern himself with that—Caroline was incapable of making a restaurant anything but wonderful-looking. It had the feel of the original Jack's but, as with each of the spin-offs, there was a vague regional atmosphere to it. Jack was never quite able to put his finger on how she managed this. Tonight, he suspected, it was the flowers and the pastel colors that somehow gave the restaurant a slightly Southern feel.

The employees were all in place, as was the complicated management structure unique to the restaurant business. They'd found the morning manager at a local bed-and-breakfast that had recently been sold. The night manager was Bella, from the Miami Jack's. A treasure. Jack had no reservations about leaving everything in her capable hands. The chef was solid. He'd been the sous chef in the Chicago Jack's and was more than ready to step up to his own kitchen. He was not intimidated by running a large staff and he seemed to be a good manager as well as a genuine talent. The assistant manager, the beverage manager, and the special-events manager were all young and relatively inexperienced but were clearly gems. Jack did not like maitre d's and he never had one in any of his restaurants. He thought of maitre d's as money-grubbing bodyguards, imperious and bribable. Instead, he had what he called anchors, and they ran the front of the restaurant—they knew how to juggle the seating, the overbooking, the walk-ins, and they knew how to deal with the extreme anxiety that came with dictating the flow of the restaurant on a nightly basis. Jack and Caroline took particular care when hiring anchors. These people had to be smart, they had to have pride, they had to be driven to make people happy. A restaurant's reputation was based on its staff's interaction with its customers. And not just at the top. That's why, for the new place, they had also hired servers and bussers who were all experienced, all happy to have stepped up in class and even happier to have an employer who provided health insurance. Watching them all prepare now—vacuuming, buffing the tables, folding the napkins, cleaning menus, test-ing the volume of the jazz that would be playing over the speakers throughout the evening—Jack was pleased and proud. Caroline seemed to have done an extraordinary job in this area. He ran down his usual list, tried to find any-thing that was missing, that wasn't being done. He couldn't come up with one thing.

5 P.M.

They had their first staff meeting.

"I just want to run over a few things," Jack began, "before Chef Dave serves the staff dinner, which I happened to take a taste of and I can assure you that it's not too shabby." That drew a few nods of approval. "We've got a few VIPs coming tonight. They will need some special service and attention but what I want to stress is that Jack's reputation is not based on the way we treat our VIPs. It's based on the way we treat our regular customers. Tonight, for instance, the tables outside will be for noninvited guests; we're nothing if not democratic. It's a gorgeous night and my guess is we'll have a huge crowd using the patio, not just for dinner but as a bar area. I want the same attention paid to those customers as you'll be paying to the mayor, the governor, and the other guys who, I promise, will be seriously undertipping you." That got more than a few nods. It got knowing murmurs and chuckles. Jack thanked everyone for all their hard work, then Caroline said a few words. She told them that she'd just made a deal with the best local cleaner, so they shouldn't be overly concerned with stains on their uniform jackets. She discussed a minor problem they were having with space for the dry storage and one of the three cold rooms. And announced that they would all have to be trained in CPR over the next few months. They were shown how best to utilize the mirrors that were strategically placed around the room—under-the-table sex was always the most common distraction that had to be monitored—and they all knew to look for the criers, the drunks, and the yellers. They were also shown the high-profile tables, the visible ones for the VIPs who wanted to flaunt their success, and the two tables in the back for any VIPs who didn't want to be noticed.

When it was over, Chef Dave and the servers brought out the food. Staff dinner was that night's special. Jack took a bite and it was delicious, but even after all the times he'd been through this, he was too nervous to eat. He did notice, with a smile, that Caroline helped herself to seconds.

5:30 P.M.

Caroline sat down with the two anchors to go over the seating for the night. There would be different pressures and problems tonight. There were no dinner walk-ins or late reservations since everyone inside was an invited guest. Still, seating was tricky. The governor and the mayor obviously had to have key tables. As did several of the local businessmen. A few politicians were coming up from Washington and Jack knew that the *Washington Post* restaurant critic had wangled an invitation and was going to be attending, using one of the five pseudonyms she'd been known to use and that had been circulated on the Internet to local restaurant personnel. The chef came out of the kitchen to discuss with the anchors how best to handle the critic. He agreed to make two of everything that the critic ordered as well as two of everything that anyone at the critic's table ordered, just in case something went wrong in the preparation of one of the dishes. The anchor instructed the wait staff as to exactly where the critic would be seated and the bussers were told to make sure there were no cracks or imperfections in any of the plates used for her meal. Then they went over the notation system for the lineup at the door. The lineup—the list of who was dining that night, along with the table arrangements—was used to determine who would sit where and what special attention had to be paid to whom. Caroline went over the system used at all the other Jack's around the country: when anyone called to make a reservation, his or her name was immediately placed into the computer. Any information that could be ascertained, either on the first visit or any future visits, would also be entered. Relevant data would then be put into the lineup, in the area known as the Guest Detail Sheet. Caroline ticked off the information she considered important to note for the GDS: the diner's job, if interesting or special; if the customer was a regular (here or at any of the other Jack's around the country—easy to find out because the database was cross-referenced for all the restaurants); regular dining companions; type of wine preferred; time restrictions; any personal relations with the staff. Tonight, in Charlottesville, the most interesting bit of personal service needed was that a congressman was coming down from D.C. His wife was short and she'd requested that a cushion be placed on her seat so she'd look taller. But it had to be discreet. No one was to know she was sitting on something that would add a couple of inches to her height.

The front-of-the-restaurant staff did not seem particularly rattled by Caroline's last-minute summary. When it was over, the mood was surprisingly calm and Jack felt that yet another piece of the puzzle had slipped perfectly into place.

6:20 P.M.

Jack and Caroline went to the private upstairs office, a small room with a computer and a leather couch, and a large window that overlooked the front of the brick-lined mall.

While they were in town, it was theirs. When they were away, it was to be used by the two site managers. At the restaurant in New York, Jack had a closed-circuit camera installed downstairs in the dining room. The monitor was in the office. From there he could observe the entire scene, watch both customers and employees to make sure everything was going smoothly. Caroline had dissuaded him from doing that here. The place was too small, she'd said. They couldn't see anything from upstairs that they couldn't see downstairs. As he eased down onto the small love-seat-sized sofa, he missed having the monitor. He felt edgy, as if one small detail was missing. He tried to picture the downstairs in his mind, to visualize what was nagging at him. . . .

"Shit," Jack said. "I forgot to talk to Emile about pouring the wine. Bella said that he seemed to be a little slow."

"Relax," Caroline said. "It can wait a few minutes. Talk to him when we go down. And it's not a tragedy if Emile's a little slow. People *do* pour their own wine."

"Not at Jack's," he told her.

"No," she said. "Not at Jack's." With an affectionate smile, she said, "Will you allow *me* to pour for you?"

"Yes," he said. "I think that's allowable."

She popped open a bottle of Dom Pérignon that she'd put on ice several hours earlier. They clinked glasses, each took a sip.

"It's not fair, you know," Jack said.

"What?" she asked.

"There's something on your mind."

"What's unfair about that?"

"You always know what I'm thinking and I have no idea what's going on inside that head of yours."

That drew a real smile. "Finally, I'm a woman of mystery," she said. "That's always been my goal in life."

"So tell me, woman of mystery. What would be the first thing you'd buy if we were very, very, very rich?"

"What kind of question is that?"

"Just curious. Let's say we sold the restaurants and made a killing. You could go anywhere, you could buy just about anything. Come on, you never thought about something like this?"

"Okay," she admitted. "I do know. I'd buy something incredibly beautiful."

"New house?"

"God forbid, I never want to leave our apartment. No, I'd buy something . . . permanent. Something that I could look at all the time and know it was home waiting for me. Something that I'd know would last forever and never change." He raised his eyebrows, waiting for the revelation. "I'd buy a Hopper," she said. "If I could. One of his early cityscapes. I'd put it right over the fireplace and I'd know how I was changing by how I reacted to it over time. I'd know I was happy if I only saw the beauty. Or I'd know something was wrong if what I felt most was the despair or the loneliness."

"Art as emotional compass?"

"You asked," she said. "You asked and that's what I'd buy. Now how about you?"

"That's easy," he told her.

"Minority share in the Knicks?"

He shook his head. "I'd buy something incredibly beautiful, too."

"Château in France?"

"This."

He reached into his pocket, brought out a thin, black box and pressed it into her hand.

"What is it?"

"Open it."

She did and he was pleased—he'd never heard her gasp before.

"Oh, my God, Jack, it's . . . it's . . ."

"Spectacular?"

"Yes. It is *very* spectacular. Are you nuts? It must have cost a fortune."

"It did," he agreed. "Happy opening."

She pulled a necklace out of the box, held it up, let it dangle from her fingers as she stared at it in awe. It was a choker, a perfect circle of diamonds that sparkled magnificently even in the dull overhead light of the office.

"Like it?" he asked.

"I've never seen anything so beautiful. I really can't believe it. Jack, you shouldn't have."

"Does it make up for forgetting the goddamn rifle?"

"I *still* can't believe you forgot it. I reminded you again *right* before you left . . ."

"Does this make up for it?"

"Yes. It makes up for it." She smiled a lustrous smile. "But just barely."

"Put it on."

She slipped the necklace around her throat, reached behind her to fasten the clasp. Then she turned to face him.

"It's a good match," he said.

They both leaned forward and their lips met. It was supposed to be a quick kiss, a seal on the upcoming evening, except Jack raised his eyes, saw something in hers, not sure quite what, but it made him lean in closer and the kiss lingered. Their lips parted, their tongues met, and suddenly one of her hands was behind his neck and both his arms were around her and they were clutching each other, merging their bodies as if trying to become one. When they finally broke apart, the kiss ended first, their mouths very gently separating; then they slowly released each other, their bodies gradually moving backward, first their heads, then their chests, and finally their hips and legs.

"When this night is over, I think we might have to make some serious love," Jack said.

"You just might be on to something," she agreed. "If the night's ever over."

And then it was time to get ready. The necklace stayed around her neck but her boots came off, then her jeans and work shirt. In only a few moments, it seemed, she was glorious in a simple, short black Krizia dress and he looked the perfect host in his Armani tux.

She tied his tie, something he had never managed to master, looping the black silk into a graceful bow. He stood back, admired himself briefly in the mirror, turned, and gave her one last kiss, this one light and quick.

"Let's go rock and roll," he said.

7:32 P.M.

"Governor, it's so nice to see you."

"Caroline, you look even more beautiful than usual. How is that possible?"

"Governor, I'd like to introduce you to the woman you really need to flatter. This is Wendy and she's the one who'll get you your table in the future."

"Ah. Then let me turn my attention to the *real* power."

The anchor laughed and blushed just slightly. "Here's my card, Governor. Please call me directly whenever you need anything."

A delighted smile in Caroline's direction. "I like her already, Caroline."

"We aim to please, Governor. We aim to please."

7:38 P.M.

It was time. No more Before. Now it was During.

The magic invitation had been used. It had worked. Of course it had worked. It was magic.

Everything was working.

Tonight, everything was magic.

The restaurant was already getting crowded and the sidewalk in front was jammed with people. Some of the key guests had arrived. Limos were parking at the east end of the mall. It was like a giant party. People were drinking, laughing, talking a mile a minute. It was happening. It was definitely time.

As long as they did what they were supposed to, as long as they stuck to the schedule. But they would. They had to. And now it was time to move. It was essential to move. Now.

It was not difficult to maneuver through the drinkers. There was no reason to think anyone would notice. There was absolutely no reason to notice a thing.

The guy at the front of the restaurant was so damn nice. The bathroom? Of course. Right through there, behind the bar and to the left. Right next to the stairway.

The stairway to the office.

Head down, don't make eye contact with anyone now. Don't bump into anyone. Don't knock over a drink. Don't draw attention. There she is. Right there, over by the bar. Just as she's supposed to be. I can practically touch her. No, don't raise your head. Don't do it. No attention now. None. Leave her be. Leave her be for now.

Go through the right door. No one inside. Perfect. Nice bathroom. Very nice. So clean. What was this stone? Marble? Yeah, maybe. Must have been expensive. Everything must have been expensive in this place.

Oh, it's just the way you planned it, isn't it? Exactly the way you imagined it in your head.

You are very, very smart. You are very, very, very smart.

Go into the stall now. It's part of the Plan. Close the door. Now just wait.

It's going to happen soon. Very soon. They wouldn't dare let you down. So just wait. All you have to do is wait.

No, no, what are you thinking? That's not all you have to do. You have to check the gun.

Good. Fully loaded. Same as it was the other ten times you checked it. All ready.

Now all you have to do is wait. Wait.

Wait . . .

8:14 P.M.

"Let's go, people, stop the gabbing. We're falling behind schedule."

"Sorry, Chef."

"Don't be sorry. Just hold the talk till after dinner. We're way behind on the side dishes for the meat station."

A waiter careened through the swinging door to the kitchen. "I can't believe it. Everyone's ordering at exactly the same goddamn time."

"What did you expect? They all *sat* at the same goddamn time."

"Christ, it's hot in here. What happened to the ventilation?"

"All right, all right, what's the pecking order, people?"

"You have some leeway with table thirty-two. A couple of lovebirds. They're practically fucking at the table—they won't care *how* long they wait for food."

"Table twelve's the mayor. He's gabbing like he'll never stop and everyone else around him's drinking like a fish so they don't kill themselves. We can hold off on them, too."

"Okay, people, look at the shrimp. It's getting cold! Cover it, cover it! Do you hear me, Fish, cover the fucking shrimp! Jesus!"

8:19 P.M.

Eleven minutes to go.

Four people in and out of the bathroom so far. Not one even noticed there was anyone else already in there.

Still eleven minutes . . . wait a second! Oh, shit . . . Christ, goddamnit, the watch, it isn't working! It isn't fucking working!

Oh, no, it's okay . . . it's okay. It's fine. The second hand's moving. Everything's okay. It was just my imagination. See? That'll show the One. He always says I don't have an imagination. Well, let's see him say that now. Let's see him try to say it.

Why is everything so slow? It's like everything here is all in slow motion. But the second hand is definitely moving. Things are going forward. It's all going to happen just the way I imagined it. All I have to do is keep waiting.

Just keep waiting . . .

8:28 P.M.

Jack stared over at the table in the far corner of the restaurant. Table 54. He pulled the server from that station over to the side.

"Watch those two guys, will you?"

"Yes, sir." The server turned. He saw two men, both fairly broad. One was quite tall with blond hair, the other shorter and darker. "What's the problem?"

"Probably nothing. They just look angry. They're arguing."

"They've both had a lot to drink. Bourbon and beer."

"I don't want anything to happen so keep your eyes on them."

"Okay."

The kid looked so concerned. Jack patted him on the back. "Relax. I'm sure I'm just oversensitive tonight. They'll calm down."

Jack patted him on the back again. He saw Caroline across the room. She was frowning, staring across the room to the table in the corner. He heard the young server say to the two men there, "Excuse me, gentlemen. Would you mind keeping your voices down, please? You're getting a little loud." He heard one of the men say, "Oh, yeah, sure. Sorry."

Jack smiled at Caroline. He thought about making love to her later that night and waved.

She waved back and he was sure she was thinking about the exact same thing.

8:29 P.M.

Okay. Get ready. Got the stocking? Right, like I'd forget it.

Then get it out. Get it ready.

It felt funny, felt so tight, tighter than in the practice sessions in front of the mirror.

It was a little hard to breathe.

No, no, it was fine. Take a deep breath. Take another. And one more. See, it's fine. Everything's just right.

The second hand is moving.

The waiting's almost over. . . .

8:30 P.M.

"Fuck you!"

"Don't say that to me."

"Why not? Fuck you!"

"I'm not kidding, goddamnit! Say it to me again, I'll break your fucking head!"

The server didn't seem to actually run, but he made it to the table in record time. "Gentlemen, please. I'm going to have to ask you to leave."

The taller man looked up. "Leave?"

"You're disturbing the other guests."

"Oh, yeah?" That was from the shorter one.

"Please. Otherwise I'll have to call the police."

It was the tall one's turn. "Oh. Well, we wouldn't want you to do that." He started to stand, then turned to the server. "I just have one more thing to say." Now he turned to the other man at the table and screamed, "Fuck you!" And then: "Fuck you, fuck you, fuck you!"

And then all hell broke loose.

8:31 P.M.

Okay, move. Go, go, go!

Out of the stall, no one in the bathroom. Out the door, no one even in the hallway.

The bar: No one's looking. They're all watching the fight. Or moving far away to help. And she's there. Still right by the bar. Right where she's supposed to be. Right where she said she'd be.

It's working. It's working, it's working, it's working!

Quick, show her the gun. Don't wave it. Not too much. Just make sure she sees it.

Oh, yeah. She sees it. And she's cool. Very cool. She's not showing much, is she? She's not showing anything. But those eyes. Look in her eyes. There, you can see it. Oh, is it terror? Please, please, please, let her be terrified.

No. No, it isn't terror. Amazing.

It's anger.

Okay, gotta move. Make her move. Fast!

Yes! She's moving.

No more waiting. Ever again.

Even if she's not terrified, it's working.

Oh, God, it's fucking working.

8:32 P.M.

Customers had been trying not to pay attention to the harsh words. But at the sound of the crash, everyone turned.

When the tall man at table 54 screamed his last "Fuck you!" the smaller man picked up his water glass and threw it. The tall man ducked and the glass exploded against the wall behind him. The woman at the next table screamed as glass shards rebounded and cascaded through the air, one of them imbedding itself in her bare shoulder. By the time Jack was halfway across the room, he could see blood streaming onto her dress and the tablecloth.

People scrambled out of the way as the tall man upended his table, sending the shorter man and the server flying. The tall man then dove onto the floor, swinging his fists. The two men were rolling on the floor now, trying to kill each other. They were spewing obscenities and kicking wildly. Now they were on their feet, stumbling into another table.

Another woman screamed.

Three waiters and three customers were trying to pull them apart.

The anchor was on the phone with the police.

The mayor and governor were heading toward the front door.

The two men were in a brutal rage. Three servers were bleeding, one profusely, his nose clearly broken. Several tables were overturned now. Food and silverware had spilled onto the floor. The violence seemed to have frozen everyone in the restaurant.

Jack was about to reach the fight, about to join the melee and try to break it up, when he turned. An instinct. A protective instinct. And as he turned he saw Caroline, just the back of her dress and her right leg, disappearing up the stairs. Right behind her was someone dressed in black. That person, too, disappeared. But there was something odd about the person's face. What was it? It seemed hidden, strangely faded, like there was something pulled over his head, a kind of gauze. And there was something in his hand. Jack definitely caught a glimpse of something in his hand.

Something metallic.

Jack turned from the fight on the floor and sprinted through the dining room.

He reached the stairs, no one even noticing his mad dash because the fight had escalated, had turned into two raging animals engaged in battle.

Jack ran up the stairs, two at a time. He reached the door to the office, grabbed the doorknob, threw it open . . .

8:36 P.M.

Yes, yes, it was going to work.

No one had seen them. No one had noticed. And she was scared now. Oh, yes, she was. She'd do anything. Anything at all that needed to be done.

The gun waved and she moved into the corner. Now everything was for the taking.

But what? What to take?

What was that noise? Running. Yes. Someone running upstairs. Don't worry. It won't matter. You're in control. It will be easy. This will be easy.

The other thing will be easy, too. No need to think too hard over what to take. Not really. It was very easy.

There was only one thing to be taken.

8:37 P.M.

Jack threw himself through the door and the first thing he saw was Caroline. She was standing in the corner and she looked shrunken, devastated, as if someone had yanked her entire life away from her. Then he saw the figure at the desk, but only for a second. He saw the gun. And he saw the mask.

A stocking, not gauze. A stocking pulled tightly over the face. The features were a blur. And then the whole world was a blur. Before Jack could turn, before he could react, the gun slammed down over his head. The blow was extraordinarily strong and he stumbled back, fell onto the love seat. He tried to get up, to offer some kind of attack, but he was overwhelmed by a spasm of nausea. He tried again to raise himself, knew he had to do something, couldn't just stand there, not again, then the room spun around him, faster and faster now, and the pain made him fall forward onto the floor.

"We don't keep any money up here."

That sounded like Caroline. Yes, it had to be Caroline. But everything was so fuzzy. Even the sound was distorted. The voice sounded like a record played at the wrong, slow speed.

"This kind of restaurant, we don't keep very much cash."

Still Caroline. That should still be Caroline talking. Then a jumble of words, some came fast, some seemed so slow.

"The bar . . . cash register . . . only place we have money."

Then he thought he heard, still Caroline: ". . . get it . . . two, three thousand . . . get it for you . . ."

And then a roar washed over the room. Was this Caroline? No, it was deeper. Angrier. He heard this word: *More*. And again, deeper and angrier: *More. Ruin. Why.*

And these words: *Bitch. Whore.*

Cunt.

Jack tried to get up. He turned his head and the movement was excruciating. More words spewed out now. But they were nonsense. Nonsense from a madman.

Tear down the wool.
What did that mean?
Wooly here . . . the will is strong . . . wool candy broken . . .
What did it mean! Why couldn't he understand?
Wooly . . . candy . . . forever . . .
He saw the person in the mask move toward Caroline. Saw him reach for her. Saw him grab the necklace, the beautiful diamond necklace, rip it from Caroline's neck. Saw his hand flash forward again, heard the noise as his fist cracked against Caroline's face. Heard her scream. And Jack threw himself upward now. He had to move. He *had* to. The pain sliced through him. It rocked his head back and he saw a flash of light. He knew there was no light like that, not in this room, it had to be pain that was blinding him, but he could fight the pain, he *had* to fight the pain, so he kept going and his arms found flesh, he knocked the robber back, he was sure he did that. And then there was an explosion. Loud. Right inside his head. And there was more pain. A new pain. It frightened him. Then there was another explosion. This one quieter. And a third, immediately after. Quieter still.

And then his fear was gone because suddenly there was no pain. Just a softness. Like some sort of pleasant dream. And no more blinding light. Instead, a gentle white cloud. He heard Caroline again. Why was she screaming? It was over now, wasn't it? There was nothing to be frightened about. There was no more pain.

He reached for her, to show her that it was all right. To show her that she was safe. But he couldn't seem to grab hold of her. She seemed to melt away from him.

Now he felt something strange. It was as if something was seeping out of him. He couldn't tell what it was. It felt good, though, that's what was so strange. He knew it was bad but it felt so very, very good.

And suddenly he knew what it was that was escaping from inside of him. What it was that was leaving, rushing away in a flood now, never to return.

It was his life itself that was deserting him.

He heard one last thing as he slid limply onto the floor. One final explosion. This one didn't frighten him at all. It was too distant. Too quiet. So he figured he had to be wrong. It wasn't an explosion. It was just a dream.

Just a nice, quiet, painless dream.

In his dream Jack reached again for Caroline. But she was gone. Jack closed his eyes.

And the dream took him into a deep, still, never-ending darkness.

Okay, everybody. It's time to put our Humpty Dumpty back together again. He's lost four liters of blood, mostly in the pelvis and hip. If we're going to keep him alive, first thing we've got to do is keep his fluids replenished. We're going to make the switch from the plasma expanders and saline tubes to the large bore. Now! This mother needs some blood and fast. He's leaking all over the fucking place."

Those were the last words spoken for the next several minutes while the large bore tubes replaced the smaller emergency tubes that had been frantically administered by the guys in the ambulance. Bigger catheters were sutured expertly into the arteries and neck. It was like a circle of serious and flawless quilters doing repair work on a worthless and torn rug. Hands moved nimbly up and down, weaving almost in unison, sealing the lifelines into place. Once the stitching was done, the catheters were hooked up to IV's and soon blood was flowing back into the unmoving body instead of just out.

The room was awash in the blood that had escaped, as were the doctors and nurses flocked around the table. The lead surgeon, Dr. Harold Solomon, shrugged his left shoulder up to wipe a splash of reddish brown from his cheek. He took a long, deep breath, exhaled through his nose as an athlete might, about to expend one last great burst of energy, and spoke quietly, quickly, and emotionlessly to the now still room. He could have been a dock foreman detailing cargo contents and shifts for union members.

"All right. We've got multiple gunshot wounds. One shot took out the right pelvis. Another the right hip. The third got the left knee. In the hip we've got a high-velocity fracture. We're gonna put in a reconstructive plate. Nothing unusual, we've all done it before. The pelvis is potentially life-threatening. We've got a communuted superior rami fracture with extension into the iliac wing. The bullet hit in the midpelvis and, besides shattering the bone, it's screwed up a lot of other things. The most crucial is that the bladder's been ruptured and that's where we've got the massive bleeding. We're going to work there first because, frankly, I don't know if he's gonna survive it, so why waste everything else. For the knee, there's a super condular fracture of the left femur. If he's still around, we'll do a similar type of reconstruction at the hip with plates and screws. All set?"

They were.

The initial surgery took eight hours and forty minutes.

The first step was to build an external fixater for the pelvis. It looked like an old-fashioned toy Erector set, a complex layering of pipes, joints, and hinges. It was a means of both elevating the pelvis—propping it up—and preventing it from splintering completely. Its essential function was to provide enough room for the bladder surgeon to go in and repair the punctured organ. If the external fixater didn't hold, the patient was dead.

The group hovering over the patient were remarkably relaxed and casual. As they worked, a stream of chatter replaced the initial quiet. There were questions about the Redskins front line and the sexual orientation of an orthopedic nurse who was not present for this surgery and there were complaints about the new vending machines in the cafeteria—there was general agreement that the hot whipped mocha concoction tasted like a combination of chalk and urine. This part of the surgical procedure was no different from the way a master carpenter put up shelves. It was done confidently, skillfully, and purely mechanically, with no thought of error. There was no science involved and zero room for interpretation. Once the decisions were made on how to proceed, this was hammer-and-nails stuff, no more emotionally involving than gluing a broken piece of china back together. The pride came from how seamlessly the pieces were restored.

When the external fixater was in place and stable, the bladder surgeon, Dr. Mugg, moved in for his turn. He was not the most popular person in the local medical community. He tended to lecture while he worked—his nickname in the halls was Dr. Smug—and several months ago he'd managed to patent a particular technique of suturing. No other surgeon in the country could now use this method without paying him a substantial royalty on each operation. As a result, Dr. Smug was not only more arrogant than ever, he was driving a new Ferrari and buying a six-bedroom weekend house on the Maryland shore. But his hands moved smoothly and surely, and however much his mouth motored, his eyes never wavered. In just over two and a half hours, Dr. Mugg turned his back on the patient and said, "It's as good as it gets. It'll take about a week to heal, then we can go back in and do an open reduction and internal fixation. He's one lucky bastard that I was in town." Without saying anything else, he left the room. The abdomen and bladder were, for the moment, whole and stable.

Now it was time for the orthopedic traumatologist, Dr. Solomon, to step back up to the table and begin to reconstruct the hip.

The bullet had completely reshaped the bone. At first, Dr. Solomon thought it might be necessary to do a replacement, but enough of the original structure around the acetabulum of the hipbone had survived so that a combination of plates and screws would suffice.

The doctor had, before entering medical school, considered becoming an architect. He was a visual person and also tended to concentrate on the way things functioned. So when he looked at an object, his mind would take him below the surface; he concentrated on structure, viewing most things as blueprints. This vaguely Platonic overview—he more often than not saw the way a thing worked rather than the thing itself—not only helped him focus when operating, it kept things on a much more objective basis. It allowed him to disassociate from the human element and concentrate on the structural work at hand. So while he went through the process of repairing this nearly destroyed hip, his eyes did not see the tissue he was slicing through nor the bone he was breaking and remaking. He saw, instead, a precise, neatly drawn architectural plan of the body.

Working from that plan in his mind, he drilled two holes into the head of the femur, inserted two screws, and attached a reconstructive plate that spanned the entire fracture. When the plate was finally in place and immovable, he looked up to see the admiring eyes of his coworkers. The blueprint faded from his mind and the reality intruded. He saw the patient, immobile on the operating table. He wondered when he'd get the details of the shooting, began to imagine the scenario that had led to this kind of destruction, then immediately shook the thoughts out of his head. It was no time to personalize. The left knee still had to be reconstructed.

Although Dr. Solomon had been operating for almost twelve hours that day, there was no hint of exhaustion in his body or his mind. So, with a blueprint of the new area firmly in place, he again began drilling, this time into the expanded distal end of the femur that articulated with the tibia. When that was done, more screws were inserted and another reconstructive plate was attached.

At 6:35 in the morning, the operating team was done.

One nurse had to rush immediately into another surgery—a misaimed bullet in a family feud had passed by the spinal cord of a fourteen-year-old girl. The doctors did not yet know if the cord was bruised or ripped. If bruised, the chances for complete healing were good. If ripped, the girl would never walk again.

One intern made it as far as the first chair he came to in the hospital hallway. There he sat, stretched out, and fell soundly asleep.

Dr. Solomon's first act, when leaving the emergency room, was to head to the cafeteria, put seventy-five cents into the coffee vending machine, get himself a Styrofoam cup of the godawful mocha concoction, then go to sit on the curb outside the side door of the hospital and smoke a cigarette. After fifteen minutes and a second smoke, he stood wearily and headed to his car. By that time he'd already been informed that if the patient lived through the next week— a fifty-fifty chance at best—and the bladder healed properly, Dr. Mugg would, as he'd announced, perform the open reduction and internal fixation of the bladder and then he, Dr. Solomon, would return with the patient to the operating room for a formal plating of the pelvis. That meant, literally, lining him up like a jigsaw puzzle and making sure the skeletal structure was back in the proper place. After that, a balloon would temporarily be placed inside the bladder, the patient would stay several more days in their care, until he was hemodynamically stable, and then he'd be helicoptered back to New York City and the Hospital for Special Surgery, where he would be placed under the care of his own orthopedic surgeon.

Dr. Solomon knew he would never see the patient again after that. Knew he would never find out what his life would become. That didn't particularly bother the doctor. He'd done his job. And if the man lived, the next six to twelve months of his life would be about one thing and one thing only: pain. Harold Solomon was not much interested in pain. He much preferred the contained and docile sterility of the operating room to the prolonged agony of the recuperation period. No, his job was basically over, and so was his involvement. But he did stop walking about fifty feet from his car, turn, and briskly return to the hospital. He went to the newsstand, bought the morning paper. He might never know about his patient's future but he decided he wanted to know about his past. Wanted to know what had brought him to the brink of destruction. At the very least, before he went home to his comfortable three-bedroom house with the little brick patio in the backyard and the toilet that wouldn't stop running and the neighbor who was without question a Peeping Tom and his fiancée who would most certainly be annoyed that once again he'd been out all night, Dr. Harold Solomon wanted to know whose life he'd just done his damnedest to save.

Jack Keller often thought about the exact moment when he realized he had not died. It was when he heard four short and simple words. The most basic and unpoetic of questions:

"Can you hear me?"

And, yes, of course he could. It was a woman's voice, clear and sweet as could be. A tiny bit hoarse but so soothing and gentle. The voice warmed him, made him glow inside. But he didn't know who was speaking. He couldn't see her. And she sounded so far away. Who was she? That's what he remembered wondering. She seemed so nice. So familiar . . .

"Can you hear me?"

He thought he'd answered but maybe he hadn't. *Yes*, he said, *I can hear you. But who are you?*

"Jack, *please* tell me you can hear what I'm saying."

Yes, yes, yes. I said I can hear you. Why can't you hear me?

"Then just listen to me, Jack."

Why are you doing this to me? Why can't you understand what I'm saying? And even as he screamed the words, he knew the answer: *Because I'm saying nothing. It's all only in my head. I'm not speaking, I'm thinking. I'm not making any noise. But why not? How can that be? What's happening?*

"You're going to be all right, Jack."

That's when he recognized the voice. The wonderful voice that comforted him as strongly and physically as if it were a cool hand pressed against his feverish forehead. It was Caroline. How could he not have recognized her? And why couldn't he see her? Where was she? Where was *he*?

Suddenly the voice became a whisper, and it was so close by he could feel her magical breath warming his ear.

"You *have* to be all right, Jack. Do you understand? I *need* you to be all right."

He felt her holding his hand, squeezing it in hers. He couldn't feel any other part of his body, it was as if the rest of him didn't exist, but he could feel the pressure on the back of his hand, feel her thumb digging urgently into his palm.

"I love you. I love you now and I will always love you and I need you to be all right so I can show you just how *much* I love you."

He tried once again to answer her but he couldn't. And then he couldn't hear her anymore either. It was as if he were being covered in a thick fog. He tried to reach for her, tried to bring her back, but there was nothing there. She was gone and he was alone.

It was only much later that Jack Keller decided there were just two things that had kept him alive.

One, of course, was Caroline. Of that he was absolutely certain.

For she had returned after that first visit. Many times. Both in Virginia and in New York, after he was able to be transferred. And every time he felt her near him, he became stronger, more determined to fight whatever it was that was pinning him down and trying to smother him. When she was by his side she would hold his hand and touch his cheek, whisper to him, will him on and beg him to endure the agony because there was still so much pleasure ahead of them. To coax him into the future, she would talk about the past, about the time they'd spent together, and, although he still couldn't see her, he knew by her words that she was smiling and that she looked as beautiful as she could look, which was quite beautiful indeed.

"Do you remember the first time we made love?" she asked. And, yes, he most definitely remembered, every little detail. It was not possible to forget something so sublime, but he enjoyed listening to her tell it; the remembering made him happy, as if they were able to make love once again, after all these years, for the very first time. "I was so nervous," she went on. "But a different kind of nervous. Not a virginal nervousness, God knows, that was hardly the case, but I'd never made love with anyone when I knew it was so *important*. It wasn't just a date and we weren't just having sex, we were testing out the viability of our permanence. It doesn't sound very romantic, I know, but that's really what I thought, even then. And it was romantic, because somehow I knew that you were thinking the same thing. And if I didn't please you or somehow you were disappointed, well . . . I didn't think I'd be able to bear it. The idea that you wouldn't please *me* was inconceivable. I was so *mad* for you. Could you tell? No, probably not. Or maybe just a little. I didn't let on, at least not too much. I was afraid. Although I couldn't even tell you what I was afraid *of.* Maybe I was already afraid of how much I was in love with you.

"Do you remember? We went back to your dorm room. And you'd put candles all around. You'd bought a good bottle of wine. French, *very* ritzy. Put on Joni Mitchell. You didn't even like her, but you knew I did. And do you remember how we talked? How we knew we were there to make love? It was definitely going to happen, so there was no rush, and we just talked and talked for hours and hours. Lying on your bed, sometimes touching, sometimes not. And then there I was, lying up against you, in your arms, and we were still just talking until I kissed you. I couldn't stand it anymore; I just had to do it. Then I put your hand on my breast, I remember that. And then your hands were everywhere. So gentle. So sexy. We kissed and touched and made love and listened to Joni Mitchell and we didn't stop until sometime the next morning. I can still remember everything. Not just remember but *feel.* Every touch. Every kiss. It was fun, wasn't it, being young . . ."

Another time she came and sat and stroked him and talked about the first time she was pregnant.

"I hardly gained any weight and I know that deep down you didn't think there was really a child in there. But there was, and when I told you I thought it was time, when I was in such pain, remember how terrified you were? You kept making jokes and acting so blasé but I knew you were afraid for me, afraid it would hurt, afraid something would happen. I thought you knew right from the beginning that it had all gone wrong. And I remember you said you wished you could go through it instead because you knew I was so scared of the pain. I thought that was the sweetest thing I'd ever heard, you wanting to take my pain. And in a way you did because in the room, I can still see you, you were in such agony watching me. Here I was, trying to have this baby, and I just kept saying to you, 'It's okay, I'm fine, it's not so bad,' trying to comfort you. I can still remember your face when . . . when we knew. The doctor told you, spoke directly to you, and I knew it was devastating but you were staring down at me, making sure I was all right. I'd never had anyone look at me that way. I remember when I was a freshman, before I knew you, I broke my arm. Riding in Central Park. I needed an operation, had to have pins put in, kind of a big deal. And I called Mother and Daddy to tell them. I thought at least one of them would fly up to New York to, you know, take care of me. I remember, when it was time to get off the phone—by then I knew they weren't even thinking of coming up—Daddy said, 'Call us after the operation and let us know how you feel.' I didn't say anything, but I wanted to say, 'No! *You* call *me!*' But they didn't. I never had anyone who thought to call me until I met you. Only you wouldn't just call, you'd *be* there. And if you could, you'd even hurt *for* me." She was quiet for a little bit. Jack could hear her breathing. He couldn't tell if this memory had made her sad or happy or both. When she spoke again, it was with a new tenderness, but also with a quiet sense of regret. "I used to think that maybe it was right that we never had children, Jack. We were so much in love with each other, maybe we wouldn't have had enough left over for anyone else. I used to think that we had a finite amount of love in us—not just us, *people,* I mean. *All* of us. That we could use it up and when it was gone we wouldn't have enough for anything else, anyone new. When you can talk, Jack, I want you to tell me if that's true. If we're all in danger of running out of love . . ."

Yes, he knew that Caroline had kept him going. And it wasn't just her love. Or her patience. When he listened to her talk—about them, about the restaurants, about the life they'd shared—he understood that they were not just friends or lovers or husband and wife. They were *partners,* had been since they'd first met, in everything, and he knew he couldn't just disappear and leave her alone. It made him strong. And it made him fight. He couldn't end the partnership by up and dying on her.

There was another thing, too. A second thing that had saved him.

It was what Dr. Feldman told him.

When the pain was excruciating. When he realized that pain couldn't possibly get any worse.

That came after the period when he didn't know the difference between dream and reality. Even now, he wasn't exactly sure how long that period had lasted. Days, perhaps. More likely weeks. He heard voices sometimes, garbled sounds that pierced his thick fog. And he saw faces, bending over him, standing above him. Occasionally he felt things. Poking. Or movement; once he was sure that someone was turning him over. Another time he felt as if someone was walking him around a room, manipulating him as if he were a marionette. He tried to speak sometimes. Often he thought he *was* speaking. But no one ever seemed to understand him.

At some point, the fog began to lift. He was not yet anchored to the real world but he could, from time to time, touch down upon it. He would drift. Couldn't stop. Suddenly, there would be a flash of color, and with a start he would realize that he was looking at the back of his own flesh-colored hand. It was paler than he remembered, but it had texture. And it was startlingly vivid. He watched his fingers move and he could tell they were part of him, and somehow it seemed miraculous that wherever he was, whatever had happened to him, he was able to think, somewhere in the recesses of his brain, *Move,* and his fingers would follow instructions. They would wiggle and bend, they would obey, before he fell back into his fog, exhausted and drained.

Soon after, the jumble of noises around him turned into words. Then, occasionally, sentences. He kept hearing the word "accident" and realized it was referring to him. *After the accident,* he heard. Or: *Since the accident . . . It's a result of the accident . . . The trauma of an accident like that . . .* And he wanted to scream, *What are you talking about? It was no* accident. *It was not an accident! It was human savagery, unleashed and unfiltered.* But it took more time before the sounds that came out of his throat began to be heard and understood. The first time he said the word "thirsty" and someone appeared, a black woman, dressed all in white, to pick up his head and give him a drink of water, he wept; tears of relief streamed down his cheeks.

Every few days, something new began to come back to him. Then it was every day, and soon, hour by hour. The room came into focus. Details were remembered—words and numbers and places and names.

But when reality came flitting into Jack's new world, so did the extraordinary pain.

First they would make him move while he was still in the bed. Turn him over, gently twist his legs and his arms. The nurses would explain what they were doing. "Don't want to get thrombosis," one of them would say. Then when another one came to move him the next time, it would be, "This is so we don't get a pulmonary embolism. We don't want a stroke, do we?" Jack didn't give a shit if he got a stroke. He certainly didn't give a shit if *she* got a stroke. All he cared about was that the pain go away. Because it flooded his entire being and dominated every waking moment and made him yearn for blessed sleep and, yes, even death.

He was forced into a wheelchair as soon as he regained consciousness. "You've got to be mobile," a nurse would tell him. And all he could think was: *Please, let me die so I don't have to feel any more pain.*

Jack knew he'd never forget the surgeon's words, not as long as he lived, because they changed everything. Good old Doc Feldman—well, not really so old, a year younger than Jack. And already the best orthopedic surgeon in New York City. Jack had been transferred back to New York, although he didn't remember any of the movement or the flight, as soon as he was stable, and placed in the intensive care unit of the Hospital for Special Surgery on East

Seventieth Street. Feldman had performed a shoulder operation on Jack years before—nothing too complicated, a torn
rotator cuff and bone spur—but he did a wonderful job
and after that he began coming to the restaurant. He was
usually with an attractive woman and once or twice the four
of them—Feldman, his date, Jack, and Caroline—social-
ized. The life-changing words came when the doc was
making his hospital rounds and saw his patient and friend
lying there, unmoving. He leaned over the bed, didn't touch
him, no attempt at bedside manner; a soothing demeanor
was not important to Andy Feldman. He didn't even check
to see if the still body lying flat on the mattress was awake.
Just said, very matter-of-fact, "I know you don't feel it, Jack,
but you're lucky. Because the human brain is a remarkable
thing. It can't do what you want most right now. It can't *prevent* pain; nothing can do that. But it does something almost
as good. It won't *remember* pain. I promise you, it won't
allow you to *ever,* not even for a moment, remember what
you're feeling right now."

That's when Jack knew he'd truly survive, understood
that he'd make it. If he'd been told that the agony was permanent, thought for a minute that he'd wake up a year later,
two years later, *anytime* later, and there it would still be,
unchanged, enveloping him, invading his body, he would
have killed himself.

Once Jack knew that he would live, he could allow himself
to return to the past. The opening in Charlottesville. The
fight in the restaurant. Running toward the stairs and rushing into the upstairs office. He could let that remarkable

brain remember what had happened to him. As it did, the world began to make a little more sense.

And then all sense was taken away from him.

At first he didn't believe them. They were lying. They had to be. But they were so calm, so sure of themselves. So understanding and so pitying. So unrelenting.

They told him over and over again until he began to believe. They showed him newspaper articles and a *Talk* magazine story. They even had Dom come and say, yes, they were telling the truth, then he'd put his head down on Jack's chest and sobbed and sobbed.

And then Jack knew.

Caroline had not cooled his fever with the touch of her hand. She had not urged him back to life with her loving whispers. Those were the drugs, they explained. He'd been hallucinating. She had not been beside him in the hospital at all.

Because that night, the night of *the accident*, that final sound he'd heard before he'd passed out, that most distant of the explosions . . . it had not been in the distance. And it had not been an explosion.

It was a gunshot. A fourth shot, after the ones that had sliced through his hip and knee and abdomen and ripped him apart.

More human savagery. Meant to destroy. To erase. To kill.

No, there was no more sense to the world Jack returned to. Because he had indeed been lucky. He had survived his wounds.

But Caroline had not.

She had been shot once, in the head.

And then picked up and thrown through the office window.

The shot had killed her, he was told. She was dead before the two-story fall down to the bricks below.

That news did not surprise Jack, when he was conscious and able to absorb it. He knew the shot was meant to kill.

Just as he knew what the fall was.

A message from someone who knew about his past.

A warning.

From someone letting him know what his future would hold.

Before had gone so well.

During had been just fine.

But now After. It was all going wrong.

Oh, the first part was smooth enough. Meet them as planned, watch the pleased look on their faces, then the surprise in their eyes. Two quick shots. Quick. Relaxed. That was just swell.

And everyone was confused as hell. No one had a clue. No motive, no fingerprints. Clean as a whistle.

But it was supposed to be done. Before, During, After, Over. That was the Plan.

And now look what happened.

There they were, both of them in the room. Both ready for the taking. Even better than the Plan.

But he hadn't died. It was in the paper. Right there in black and white. After all that, Jack Keller had lived.

So it wasn't over. Not really. Not yet.

Now it was Before, During, After . . .

And Just Beginning.

BOOK THREE

THE
THIRD
FALL

SIX MONTHS LATER

2000 - 2001

" **J** ack . . ."

Jack looked up, distracted. As he did, he felt a slit of cold air slither across the back of his neck and he shivered.

"Jack?"

It took him a moment to focus, frustrated that he'd only managed to get a quarter of the way through the newspaper article he was reading. Sitting at the small, round wrought-iron table on the terrace of his penthouse apartment, he'd been startled to hear the soft voice calling his name. Something told him that he'd been called three or four times already.

"It's too cold to be sitting out there," the voice said. "Why don't you come in now?"

It was Mattie, the housekeeper who'd been with them for twelve years. Talking to him tenderly, the way a nanny speaks to a favorite but willful child. When Caroline was alive, the rail-thin black woman with the round glasses and silvery hair used to come every Tuesday and Friday, did the cleaning and shopping and any errands that needed doing. Since the shooting, she'd come in every day to look after him. He hadn't asked, she just appeared on a Monday and said, "I changed my schedule." Never asked him if he'd wanted her in more often, never asked about money. Just took over and added cooking to her other responsibilities. For the first two months, he had someone living with him. A male nurse named Willie. But that didn't matter. Mattie began showing up at nine every morning. When she realized that Jack had trouble sleeping through the night, that he almost always woke earlier, she showed up at eight or seven, sometimes as early as six, so she could prepare his breakfast and make coffee. She had a key to the apartment, could let herself in whenever she pleased. Jack had recently discovered that from time to time she returned in the middle of the night. He'd awakened at two o'clock one morning to find her sitting in the living room, watching television with the sound turned down so low it was barely audible. He hadn't gotten out of bed, just sensed that someone was in the apartment other than Willie. When he called out, an embarrassed Mattie came into his bedroom. She came once in a while, she told him, just to check up on him, to make sure he was all right because she knew he'd never call her that late, even if he needed something. She knew Willie could handle any emergency, but she didn't trust him to do the little things, she said. Dear, dear Mattie. Jack thought that she missed Caroline almost as much as he did. And she looked so frightened for him now, watching him from inside the living room. So sad.

"They say it's going to rain. Maybe sleet. Why don't you just come in where it's warm?"

"I'm all right, Mattie," he said. But that didn't satisfy her. She stood, left hand on her hip, staring out at him, frowning through the halfway-open sliding glass door. "I'll be in in a few minutes. How's that?"

"Are you telling me the truth?" Her voice was edgeless, in no way accusing, almost a singsong.

"I promise."

"Five minutes?"

"Yes. No more than five minutes."

She nodded, not a hundred-percent pleased but accepting the compromise as the best she was going to get.

As soon as she'd walked briskly back to the kitchen, Jack returned to the routine he'd kept every morning since getting home from the hospital. It was the first thing he did each day: sit on his balcony and read the Charlottesville newspaper's account of Caroline's murder.

The location was important to him. They had bought the apartment because of this terrace, with all that it symbolized, so it didn't matter what the weather was. If it was raining, he had Mattie put up the umbrella that Caroline had installed as a sunshade. If it was cold, he put on a sweater. When he thought about his marriage, when he thought about *them,* he pictured the two of them sitting at this wrought-iron table, set up as close to the ledge as he could bring himself to go—over the years, he had learned his limit; his seat was exactly eight feet from the edge—having a gracious and comfortable breakfast, their knees brushing against each other, her hand grazing the top of his as she reached for a piece of toast or a spoonful of jam.

Having lost his concentration as a result of Mattie's interruption, Jack started over at the beginning of the article, painstakingly reading every word from the first sentence to the last. As always, he tried desperately to find some sort of meaning or solace, even something as simple as order, in what he read. But, as always, by the time he reached the end of the article, he found only randomness and chaos and infinite sadness.

From the front page of the
Charlottesville *Constitution, April 2:*

. . . It is not known whether the suspect attended the party for Jack's opening, so it is not known exactly how he gained entrance to the office. Police believe that after the shooting, the suspect did not descend into the main room of the restaurant but instead climbed out the office window and pulled himself up onto the roof of the building. From there, he likely lowered himself onto an adjoining garden balcony, from which he would have had easy access to Water Street, where there are several nearby parking areas and it would not have been difficult to have a car waiting.

Police say they are putting all local resources into finding the suspect and they expect an arrest shortly.

Jack carefully folded the newspaper back up and set it down on the heavy iron chair next to him. Leaning forward, he reached for the coffeepot, stretching toward the center of the table. As he did, he instinctively flinched, but it was too late. He had been lost in his own reflections, so he was not quite prepared for the bolt of agony that arrived, streaking down from his right hip and magically running across his body to thunder through the joint of his left knee. Jack closed his eyes, realized he had hold of the coffeepot and that his hand was shaking, sudden, jarring tremors, so he forced his eyes open again, put the coffee down as slowly as he could manage. He took a deep breath, waited a full thirty seconds, forced himself to focus on the ticking second hand, then he steeled himself, reached for the pot once more. The pain came again but he was fully prepared for it this time and held on to the coffee, even grabbed hold of his cup and poured himself a second helping. He managed to drink it, at least a couple of quick sips, before the tremors in his hand made him set the cup down.

He stayed motionless, still as could be, until the pain became manageable. As he sat, frozen, he realized that among the many things that had changed for him over the past months, the biggest change by far was the pain. Yes, he could deal with it. It was not the kind of excruciating, mind-numbing pain he'd faced at the beginning of his rehab, when the simple act of turning over in bed seemed impossible and the gentlest of steps felt as if a sledgehammer were shattering his bones and a drill boring into his nerve endings. Nor was it as absolutely omnipresent as it had been after the shooting. He now had moments of relief, long minutes when his body was calm and peaceful, and he could almost sleep through the night now. But still, the pain dominated his life as nothing else ever had. He made no movements without being aware of it. He rarely had a thought that was totally separate from it. And most of all, he realized that he was afraid of it. Afraid of how much it limited him. Afraid of how mortal it made him feel. And just plain fucking afraid of how much it hurt.

Now it had subsided to the point where he could gingerly reach for the second newspaper, perched on the chair to his right. It was a much easier movement for him. He picked it up, hesitated, waiting to see how bad the next wave would be; finding it to be relatively minor, he turned to the article he already knew by heart and went on to the next step of his daily routine.

From the front page of the
Charlottesville *Constitution, April 4:*

TWO MORE MURDERS POSSIBLY CONNECTED TO RESTAURANT SLAYING

The dead bodies of two men were found in a car last night and police are investigating whether or not there is a link to the April 1 murder of restaurateur Caroline Keller in the Jack's restaurant in the Downtown Mall. Both men had been shot once in the back of the head. They are believed to be the same men who engaged in a fistfight in the restaurant the night of Mrs. Keller's murder and her husband, Jack Keller's, shooting.

The car was discovered in the parking lot of a deserted Dunkin' Donuts on Highway 29 just south of Danville, Virginia, by Ned Rodrigue. Mr. Rodrigue was on his way to Roanoke, approximately 17 miles north of where the bodies were found. He pulled into the parking lot of the restaurant, which has been closed for several months, due to illness. Feeling light-headed, he got out of his car, hoping the fresh air would make him feel better. There was one other car in the lot and when Mr. Rodrigue walked by it, he noticed what he thought was someone asleep at the wheel. On closer inspection, Mr. Rodrigue saw a second body as well and immediately called the police.

Although police officials refuse to reveal the names of the two dead men, a reliable source has one of them being tentatively identified as Raymond Kutchler. There was a reservation in Mr. Kutchler's name for the opening night of Jack's restaurant and it is believed that he attended that dinner with a male friend. During the course of the evening, Mr. Kutchler and his friend engaged in a shouting match which turned into a full-scale brawl. Police believe it was during the course of this brawl that Mr. and Mrs. Keller were attacked.

Eyewitnesses say that the fight between Mr. Kutchler and his dinner companion was vitriolic and violent. If it is indeed these two men who were found dead, police are at a loss to explain why, after such a battle, they would be in the same car. They also offered no theories as to the connection between the latest two murders and the shooting in the restaurant.

Jack gingerly placed the newspaper on the table to the right of his coffee cup and picked up the third paper from the chair next to him. This story was a concise summation of the prior two, adding previously unknown facts and whatever conclusions were possible. Once again, as he read, despite his intimate knowledge of the details, a wave of incredulity washed over him as if he were absorbing the information for the first time.

From the front page of the
Charlottesville *Constitution, April 21:*

POLICE AT DEAD END IN RESTAURANT MURDERS

The mystery surrounding the death of Caroline Keller and the shooting of her husband, Jack Keller, grows deeper and deeper. Bizarre facts keep emerging but police admitted today that they have had no luck making connections between any of the people, places, or events that seem as if they must be linked. "We're as unsatisfied as the public must be by our conclusions up to this point," said Charlottesville police chief Phil Eagle. "But, unfortunately, the trail we've been following is as cold as an icebox. While we are confident that there will eventually be a break in the case, and while we will continue to pursue every avenue, at the moment we have no new leads and nothing on which to speculate, either publicly or privately."

The events to which Chief Eagle refers began on April 1 at a gala opening-night dinner at Jack's restaurant in Charlottesville . . .

As he read, Jack began to drift. It was no longer necessary to read every word. He knew it by heart.

The article, yet again, recounted the details of the opening and the fight between the customer Raymond Kutchler and his guest. It talked about the police arriving, too late to break up the fight, and then hearing a crash, rushing outside to find Caroline's body on the brick patio. . . . The cops charging upstairs to find Jack . . . It said that Caroline's valuable diamond necklace was missing and presumed stolen. . . . The murder of the two men in the car in the Dunkin' Donuts parking lot . . .

This story confirmed the identity of the men in the car as Kutchler and his guest. But it also revealed that Kutchler was a pseudonym. The man's real name was Robert Haywood; his dinner companion, and fellow murder victim, was Trent Neufield. And they were boys, really. Students and members of the football team at Virginia State University.

Jack remembered the police coming to him, trying to find any link between him and Caroline and the two students. They found none, direct or otherwise. They could not figure out why the pseudonyms were used. Or why they'd received the invitation. And, ultimately, they could not solve the final piece of the puzzle, either—why were Haywood and Neufield murdered? What was their connection to the robbery and its violent aftermath?

All that was included in the article. But there was more to it than the newspaper reported. There always was, of course.

At first, Jack himself had been a suspect. While he was still loaded with painkillers—and thus, he guessed, more

susceptible to telling the truth—the police had tried to find
some kind of motive for him to murder his wife. Over doctors' objections, they grilled him about his story, making
him repeat details and observations over and over again.
They questioned him about his relationship with Caroline,
asked him if he'd ever had an affair. He realized he must
have been susceptible because he told them that he had,
which was true. A brief one, years earlier, when he'd been in
London. The woman's name was Emma and she was
English, and he hadn't seen her in years. He'd barely seen her
even when they'd had their fling, which was all it was. Brief
and meaningless and long, long over. Thinking about touching another woman, when he knew that he could never
touch Caroline again, made him weep, and the police realized they'd stepped over the line, so they left him alone and
never again questioned him about his marriage.

When he was well enough, Jack must have spent fifty
hours talking to more cops and, eventually, to private detectives, trying to piece together what had really happened. He
even hired an ex-FBI agent who'd written two bestselling
books about his cases. They all had the same theories. And
none of them could link those theories to any facts.

They were all certain there was a connection between the
Haywood-Neufield fight and the shooting in the office. It
was a common robbery ploy, Jack learned. Start a distraction, draw everyone's attention away from the real target,
and then move in on that target. The target that night had
obviously been Caroline. Or possibly Caroline's necklace.
And there was the first missing fact: no tie could be found

between anyone who had known about the necklace and the robbery/shooting. Jack had shown Caroline's mother his gift and she, in turn, had told both of her other daughters about it. None of them was at the opening, though. Caroline's mother was suffering from terrible arthritis and did not feel up to sitting through a dinner. Llewellyn was on a family vacation with her husband and children. Susanna Rae, staying, as always, in character, simply responded with a "not attending" and never showed up. All were officially ruled out as suspects almost immediately. For several days— a period Jack chalked up to his delirium—his mind kept coming back to Susanna. But when he was more rooted in reality, he realized that as bitter and unpleasant as she was capable of being, she was not capable of being involved in something this horrendous. Several staff members had been told about the necklace moments before the evening officially began—Caroline had shown the jewelry proudly when she went downstairs—but all investigations there were dead ends. The idea of this as an inside job was eventually dismissed and Jack believed that was the correct decision.

No one could establish a connection between the two students and the unknown shooter. Nor could anyone find any link to "Raymond Kutchler" and anyone at the restaurant. Caroline had been in charge of the final invitation list—she had taken suggestions from everyone ranging from Jack to the restaurant managers to the local Chamber of Commerce, but ultimately the list was hers. When it had been time to send out the formal invitations, she'd given the restaurant secretary several sheets of yellow legal paper with handwritten names and addresses on it. Kutchler's name and address were on it—"Raymond Kutchler plus Guest"— written in Caroline's perfect and careful scrawl. The address checked out as false, and so there was another missing fact: How had Kutchler/Haywood received his invitation if not through the mail?

The assumption was that Kutchler/Haywood and Neufield had been killed by the same person who'd murdered Caroline and shot Jack, but again no leads emerged from this probe. No one who knew the two dead men could come up with even a remote idea about how they'd gotten invited to the opening. Not one person who knew them could envision any connection at all to the Kellers or anyone who worked in the restaurant.

Although all investigators assumed the killer was a man, at some point Jack realized that he could not even say *that* for certain. Due to the deep concussion he'd received as soon as he'd entered the office, the voices he'd heard were distant and dreamlike—in retrospect many of the words were gibberish—and of no distinct gender.

So here was the most crucial missing fact of all: Who was the third person in the office that night? Who had put three bullets into Jack and one fatal bullet into his wife?

And why was Caroline thrown out the window after she'd been shot? Police, as well as Jack's private investigators, dismissed any real connection to Joan Keller's death. One cop claimed it was an unfortunate coincidence. One theorized that the murderer might have known about Jack's mother's death and gone the copycat route.

Jack knew better, though. He knew it was the uprising of the ghosts.

There were so many unknowns. And only one thing that could not be questioned: Lives had changed. Been ruined. Ended.

There was one more news story for Jack to read before he went inside. It was in the business section of that morning's *New York Times.* He'd already read it once. After the first paragraph, it was just a rehash of the shooting and the fact that the suspect was never found, as well as an update on Jack's recovery. He had no need to read that material again; the *Times* reporting was not as detailed or accurate as the local Virginia paper. But he did read the first few paragraphs again. He wanted the quick hit of reality that the words gave him.

From page D1 of the Business Section of the
New York Times, *September 25:*

Jack's Restaurant Deal Concluded

Leonard R. McGirk, an executive vice-president for Restaurants United, announced today that the Dallas, Texas–based consortium has signed a contract to assume complete ownership of Jack's restaurants. The negotiations have been ongoing and, according to Mr. McGirk, the terms were settled upon over two months ago. "The deal would have been closed soon after the first of year," Mr. McGirk said, "except both sides had lawyers who wanted to make sure every *t* was crossed and every potato was fried." Mr. McGirk said that one of the key elements to the deal, which both sides wanted, was figuring out a way to keep Jack Keller, the founder of the restaurant chain, involved as a consultant. Neither side would reveal the terms of the sale, but it is estimated to be in excess of twenty-five million dollars.

The original Jack's, based in Manhattan, has long been a popular eatery and watering hole for the city's top athletes, politicians, and celebrities. Over the past twenty years, the owner, Jack Keller, has built upon the restaurant's cache and popularity to open six additional restaurants around the world. There is currently a Jack's in London, Paris, Los Angeles, Chicago, Miami, and Charlottesville.

The Charlottesville restaurant, which opened in April of last year, was the scene of a tragic shooting, in which Mr. Keller's wife, Caroline, was killed and Mr. Keller was . . .

Jack put the paper down.

Jack's Restaurant Deal Concluded.

It was done now. No last chance to renege. The person he had loved the most—Caroline—had been murdered and her death made him despise the *thing* he'd loved the most—the restaurant. He couldn't bear to go into Jack's, couldn't stand to talk about it; it made him too sad to even think about it. So he'd sold it. The whole thing.

Dom had tried to talk him out of it. "What'll you *do?*" he'd said.

"I'll be rich," Jack responded. "I'll do whatever I want to do." But even as he said it, he knew it was a lie. There was nothing left for him to want to do. Nothing left that he cared about. His wife, his business, even his body, gone. The only life he'd ever wanted, gone.

Gone is gone.

Through his fog, Jack realized that Mattie was once more speaking to him.

"I know, I know," he said. "I'm coming in."

"I'm not bugging you," she told him. "You're a grown man. I'm just telling you they called from downstairs; you've got company on the way up."

"Who?" he said, and there was genuine surprise in his voice. Jack did not have many people just pop in to say hello.

"You'll be happy to see him, that's all I'm saying," Mattie answered. "Now please get in here so I can close the damn door and stop *myself* from freezing to death."

Jack nodded, put his hands down at his sides, and as his fingertips grazed cold steel spokes he had the same astonished thought that had sprung to mind every single day since he'd been home from the hospital:

Jesus Christ, I'm in a wheelchair.

He still had not mastered the workings of the chair, still felt awkward as his fingers groped for the wheels and spun them backward, rolling the chair away from the table. As he was trying to turn it around, it lurched forward a few inches toward the restraining wall and Jack felt his stomach clench. For the briefest of moments, his terrible fear of heights overcame him and he saw the picture that had flashed through his head so often: getting too close to the wall, somehow toppling over, then falling, tumbling through the air, the ground rushing up to meet him. The picture in his mind was far too real, not at all dreamlike but vivid and crystal clear; it made him dizzy and sick. He quickly turned his chair, was able to shake away the vision as he looked down at the terrace floor, away from the wall. He took a quick breath, in and out, then another, and maneuvered the chair so it would roll safely through the sliding door to the living room. That was when he heard the familiar voice:

"What the hell are you doing out there, freezin' your balls off?"

Dom, in baggy beige chinos and a bulky white Irish knit sweater, was standing there, looking out at him.

"I told him, Mr. Dom." Mattie was behind him. "He won't listen to me."

"I listen to both of you," Jack mumbled. "I just try not to pay too much attention."

"Get inside, you asshole. I got a surprise for you."

Jack propelled the chair forward. As soon as he was inside, Mattie skipped out to retrieve the newspapers and then, quickly stepping back in, she slid the balcony door shut, locked it, and headed for another room.

"So," Dom said, and Jack could immediately hear the forced casual tone in his voice. "How ya feelin'?"

"I feel better."

"Oh." Dom tugged at the side of his sweater, yanking at a long, loose thread, trying to break it off, managing only to unravel it even further. "What I mean is, how are you *feeling?*"

"Are we talking psychological scars now instead of physical ones?"

"Goddamnit, Jack. You know I'm not good at this shit. I'm just trying to figure out how the fuck you're doin'."

"Is this the surprise? You're revealing your sensitive, feminine side?"

"No." The voice came from the entryway by the elevator. The person speaking was just out of view. It took Jack a moment to recognize the voice, which he did a split second before the speaker stepped into the living room. "*I'm* the surprise."

Jack stared in silence at the young man standing in his apartment. He was maybe six-one but he seemed even taller. He filled up the room, not with size but with his presence. He wore jeans and a light blue hooded sweatshirt, the hood drooping down his back, and black-and-white Nike running shoes. Even under the sweatshirt, Jack could see that he was lean and in great shape. His sleeves were pushed up just below his elbows and his forearms were ripped; standing there, he nervously clenched and unclenched his hand and each time he did, the veins on his arms popped and a muscle rippled. His hair was a light brown and slightly too long and shaggy. It looked messy but calculatingly so. He wore no jewelry, not even a watch. But around his neck was a thin, black cloth string that carried a tiny cell phone. There was a nervous expression on his face, which he was attempting to hide behind questioning eyes and a casual grin. All in all, he was extraordinarily good-looking and, even with his tapping foot and twitching hand, there was a palpable air of confidence radiating from him.

When Jack finally spoke, he was surprised at how hoarse his voice was. It felt as if he hadn't spoken in days. "Congratulations. You've stunned me into silence."

"He showed up at the market yesterday," Dom said.

"So," Jack said. "How are you, Kid? It's been a while."

"It's been too long. I know. No, that sounds ridiculous. I mean, it sounds too . . . unimportant. I'm sorry. I don't have any real excuse for what I did . . . for disappearing like that, not being in touch. I've been away. . . ."

"You've been away almost *five years.*"

"I know."

"No details?"

"You'll get 'em. There's plenty of time for details."

"I take it that means you're back. From wherever you've been."

"Yeah, I'm back. I'm definitely back."

There was an awkward pause, neither man knowing quite what to say. Dom broke the silence.

"Ask him *why* he's back, Jackie."

"There's a reason?"

"There's a reason," Kid said. "At least there's a reason why I'm standing in the living room right now."

"Just ask him, will ya," Dom said.

"Okay." Jack shrugged and his eyes met Kid's straight on. "Why are you back—*in the living room right now?*"

Kid smiled for the first time since arriving at the apartment. It was a broad, penetrating smile that revealed white teeth and genuine pleasure. And the cocky, I've-got-the-world-by-the-balls attitude that Jack had seen since the man in front of him had been a small boy.

"I'm your new guardian angel," Kid Demeter said to Jack Keller, and the smile broadened and lingered, looked as if it would stay on his face forever. "I'm here to take away your pain."

"**A**ll right, I want you to say when it hurts."

"When."

Jack could feel the sweat breaking out on his forehead. Little beads popping up and starting to stream down toward his eyes.

"*When.*"

Now the back of his neck was damp. And he could feel his shoulders tense up and his lower back start to ache. No, more than ache. A stabbing jolt . . .

"*When,* goddamnit!"

"I haven't done anything yet, Mr. Keller. We haven't started."

It was the day after Kid had first shown up at the apartment with Dom. Following his proclamation that he was there to heal Jack, the three of them sat down and talked for two hours. It was a strangely nonpersonal conversation. Jack and Dom kept pressing but Kid shied away from any details about his life that didn't have to do with the specific reason he was there.

"I dropped out of St. John's after my junior year," he explained. "I know you know that; I remember the conversation."

"Yes, I remember it, too," Jack said. "I remember the conversation and I remember that you disappeared."

"First of all, I didn't disappear. I disappeared from *here*. That's two different things. And I don't want to go into that right now. It's gonna be hard enough trying to convince you to let me do what I want to do. So let's come back to that."

"To the past?"

"Yeah. Let's come back to the past some other time."

"He's right, Jackie. Let him explain what he wants."

Jack nodded and Kid continued.

"I traveled around for a while. About a year, just trying different things. And then I got a job in a gym. You know I've always been into that."

"You're in good shape, I'll give you that."

"Uh-uh. I'm in *great* shape. I'm a jock, I've always stayed in shape. Always been kind of obsessed with it. But when I started at this gym it became even more of an obsession. And then it turned into something else. I became just as obsessed with getting *other* people in shape."

"You're a personal trainer?"

"I was. In a way, I still am, but that was just the first stage. I realized I could do more than just get people in shape. I could . . . make them better."

"Better, how?"

"I had the knack; I don't know how else to put it. If they came to me with a bad back, I could fix it. If somebody had an operation on their arm and couldn't bend it, they could after working with me for a while. It was exciting to me, it really was. People would come to me sort of . . . incomplete . . . and they'd leave whole. After a while, that's all I liked doing. I mean, I'd get started with someone, someone who needed my help, and work with him for hours. I could work all day; it was like I couldn't stop until the people I was working with reached their limits. And what happened is I started getting bored working with yuppies who wanted washboard abs and lawyers who wanted to get in shape so they could find someone to cheat on their wives with. So I went back to school."

"To do what?"

"To become a physical therapist. I got my B.A. first. Had to. Then I got my master's in PT. It was a two-year program and, oh, man, you guys won't believe the shit I had to take. A year of physics, a year of chem, two years of biology. It was brutal."

"You took physics?" Dom said in an incredulous growl.

"Yeah."

"So say something in physics."

"Dom, I don't think I can."

"Come on. Make an old guy happy."

Kid looked at Jack and good-naturedly rolled his eyes. Then he turned back to Dom and said, "How about if I explain what an energy level is?"

"Sounds good."

"Okay. An energy level is one of a quantized series of states in which matter may exist, each having constant energy and separated from others in the series by finite quantities of energy. How's that?"

"Holy shit," Dom said.

"Where was all this?" Jack asked. "I mean, where you got

your master's and learned about energy levels and discovered you had the knack?"

Kid ignored the barbed tone lurking at the back of Jack's question. "Maryland. That's where I was so that's just where I stayed. Maryland State. Finished my B.A. there."

"How'd you pay for it?" Jack asked quietly.

Kid didn't back down from the hurt underneath these words. "I worked. As a trainer. And I got a partial wrestling scholarship that turned into a full."

"Since when are you a wrestler?" Dom demanded.

"Thought I'd try my hand at it and I liked it. Fast and strong, why not? We even had one nationally televised match on ESPN . . . well, okay, the Deuce, against N.C. State. I always thought maybe you guys were watching, saw me."

"How'd ya do?" Dom wanted to know.

"I didn't disgrace you, don't worry. Pinned a guy who was nationally ranked." Kid turned to Jack now. He hesitated, as if afraid of the answer he was going to get. Then he plunged ahead, the cockiness back. "So? Now you got my story. You gonna let me help you?"

"You think you can heal me?" Jack asked.

"I *know* I can." When Jack didn't respond, when he glanced dubiously at Dom, Kid's voice got louder. He was ready to bounce off of the sofa. "It's what I do."

"I'm kind of an extreme case," Jack said slowly. "I don't just have a bad back or a hurt arm."

"Oh, come on, I've worked with people a lot worse off than you. Mangled arms, guys who've had their legs crushed in a car accident . . ."

"I appreciate it, Kid. But I don't think so."

"Why not?"

"I just don't think so."

"What are you afraid of?"

Jack recoiled, bit off the angry words that were about to flow. "I'm afraid of a lot of things right now. And if I were you, I wouldn't take that tone with me."

"You're not just afraid, you're feelin' sorry for yourself. That's a bad combination."

"That's enough, Kid," Dom said. "That's more than enough."

"Hey, I've done this a lot. You get a feel for people, see who has it in 'em to fight back. Look at you," Kid said, staring at Jack. "Still in that wheelchair. You should've gotten rid of that thing already! Months ago!"

"I don't use it all the time."

"You shouldn't use it at all!"

"You don't know the kind of pain I've gone through. I'm *going* through."

"Yeah, I do know." Kid's voice was loud. It resonated through the apartment. "It's what I'm trying to tell you—I can get rid of it."

"I don't think so."

"Because you don't *want* to get rid of it!"

"Kid!" This was from Dom. He was angry now, and standing. "I said that's enough. You said enough, so don't say no more."

Kid's face was flushed. He was angry and he took a deep breath to calm himself. "All right. I'm sorry I got excited," he said, quieter now. Then he turned to Jack. "But I don't take back what I said. I can make you better. Only you have to want to *get* better. And I don't think you do. I think your pain is all you've got right now and you're afraid of what'll happen next after it's gone."

There was a long silence. Kid finally grabbed his jacket from the back of the couch, stood, and headed to the front door. Jack let him get halfway to the elevator before he spoke, evenly and softly.

"That may be the worst thing anyone's ever said to me." He looked down at the wheelchair, and when he lifted his head, Kid had stepped back into the room. Their eyes locked. "But it's also true. I'm terrified of what's going to happen next."

"Then let me help you," Kid said. "Please. You saved my life, both of you guys, after my dad died. I've fucked up big-time, I know that. I've been wanting to call you ever since I heard what happened and I didn't because . . . well . . . just for this reason: I didn't think you'd want me anymore. There are things you don't understand about why I left, things you'll never understand, and I don't blame you for not trusting me, but I can do something. I can do for you what you did for me. I can give you your life back."

When Jack said nothing, Kid shook his head sadly. The look on his face showed that he knew he'd failed.

"He believes you, Kid," Dom said. "You don't have to look like that. Right now it ain't personal. He's just tryin' to figure out if he *wants* his life back."

Jack looked up sharply. His eyes met Dom's. The old man

said nothing more, but he didn't have to. He was challenging Jack to disagree with him. And even at age seventy-five, even with one arm, Dom was a tough guy to challenge. Jack turned away from the grizzled old face and now stared at Kid's young one.

"You'd better know what the hell you're doing," Jack said.

KID DID KNOW what he was doing. And twenty-four hours later, he had Jack lying on his back on the floor of Jack's living room.

"Don't worry. I'm not going to start working you out yet, you're at least a couple of weeks from that. We're gonna start with ultrasound and ultrastim. I've already ordered the machine; it'll be delivered tomorrow."

"I'm paying for this, I assume."

"You can afford it, stop whining. My goal is to eventually set you up with the ultimate home gym. You're gonna *want* to work out, you're gonna *want* to put yourself through the agony."

"This does not sound likely to me."

"I know you. I know what'll happen when you start to see what you're capable of doing."

Jack grunted noncommittally. "What the hell's ultrastim?"

Kid's face lit up. He was the teacher now, explaining a life-changing insight to a disbelieving student. "I got you an ultrasound-slash-ultrastim machine. It's an electrical charge that goes into your muscles. It stimulates the hard-to-get interior muscles."

"It works?"

"It works. In school, we had to do this experiment. You cut a frog's leg off, put it on a hook to elongate it, shock it with current—and that causes contractions."

"Sounds like a fun experiment."

"It's an important one. It proves that an electrical charge predetermines muscular contractions. And that's what we've got to do with you 'cause my guess is there's been so much atrophy."

"So in this particular experiment, I'm the frog."

"Oh, yeah," Kid said. "You are definitely the frog." He grinned. "Now all I'm gonna do right now is stretch you out. Nothing hard, you don't have to do anything except let me do a little pushing and pulling. I want to determine your level of flexibility." Jack nodded his okay. Kid stretched Jack's right leg flat on the ground, putting his hand on Jack's thigh to keep the leg pinned down. "Straighten the left leg and extend it straight out toward me," he said, and when Jack did that, Kid took hold of it from the arch of Jack's foot and lifted it about six inches off the ground. "All right, I want you to say when it hurts."

"When."

Kid flexed Jack's foot so it was pointing upward. Sweat began pouring down Jack's face as he lay sprawled on the mat on his living room floor.

"When . . ."

Kid pressed down more firmly on Jack's right thigh, rendering it immobile.

"*When*, goddamnit!"

"I haven't done anything yet. You might want to hold off complaining until we start."

The sweat had soaked through Jack's clothes. The fear had taken hold. The expectation of pain. Kid began inching Jack's left leg up, slowly and carefully, an inch or two at a time.

"You know, Kid . . ." Jack's breathing was getting heavier ". . . you're still on thin ice. I'd try to hide your . . ." his breathing grew even more labored ". . . naturally . . . snotty . . . personality . . . Oh, shit . . . if I were you. At least for a little while longer . . . that's far enough!"

Kid ignored him. Slowly, he kept raising Jack's leg.

"Kid . . . stop."

"Just a little bit more. You can do it."

"I can't! Stop!"

Kid raised the leg another inch. It was maybe three feet off the ground, extended straight out.

Jack's voice got louder, more urgent. "Don't go any further . . ."

"One more inch."

"Let it go! Put it back down!"

Kid moved it just a fraction of an inch this time and Jack screamed. Kid stopped the movement, but he made no motion to release the leg. He held it in place as Jack turned red in the face and swore.

"Put it down! . . . Fuck you! . . . *Fuck you!*" The sweat was pouring off his face. His shirt was sopping wet now and his arms, which were by his sides, were shaking.

"Keep breathing, Jack. Deep breath."

"Put it down! . . . Goddamn it! *Let go!*"

Kid nodded, as if seeing what he wanted to see, and slowly eased the leg back down. When it touched the floor, he released it. Jack's entire body sagged. He used the cuff of his shirt to wipe his forehead and his breathing was so labored he couldn't speak. Kid looked down at him, spoke slowly.

"You gotta go ten seconds past the scream, Jack. That's the program. It won't always hurt like that, but it'll always hurt. That's how you're gonna get better."

Jack's breathing was under control. It took him another moment before he spoke. "I've missed you," he said weakly. "You son of a bitch."

"**O**kay, I'm going to try to explain to you exactly what's going to happen. Not just today but over the next few weeks and months."

Jack was sitting in his wheelchair. He and Kid were in what had been, until the night before, Jack and Caroline's home office, a small room, maybe fourteen-by-fourteen, off the kitchen. It was now furnished with padded benches, thick floor mats, dumbbells, barbells, and state-of-the-art Universal weight machines. Kid wanted this to be their retreat, he said. He wanted it to be a separate world where Jack felt safe, someplace soothing and calm and yet strong, where he could believe he was on the road to recovery.

"Come here, I'm gonna show you something." Kid reached over and put the cane, which was hanging over the back of the wheelchair, into Jack's hand. Then he grabbed Jack's other hand and gently pulled him up to a standing position. "You can't bear weight on this leg yet, can you?"

"Very little."

Kid nodded, as if this somehow pleased him. "Lie down on this mat."

"Kid, is this really—"

"Come on, Jack. Lie down."

Jack nodded and Kid put his hand behind Jack's back. Jack eased himself down as best he could but ultimately had to trust himself to Kid. Kid lowered him to the mat and Jack lay on his back, staring up at the ceiling.

"Okay," Kid said. "Keep your head down. Put your arms by your sides, palms down." He waited until Jack complied. "Now lift your leg ten times."

"What do you mean, lift it?"

"Just straight up and down. That's all. Nothing hard. All you have to do is lift your leg ten times. As high as you can. Either leg. Your choice."

Jack stayed motionless for a moment, then lifted his right leg into the air. It rose about two feet, then he slowly lowered it back down to the mat. He rested it there for three seconds, then lifted it again. Again it went about two feet high, then slowly went back down.

"Eight more to go," Kid said. "No resting in between."

Jack made it to seven lifts. After that, totally flat on his back, he shook his head slowly from side to side. He was finished.

"You look exhausted."

Jack was so tired he couldn't even answer. All he did was nod.

"Okay," Kid said, "now stand up."

Jack took a deep breath, finally was able to say, "You know I can't get up from this position."

"So let me get this straight," Kid said. "You can't get up from the floor and you can't even lift your leg ten times in a row. With no weight attached to it."

"Are all our conversations going to end with me saying fuck you?"

"No. I just want to show you something. You watching?"

"I'm lying on the goddamn floor, Kid, doing my best carrot impersonation. What else do you think I'm doing but watching?"

Kid went to the barbell that was lying on the floor, rolled up against the wall under the room's two small windows. He moved the bar to the center of the room, went to the rack in the corner and pulled off two weights. He attached one of them to each end of the barbell, bent down as if to lift it, then stopped and went back to the rack. He took two more weights and added them to the bar.

"Watch me, Jack."

He put his feet shoulder-width apart and positioned himself so his shins were practically touching the bar. Then he bent down and grasped it, his palms down. Kid's body revealed no tension; there was no apprehension or even hint of strain to come. His legs bent so his thighs were almost parallel to the floor. With his head up and his arms extended straight down, he inhaled deeply and suddenly and, seemingly in one motion, lifted the bar up past his waist and, flipping it so his hands were now underneath it, to shoulder height. He was standing perfectly erect and the bar was resting on his chest. He was not breathing hard and there was no outward sign of exertion.

"This is called a 'clean,' " Kid said. "It's the hardest weight exercise there is. I'm doing two hundred pounds. That's a serious weight."

"And you're showing this to me because . . . ?"

"Because you're gonna be able to do this. With this exact weight."

"Kid, I can't even stand up by myself, as you've so kindly pointed out."

Kid exhaled deeply and, in one motion, returned the bar to the floor. The weight touched down so softly it barely made a sound.

"A year from today, Jack. Mark it down in your calendar. That's the day you clean two hundred. You're not going to be as good as new, you're gonna be *twice* as good as you ever were."

Jack didn't say anything. He just motioned for Kid to help him up. When he was safely back in his chair, he looked up at Kid and said quietly, "How long have you been back?"

"A year," Kid told him. His voice was just as muted as Jack's. "I came back a year ago."

Jack looked down, shook his head as if clearing away a physical pain. "What the hell have you been doing this whole time?"

"I told you. Keeping my head above water."

"I could have helped," Jack said. "When did I ever refuse to help you?"

"Never. That's one of the reasons I didn't call. I needed to do this on my own."

"What are the other reasons?"

"Let me hook you up to the machine now, Jack."

There was silence between them until Kid moved to something that looked a bit too much like R2-D2. It was the ultrasound-ultrastim machine. "You won't feel anything at first. I'm starting really low. Gradually you'll feel a kind of prickly sensation." Kid now attached Jack to the machine. Wires led out to directly above his left knee and just above his right hip. "I just want this to be nice and soothing for now."

"Doesn't seem right," Jack muttered sarcastically. "You're giving me something where there's no agony."

"Don't worry," Kid said. "The agony'll come soon enough." And then with a half laugh and a shrug of his shoulders, he said, so quietly that Jack could barely make out the words, "And the strange part is you're gonna start to like it."

I n the months since Caroline had died, Jack had spoken very little about her. He accepted awkward condolences with a quiet thank-you or a silent nod of the head and he rarely reminisced about her, even with Dom, who spoke to or saw him every day, or Herb Bloomfield, his lawyer, who called him every other day—Jack decided that his lawyer friend had to have had his secretary put "Call Jack, see how he's doing" on his calendar, blocking off five minutes three times a week as if it were a business appointment.

But he thought about Caroline a lot. If the truth were known, almost constantly. Little things would bring memories rushing back. He'd look out from his balcony and see a fir tree flourishing in the park and he'd remember a trip to Vermont; it was snowing, and they went cross-country skiing through miles of perfect firs. From his perch above Manhattan, Jack would smell the exquisite mix of minty fir needles and newly cut wood and fresh Vermont air. And he would see Caroline in her ludicrously bright orange parka, slithering along the dirty white paths of the forest.

He'd watch TV and see a pregnant woman on a mindless sitcom and he'd remember how Caroline cried when she told him she was pregnant and, when he went to hug her, how she'd waved her hands, a totally feminine gesture, embarrassed at her tears, which were brought on by a combination of bliss and fear and raging hormones. Then he'd remember all their promises to each other, how they'd love and honor and always be kind to each other. How they'd be friends, not just lovers. He'd kept all the promises he'd ever made to her, he thought. Except for the most important one, the one about keeping her safe and happy forever.

Jack had played the scene in Charlottesville over many times in his head. *What if he hadn't barged in on them? What if he'd done it differently? What if he'd managed to overcome the brutal blow to the head and talk to the killer? What if he hadn't let Caroline talk him out of having a TV monitor—maybe they'd have a face for the killer. What if . . .*

It was the last "what if" that usually stopped Jack cold. Especially as it was the same one that had haunted him ever since he'd seen his mother die.

What if he'd been killed instead of her?

What if . . .

"You ready to boogie, Jack?"

Jack looked up, his regretful reverie over. Kid stood in the entryway, on the edge of the living room, looking in at him.

"How'd you get in?"

"The key," Kid said. "From when I cleaned out the office. I drove here, so I just parked in the garage and came up."

"You have a car?"

"Borrowed a friend's," Kid said. "I'm running around all day today and it's a lot cheaper than cabs." He dug into his pocket, pulled the small, squat elevator key out, and held it in his palm. "Where do you want me to put it?"

"It's Mattie's," Jack told him. "Put it on the little table there so I'll remember to give it back to her."

Kid nodded, placed it on the side table in the hallway. "You're looking pretty serious today."

"I'm feeling pretty serious today."

"Thinking too much is bad for you, Jack."

"It depends what it is you're thinking, doesn't it?"

"Oh, right. Sorry. I guess you were sittin' in here just thinking your happy thoughts."

"I'm paying you to be my physical trainer, not a psychiatrist."

"Sometimes they go hand in hand."

"But not this time," Jack told him.

"Okay." Kid shrugged, sloughing off any acknowledgment of Jack's self-pity. "Then let's get physical."

OVER THE NEXT month, Jack learned that his pain was inextricably tied to his improvement. And Kid was right. He'd begun to enjoy it in a strange and elusive way. As excruciating as it was, he could feel it bringing him slowly, inch by inch, closer to life.

Kid came, without fail, five days a week. Seven o'clock every morning, and they spent an hour together, sometimes two, Kid pushing Jack as hard as he would let himself be pushed. And then he'd give Jack another hour's worth of work to do on his own, a specific plan to do every afternoon. More exercises. More pushing. More pain.

Sometimes, when he had the time, Kid even came back in the afternoon to oversee the second session. And often he'd show up on the weekend, occasionally cajoling Jack into an extra workout.

While they worked together, they talked. Gradually, Kid let his reserves down, began to open up and fill Jack in on his past. He also began to let Jack into his present. Jack, in turn, realized how much he'd missed the regular human contact he'd grown accustomed to at the restaurant, how much he'd missed having a daily dialogue with someone. The relationship they'd had years ago began to establish itself again. Kid began to rely on Jack to act as the father he'd lost at such a young age. And Jack began to think of Kid the way he had when Kid was a teenager—as his own son.

The ice was broken ten days into the training session.

"Come on. Push yourself!" Kid was exhorting him. Jack was curling two-pound weights, which felt as if they were two hundred pounds. "Does it hurt?" Kid asked.

"Christ, yes."

"Good, it's *supposed* to hurt. It's not your injury—it's *surprise*. Now give me more!"

"Eleven . . ." Jack breathed. And, arms trembling, eyes closed in concentration, he slowly forced his body to repeat the exercise one more time. "Twelve . . ." And then all the air swept out of him. His arms dropped to his sides and the weights dangled until Kid swooped them up. Jack sat for a minute, breathing heavily, then Kid handed him a bottle of water, which Jack raised gratefully to his lips then took a long swig.

"You can't be afraid to fail," Kid said. "It's the paradox of training. You have to *embrace* failure. You have to work until you *do* fail. If you don't fail, you don't get strong."

Jack, exhausted, nodded. He got it. He didn't like it, but he sure as hell got it.

The cell phone hanging from Kid's neck emitted a bird-like chirp of a ring.

"Excuse me," Kid said, then spoke quietly into the phone. Jack heard only Kid's end of the conversation. "Hey . . . Yeah, that's why I left the message. . . . I'm really, really sorry. . . . I know, but I got a management seminar at four, then I promised to fill in for Kim at the Saddle. . . . Yeah, Friday, I promise . . . I *promise* . . . You're the best. Bye-bye."

He hung up, turned back to Jack. "All right, let's do the last set."

"Management seminar?" Jack asked.

Kid nodded, almost sheepishly. "I'm getting my MBA."

"You're shitting me."

"For real."

"Why didn't you tell me? And do they know you left most of your brains on the football field?"

Kid shrugged. "It's NYU—I'm on a minority scholarship for slow white quarterbacks who couldn't hit the side of a barn. And *that's* why I didn't tell you."

"What are you going to do with it?"

"I've got an idea." Before Jack could get out a word, Kid said, "Yes, I'll talk to you about it. But when I'm ready. When I've got the thing really planned out."

"But there is a *thing?*"

"I think so," Kid said. "I really do think so. Now stop stalling."

Jack did twelve more reps of light curls. He didn't pause at eight this time, didn't need the break, just gritted his teeth and kept going.

"You're my idol, Jack. That was very impressive."

Jack accepted the compliment with a quick nod. It took him a few seconds to gather himself before he could speak. "How are you paying for it? For grad school?"

"By the hour." Kid tapped his cell phone. "I'm back to personal training and that's why I hate bailing on a client. But she lives in Park Slope, way the hell out, and it's the Entertainer's birthday—and you do *not* disappoint *her*, believe me."

"Who the hell is the Entertainer?"

Kid breathed out a little laugh and said matter-of-factly, "She's a member of the Team."

"Okay. Let's keep going. What the hell is the Team?"

"Sorry. It's kind of a joke. They're the women I go out with."

"Plural?"

Kid nodded. "These days, it seems like it."

"At the same time?"

"I don't seem to be too good at the one-on-one thing. At least, well . . ." He shook his head. Something he wasn't ready to talk about. "So, yeah, I guess, at the same time."

"I didn't know you were such a stud."

"It's not always by choice. But for the moment it's what I've got instead of . . ." Kid stopped, bit off his words, and turned his head away from Jack.

Jack took a deep breath, then finished the sentence. "It's what you've got instead of a wife and a home, instead of a family."

Their eyes met now. And Kid nodded.

"It's what *you've got* instead of what *I had*," Jack finished.

"I'm sorry," Kid said.

"I think these weights are too light" was all Jack said in response. "Next time let's move up to five pounds."

TWO DAYS LATER, Kid's cell phone rang again in the middle of the workout.

"I won't answer it. She can wait," he said.

"How do you know it's a she?"

"It's *always* a she."

"Kid, I'm now officially intrigued."

"With my love life?"

Jack nodded. "Who's on this . . . this *team?*"

"I feel funny talking about this to you."

"Consider it part of the therapy," Jack told him. "I've been thinking about it. It might be good to hear about what's going on in the real world."

Kid held back the smile. But his eyes gloated. "You're paying me to be your physical trainer," he said, "not your psychiatrist."

Jack gave a grudging smile back. "Sometimes they go hand in hand," he said.

Kid hesitated, then said, "Okay. But it did start as a kind of goof. One day I realized I was seeing a lot of women. Four, five, six of them. And individually they were okay but when you put them all together, took the best of what each one had to offer, well, they made a kind of perfect woman. It was like a baseball team, you know. You don't need a real star as long as you've got a real team."

"So what's the lineup?"

"It's fluid. And you gotta be flexible. Like I said, you can't just go out with the MVP's all the time."

"That's very magnanimous of you."

"Just being practical. You gotta go with your occasional gritty veterans, a designated hitter or two, the franchise player . . ."

"And the Entertainer? She a franchise player?"

Kid shook his head. "Short relief. My closer."

"You're unbelievable. What's her name?"

"No names, Jack. Trainer's code."

"What are you talking about?"

"For real. I'm telling you personal stuff about her, maybe about some of the others. I mean, I know you won't go gossiping or talking about this, but you never know, you might meet one of them someday and I wouldn't want to embarrass her."

"That's very gentlemanly."

"Good for business, too. It won't help me get work if people know I'm out spilling my guts about them to all my clients. I'll tell you about them, but it's all nicknames—the Entertainer, the Mortician, Samsonite, the Rookie . . ."

"Very descriptive."

"There's some logic behind it," Kid admitted. "I'm pretty

careful about my nicknames. I pick 'em for a reason. The Rookie'll change—that's just until I know more about her, until I can really peg her."

"Are all these women clients?"

"Most of them, yeah."

"That's how you meet them?"

"Mostly. Sometimes at clubs, after-hours places. Bars. I met the Rookie at an after-hours club, then saw her again in an art gallery. Sometimes I meet 'em just walking down the street." He grinned. "What can I say? Women like me."

"Keep going."

"Gimme fifteen leg lifts and we'll gab."

Jack began to strain, sitting on the Universal leg-lift machine. As the small stack of weights slowly began to rise and fall, Kid began to elaborate.

"So there's the Entertainer, you know about her."

"I don't know *anything* about her."

"What do you *want* to know?"

"*Something*. What does she do?"

"She's a dancer."

"A few more details, please."

Kid thought for a moment. "Okay. She's got a great body, she chews with her mouth open sometimes, which drives me a little crazy, she surprises you sometimes with how smart she is, and she's a little bit sad."

"Why sad?"

"Because she has to live a secret life." When he saw Jack's look of confusion, he went on. "She's got things she can't tell anybody."

"Not even herself."

It wasn't a question and Kid nodded, pleased that Jack understood so quickly. "Especially herself."

"That *is* sad," Jack said.

"The saddest thing there is," Kid said, and Jack was suddenly surprised to realize that this wasn't really part of the conversation, that this was, in part, Kid talking directly to Kid. Then his eyes focused back on Jack and he put another two-pound weight on the machine. "But, hey," he said, "that's what makes her an interesting closer. Great stuff—but she's too damn wild to depend on."

SEVERAL MORE WEEKS passed and Jack's body was aching all the time now. But it was an ache that excited him. He could feel his body responding, getting stronger. It seemed as if strength was surging back into him almost on a daily basis. It made him work harder, force his body to absorb more punishment. It made him realize the possibilities and hunger for more of what he was just beginning to taste.

It was in the middle of one particularly grueling session, perhaps the biggest push he'd made yet, that Mattie wandered into the workout room.

"I'm sorry to interrupt," she said, "but I'm off to the store. Is there anything special you want me to get?" she asked Jack. His only response was a weak wave of the hand, grateful that she'd rescued him, giving him a few seconds respite from the torture Kid was putting him through.

"Mattie," Kid said. "How is it you haven't aged a day since I first met you?"

"Stop messing with me," she said, but she grinned as she said it. She could not get angry at Kid. She had told Jack several times how glad she was that he was back. How much livelier the apartment had seemed since he'd returned.

"And you've gotten even more beautiful," Kid told her. "What's the secret? A pact with the devil?"

"I'll give you the devil," she said, but her grin grew even wider. "This is your last chance to tell me what you want."

"Whatever you get is fine with me," Jack told her.

She turned to Kid and said sternly, "And you don't deserve anything special"—she wagged her finger at him now—"but I'll *think* about buying you something too if you tell me what you like. No promises now, but I'll think on it."

"A weekend with you on a romantic island, that's all I want."

Mattie swatted at him with her hand. "You are *bad*," she said, but she had an extra little skip in her step as she headed toward the front door.

"She likes you," Jack said when Mattie was gone.

"She's got good taste."

"She does. Mattie's very fussy about who she approves of."

"She was always nice to me. I think she used to feel sorry for me. She always used to ask me about my mom, making sure she was okay. And she used to want me to talk about my dad, too. I remember one time she told me that when her dad died, she tried not to think about him. She thought that would make the pain go away. But then she realized that only made the pain worse. What made it better was to remember."

"That's good advice. Hard to follow, but good."

"I guess. I still find the forgetting a lot easier."

"What is it you're trying to forget, Kid? What the hell's been so hard for you?"

Kid looked down at the barbell on the floor. "It shows, huh?"

"Something shows. I don't have a clue what, though."

Kid said nothing for a few moments. Then, as he bent down to add weights to the barbell, he turned to Jack and said, "Do you miss her? I mean, do you miss her all the time?"

"Yes." Jack was surprised how quickly he blurted out the word. He thought he'd tell Kid to stick to his team and leave him the hell alone. But suddenly he found he *wanted* to talk about Caroline. Maybe it was hearing Mattie's advice. Memories were welling up inside him and he felt an overpowering urge to get them out into the open. "It's almost unbelievable how much I miss her."

"I miss her, too."

Jack swallowed hard. "I think anyone who ever met her would have to miss Caroline."

Kid nodded solemnly at that. "Do you think you'll ever . . . it sounds so jerky when I say it out loud, like a song, but . . ."

"Do I think I'll ever fall in love again?"

"Yeah. That's what I was trying to ask."

"Kid, a few weeks ago, I wasn't sure I'd ever leave my apartment again. I haven't had much time to think about falling in love."

"But now that you know you're going to get better, back to normal . . ."

"Hold on. I don't know that. I can lift ten pounds and not pass out; that's not the same as being normal."

"Jack, you know it. It's a process but it's happening. I can see in your eyes that you're starting to know it. I told you that I'm going to bring you back so take it as fact."

"Okay," Jack said. "I'll take it as fact for this conversation."

"Good enough. So you know your body's going to be fine. Normal. *Better* than normal. What about the rest of you?"

Jack didn't answer but not because he didn't have one. It's that he was overwhelmed with his realization. "I think you can heal my body," he finally said, "but I think my heart is broken forever. We were like one person in a lot of ways. And when she died, enough of me died, too, that the whole can't be brought back to life."

"I'm gonna make you whole, Jack." The words were soft but they rang with passion and conviction. "I really am. And then maybe, somehow, the dead part can come back to life again. I want it to come back to life more than I've ever wanted anything before, ever."

"Who are we talking about now," Jack asked. "You or me?"

This time Kid said nothing. Just pointed to the weights, expressionless, as Jack reached for them and began to take one step closer to being whole.

t was happening again. He hadn't learned.

What did it take for Jack Keller to learn?

What did it take before he understood that you don't steal what belongs to others? How many deaths and accidents before he realized?

One more, at least.

One more death.

Then one more chance.

Then maybe, just maybe, this could all be over. If not . . .

Well.

There'd be no more chances.

But many more people would die.

EIGHTEEN

The end of the year was cold and snowy. The beginning of winter turned New York into its most common role: the ultimate urban contradiction. The buildings shimmered and lit up the skies as if they were alive. The city was clean and fresh and vibrating with activity; it begged to be explored and appreciated but tourists and shoppers made movement impossibly difficult. One had to swivel one's neck to stare at the extraordinary beauty all around, but one swivel too many would ensure a plunging step into a curbside pile of ankle-high brown icy slush.

Christmas was difficult, but Jack took Mattie's advice to heart. The week between the twenty-fifth and the first was spent drinking excellent wine, eating well, and spending long nights with Dom, Kid, and a few select visitors reminiscing about Caroline and the many good times past. Jack also realized he was beginning to look forward to more good times in the future. The realization both thrilled him and worried him. And made him feel more than a little guilty, a feeling that he alternately fought against and succumbed to.

What if . . .

On New Year's Eve, Jack and Dom went out to Daniel, the best restaurant in New York. Dom's treat. Kid was invited but he was spending it with a member of the Team. He was evasive, didn't want to tell Jack which one. Finally he confessed he was seeing two women. The Mortician was early. Then, after midnight, he was meeting the Entertainer, when she got off work. Jack just shook his head, said he hoped that Kid knew what he was doing. For the first time, Kid didn't make a smart-aleck comment back. He shrugged, as if he wasn't really sure that he did.

January second was a different kind of celebration. Dom came up, as did Kid and Mattie, and at three o'clock they stood and cheered as a man from Goodwill came up to the apartment and picked up Jack's wheelchair. He didn't need it anymore. "Come back in another month," Kid told the guy. "We got a couple of canes we won't be needing either."

A couple of weeks after that, Kid stepped out of the elevator to find Jack waiting for him excitedly. He headed, as usual, straight for the exercise room but Jack stopped him, ushered him into the living room. It took Kid a moment to notice but he was led to it by Jack's stare.

What Jack was staring at was a new painting that had been hung on the living room wall. It stood all by itself, bathed in a soft light that came from up on the ceiling. It was not large, maybe two feet by three feet. But it managed to dominate the room and when Kid turned to look at his friend and patient, Jack's eyes were moist.

"Do you know what it is?" he asked Kid.

Kid nodded. "A Hopper. I never saw one in person before."

"I didn't think I was ready to get it. But I've had feelers out for a while and I heard it was up for auction . . . and I decided the time was right."

"Right for what?"

"To do something I was supposed to do. Keep a kind of promise. To have something really beautiful to look at."

"Do you think it's beautiful?"

Surprised, Jack said, "Don't you?"

Kid shrugged and in a high-toned voice said, "I regard Edward Hopper as the depressive's Norman Rockwell."

Jack's jaw practically dropped to the floor. "*What!*"

Kid grinned. "Jack," he said, "I don't know shit about art. I'm just quoting."

"A member of your fucking team?"

Kid nodded. "The Rookie. She has very strong feelings about art."

"Do me a favor and tell her to go fuck herself."

Kid laughed. "You don't want to mess with her, Jack. Not with what I've just learned about her."

"Your goddamn team," Jack mumbled. "I don't think they even exist."

Still laughing, Kid said, "They exist, all right. Hey, the Rookie was even written up in yesterday's *Times*. She's famous."

"Well, don't ever bring her here. Don't ever let her see my goddamn Hopper!"

"I'm just kidding, Jack. I think it's very beautiful. And I'm sure she would, too."

"Your goddamn team," Jack said again.

"It's incredibly beautiful, Jack. I swear." And when Jack raised his eyebrow questioningly, Kid said, sincerely, "Really. It's really, really beautiful."

Jack frowned. Then nodded, accepting Kid's last words. "Okay, you can stay," he said. And mumbled, one more time: "Your goddamn team."

IT WAS MID-FEBRUARY when Kid came in for a morning session looking as if he'd been up all night. Jack soon ascertained that he had.

"The Mortician," Kid said, as if that were all the explanation needed. When Jack waved his hand, a silent "let's have a bit more detail" gesture, Kid added, "It was a special night."

"What kind of special?" Jack wasn't about to let him off the hook. For one thing, talking about Kid's life helped him get through the workouts. Talking about Kid's sex life made him extraordinarily curious. And, he had to admit to himself, it was beginning to make him somewhat envious.

Kid was clearly uncomfortable. His shoulders moved and his neck shifted under the confines of his T-shirt. "She's too involved in the relationship. Emotionally."

"That's what made it special? You dumped her?"

"No." Kid laughed nervously. "She helped me move to a new apartment. Helped set things up."

"Congratulations. Where is it?"

"Tribeca. On Duane."

"Nice."

"Yeah, it is, but . . . I don't know. I don't know if I should have let her help so much."

"Why not?" Jack asked.

"She's very . . . controlling. She's in a situation where she's not in control of a lot of things in her own life, so she tends to hold on to the things she *can* control."

"And you're one of those things?"

"No. But she thinks I am. Or at least she'd like me to be."

"Here's my advice. Get out now."

Kid looked somber. "Yeah, well, the Mortician's not so easy to break up with. She's got some really nasty friends and I don't think I want to piss them off just yet."

"It sounds like you're *afraid* to get out of this."

"A little bit, I guess. I'm a little afraid of her."

"She sounds lovely, Kid. I'm glad to see you're going out with class."

"She's not my usual type, that's for sure. But she's got a lot of experience and I like that and, well . . . she *is* classy. She's got a lot to offer."

"So she's still on the Team. Even though she scares you."

"I don't know for how much longer but, yeah, she's still on the Team."

"Who else is still on? And who else scares you?"

"They *all* scare me, Jack. And let's start with shoulder presses."

"Don't change the subject."

"Don't dick around on my time. I'll talk, you work."

They moved to the Universal machine. Jack positioned himself, sitting, in front of it, Kid set the proper weights, and Jack began to lift. After six reps, he managed to breathe out,

"I'm waiting." And at eight reps he said, "I'm still waiting. All I know is the Entertainer, the Mortician and—"

"God, you're a pain in the ass."

"That's fifteen." Jack allowed himself to slump against the back of the seat. "Talk."

"Okay. Right now there's the Entertainer, the Mortician, the Murderess . . . she's great. She's really special."

"Hold on. She *killed* somebody?"

"It's a nickname, Jack. That's all."

"Well, it had to come from somewhere."

"There was an accident, when she was a kid. That's all it was. At least that's all I'm gonna tell you. But she's definitely still scarred by it. Seriously scarred." He raised his eyebrows conspiratorially. "Sexily scarred. Second set."

Jack moved forward in the seat, struggled with the first lift, fell into a more manageable rhythm for the next round of fifteen reps.

"Is that it? Three women right now?"

"No," Kid said. "There's more. An old one. I thought it was over a long time ago but—" he hesitated, chewed on his lower lip before continuing—"it's not."

"Back in the picture?"

"Not as far as I'm concerned, but . . ." He didn't have to finish the sentence. Jack understood the implication.

"Got your very own stalker, huh?"

"Not exactly. But kind of."

"Nickname?"

"The Mistake."

"Not very encouraging."

"No. It really was a long time ago. Back when my father died. Right after. I went to a party and I was pretty down and we just started talking. I started crying, I couldn't help it . . ."

"A comfort fuck?"

"God, no. It wasn't anything like that. No fucking at all. It just got . . ." Kid shook his head, looking for the right word.

"Intimate?"

He nodded. "Yeah. Intimate. No sex but weirdly sexual. Very loving but . . . no love."

"At least on your part." And when Kid nodded again, Jack said, "Mistakes come back to haunt you."

"More than I ever thought possible," Kid said.

"What else is haunting you?" Jack asked, and suddenly they were not just bantering.

"I thought we were talking about the Team."

"Is that what you want to talk about?"

"I haven't finished."

Disappointed, Jack backed off. "Okay. Who else is there?"

"There's Samsonite . . ."

"A hard case?" Jack asked.

"Very true. But not where I got the nickname." He paused, proud of this one. "She comes with too much baggage."

"What kind of baggage?"

"She's a Slash."

"Come again?"

Jack finished the last rep and dropped the weight. Kid gave him a look of approval, added ten more pounds to the machine.

"You know, a Slash. People who want to be somebody else. People who have to pretend to be one thing so they can live with what they really are. Samsonite wants to be Courtney Love but for now she's a singer-slash-bartender-slash-dealer."

"She sounds delightful, too."

"She's not boring, that's for sure."

"And will she ever be Courtney Love?"

"Nah," Kid said. "That's the thing. It's like I told you about the Entertainer. She lives with too many secrets. Can't tell people what she's done, can't tell people what she does. Can't tell herself, either. And definitely can't tell herself what she's going to *be*. That's why she's a Slash. Samsonite and the Murderess, too. The Mistake. Even the Mortician. She's better off than the others in a lot of ways but she's definitely a Slash. It's the only way to pretend you're not going to end up the way you know you're going to end up. In my world, Slashes never get to be what they really want."

"You think your world is so different from mine?" Jack asked quietly.

"Very different." Kid smiled now, a sad and knowing smile. "In my world, we're *all* Slashes."

KID HAD JACK concentrating on his abs this session, a whole series of crunches.

"I've been thinking about what you said," Jack managed as he curled himself up and back. "About the Team."

"Which part?"

"All of it. What I want to know is, is it satisfying?"

"It's different, Jack. It's not your style. It's not something you ever could have done. But for me, it's the best I'm going to get. And at least it's fun."

"You ever been in love, Kid? As compared to being in lust?"

Kid stayed silent a long time. Long enough that Jack thought he wasn't going to answer. Possibly hadn't even heard him.

"I said, have you ever—"

"Yeah," Kid said very slowly. "I've been in love." He went a long time again before speaking, and then added, "The Destination."

"Good nickname."

Kid smiled sadly. "Came from something I read somewhere. In a magazine. It said Topeka's a town, Cleveland's a city, but Rome's a destination."

"Nice."

"She *was* a destination, too. Something to wish for. Something to aspire to."

"What happened to her?"

Kid coughed into his fist, then took a deep breath. The words he spoke were obviously painful for him. "She ended it."

Jack managed to twist himself so his right elbow touched the outside of his left knee. "Almost unimaginable."

"Yeah, well. She did."

"For another man?"

"I never asked," Kid said. "Didn't matter to me why. It only mattered that it was over."

"Come on. You weren't curious? You didn't even want a chance to convince her?"

"I knew what was going on. It was her decision to make and once she made it . . ." Kid shrugged. "She was out of my league, really. It was down in Maryland and the thing is, she had a real life without me. The other members of the Team, they kind of need me. For all different reasons—to help them do something, to help them escape something, give them some security—but the Destination . . . it was different. She *thought* she needed me but then she realized she didn't and I knew it and that's why I didn't have to ask."

"Rome's not the only destination, you know."

"Well," Kid said, "I don't think I have much chance of going to Paris or London or Vienna. That's the thing about a Slash. We usually know where we want to go, we just don't have any way of getting there."

As Jack finished his set and fell back onto the slant board, breathing hard, Kid said, "They all live on the edge. What do you think that says about me?"

"I'm sorry," Jack said. "I wasn't paying attention. I'm too busy cramping and practically vomiting. Who are we talking about now?"

"The Team. What do you think it means that they're all kind of"—he watched Jack lurch forward, beginning his next set—"twisted?"

"It means you have shitty taste in women" was the response.

"No. They're all great. Really. They're all interesting and weird and amazing-looking. But they all have these *flaws*.

They're all . . ." He thought for a moment, trying to come up with the right word. It didn't take him long. "Dangerous" is what he came up with. "They're all dangerous."

"Dangerous, how?" When Kid didn't answer immediately, Jack asked, "What kind of flaws?"

"It's hard for me to describe. Well, Samsonite's easy; she's just way too crazy. She's a druggie. Drinks too much. Pretty paranoid, pretty generally wacko. I met her at a club, an after-hours place. She was working there, still does, and I started talking to her and she says, 'Can I ask you a question?' I go, 'Sure,' and she says, 'I got a bet with a friend. A hundred bucks. I said that Mount Rushmore was a natural rock formation and she says it's a sculpture.' So I broke it to her that it wasn't purely an act of nature that Abe and the boys are up on the cliff there in perfect detail and she can't believe it. First she gets furious, thinks I'm lying. Then she decides I'm in on it with her friend, and that I'm splitting the money. Finally, I convince her I don't even know who her friend is, I don't even know who *she* is, and I'm telling her the truth. So what does she do? She asks if she can borrow a hundred bucks so she can pay off the bet."

"Kid, I don't want to put down your very fine circle of friends, but what's the attraction for you to someone who thinks Mount Rushmore is a natural rock formation?"

"You have to see her, Jack."

"So it's just physical?"

"Just?" Kid shook his head slowly. "No. That doesn't begin to describe it. I mean, yeah, sure, it's *very* physical, with Samsonite it's kind of scarily physical, but these women—all of them—they're almost *perfect,* I mean, really perfect physical specimens. And they're working all the time to get themselves even closer to perfect."

"As long as it's not superficial."

"Give me some slack here. It's not totally superficial. It's not only their looks. They're sensual. They're hungry. They *want* things—I don't know how else to describe it—and their want is just overpowering. At least to me it is." Kid laughed, an attempt to brush away his sudden seriousness. "It's another difference between our worlds, Jack. You live in a kind of rational one, where thinking and responsibility and work are what count. Me, I'm surrounded by all these people who'll do anything to make themselves beautiful or get rich or—"

"Or just get whatever it is they want." When Kid nodded, Jack said, "I think I met one of those. Down in Charlottesville."

"Yeah," Kid answered. "I guess maybe you did."

Jack finished his third set of crunches and lay still on the board, not even having the energy to speak for a long while. When Kid asked, "You want to try a fourth set? Really go for the burn?" Jack waved him away and Kid must have seen the look in his eye because for once he didn't press him. He stepped back and let Jack do his best to recuperate.

Within seconds, Jack forced himself to sit up. Rubbing out the cramp that now gripped his stomach, he turned to Kid and said, "These people . . . your Slashes . . . your Team . . . doing anything to get what they want . . . is that what makes them dangerous?"

Kid thought for a moment. "No," he said. "What makes the Team so dangerous is what they do when they *don't* get what they want."

NINETEEN

THE TEAM

SAMSONITE

Where was she?

Oh shit oh shit oh shit, oh God, where the hell was she . . .

Oh. Yeah.

She was home.

Jesus Christ, she was in her very own apartment. How the hell could she not recognize that? Oh, well. Wasn't the first time. Probably wouldn't be the last.

For one horrible moment she'd thought she was home in Russia, not home in America. That happened to her sometimes. Usually in the middle of the night. When there were shadows. Shadows reminded her of Moscow. She'd left when she was fourteen but somehow she knew that shadows would *always* remind her of Moscow. She didn't think she'd ever escape those shadows. The lack of food. Eight people in an apartment that made this one look like fucking Buckingham Palace. The cold and the grayness and the old men who wanted blow jobs in exchange for fucking cigarette lighters . . .

She reached over to her right, groping for the top of the orange crate that served as her bed table, hoping to find a cigarette. Her arm brushed across something hard and she heard a quiet moan and the thing next to her moved and—

Jesus Christ. She wasn't alone.

Who the hell was *he?*

Oh, yeah. She knew him.

Yeah. She *liked* him. He was nice. A nice guy.

Kid.

He was doing something for her. A favor.

What the hell was he going to do?

He was good-looking, that was for sure. Had a major body. Oh, God, they'd had amazing sex, now she remembered. And now he shifted slightly next to her, onto his side, and she saw the deep scratches on his back. How had *those* gotten there?

Oh, yeah. *She'd* done that. And remembering, she started to laugh, but the laugh turned into a cough and she really started hacking, so she swung her bare legs out of the bed and half ran, half staggered into the kitchen to grab a cigarette because she suddenly remembered she'd left a pack by the sink.

On her way in, she stumbled over one of her boots, which had been discarded and tossed aside sometime the night before. Her eyes flickered briefly, searching for the other one, but she couldn't find it. Had to be in there somewhere, she decided. Didn't it? Maybe it didn't. Oh, well. Who cared.

Leaning against the countertop, she inhaled deeply. Felt a

lot better. Then she realized that her foot hurt and she looked down. Jesus Christ, she was bleeding. She'd stepped on a piece of glass. How the hell did glass get all over the kitchen floor?

Oh, yeah. She'd broken a bottle. Vodka. Two more Russian things she couldn't escape: vodka and her goddamn accent.

Was that last night? Jesus fucking Christ . . .

What was that? What was that noise?

Oh, yeah. She wasn't alone. She'd forgotten. The nice guy. Kid . . .

She wondered if she had any more drugs in the apartment or if she'd have to go out and find some. Another better thing about America. In America you could go to a club and find some rich guy who had drugs and all you had to do was fuck him. In Moscow you had to *beg* for drugs. And then you had to fuck the guy anyway.

Jesus. Her foot was bleeding pretty badly.

She could see her reflection in the window. The kitchen window that looked over a dismal alleyway. A dismal alley on a dismal block in a dismal city. The alley looked like shit. But she looked mighty fine. Mighty fine.

She stared at the shadowy reflection in the dirt-streaked window. At her naked body, so thin and perfect, absolutely flawless, and she licked her lips. She watched the reflection as she put one hand on the countertop to balance herself, lifted her right leg, looked at the bottom of her bare foot. She picked the small piece of glass out of her heel, vaguely felt a stinging sensation.

She stood there on one leg in the kitchen, naked, a small stream of blood trickling onto the floor from the bottom of her foot, staring, transfixed, at her image in the window, flickering and shining in the gray morning light.

What the hell was that?

Oh, yeah. Christ, how could she keep forgetting? That *guy* was there, in her bed.

That guy who was going to do something for her. What the hell was he going to do?

Wait . . . hold on a second! She remembered! All right! Fuckin' A! She remembered! It was something great. He was going to do something *major* for her.

What the hell was it again?

Oh, yeah.

He was going to save her fucking life.

THE MORTICIAN

It was on the first night of her honeymoon that she realized she did not like her husband.

No, it was more than that.

By midnight, within ten hours of their exchanging marriage vows, she knew that she hated him.

She didn't panic when she realized her mistake; she was not the panicking type. But it surprised her that she'd been so wrong, so off in her perception. After all, she was not a kid when they met, certainly not naive, but she had never been pursued by a man like Joe. He'd been so single-minded, so overwhelming. She was twenty-six years old when he spotted her working in Tiffany's. He was fourteen years older and not exactly handsome, but thickly sensual and solemnly charming. He'd come in to buy a piece of jewelry for another woman, she assumed his wife, but with no prompting he said he wasn't married, that he'd never been married. She thought he was lying—she could see instantly how he looked at her, the way his eyes betrayed his cool demeanor and revealed his desire for her—but it turned out he was telling the truth. Forty years old and never married. Okay. Fine. The jewelry was for a girlfriend. "She looks like you," he said, "only not as good. Not as . . ." He hesitated, he couldn't find the right word, and then he came up with it: "Elegant." Then he told her to pick out something that she liked, something that would look right on her; he could tell from that if he wanted to buy it. When she asked him the price range, he smiled. It wasn't an arrogant smile or a pretentious one. She liked his smile. It dazzled her and made her a little weak because it was the smile of someone who was used to getting absolutely everything he wanted. He didn't have to say anything after that smile. She knew it meant that the price didn't matter. That the price *never* mattered.

She picked out a diamond necklace. It was something she'd neither craved nor particularly admired, but it was something she appreciated as beautiful. It was cold and very expensive and perfectly crafted. She put it around her neck, her arms snaking over the top of her back to effortlessly close the clasp. She let her arms linger in the air for just a moment, feeling her own thick hair envelop and hide her fingers, and she saw his eyes flicker, taking her in from head to toe. Her legs, which were spectacular and long and quite visible through the waist-high slit in her full-length skirt. Her breasts, which were full and firm. Her porcelain skin, looking as if it was untouched by the sun, gleaming even whiter against her dark, dark hair, which hung straight down to her shoulders. All it took was those few seconds, that pose, she could feel it. Then her arms unfurled from behind her neck, came back down to her sides, and his eyes settled on the necklace. The diamonds no longer looked cold and distant. They were hot and steamy against her pale skin.

He nodded. Again, no words were necessary. He handed her his credit card and when she lifted her hands again, went to remove the necklace, he reached out and stopped her. Put one hand on her elbow and said, "No. It's for you now."

Three months later, she quit her job.

Six months after that, they were married.

She'd known what he did for a living before the wedding. And it didn't bother her. The fact that he was always in the news was a little troubling—she was a fairly private person and she knew that things would be different now—but it was also exciting. And that's really what she was about, she knew that. Not money. Not sex. Not love. Excitement. The day after their engagement, her photo was on the front page of the *Post*, and three old friends whom she hadn't seen in several months called her to say *Do you know what you're doing?* She did know. And she didn't care. She didn't think he was any different from any other successful business-man. She had no problem with the morality of what he did or that she was about to become a part of it. She had no problem with anything until the wedding.

They spent almost all their time together in the several months before the big event. They talked incessantly—he was bright and witty and surprisingly learned. He made her feel ignorant and during that period she began to read again. History, mostly, which he encouraged, but novels, too. And biographies of businessmen and politicians and leaders of social movements. He liked to entertain and she proved her-self a good hostess. She could be warm and inviting as well as invisible, and she had an instinctive awareness when each talent was needed. Sex between them was fine. Not the best she'd ever had but passionate and quite physical and some-times romantic because they really were in love.

The ceremony was at a grandiose Catholic church in mid-Long Island; the party was at Joe's father's estate nearby. An elegant and tasteful affair. Perhaps five hundred people, maybe ten of whom were her friends. She knew that after the marriage those friendships would fade and, before long, disappear, but that was all right with her, too. She didn't care.

What she did care about happened while they were cut-ting the wedding cake.

He'd put the ring on her finger, they'd taken their vows. Their kiss was long and lingering and people cheered and applauded. They danced, a wonderful-looking couple glid-ing across the floor, then they moved to the table with the three-tier chocolate cherry creation. She picked up the knife, smiling and loving, went to cut the dessert, but he moved so quickly, his hand just shot out, grabbing hers, covering it. And suddenly she realized she couldn't move her hand, he was squeezing it, and very quietly he said, "Not by yourself. With me. We do it together. You don't do anything by yourself. Not now, not ever again."

For a moment she thought he was kidding. She smiled questioningly and said, "Honey, what are you . . . ?" She didn't finish her sentence because she didn't have to. By then she'd seen the look in his eyes. And it terrified her. Made her knees buckle. He thought it was all the excitement. He thought it was the overpowering pleasure of the moment. But it wasn't.

What she saw when she looked in his eyes was: *You're mine.*

She'd become a possession. *His* possession.

They got on the plane several hours later, flew down to Peter Island in the Caribbean, where they had a spectacular four-bedroom villa overlooking the sea, on top of the hillside, with a cook and a maid and a chauffeur to take them to the beach or to town for shopping, all just for the two of them. They ate slowly and kissed and groped each other during the marvelous dinner, then they made love, slowly and lovingly. It was so wonderful she thought that maybe she was way off base; he *had* been joking when they'd stood at the wedding cake. The thought made her happy, so she kissed him, started babbling, just because she was so relieved. She told him what she'd been thinking about doing with the house, she didn't want a decorator, *she* would do it, if it took longer so be it, but they'd be sure to love everything that was around them—

And that's when he spoke. Said those words that chilled her to the bone.

"When we have our kids," he said, "the names are already picked out."

She didn't understand at first. But she stopped her babbling and just said, "What?"

So he repeated it. And when she looked at him, confused, he said, matter-of-factly, "I just want you to know that everything's decided already. Today, tomorrow, two years from now. It's already done. Do you understand what I'm saying?"

She did indeed. She understood all too well. What he was saying was: *You belong to me.* That's what his eyes had said at the wedding, and that's what he was saying there, by the sea, while they were naked on the floor of the villa. It's what his eyes would always say now, and she knew it was true.

She did belong to him. And she hated it.

She hated him because of it.

She had her first affair the day before their first wedding anniversary.

It wasn't an easy thing to arrange, not at the beginning. She couldn't stay too close to home. But she'd gone back to school to finish her college degree and there, at NYU, in an undergraduate business class, she seduced her professor. He didn't know who she was, who Joe was, and the affair lasted a month until he found out. She didn't mind when he said he couldn't see her anymore. She was already bored with him. And she already knew she was going to get an *A* in the class.

It was not a spectacular affair, as far as affairs go, but it was exhilarating to her. Remarkably freeing. She went back to Joe with her mind at ease after that month, threw herself into the role of wife, knowing that he had lost a little piece of her, that she had regained just a small fragment of her own self.

Eighteen years later, she was older than Joe was when they'd first met. She was forty-four now and still having affairs. One a year.

She still looked great. Possibly even better than when she was twenty-six. Joe told her that all the time. He couldn't believe it. "Look at me," he'd say. "I've gained thirty pounds and my hair's as white as Santa's. But you . . ." And then he'd smile that same confident smile. "You look exactly the same. Even *more* beautiful."

Then his eyes would shine with pride.

And ownership.

Of course, her beauty wasn't without effort. She'd had a personal trainer for six years now. The latest one came to the apartment three times a week, sometimes even to the Long Island house, although usually when Joe was away. His workout was brutal. She ached constantly. But the results were splendid. Her body was back to what it had once been, before Joe, before the kids, before the eighteen years had somehow slipped away.

She was mad for the trainer. He was quite lovely. And he was gloriously young.

The first time he didn't show up for an appointment—he called to cancel early that morning—she pouted. She missed him throughout the entire day. She was unhappy. Several weeks later, he canceled again, a Friday session, and she was angry. Miserable. She didn't sleep that night and even Joe noticed that something was wrong. Her anger stayed with her all weekend, until she saw him again early Monday afternoon. Kid Demeter walked in the door and she was happy again. Relaxed.

After that, she began to think about him often. She would lie in bed, Joe curled up next to her, and she would be thinking about the boy. There was something special about him. As if there was much, much more to him than what she was allowed to see. And soon she had seen quite a bit.

Most of her affairs lasted no more than a month. That was all she desired. Anything more than that could get complicated and messy and she desired no complications or mess in her life. But her affair with the trainer had gone on for nearly a year now. And she was addicted. When he wasn't there, she craved him. When he was there, she dreaded his leaving. She bought him things, took him places, tried to please him, and the only subject that was off-limits was the future because he was young and she was not and no matter how spectacular she looked, she could not be a part of his future.

For them there was no future.

Which meant for *her* there was no future.

Sometimes, late at night, she forced herself to think about that. She made herself focus on what she would do if he ever left her.

The answer surprised her. And disturbed her. For she had no answer.

It was unimaginable.

It would never happen, she finally decided. *Could* never happen.

She owned him. He belonged to her. He was *hers*.

At last, she had her own possession. And one did not just let one's possessions up and go. Disappear. Who knew that better than she did?

No, being left was not acceptable. It was too horrible. Too painful.

Unimaginable.

THE ENTERTAINER

She was very pretty. *Muy bonita.*

Really and truly. *Es verdad.*

Very, very pretty. *Muy muy bonita.*

She knew that she was, and she was more than willing to take advantage of it. How could she not? She saw how heads turned when she walked down the street, especially when she wore that little black skirt and the gray tank top, the one that just managed to reveal the thin ripple of muscle on her shoulder and down her back. And she knew that her body was superb, as good as it had ever been. Why shouldn't it be? She worked out two or three hours a day now, so her arms and legs were hard and thin, her stomach was cut and flat. Her breasts weren't large, but they were fine. Everyone told her to make them bigger, to have the surgery, all the other girls did, but she just couldn't bring herself to do it. She liked her breasts, her little *chi chi*s, liked that they were really her. She lost some customers because they were too small but she didn't really care. She wasn't going to start slicing herself up, changing herself. She really and truly would not do that. At least not yet.

Men wanted her, that was clear. And because of that she could get them to give her almost anything she wanted. Presents. Expensive dinners. Or just good old-fashioned money. One man, old, in his forties, probably, maybe even his fifties, with a paunch and saggy chicken skin on his chin and neck, wanted to give her an apartment. He was Indian, she thought. Maybe Arab. She wasn't sure. She just knew he was dark, much darker than her, and had an accent and that saggy skin. She already had an apartment, though, a nice one, with a view of the East River. It was the one thing she paid for herself. She liked paying for it. Really and truly. It made her feel grown-up and as safe as she could ever feel. So she told the dark old man that she didn't want his apartment. It was the only thing of any importance that she'd ever turned down. She thought it would make her feel good, turning it down, paying her own way, but it didn't. It only made her feel sad.

It made her sad, too, that she could get men to beg and humiliate themselves just to touch her. But it also excited her, made her feel powerful, at least for a while. When it was over, she'd just feel empty again. It was like when she was little. When her dad would come into her room at night, when everyone else was asleep. She saw what she could do to him. She would tease him and his eyes would harden; they wouldn't stare *at* her, they'd stare *into* her. She would run her little hand across his neck and call him funny names and she could feel him tense, but more than that, she could feel him succumb to her. She could tell that he liked her, even though he rarely said it. She could tell that he loved her, really and truly loved her, even though he *never* said it. She could tell, even at that age, that he wanted her for some overwhelming and incomprehensible purpose. He never said anything about that, either, but he didn't have to. She saw it in his eyes when they burned into her. He said nothing but his eyes said *por favor*.

He never touched her, though. He never got the chance. Her mother also saw the look in his eyes and one day said something about it. Soon after that, her father was gone. She was allowed to see him, but only when another grown-up was present. At first, he came once a week. Soon, every two or three weeks. Then, less often than that. Finally he just stopped coming. Her mother said she was lucky. They were all lucky. Particularly so when, less than a year after the divorce, a new man came into their lives and her mother remarried. A wonderful man. A pillar of the community. A man devoted to his new family, her mother said. So proper. And good. And moral.

And white. So very white, which is why her dear *madre* thought he was so perfect. So clean.

But she wasn't surprised when her stepfather came into her room that first time, that night when everything changed. He had been nothing but kind to her. Helped her with her homework. Smoothed things out when her mother got impatient with her. She liked him fine, decided she could probably grow to love him. But she'd seen that same look in his eyes.

Por favor.

Only he said it in English. Said it the way a white man would say it.

She wasn't unhappy when he got down on his knees and whispered that he'd do anything for her. He pleaded and cajoled and stroked her hair, so soft, so gently, and yet she knew that she couldn't pull away, that he wouldn't *let* her pull away. He'd do anything for her, he said, over and over again, if she'd only do one little thing for him. One little tiny thing that would make him so happy. So she did, that night and many nights after that. It always made him happy, just as he'd said, and she never felt ashamed. It thrilled her and made her proud. Until he'd go away and ignore her. Or worse, yell at her. And sometimes hit her. That was always in the daytime. Then he'd be back in the middle of the night, sorrowful and repentant and begging her to be his little girl and let him love her. She tried telling her mother but her mother wouldn't hear a word of it. Didn't believe her. Refused to even listen because it was impossible for this man to be unclean. So she stopped talking about it and just accepted it as a fact of life. She liked the pleasure and could put up with the pain. It went on for a long time, the begging and the yelling and the hitting and the loving. Until eventually it was no longer thrilling. Eventually it just made her feel empty, like everything else.

Really and truly empty.

When she first started her job, she didn't let the men touch her. Just teased them. And flirted, of course. Then, somehow, that stopped, the barrier disappeared, and they were grabbing her, pawing her, breathing hard and rolling their eyes back like they were having a fit. At some point, she realized that the touching meant nothing to her. So she allowed it. And while she would still get sad and empty, it was all somehow funny to her, too. When she would see them, so hungry for her, so hungry for *everything*, she would laugh. Sometimes to herself, sometimes right in their face. It never seemed to bother them, the laughter. As long as they got what they wanted. That was the number-one lesson she'd learned over the past three years: nothing matters as long as you get what you want.

She didn't know how long this life could go on. She feared that it would come to an end, and sooner rather than later. Because she knew something. She had a secret. A secret that terrified her. Really and truly frightened her. Kept her awake at night. Sometimes made her break into a cold sweat when all she was doing was sitting on the white, fluffy couch in her living room, having a cup of tea with her feet tucked under her. She was certain that no one knew this secret other than her. She was sure that no one even suspected it. But there it was, and she lived with it every minute, until it got bigger and bigger and now it gnawed at her day and night and scared her and made her sweat.

Oh, yes, she was pretty.

But she wasn't pretty *enough*.

Her nose was too large and pushed off to the side, ever so slightly. Her teeth were excellent, white and even, but her gums were too prominent. When her lips curled back, they showed too much of her pink gums and she hated that. It's why she rarely smiled.

She wasn't crazy about her skin, either. It was dry, no matter how much expensive moisturizer she kept on it, and it wasn't smooth. There were imperfections, little bumps and hairs; when she stared at it under the bright lights of her makeup mirror it sometimes made her sick. Really and truly ill. She would stare at the magnified flaws in her skin for five minutes, ten minutes, sometimes as long as half an hour, and then her stomach would hurt and she'd have to lie down. And when she'd lie down, she'd think about her hips, how they were too wide, they really and truly were. Oh, no one could tell now, but she knew what was going to happen in another ten years. That might seem like an eternity, but it had already been three years since she'd come to New York and that had gone by in a flash. It seemed like yesterday. So she knew that any minute her hips would widen and her triceps would sag and she'd have her mother's body and once that happened, men wouldn't love her, they'd leave her, just like they left her mother. . . .

No. She couldn't go there. Once that happened, everything would change. But for now, it was her secret. No one else knew what would happen as she got older. The same way no one knew what she was like before. All they knew was what she was now. *Muy muy bonita* with a perfect body and small *chi chi*s that were still her own.

Then she found out that one other person knew. Just one. She had told him about her past, about her father and the way he crept into her room at night. About her parents' divorce and her stepfather and her mother's religious conversion, and her sister's suicide and her other sister's drinking. Yeah, she was the one who revealed to him what she'd been. But he'd figured out on his own what she was going to become. Somehow, he'd seen it for himself. Watched her as she stared at her own face in the mirror. And when she turned to him, realizing that he was there, in the bathroom doorway, he'd said, "Scared." Said it very plain and simple. Not really a question, much more definite than that. More of an answer.

"Why should I be scared?" she asked, and flipped her streaked blonde hair. Men melted when she flipped her hair. Especially since it had been streaked.

He didn't melt, though. Just stared at her for another few seconds. And then said, "Because you're smart enough to know what's going to happen to you."

She wanted to ask: *What do you mean? What's going to happen to me?* But she didn't, because he was right. She already knew.

Just as he knew that she wasn't pretty enough.

That was the first time it occurred to her that she was in love with Kid.

It was also the first time she realized what she was capable of.

It was the first time she thought she could kill him.

Es verdad.

Really and truly kill him.

THE MURDERESS

She couldn't believe her life was turning out so well.

So far, it had been a dream of a day. She woke up, alone and liking it. Went for a run, did the entire Central Park reservoir twice around. She ran easily, with her mind clear, able to concentrate on exactly what she was doing: putting one foot in front of the other, breathing deeply, in and out. She kept her own pace, competed against no one. Ran out of the park until she was half a block from her apartment building—she adored living on the Upper West Side; what could be better?—then walked briskly the rest of the way, smiled at her doorman, rode up in the quiet elevator, stepped back into the apartment she loved so much. She spent a minute stepping through the apartment, touching the art on the walls, the piece of fabric from India that had been mounted and framed and hung in the living room over the elegant Shabby Chic couch. Touching them made them real to her. The way her life was now real to her.

She had ground the dark, French Roast coffee beans the night before and put the powder in the top of the gleaming black Cuisinart coffee maker, along with a dash of cinnamon and a touch of vanilla, so all she had to do was pour in four cups' worth of water and flick the switch. The aroma of brewing coffee immediately filled the kitchen while she yanked her sweaty clothes off, dropped them on the living room floor and left them there, ran in and took a hot shower, let the steaming water, pleasant little stings of heat, rain down on her body while she scrubbed herself clean and shampooed her hair vigorously, twice.

Her clothes had been laid out the night before—organized was better, she had long ago concluded—and she stepped into the suit she'd decided to wear that day to work. She wouldn't get home before the party she was hosting that night, so this outfit would have to suffice for both. The black pinstriped skirt was short enough to be revealing and sexy but loose enough to be tasteful. The matching jacket was conservative but beautifully tapered. She buttoned it to within two buttons of the top, revealing only her long, graceful neck and the very top of her angular chest. To counter the conservatism of the cut and fabric, she wore no shirt underneath. Let everyone wonder. She had concluded something else long ago: mystery was also better.

She wore two-inch heels. She'd be on her feet all day, but she decided against flats, went with the Manolo Blahnik slingbacks that had been such an extravagance when she'd bought them. The extra inches boosted her up to five foot five and that, she decided, was a respectable height.

Her reddish hair—once a mousy brown, now lightly hennaed so it had a coppery glow—was layered and cut short. She'd had it touched up the day before. She wanted everything to be in place for tonight. Tonight was meant to be special.

She nudged the toe of her right shoe under her running shirt and sweatpants and kicked them up in the air. Cupping her hands and catching them expertly, she dropped them in the hamper in the hallway closet, went back into the kitchen and had two cups of black coffee—why, she wondered, does four cups of water always make only two and a half cups of coffee—while she read the *Times*, which had been delivered to her front door.

Even the long subway ride down to work had been particularly nice. A very handsome guy eyed her appreciatively the whole way down. He was around her age, wore expensive jeans and a pressed and firmly starched white shirt, and there was nothing leering about his stare. He got off the train before she did and he smiled at her, an appreciative smile, acknowledging the fact that she looked good and that it was nice to see someone who looked good.

Work, too, had been easy so far. She'd made the sale she'd been hoping all week to make. The clients had been indecisive but ultimately had trusted both her taste and her assessment that the piece they were buying was going to appreciate substantially in value. She was thrilled when they'd finally said okay; she didn't even bother to try hiding her pleasure. She had a bottle of Perrier Jouët sent to their apartment with a note that read, "You made the right choice. Drink this while enjoying your new purchase," and she received a dozen roses from them—sent before they could have received her gift—with a note that said, "Thanks for making our lives easier and more pleasurable."

She had a delicious little lunch right around the corner— turkey on black bread with Brie and honey mustard—and then a cappuccino with skim milk at the Italian coffee place a block farther away, one of the last neighborhoody places, sad to say, left in that part of SoHo. Gianni, the usually grouchy seventy-ish counterman, even threw in a chocolate biscotti, saying, "On you it looks good."

It was only toward the end that the dream of a day took a rocky turn. She was on the phone, doing a favor for another customer, giving some advice to a young artist who was looking for a place to display, when she heard the front door open and he walked in. Flustered, she didn't get off the phone, talked to the artist for perhaps five more minutes. Knowing she was being rude but not really caring, not knowing what else to do exactly. Then the conversation was exhausted and she hung up, had to deal with the situation.

"I wanted to see you," he said.

He looked good. Of course, he always looked good. This was him at his best, though. Tight jeans worn over a pair of brown cowboy boots, a yellow T-shirt. A light beige suede jacket. Hair mussed. Why couldn't he ever keep his hair combed?

"You know I'm happy to see you. But we've been through all this," she told him.

"This is different," Kid said. "It's not what you think. I just need to talk."

She smiled, not exactly believing that all he wanted to do was talk.

He saw her smile and said, without smiling in return, "I need help."

"What kind of help?" she asked and now she believed him because she'd never seen him quite so serious.

"Can you meet me later? Tonight?"

"I can't," she said, and felt as if she were lying but she wasn't. Tonight was too important and she couldn't leave. When he kept staring at her, she repeated it, stressing the word so he'd at least try to understand, "I *can't*."

He still said nothing, and in the silence she thought, *He knows so much about me. More than almost anyone.* Then she thought, *What he could do with what he knows. What he could do . . .*

"Please," he said. The word was so faint that she wasn't sure she had heard it at all. Then he said it again, firmer. *"Please."*

"I'm sorry," she told him, and she couldn't believe the words were coming out of her mouth. She was being so strong. Or was she being cruel? Or worse, self-destructive?

She watched him turn, disappointed and hurt, and go out the door, saunter away down the cobblestone street. He *did* tend to saunter.

The phone rang again. It was the artist-in-waiting, with a couple more questions. She gave him answers but she didn't really hear the questions. She was too busy thinking about the end of her perfect day, and what it meant, him being hurt like this. She realized that she would have to go see him one day. Soon. And she realized what she was going to have to do.

And why.

I n mid-March, Kid said it was time to begin the final push.

"You are now strong enough to begin phase four," Kid announced. "What I think is that if you stopped now, stopped progressing, I mean, you could live like this. Your body is basically back to normal, your injuries are pretty much healed. There's pain, I know, but it's manageable pain."

Jack thought this over and nodded. "Most of the time it is."

"You can live like this but I don't want you to. You shouldn't have to," Kid went on. "The problem, at this level, isn't so much the pain itself as the fear that goes with it. It's no longer a question of healing, it's a question of strengthening. It's a question of how strong can we make you and the answer is you have to be strong enough to eradicate the fear."

"What's that on your arm?"

Kid glanced down. Peeking out from the bottom of his T-shirt sleeve was a hint of a white bandage. "It's nothing," he said.

"What happened?"

Kid hesitated. "A cut."

"How?"

Now Kid fidgeted. He bit his lower lip, chewed it until it turned white, swiveled his head uncomfortably and finally said, "The Mortician."

"She *cut* you?"

"I . . . I talked about the idea of breaking up. She got upset and—"

"Kid, did she do that with a knife?"

Kid nodded. "It was mostly an accident."

"I think this is getting out of hand."

"Look, can we not talk about this? I don't want to talk about the Team anymore."

"Why not?"

Kid now pulled out a small chart. "There are six hundred muscle groups in the body, comprising forty percent of your body weight—"

"What's happening that you don't want to talk about?"

Ignoring him, Kid went on, looking only at his chart. "We're gonna go to town on those muscles now."

"Kid—"

"No!"

Jack was startled by the vehemence behind Kid's shout. He said nothing until Kid looked up and their eyes met. Then Jack nodded. While he nodded, the thought that was in his head was: *He ran before. I don't want him to run again. Something's going on and I don't understand it—but I don't want to push him away. I don't want him running.* So he didn't go beyond the nod, which let Kid know that he was willing to drop the subject.

"Here's a schedule." Kid tapped his chart again. But before he could go any further, Mattie came running into the room.

She looked around frantically, expecting to find something wrong, and was surprised that the room was calm. "What was that screaming?" she said, and though her voice was even, her eyes were fierce. Her anger was directed at Kid, and when he didn't answer she said, "Don't you start screaming and upsetting things," she said.

"It's all right, Mattie," Jack told her.

"I don't want him screaming at you. And I don't want him hurting you more than you already been hurt." She faced Kid again. "You understand what I'm telling you?"

"Yes," Kid said, all force gone from his voice.

"You hurt him once. And you are not going to do it again."

"You're right. I'm sorry."

She stood in the doorway, scowling, until Jack said, "It's really okay. I swear."

Mattie nodded, satisfied that she'd done her job, turned, and headed back to the kitchen. There was an awkward silence in the room until Kid said, "She protects you."

"Yes."

"Well, she's right to."

"Right or not, I'm glad she does."

Kid cleared his throat, tapped his chart again, and said, "Okay, for now, we're gonna follow this four times a week."

Jack frowned and looked over the chart in Kid's hand. There were all sorts of columns, neatly printed out on a computer. The exercises were impossible. Kid wanted him to do things he could not do.

"You *are* joking, right?" he asked Kid. "You want me to run?"

"We're not gonna get there tomorrow, Jack. But a year from now, yeah, I think you'll be able to do all this. And you don't have to run a ten-minute mile. We can start at fifteen. Or twenty. I just want you to get on the treadmill and—"

"You're completely out of your mind."

"When are you gonna learn to trust me?"

"I trust you."

"You don't." Kid's voice had no anger in it now, just a quiet determination that was as strong as the day he'd shown up in the living room and challenged Jack to get well, challenged him to fight back against the pain. "I'm serious. How can you not believe me when I say you're going to do something? How can you not trust me after all this?"

Jack took a long time before saying, "Kid, to be perfectly honest, I think I had all my trust shot and cut out of me."

Jack could see the hurt on his face. But Kid just nodded and said, "Okay, will you at least try the treadmill? I promise we'll go slow. All you have to do is say when it hurts and I'll stop."

Jack didn't say anything. But he stepped onto the treadmill and, as Kid pressed the start button, he began walking, gradually picking up speed, then a bit more, and then more until he was moving at a light jogging pace. He waited for the pain to come crashing into his hip but it didn't. It was there, but not a crash, more of a wave, and for a moment he broke stride. But he saw Kid watching him and he thought he could run through this particular pain. He knew he'd ache like hell the next day and the one after that. But it was okay. He could do this. He was running. It was the slowest damn run in history but he was running.

"I met someone," Kid said quietly. "It's been pretty intense."

"A new Destination?"

"It's the perfect nickname for her," Kid said. "In every possible way."

"Congratulations."

"Except . . . There are things about her . . . I don't know how to put it."

"She's another one who scares you?"

Kid did his best to smile but he only managed a glum shrug. "Jack," he said, "everyone I know right now scares me. This one, the new Destination . . . I don't think she's what I thought she was."

"Do you want to tell me what's going on," Jack asked, "or are we just going to keep talking in riddles?"

"I do." Kid nodded, as if making a decision. "And I will. Soon. There's a lot I understand now, but I just have to figure a few more things out. Then I'll tell you everything."

"Well, in the meantime, can I stop running? I think I'm going to pass out."

"Lemme tell you a story," Kid said as Jack moved at his easy pace. Kid's voice was calm now, and soft. Jack knew that tone was as close as he'd get to an apology for Kid's unwillingness to bring him into his personal life. "When I was playing football, in high school, we were playing this huge team. I'm talkin' *huge;* their line averaged two hundred and eighty pounds and ours was maybe two-twenty-five, two-thirty. We thought we were gonna get slaughtered. But our coach said we could win. He said if we could keep it close till the fourth quarter, our aerobic training would kick in. We were in much better shape, he said, and they'd get tired and, even as big as they were, once they were tired, we'd be able to outmuscle them. And you know what? He was right. We beat 'em. And in the fourth quarter, we stomped all over those big fuckers."

"That's good to know. Maybe I'll re-enroll in high school and try out for the football team."

"I'm just saying that running's important. You never know what you're going to come up against out there, Jack." Kid's voice got even quieter, seemed to come from someplace far away. "You just never know," he said, "what kind of huge fuckers you're going to come up against."

T here she was, totally unsuspecting.

You didn't have to know her, just by looking at her you could tell she was a nice woman. There was something so warm and pleasant about her. So likeable. She was clearly a very loving and caring person. It was all over her face, in the way she walked, as if she were hugging the whole world in her bony arms. It was nice to see. It was comforting in a way.

And that must be her husband. He looked like a nice guy, too. He was using a cane to help him walk. Wonder what happened to him? An accident, maybe. Maybe even Nam. He was limping pretty badly. Husky. That couldn't help his leg. Probably went two-ten, two-twenty. Maybe five-nine. He could lose a few pounds, sure, but he looked pretty happy so maybe he was one of those guys who didn't mind what he looked like or that he had to struggle along with a limp.

She looked happy too. Why shouldn't she? It was a beautiful day, cold and crisp and clear, and she had a nice husband who picked her up at the bus stop on her way back from work and walked her home, even with his bad leg. You didn't see too many couples like that anymore, did you? No, you definitely didn't. People just weren't that considerate anymore. People didn't do things like they used to, like they were supposed to.

It didn't seem right what had to be done. But it was necessary. Why should this nice couple be the only happy ones? Didn't they deserve their own happiness, too? You better believe it. And wasn't everyone else trying to steal their happiness right away from them? They damn sure were. Well, maybe not everybody. Maybe that was an exaggeration. There was no way to be positive about everybody. But better safe than sorry.

That was a good slogan, wasn't it? No, not a slogan. What was it called? A saying? Maybe. No, a motto! That's what it was. A really good motto: Better safe than sorry.

The black couple passed an older black woman coming out of a building. The older woman said, "I was just knockin' on your door, Mathilda." Mathilda was so nice, she looked unhappy that she wasn't there for this woman when she knocked. And she said, "Well, we're home for the night now so you can knock any time you like." The older woman said she would and then the black couple climbed up the three thick, concrete stairs that led to a pretty nice building, red brick, maybe twelve stories, two houses off Lenox Avenue.

That's where she lived.

Oh, this was easy.

It really was easy.

It was easy to park the black Pathfinder on Lenox Avenue at six o'clock the next morning—early, sure, but better safe than sorry.

It was easy to spot Mathilda and her husband when they emerged at 7:30, it was easy to follow them as they walked three blocks to the bus stop, and it was easy to watch as they kissed good-bye and then the husky husband headed back home.

It was easy to follow the bus down Fifth Avenue and then to jump ahead of it because there was no question where she was headed. There was no need to even double-park. Amazing. A car parked on Madison pulled away and the spot was just big enough for the Pathfinder to pull in. There was even twenty minutes left on the meter.

It was easy to wait on the corner for exactly eight minutes until the right bus arrived and it was easy to step up behind Mathilda and guide her, well, force her, okay, into Central Park, just steps away from the bus stop.

No one paid any attention at all, so it was very easy to push her behind the bushes and cut her throat before she even knew what was happening.

It was easy to take the money that was in her wallet. And not only easy, smart, because it made it look like a robbery.

But best of all, it was easy to go through her purse and find exactly what was needed.

Well, to be honest, that might be an exaggeration. It might not even be needed.

But let's face it. It probably would.

And, besides, it was always good to have another magic invitation. Another way to make absolutely sure their dream would come true.

Better safe than sorry, right?

That sure was a good motto.

"That's funny," Jack said. And when Kid looked at him curiously, Jack asked, "What time is it?"

"A couple of minutes after nine. Damn, I gotta get going. I got a session at Hanson's."

"What's Hanson's?"

"A gym down in SoHo. I train people there sometimes. Good facility." He swept his hand over Jack's home gym. "Not everyone's got the setup you've got here, you know."

"I'm worried. It's not like Mattie to be late."

"Maybe she's sick."

"She'd call."

Kid shrugged. "Traffic, maybe."

At ten, really worried now, Jack pulled out his Palm Pilot and used the stylus to click on the name Mattie Strickland. He dialed the number on his cordless phone and when a woman's voice answered, he said, "Mattie?"

The woman on the other end of the phone was crying and he couldn't understand what she was saying.

"Is Mattie there? This is Jack Keller. She was supposed to be . . ."

And now the woman started crying even harder. "Oh, Mr. Keller," the woman said. "Mattie was always goin' on with the nicest things about you. . . ."

"What's going on?" Jack said. "Is her husband there? Could I speak to him?"

"He's here," the woman answered, still sobbing. "But he can't come to the phone. He can't talk now. I'm their neighbor," she said. "I'm not talkin' too good myself but I'm answerin' the phone for a while. Until the children can get here."

"Please tell me what's going on. Is Mattie okay?"

"Mattie's dead. Killed," the woman cried. "Mugged right on her way to work. They took the money in her purse and killed her. . . ."

The woman went on, giving as many details as she could, but Jack barely heard another word. He was only vaguely aware of saying good-bye, saying that he'd be in touch and would do whatever he could to help. And when he hung up, dizzy from the news about the woman who'd been so kind to him and had cared for him for so long, the only thing he could think about was how many dangerous people there were out there in the world, how many Slashes desperate to take whatever they needed.

Whatever they wanted.

B y the middle of April, Mattie's funeral had come and gone and, as always, with time, a sense of order had reasserted itself into daily life.

Jack, Dom, and Kid had all gone to the service, where Jack had spoken to Mattie's husband. "I know this doesn't begin to ease what you're going through," he said, "but I want you to know that Mattie's salary will be paid every week for the rest of your life."

"Thank you, sir," he said to Jack.

"If there's anything I can do. Anything at all . . ."

"Thank you, sir," he said again, "thank you," and grabbed Jack's hand, squeezing it hard. Jack recognized the sound in the man's voice. He knew it from his own voice: it was the sound of indescribable and unsharable loss.

Jack found that his therapy with Kid, the sheer physicality of it, was of enormous help in coping with this latest tragedy. He could concentrate on his body for hours at a time without having to worry about his heart.

On April twelfth, the thermometer reached seventy-two degrees. After running a thirteen-minute mile, Jack, sore as hell, stepped off the treadmill and Kid said, "We've got a little treat today."

With that, Kid walked Jack out to the balcony, where he'd set up the barbells and dumbbells they were going to use that day. "I figure for the summer we can move the whole gym out here, the machines and everything. The awning'll cover the stuff in case it rains, but you can run and lift and bike outside. It'll be nice sweating in real air instead of air-conditioning. For now, we might as well use it for free weights."

The day was spectacular and Jack breathed in the city air and surveyed the enveloping green view, a green that was now dotted with color from the first planting of tulips and the crush of pedestrians happy to be outside strolling and jogging and even dozing on benches.

The workout was a pleasure. Invigorating. Jack did little but concentrate on what he was doing. He was relatively free of any contemplative thoughts, instead just enjoying the warmth of the sun hitting him and the ease of his movements. He vaguely noticed that Kid seemed restless. He was pacing. And while Jack did his biceps curls, Kid was furiously pumping heavy iron. He wasn't paying full attention to Jack, which was rare. He was straining, forcing himself to bench four hundred pounds, hurling heavy grunts and muscling aching moans into the air; then he grabbed a barbell, put it behind his neck with two hundred pounds of weight attached, and rapidly squatted out fifteen reps. Even that didn't quite do it. As Jack finished up the last of his exercises, Kid still looked like a coiled spring waiting to explode.

"What's up with you?" Jack finally asked. He was down from the high of his own workout, the world was back in normal focus, and now he saw that there was indeed something troubling Kid. This was not just restless energy he was seeing.

"Things are comin' down."

"The Team?"

"A little bit. Maybe."

"The Mistake."

"Jesus, you don't forget anything, do you? Yeah, it's gotten even weirder. The more I find out . . ." Kid's voice trailed off.

"What else?" Jack asked.

"A whole bunch of things."

"Like what?"

"School. Finals. I'm training a lot of people. And . . . and I want to bring you something, something I want to show you. I mentioned it before. The MBA, my idea . . ."

"Whenever you want."

Kid was nervous. His words were coming out faster than usual. And Jack thought that the sweat on his forehead was from more than his quick and brutal workout. "I'm working up a plan. I'll put it down on paper. You don't have to like it or anything. I mean, you can be honest, but I really want you to like it. Or at least take it seriously, okay? It's really important to me that you take it seriously."

"Kid, when did I ever not take you seriously?"

Kid let some air whoosh out of him. Jack's words seemed to relax him. "Never, I guess." He chewed on his lip, thinking. "It's gonna take me a little while to get it right. A few weeks at least, maybe a month."

"Bring it to me whenever you're ready. Whenever you think it's right. I'll take it seriously and I'll be honest and I'll be blunt. How's that?"

"That's good," Kid said. "That's real good." He hesitated. "And, look, it's not just me. It involves my buddy Bryan. You remember Bryan? From when we were kids?"

"The big guy. Your shadow."

"Yeah. Smaller now since he cut out the steroids."

"Helluva blocker. I remember."

"Well . . .." Kid was back to being jittery. "Maybe I can bring him. I mean, after you read this plan. For a meeting."

"You can bring whoever you want," Jack said. "I'd like to see him again. Be like old times, you guys eating enough for ten, me paying. As long as I can be just as honest. And just as blunt."

Kid looked relieved. "Yeah," he said. "That's perfect. That's completely perfect." He took a deep breath now, nodded to himself a couple of times, and Jack thought he was calming down. Kid turned away from Jack, stood near the wall at the end of the terrace, peered out curiously at something. As Kid stepped closer to the edge, Jack felt his stomach clench.

"Hey," Kid said. "Do you know you could actually walk to the next building from here?"

"No," Jack said. He didn't know if Kid could hear it, but there was definitely a tremor in his voice. As Kid bent to look over the edge, Jack felt his throat tighten. "I never—"

"Seriously. The buildings are connected. Someone could walk along this ledge and get to that rooftop. You'd have to be kind of nuts but . . ."

"Kid . . ." Jack's mouth was dry now. The image in front of him—Kid standing by the wall, leaning over—turned wavy and fuzzy, like a TV set with bad reception.

"And these gargoyles. Unbelievable. These are scary-looking motherfuckers. I never even noticed them before! God, they're huge."

"Kid . . ."

And then it happened. Kid took yet another step closer to the restraining wall and with one sudden motion, one fluid jump, leapt up to stand on it.

Jack screamed.

Or at least he thought he did. He *tried* to scream but no sound came out. He saw Kid perched on the ledge, standing on the precipice, and his own legs turned wobbly. He wanted to call out but he couldn't. It was as if a hand had clamped down over his mouth. He looked up at the sky and saw the bright sun shining down, only it was spinning, going sideways, whirling around the clouds and getting brighter, turning everything a bleached-out white. And he saw a figure—he knew it wasn't real, *couldn't* be real—but he saw it anyway: a boy with feathered wings, flying by the sun, then falling, plummeting, waving his hands wildly trying to keep himself aloft, but failing. Falling even faster. Falling . . .

Jack felt himself choking, no air was coming in, and he remembered: *Look down . . . Look straight down . . . Grab something, hold on to something and look down . . .*

Jack gripped the bench he was sitting on, forced his head down to look at the floor of the terrace. He closed his eyes then and waited for the dizziness to pass, for the heaving in his stomach to stop and the panic to disappear.

He heard Kid's voice calling his name. Jack took a deep breath, then another, and a third. Without looking up, without opening his eyes, he tried to speak, didn't think he could, but he was surprised when he heard the words in his head come out of his throat.

"Down . . ." he gasped. "Get *down* . . ."

Still with his eyes shut tight, he heard Kid's voice, totally calm and unhurried. "Jack," he said. "Jack. It's okay."

Jack opened his eyes. The dizziness had passed. But still he didn't look up. His mind took him, without looking, to the ledge, and he pictured Kid standing there, looking over the city, nothing to stop him from toppling, and Jack thought he was going to throw up. He shut his eyes again, tried to force the image out of his head, the image of Kid tumbling in a free fall through the air, down . . . down . . . And then it wasn't Kid who was falling, it was Jack. In the image, his eyes were open and he was screaming, but there was nothing to see and there was no noise. . . .

"Jack." It was Kid's voice. "Open your eyes."

Jack didn't move.

"Nothing's going to happen, Jack. I'm not going to fall."

Jack's eyes fluttered open. But he didn't move. Didn't look up.

"You only fall if you want to fall," Kid said. "Please. Just open your eyes and look."

Jack breathed in slowly. He knew it was foolish, he felt weak and stupid. But his brain had no control over what he was feeling. This was pure terror, an uncontrollable phobia. The idea of being so close to the edge . . .

"You only fall if you want to fall, Jack. Please. Just look up."

Jack exhaled now. He felt as if he'd been holding his breath forever. Slowly he lifted his head up. Kid was standing on the wall of the terrace, facing Jack. His back was to the park, to the city and the street below. Jack trembled, forced himself not to turn away. He could see the sky in the background, the blue with white clouds, Kid silhouetted against the distant green of the park and the brown peaks of the West Side buildings. Jack's hands were shaking. And his right foot couldn't stop tapping.

"I'm sorry. I wasn't thinking. I forgot about . . . everything. But I'm not afraid of heights, Jack. This doesn't bother me."

Jack's voice was faint. It was as if he had a fever, some deadly flu that had weakened his body, sapped him of any muscle control. "Come down now, Kid. Please come down."

This time Kid listened. He hopped off the wall, planting himself firmly back on the terrace. He walked over to Jack and as soon as he was away from the edge, Jack's whole body relaxed. The sweat on his neck turned cold and clammy and he wiped it away. His foot stopped moving and his hands were steady.

"I'm sorry," Kid said again. "I didn't realize . . . I didn't know it was so bad."

"I feel like an idiot," Jack said. "Jesus. But I can't help myself."

"I didn't think . . . it just doesn't bother me. I like being up there. I *like* looking down."

"Kid," Jack said, his voice still shaky. "You said you only fall if you want to fall."

"Yeah," Kid nodded. "If it's just you. If there's no one else pushing you. That's right."

"Well, that's what terrifies me. When I get close to the edge, when *anyone* goes too close, I see myself—I don't just feel it, I see it—I'm hurling myself over. I can't stop it, it feels like a magnet pulling me there. I throw myself over and I see myself falling. And falling . . ."

"I'm sorry, Jack. I didn't understand."

"It's okay." Another deep breath. "I'm okay now."

"You want me to get you something to drink?"

"No," Jack said. Now he forced himself to stand. He could manage, but he was not at full strength yet. "Let's just go inside."

Kid took his arm, opened the sliding door that led into the living room.

"You only fall if you want to fall," Jack repeated slowly. "Is that really what you think?"

"Yeah," Kid said. "That's really what I think."

"I don't want to fall," Jack told him. "I really don't. But I just don't think I can stop myself."

SAMSONITE

How could this be?

Wasn't this plan so brilliant? She was *sure* it was.

It had been fucking simple and fucking brilliant.

She'd been amazed that she'd ever been so fucking smart to have thought of something that was so fucking simple and brilliant.

Even now she was still amazed. It was a fucking brilliant plan; that's all there was to it.

Except it didn't work.

What a motherfucker.

Oh, well. It had been that kind of a day all around. Nothing fucking worked. No big surprise there. *Every* day was pretty much that kind of day, now that she thought of it. That's what had made her plan so great. It was gonna make the days a little more bearable. Or make *one* day more bearable, anyway. That would've been enough, wouldn't it? You bet it would. Fucking A. That would've really been something. One bearable fucking day in America . . .

Wait. Now that she thought some more, yesterday was not a bad day at all. Yesterday was pretty damn good. She'd seen Mr. Wonderful. That's what she called Kid. He *was* pretty goddamn wonderful, too. Almost wonderful enough to make her forget that her fucking plan hadn't worked.

She remembered how powerful she'd felt when he was finished with her. How, when he was so tired and ready to fall back on the bed and lie there, she'd fucked his brains out all over again. God, yes. She'd wrapped her legs around him, squeezed him practically to death, but it didn't matter because he was so strong and so hard. *So* hard. And she remembered how surprised he was when, right in the middle, she'd whipped out those handcuffs and there he was, chained to the fucking bedpost. KGB handcuffs, she told him. Real and official and oh, man, he was angry. And she'd laughed. She hadn't laughed that hard in, what, days? Maybe even months. Because what could he do? He couldn't do *anything*. He sure as shit couldn't go anywhere. He had to let her fuck him again. And even harder, even longer. He had to . . .

How could the plan not have worked!

It was a can't-miss.

Lots of dough. *Lots* of dough. All hers for the taking. The American dream and as easy as fucking pie.

A great plan, no question about it.

Okay, maybe it had been a little risky. Shit. Now that she thought about it some more, it was even a little dangerous. Maybe a lot dangerous. And probably pretty stupid.

Good thing Mr. Wonderful was so reliable. Reliable was good. And he was more than that. He was strong. Christ, was he strong. That was even better than reliable. At least in this case.

Because maybe, just maybe, he was strong enough and reliable enough so he could stop them from killing her since her perfect plan hadn't been so fucking perfect after all. Since she'd fucked it up like she fucked up everything else.

God, it had seemed so good.

But it was just another thing that had blown up in her goddamn face, just like every other fucking thing on every other unbearable day in her goddamn unbearable fucking life.

THE MORTICIAN

He had just left, her beautiful boy. She watched him saunter down the walkway and disappear into the garden. She caught a glimpse of him again through the trees as he walked down the driveway and then again as he stepped into the waiting town car. She stared after him from the window until she realized he'd been gone for several minutes, and even though she was alone, she felt self-conscious, like a schoolgirl writing something naughty in her diary.

She could still smell him, he was still in the air, and that smell sent a shiver of excitement through her entire body. She took four quick steps, skips, really, and threw herself back onto the bed. She buried her face into the top pillow, took an enormous, deep breath in, felt her lungs swell and was overwhelmed by his scent—the light touch of the lemony Balmain cologne she'd bought for him, the powdery fragrance of his deodorant, the wonderful harshness of his sweat. Although they had just made love, hard, passionate, glorious love, she was aroused again. Squirming, she felt between her legs and she was dripping wet. She remembered running her fingernail down his arm, the way the bicep bulged and tightened. She touched the bandage there and he'd flinched. She liked him flinching, it practically made her come seeing him so vulnerable, but she told him she was sorry. Said she'd lost control. She didn't tell him that she wouldn't lose control again, though—she didn't want him to get too comfortable—but he had accepted her apology. He reached up and grabbed her and now she pictured herself on top of him, bending low, kissing his chest, working her lips down to his hard stomach. . . .

She tried to force herself to think of other things but it did no good. She wanted him again. Now. But she couldn't have him, and for a brief moment she was angry, furious, and she hated him for leaving her. Then she inhaled again, face back down in the pillow, and, feeling light-headed, she laughed out loud. She was laughing at both her exhilaration and her foolishness.

She had tried to convince him to stay for dinner. He had work to do, he said. Other clients. *Real* clients.

She was a real client, too, she reminded him. And she even offered to pay him overtime if he'd stay, shocked at her own offer, but she didn't care. She wanted him that much and she knew money was important to him. It was not important to her and she realized she was happy to throw it at him, happy to give him whatever he wanted, but he said he had to leave, that he was tempted, how could he not be tempted, but he had to be strong. He had another client who needed him and when she pouted and asked who it was he said he couldn't talk about his other clients, even with her. Yes, it was a woman, he told her. And, yes, she was young. But, no, this woman wasn't nearly as attractive as she was. And, no, there was nothing between them, she was just a client. If she needed a name, think of her as the Entertainer. That's how he referred to her when talking about her to clients. The Entertainer, because she was a dancer-slash-actress.

How do you refer to me, she asked coyly, when talking to your other clients?

I don't, he said. Then he smiled and pulled her toward him and kissed her.

And then he was gone, out into the garden and down the driveway and into the limousine that was waiting to take him away back to the life he led without her. The life she knew so little about.

She decided to learn a little bit more about his other life. She decided she *needed* to know more about it.

Now she thought about that last kiss and her giddiness disappeared. The more she thought about it, the more it seemed passionless. Like an attempt to appease her. A means of escape.

She threw her head back into the pillow one more time, hoping to breathe him in again, but his scent was gone now. There was no trace of him.

She was all alone in her room.

THE ENTERTAINER

From nine to ten that morning, she was on the StairMaster.

From 10:03 until 10:23 she was on the treadmill. Exactly two and a half miles.

After that, she did fifteen minutes of abs, fifteen minutes of stretching, then a fast one thousand meters on the rowing machine. It took her three minutes and fifty-two seconds, just seven seconds off her best time.

In the women's locker room at the elegant Chelsea Piers gym, she yanked off her running shoes and her socks, stripped off her leotard, then the tank top she wore over it, and stood in front of the long expanse of mirror. She stared at herself, watched the sweat drip from her shoulder, flexed her tricep and saw the muscle glisten under the fluorescent light. She ran her finger from the bottom of her chin, down her neck, down all the way between her breasts. Then she put her finger in her mouth, tasted her own sweat. She turned slowly, all the way around, standing on her toes, watching herself in the mirror as she spun on her bare feet. There were quite a few women in the locker room now, showering, dressing, getting ready to go back to their office jobs or their photo shoots. She knew they were starting to watch her and that excited her. She liked when all the white girls stared at her body, so she prolonged her twirl, long after seeing what she wanted to see in the mirror. Did it make them envious, what they were seeing? Did it make them horny? Did she amuse them or repulse them? She didn't much care, really and truly. As long as she did *something* to them.

The afternoon was spent shopping. She didn't need anything and that was the whole point. She bought frivolous things. But elegant. She had learned to be elegant, to have rich, white taste. She liked to tease and tart it up at the gym, get all the guys—the ones who spent their nights beating off thinking about Mariah Carey—all worked up and hot. And at the club, of course; there she loved to bare her rock-hard thighs and wear those fuck-me high heels. But in real life, she liked class. And more than that, she knew what class was. Real class. So while other girls her age were strolling Eighth Street, buying silver-plated earrings, she walked confidently up and down Madison Avenue, stopping into Fratelli Rossetti for a pair of bright-red satin open-toe shoes with a one-inch heel, and into Prada for a black purse with a red snap that exactly matched the shoes. *Two* black purses with red snaps because . . . well . . . because you just never knew when an extra would come in handy.

She had an audition at 3:30, for a soap, but it wasn't much of a part and, besides, she was really bushed, so she blew it off, went home, and instead took a short nap around four. Then, at six, she hailed a cab and went to work.

It was a good night. She slithered and pounced and kicked and was sexy as hell. She made $1,800 in tips and not one person knew that when she was slithering up against them, she was thinking about the new fabric she wanted to buy for her living room couch, or where she'd put the dry-cleaning bill because tomorrow it was time to pick everything up, or what books she was going to read lying on the beach when she took a vacation down in Florida in another month. One guy asked her her name and didn't bat an eye when she decided to goof on him and said, "Madre. Madre Teresa." He just said, "Nice name. Is it Spanish?" and she knew he thought she liked him, knew he believed there was a chance she'd give him her number and maybe even go out to dinner with him. He was a scrawny little guy with a bad haircut and bad skin, and she knew she was doing her job as well as it could be done because by the time she was through dancing for him, he'd given her a hundred and forty bucks and she'd bet her life he didn't make more than five hundred a week.

At 4:00 A.M., the club closed and she left. A taxi was waiting for her when she hit the street. Taxis were always waiting for the girls at that hour. The cabbies liked taking them home; one driver told her they all figured that sooner or later one of the girls would forget her billfold and they'd get a blow job in exchange for the ride. As far as she knew, that hadn't happened in the entire history of the world but she thought it was kind of sweet that the hope was so persistent.

At 4:20, she was sitting in the lounge at Sax, the after-hours club of the moment where most of the girls hung out. She thought Kid would be there. But he wasn't. One of his friends was, though. The sweet one. She could never remember his name; all she could remember was that he wanted a job at the club. He wanted to be a bouncer there. It never seemed to bother him that she couldn't remember even the smallest little detail about him. He was always hanging out at the club or in an after-hours place. He always seemed to be waiting for Kid. Like he was his bodyguard or something. Or his shadow. She wondered if he was as sweet as he seemed. Or if he was just dumber than shit.

She wondered if she should fuck him. Would it hurt Kid? If it would, she'd do it. But she had a feeling nothing could hurt Kid.

Well, *something* could.

She reached into her purse, fingered the switchblade that lay nestled beneath the gum and the loose cash and the lipstick. She loved the feel of it, loved just having it. One of her ex-boyfriends had given it to her over a year ago. For protection, he said. *All Spanish girls eventually need protection. Especially if they have a body like yours.* She didn't want it, not at first, but she took it, it was easier than arguing. Then she got to like having it. Then she got to love it. The noise it made when it *sssssed* open. Its sleekness. The fact that it was so beautiful and yet so deadly. She'd never had to use it and part of her hoped she never would. But part of her felt quite differently. *Quite* differently. She pulled it out of the bag now, held it under the table, and flicked the button that released the long, slim blade. *Sssssss.* She ran her finger over the flat surface of the cool steel.

That could hurt him.

Somebody had done it to him already; she'd watched him unwrap the bandage, she'd seen the jagged cut. Why couldn't she do it, too?

Touching the blade, she thought: *That could hurt him* bad.

Smiling, she closed the blade and put it back into her purse. Then she smiled across the room at Kid's friend. Waved him over with a slight movement of her index finger.

He started talking. She didn't know about what. She was busy thinking about her dry cleaning again. And then the test she was supposed to take the next day. Psychology. She already knew one of the questions: *Can you prove that there is such a thing as the pleasure principle?* Yes, she could. She most definitely could.

And then she thought about why she liked the idea of hurting Kid so much.

She didn't know. She really and truly didn't.

But it did make her smile.

THE MURDERESS

She could not remember ever being this happy.

Her life was under control for the first time since she could remember.

Business was great and as long as the economy stayed strong and the market kept going up she was sure it would stay great. She loved what she was doing and felt she was now really good at it. She trusted her eye, confident she could spot who and what was going to be hot. And other people obviously shared that confidence.

She'd just gotten back from a dizzying two weeks, one in Paris, one in London. Meeting new customers, new clients, new agents. It was her first-ever trip abroad and it was exhilarating. It was a big step up in class for her, she knew that, but she'd pulled it off. More than that—she'd flourished! In Paris she'd dined at L'Ambroisie, the most expensive restaurant she'd ever been to. She didn't pay, the client paid, but she

couldn't help sneaking a peek at the bill and she quickly figured out that it had come to almost two hundred and fifty
dollars per person. She must be getting decadent, she realized, because she decided it was worth it. It *felt* like a
two-hundred-and-fifty-dollar meal. She went to every
museum she could cram in, of course. Spent almost all of her
one entirely free afternoon in the Musée d'Orsay, stayed until
closing time. Didn't leave until the guard insisted.

In London, she spent one night pub hopping, drinking a
ton of beer, and got a little out of control. But it was okay,
nobody minded. At the end of the night, she didn't go back
to her hotel. She was having too much fun and she was
drunk and so she went back to an artist's flat, not very professional, but he'd been hitting on her all night and she
thought he was extraordinarily attractive. It had been a good
decision because their lovemaking was exceptional. They
got even drunker and screwed their brains out and as great
as that was, it was almost as good being in the flat, a loft
which was right on the Thames, way, way east, with huge
windows that looked out over the river and a part of the city
that looked like Dickens was still living there. The next day
she wasn't even hungover and someone else took her to the
Groucho Club to discuss a book idea, whether she thought
it was viable for America—and whether she might want to
write the introduction.

Her last night there, she dined all by herself. It was her
choice—she forced herself to do it, actually, since she was a
little phobic about eating in public alone. But she loved it.
Went to a chic place in Soho, the Sugar Club—a rave in the

Time Out eating/drinking guide. She didn't even bring a book or magazine to read. She just ate and thought about everything that was happening to her and let the waiters fawn over her, which they most certainly did.

Oh, God, she'd felt sophisticated.

She didn't even mind coming home. Didn't mind being bumped in the airport by people rushing to get their luggage. Or getting stuck in traffic on the LIE. She didn't mind coming home to her apartment, which seemed warm and cozy to her. She enjoyed unpacking and tossing her travel clothes in the laundry and putting on her scruffy gray sweatpants and Marc Anthony sweatshirt, which she'd bought at his concert at the Garden.

The only thing she minded was when she checked her phone machine.

Three messages from Kid. He thought she'd be back by now. He really wanted to talk to her, to see her. Would she please call.

She didn't want to call him. It was over and she'd told him that before she left. Now, after this trip, she was more determined than ever to make sure it *stayed* over. It had been fun and, yes, it had been good for her. Even her shrink said so. But it was over. She had to move onward and upward. It was time to put what she *was* behind her. Time to *become* what she was on her way toward being.

She thought she'd made it clear to him. She was positive she'd made it clear. And she didn't want to see him again to go through the whole thing one more time. She knew exactly what would happen—she'd weaken. She'd start to like him—that was never the issue—and she'd start to be attracted to him—that was certainly never the issue—and she'd start to think about everything he knew about her. She'd start to realize how he could make her life so . . . so *undesirable* again.

She thought about the messages on her machine and she started to get angry. Really angry. She decided maybe she should call her shrink but then she thought: No, I can do this on my own. I can. I just got back from Paris and London and I'm sophisticated. I can handle it by myself.

She decided the best thing was to ignore him. She wouldn't return his phone calls. Yes, that was definitely best. Otherwise she might get even angrier.

And her anger scared her. And it depressed her.

It made her remember too many things it was time to forget.

THE DESTINATION

It was strange being this close to him again. She knew where he lived, she was beginning to learn about his new life; sometimes she thought she could feel his presence. Feel *him*.

He had no idea she was around, of course. And it was better that way. It was the *only* way; she understood that. It would be a mistake to see him. It would be a disaster, in fact. He wouldn't want to think about her. He wouldn't want to see her. He wouldn't even want to know that she was alive.

She turned over in her bed. Slowly stroked the back of the man next to her, until he stirred, coming awake. She shouldn't have told him. That had been a mistake. But she thought somehow he would like it, that it would bring them even closer. It didn't, though. It had scared him. He hadn't said that but she could see it in his eyes. It had disturbed him, as if there were something sick, almost perverted about the connection.

Oh, well. It was too late now, though, wasn't it?

She often thought there should be a place where you could queue up and receive a ticket that would allow you to live certain parts of your life over again. A replay. Like in a friendly tennis match.

But there were no replays in life, were there? She was living proof of that. So was the ache in her heart. She wondered if that ache was ever going to disappear.

She was beginning to think it was a permanent part of her. A physical attachment. *We'll meet for tea? Oh, yes, I'm easy to find. I'm five-foot-six, have short black hair, gray eyes, and a large hole in my heart.*

The man's eyes were open now and he smiled at the pleasure he was receiving from her nails scraping lightly down his spine.

He was a handsome man, Kid Demeter was. She liked being in bed with him. She liked being with him, period. Hell, she just plain *liked* him.

But she was in love with Jack Keller.

And, as always, she wondered if she'd ever be able to do anything about it.

t was a Monday, the last week of a glorious May, and Dom was doing what he always did at noon on Mondays. Or 11 A.M. on Wednesdays or 4 P.M. on Fridays. He was working, quartering a baby calf, one of two requested by one of the top chefs in the city for a private party. This was Dom at his best: not only did he enjoy the work, he had charged the chef twice the going rate for these beauties and didn't even have to haggle. He looked at the man to his right, busy slicing up the second calf, and he smiled.

"You haven't lost your touch, Jackie boy."

Jack looked up, satisfied with the job he'd done. He laid the butcher knife on the table, the razor-sharp blade glistening and dripping with red. "I love these knives," he said. He stared at the row of eight, each one a different size and thickness, that Dom had lined up on one of the butcher-block tables. These knives were a good forty years old, they'd been there since Jack was a boy. Thick, dark wood handles, rough-hewn and worn but somehow elegant and light to the touch. The blades, sharpened every day, able to slice effortlessly through muscle and gristle and even bone. Jack walked over and picked up the cleaver. He turned it over, admiring it from every angle. "They're works of art, aren't they?"

"I wouldn't get carried away," Dom said. "They're nice enough. Mostly they're sharp as shit and they get the job done. But I'm glad you like 'em so much. If you ever want your old job back . . ."

"I keep forgetting who I'm talking to," Jack said, then looked at his watch. "I told him not to be late."

"Kid's never been on time since he was twelve years old," Dom told him. "Relax."

"It's just—"

"Yeah, yeah, I know what it's just. It's just that you haven't been back to the restaurant since . . ." He hesitated, saw the fear in Jack's eyes, decided to plunge ahead anyway, it was the right thing to do. ". . . since she died and you're nervous about it. You got a right to be nervous about it, pal. And guess what? You'll feel like shit for a while and then it'll get better. You gotta do it sometime so you might as well do it now. And don't think I'm tryin' to take your mind off this whole thing, but I gotta tell ya, you're walkin' just about normal now. You look really good. Who'da thought Kid'd actually know what the hell he was doin'?"

"I heard that." It was Kid. His voice came from somewhere among the hanging slabs of meat but they couldn't see him yet. Jack heard footsteps, then heard a punching sound—like fists hitting a heavy bag—and he saw one of the hanging pigs off to the side start to sway. Kid stepped out from behind the pig, rubbing his right fist. He jerked his head toward the moving pork slab. "He gave me a tough fight, but I knew he'd weaken around the seventh. I'm sorry I'm late."

Dom snorted and Kid gave Jack a "what's up with him?" look. Jack shrugged as if he had no idea.

"So what's this big business idea you're goin' off to discuss?" Dom asked. "And do I get to buy in?"

"You'll get your chance," Kid said. "If Jack thinks there's anything to it."

"I can't believe you're usin' him as the sounding board. I taught this guy everything he knows about business."

"That's true," Jack said. "That's why it's a miracle I ever made a dime."

"Nothin' but grief," Dom muttered. "Nothin' but grief..." And then both he and Jack were looking at Kid, who was standing still in the middle of the warehouse, a distant look in his eyes. He looked up questioningly at Jack, who was taking off the white apron he'd worn to slice up the calf, and Jack nodded solemnly.

"I didn't even think when I told you to meet me here... I thought you'd like it."

"I've been here since then," Kid said. "And I do like it. I don't always think about it. But today... I don't know, it just seemed to hit me." He stared down at the floor. "It was right about here, wasn't it?"

"He was slingin' a side of beef," Dom said. "On his way to the loadin' dock. No warnin', no pain, no nothin'."

"Just dead," Kid said quietly. "Forty-four years old and dead of a heart attack." His voice caught and when he spoke again he sounded angry. "He didn't take care of himself. Drank and ate every shitty thing he could put in his mouth. Just another fat slob with a beer belly! He was so goddamn stupid."

"Your dad was a good man," Dom said.

"Yeah, he was," Kid agreed. "A fat, stupid bastard but a good man."

Jack tossed the bloody apron on the floor and put his sports jacket on. "Are you ready for lunch?" he asked and put his arm around Kid's shoulder. "Let's go. We'll make a whole ghost-filled day out of it."

IT WAS STRANGE being back at Jack's but not as awful as he'd feared.

The lineup had changed somewhat, but he recognized most of the servers and even most of the bussers. The decor hadn't changed, at least not so he could tell at a first look around. It was no longer his and it was part of a giant syndicate, but it still felt like Jack's. And he was surprised at how good it was to be back inside, ghosts or no ghosts.

"I always thought this place looked classy," Kid said as they were led to their table.

"That's because Caroline designed it," Jack told him.

The chef came out of the kitchen now, saw Jack, and rushed over to hug him. "I'm hating this" was the first thing he said into Jack's ear. "Already they're in my kitchen, asking me how come I use ten pounds more of onions than they use in Chicago. What am I supposed to do?"

"Solve it," Jack told him. "I'm out."

"I thought you were a consultant."

"I am. Consultant's a fancy word for 'out.' "

"We miss you, Jack."

"I miss you guys, too."

"You want me to make something special for you?"

"As long as I get a side of Jack's Potatoes."

The chef then turned to Kid, who said, "Anything other than red meat."

Jack shrugged, a "what can I do?" gesture, and Kid said, "Hey, the body's a temple, you know," then the chef nodded and rushed back toward the kitchen.

The waitress was over in a moment and, for the first time, Jack saw Kid in action. All he did was order a sparkling water—but that's all it took.

"Is Pellegrino okay?" she asked, and if he said that it wasn't, Jack was fairly sure she'd burst into tears. Or offer to run to the store and buy him a bottle of Perrier.

"Pellegrino's fine," Kid told her and flashed a grin.

She nodded and smiled back shyly. "Can I get you anything else?"

"Like what?" Kid asked.

"I don't know," she stammered. "I guess Chef already took your order, didn't he?"

"He did," Jack said but she barely glanced over at him.

"I'll let you know if we need anything," Kid told her. "I promise." And she slid away across the floor, turning to look back at him several times before she managed to reach the bar and put their drink order in.

"Okay, I'm impressed," Jack said. "Nauseated but impressed."

"Don't be," Kid said back. "I'm thinkin' of giving up the Team."

"Excuse me, is that the sound of hearts breaking I hear?"

"I'm serious," Kid said.

"I don't think so," Jack told him. "Not after watching you with her."

Kid leaned forward, spoke quietly now. "Listen," he said. "Things have changed."

"What things?"

"The Destination. I think I have to tell you about her."

Jack didn't interrupt, he just nodded, letting Kid know that he could say absolutely anything.

"She told me something and it kind of shook me."

"Hard to imagine what would shake you."

"Yeah, I know. But this did. She told me a secret."

"Must have been some secret."

"It was. And I have to tell you a few other things. The Mistake . . . I need to find out where the Mistake was . . ."

"I'm not following."

"I know I'm not making sense. Give me a few more days. I'm really close."

Kid's eyes flicked up to look toward the front of the restaurant. He grimaced, shook his head slowly, and raised his hand in a wave. He looked back at Jack and said, "My partner's here."

Jack looked up, too, and gave a half wave toward the young man making his way through the restaurant.

"Listen," Kid said, and there was a quiet urgency to his voice that made Jack narrow his eyes. "I told her a secret, too."

"The Mistake?"

Kid looked startled but just said, "No. The Destination. She knows a lot of stuff now."

"What kind of stuff?"

"Complicated stuff. I just want you to know that. A couple of them do."

"Are you all right, Kid? You seem—"

"Yeah, I'm great . . . I'm great. But remember what I said. A couple of them know . . ."

Before Jack could ask another question, the restaurant anchor was upon them and Jack turned to greet Kid's oldest and dearest friend as he reached their table. Jack hadn't seen Bryan Bishop since he was about twenty years old, maybe four or five years ago. But the boy hadn't aged much. He still had a teenager's face and the friendly, open expression that Jack recalled as soon as he spotted him. Kid was right—Bryan had lost a lot of his size. In college he'd been huge, a lineman on the football team. Kid had said something about steroids; even at that age athletes were fed them. But those days were apparently over because, although obviously in sensational shape—he was still bigger than Kid and looked even more powerful—he was back to being normal-sized. As Bryan approached, Jack remembered him as a sort of loyal sidekick, not very polished, not nearly as bright as Kid, but ingenuous and impossible to dislike. None of those impressions changed as Bryan pulled out a chair, hesitated, then stuck his hand awkwardly in Jack's direction.

"You probably don't remember me, Mr. Keller," Bryan said, almost apologetically, as they shook hands, "but—"

"Of course I remember you, Bryan," Jack said. "I can still see that block you threw that sprung Kid. In that championship game . . ."

"Against Malloy," Bryan said, and when Jack nodded, Bryan's whole face lit up.

"Monster block," Jack said.

"I knew I always liked you, Mr. Keller," Bryan told him and Jack thought he'd never seen such a pleased grin on anyone's face.

"Doofus," Kid said now, looking in Bryan's direction, "I told you to wear a tie."

Bryan looked down at his outfit—jeans, running shoes, a muscle shirt with the words "Hanson Fitness Center" on the front, and a too-big tweedy sports jacket thrown over him—and shrugged. "I thought I looked okay," he said.

"You look fine," Jack told him and Bryan grinned sheepishly.

Jack waited until Bryan ordered—the waitress was delighted to have another opportunity to come over to the table—and then he put the manila envelope he'd been holding on top of the table. Kid, who'd given Jack his business plan three days earlier, watched nervously as Jack opened the envelope and removed a batch of papers. He smacked them down on the tablecloth, a tad flamboyantly, even he knew it, and said, "Tell me why you guys want to open a gym."

" 'Cause we always have," Bryan said excitedly, enthusiastically. "Ever since we were kids—"

"Bryan," Kid said, not too sharply but pointedly enough that the bigger man looked embarrassed and immediately stopped talking. Kid turned to Jack and spoke calmly and seriously. "It's all we've ever talked about, Jack. When we were just starting to fool around with weights and when we started playing ball and, you know, learning about the body and how things worked, it's all we wanted to do. Between the two of us, we know a lot about it. I mean, you can see what the Wall"—he stopped, then nodded his head at Bryan; the Wall was clearly Kid's longtime nickname for him—"what Bryan looks like. That actually means a lot. It's inspiring for someone to come into a gym and work out with a guy like him. And I know a lot of different things: the physical therapy, different approaches to training. And now that I'm almost done with school, I've got a good idea of what's needed on the business side—how to make this whole thing work. We think there's a real market for what we have to offer: a small, personalized gym, a little upmarket, top-of-the-line equipment, top-of-the-line trainers—class." He looked around the restaurant. "Like this place."

Jack stared at Kid, just for a moment, then nodded. "Okay," he said. "Whatever it costs, you can put me in for half."

Kid and Bryan looked at each other in stunned silence. Neither seemed able to speak until Bryan burst out: "Are you kidding?"

"I'm not kidding," Jack said.

"Half of . . . whatever it costs?" Kid asked.

"You got it."

Kid could barely get his words out. "Jack . . . this is unbelievable. I mean . . . I don't know what to say. I mean, this is really a big thing for me."

"I know it is. That's why I'm doing it."

"Thanks, Mr. Keller." Bryan was floundering. He didn't even know where to begin. "Geez . . . I never had nobody do anything like this for me before. I . . ."

"Well, I'm willing to do it. You understand that, right? Both of you. I said I'd do it and I will."

"Yeah, Jack, we understand it. We—"

"But it won't work."

Another silence fell over the table. This one was not steeped in gratitude. This was an awkward and unpleasant quiet.

"I want you to listen to me," Jack said. "Both of you."

"I don't understand," Bryan said slowly. His words were a bit thick and plodding and Jack could tell he was trying to be polite and professional. But the hurt on his face was obvious. As was the confusion. "Why won't it work?"

"It doesn't matter," Kid said quickly. And his words sounded harsh. He was practically jumping out of his seat. "He said he'd give us the money. That's all that matters."

"But why won't it work?" Bryan wanted to know. He never turned toward Kid, never took his eyes off Jack. He looked like he was going to burst into tears.

"It'll work," Kid said urgently. "I worked unbelievably fucking hard on that plan and I know it'll work."

Now Bryan turned to look at his friend. "But he said—"

"*Forget* what he said!" Kid was practically screaming now. "He'll give us the money! That's what we need! I'll *make* it work!"

"Kid," Jack said. His eyes narrowed; he was shocked at

the tone in Kid's voice. "For Christ sake, calm down and listen to me."

"It'll work, Jack! There's *no* reason it won't work!"

"There are two reasons. One, you're behind the curve. The big chains have already taken over. Reebok's got the West Side, the Vertical Club's got the East Side, Crunch has got downtown. And there are a lot of boutiques already established. I didn't just read your plan, I did some checking, talked to a few people."

"Those gyms you're talking about, they aren't real gyms," Bryan said. He spoke quietly. He was trying to absorb what Jack was saying. He was careful not to fly off the handle like Kid. "I mean, they're not serious. I've been to them. Really, Mr. Keller. They're for a bunch of phonies. We really know how to *train*."

"Bryan," Kid said. "He's giving us the money. It's okay."

"But if he doesn't think it's gonna work," Bryan said. "If he doesn't think it's gonna work . . ."

"Look," Jack said. He was trying to bring the conversation back to something manageable. He was astonished at Kid's reaction and he didn't want to let Kid's anger and frustration get out of hand. "Look at this restaurant. This place was *my* dream. I opened it because I knew I could do it right. The same way you can do a gym right. I'm not questioning that. But that's not enough. Especially not now, not these days."

"Jack, you gotta trust me on—"

"Listen to me, Kid, for God's sake!" Kid's mouth closed at the force of Jack's words. "You asked my advice and I'm giving it to you. Afterward you can do what you want. What

I'm telling you is that no matter how much I knew when I started Jack's, it wouldn't have worked without Caroline. Yeah, I knew what food to buy and how long to age which cut and I had the *idea*. The vision. I knew what I wanted. But to make it a reality . . . She had the social contacts. She had the good-looking friends who'd become models, and they started coming in, and they brought the athletes, who always want to be around the models, and the athletes got actors coming, and then *everyone* was coming because they wanted to see who else was here. And that was just the beginning. Caroline knew the right PR people, or she knew people who *knew* the right PR people, who put items in the right columns. And she knew how to get people talking, who to send a drink to, when to change the menu. Yeah, the place delivered. It was good. It was really good. But really good doesn't always matter. Sometimes it's timing and luck and a lot of other things. Do you understand what I'm saying?"

"Yeah," Kid said sullenly. "You think it's a shitty idea."

"I think it's a shitty idea for now. For *you*," Jack said. "And partly because you can do so much better."

"Jack, don't say that, *please*." It was barely a sentence, it was almost a moan that came from Kid.

"I've seen what you can do. I've seen the kind of potential you've got. My God—"

"Bryan, let's get outta here. He'll give us the money. He promised us the money no matter what."

"But he doesn't think it'll work, does he?" Bryan asked quietly.

Kid put his head down on his hands. The breath seemed to ooze out of him. "No," he said, almost in a whisper. "He doesn't think it'll work."

There was a long silence now around the table. Kid stood up, slumped to the side as if physically beaten, walked slowly but steadily away from the table and out of the restaurant. Jack stared after him in astonishment.

"It's okay, Mr. Keller."

Jack turned to Bryan, almost surprised to find him still there. "I'm sorry," he said. "I didn't expect that kind of reaction. I thought we'd have a discussion, find a way to—"

"Don't worry about it." Bryan smiled what Jack was sure was meant to be reassuringly. "You were just bein' honest, right?"

Jack forced a grin. "Just being honest."

"He'll understand. He just needs to calm down. He gets this way sometimes." He put his hand hesitantly on Jack's hand, in what was meant to be a comforting gesture. "I know how to handle him. He'll be okay. You don't have to worry."

Jack nodded. Then Bryan cleared his throat and said, "Well, I guess I better go find him." He stood up slowly from the table. Put his hand out and Jack shook it. "Thanks for everything, Mr. Keller. I'm sorry you didn't like the idea but, hey, there are other ideas, right?"

"Thanks a lot, Bryan. I really appreciate it."

Their hands then broke apart and Bryan Bishop went lumbering out of the restaurant, searching for his best friend.

Jack Keller sat at the table for another half hour, finishing his steak and his potatoes and wondering what the fuck had just happened.

The next morning, Kid was setting up the barbells on the terrace. From the living room, Jack watched him for several long minutes, then shook his head and stepped outside. Kid looked up but avoided making eye contact, said nothing, went back to his weights. Jack allowed him his petulant silence, began his warm-up routine: stretching, crunches, ten minutes on the stationary bike.

Finally, as the ten minutes were almost up, Jack took a deep breath and said, "Well, I'm glad to see you take rejection as well as ever." Kid didn't respond, so Jack continued: "And at least you keep your temper under control."

Kid threw his hands up in the air, turned to face Jack. "I'm sorry. Christ, I'm *so* unbelievably sorry. . . ."

The red "10 minutes" flashed on the bike's panel and Jack slowly let the pedals spin to a halt. "Listen, asshole. Yesterday I said there were *two* reasons why the gym might not be a great idea and you clearly weren't paying attention to the second one: *you can do better than that.* A *lot* better."

"Doing what?"

"I'm hooked up with a giant company. They might not want my opinion on Jack's menus but I can get you in their management training program. I've been giving this a lot of thought, so listen to me for just a minute. Try not to fly off the handle and try not to say anything stupid, which I know won't be easy. Six months ago, hell, six weeks ago, I would have said I was out of the business for good. But I'm feeling so much better, thanks to you, and I've been thinking that when my contract's up—I have a three-year no-compete clause—I might want to start something. Something new and exciting. I don't know exactly what, but . . . start *over* in a way. And you can come with me."

Now Kid made eye contact. When he spoke, his voice was hushed, as if he didn't want to put a jinx on what he was hearing in case it might not come true. "As what?"

"In the beginning, an overpaid schmuck. Eventually, my partner."

"You and me?"

Jack nodded, enjoying Kid's stunned tone. "It's what we talked about a long time ago, before you flew the coop. What goes around comes around, I guess. One thing I know," Jack said, "is that I'm better with a partner. The best partner I ever had is dead; that's the reality I have to face, and I'm starting to face it. So as near as I can tell, that leaves you. If you're interested. You were five years ago. I hope you are now."

"Jack . . . what do I know about restaurants?"

"You'll learn."

Kid said nothing for a long time. Then: "I want you to do me a favor."

"Christ," Jack said, "haven't I done *enough* for you?"

"No." Kid tore over to the weight rack, furiously loaded up the barbell with heavy weights. Jack stared, bewildered. In a controlled frenzy, Kid jerked the bar up and hoisted it above his head. It weighed over two hundred pounds but in his fury, Kid was holding it as if it were made of feathers. "See this?" he said, biting off the words. "You're gonna *do* this. But only if you start now. The only thing holding you back is fear. And I'm telling you, you're strong enough to get rid of the fear. You're strong enough now. *Right* now."

"I'll hurt myself. It's too soon. I don't think I can go through that again."

"You won't. You're just afraid."

"Yes," Jack said.

"Fear is your lover, Jack. Stick your tongue down her throat! Grab her!"

Jack hesitated. Then he said, "What do you want me to do?"

"Take off your back brace."

Slowly, Jack removed the heavy brace. He felt both free and afraid the moment he set it down on the ground.

"Take the brace off your knee, too."

"Kid . . ."

"You don't need it. I swear."

Jack unwrapped the knee brace. For a moment, as he paced, getting used to the feeling, he felt so light and springy it was as if gravity had stopped holding him down to this earth.

Kid now put the barbell down. He removed some of the weights at each end. Not many but some. "Don't ask how heavy it is, Jack. It doesn't matter. But it's heavy, okay? It's not easy. This is big-time stuff now."

Jack walked over to the barbell, stood over it.

"I want you to give me an upright row." Kid spoke quietly now. Soothingly. "That's all. You're not doing a clean. You don't have to lift it above your head. Just bend down, grip it like this, use your legs, and lift the bar to your waist. Give me ten reps—no—just give me five. That'll be plenty. Even three. I don't care how many you do."

Jack didn't move. He looked down at the barbell. He felt his back start to tense and spasm. Felt the ache in his knee and his hip. He began to sweat. . . .

"You are fucking Arnold," Kid said. "You are Hercules Unchained."

Jack took a deep breath, bent down, and grabbed the weight.

"All you have to do is say when it hurts, Jack. If it hurts, you can stop."

Jack nodded. He got a good grip. He closed his eyes, steeled his legs, pushed up, lifted . . .

He felt the resistance of the weight, was stunned at how heavy it was; for a moment he was out of control, thought he might topple over. Then he was standing. His arms up by his waist. His hands wrapped around the metal bar.

He opened his eyes, looked at Kid, who had a loopy grin on his face. Jack was fairly sure he had the same grin.

"Fear is your lover," Jack said in mock disgust. "Stick your tongue down her throat . . . where the hell did you come up with that one?"

"Hey, it worked, didn't it?"

"Yeah, it worked." Jack could hear the amazement in his own voice. He could feel the overwhelming relief and the release of the fear that had gripped him for the past thirteen months. "You took away my pain."

"No, Jack. *You* took away your pain."

Jack did his five reps. No pain. None. None whatsoever. It was exhilarating. As if he were drunk, drunk for the very first time. More than that, really. He felt separate from the world, for just these few moments, hovering above, free of all restraints. When he reached his limit he glanced at Kid, who knew him well, read his mind, shook his head and said, "No. Just five. Let's not push it."

Jack crouched, eased the bar down to the terrace floor. Then stood up again. He waited, still expecting it to come, but it didn't. No pain.

He turned to Kid, still not fully believing, still not accepting that it was over.

"What do you say, Jack? You want to celebrate tonight? I'll take *you* out. I'll know what I need to know by then, all the stuff I've been hinting at, and I'll tell you everything."

"Knicks play-off tonight," Jack said, his entire face bright and alive and unable to stop smiling. "Come with me. I was supposed to take Dom, but he'll understand. He just goes for the beer anyway. Seventh game against Indiana. I'll meet you at the Garden at seven. Game's at seven-thirty."

"I've got a six o'clock client."

"You can still get there by tip-off. I'll give you the ticket now." He waited. "We can celebrate afterward," he said. "You can tell me all about the new Destination. And the mysterious secrets you're going to learn tonight. And we can talk about the future."

"Okay, I'll be there," Kid told him. "I'll be there by tip-off."

"Good," Jack said. "I'm glad." He stepped forward and they shook hands. Their grips held for a long time, firmly, warmly.

"And now give me five more reps," Kid said, pointing to the barbell. And as Jack scowled, he added: "Sorry, partner, but you've got two more sets to go."

H e was flying.

At first, he thought it was beautiful.

He could feel the onrush of air sweeping over his body, whipping at his outstretched hands and bare feet. He could see over the rooftops, out into blue sky, all the way to the river, and down onto roof gardens with their splashes of early summer colors, yellow and purple and pink. And there were quick glimpses into windows as they flashed by: TV sets blinking, food being cooked, life, thought to be hidden, suddenly revealed.

Best of all, it was exquisitely quiet. Eerily, wonderfully silent.

He didn't understand what was happening. Didn't know how he could have such power. All he knew was that it was magical. Everything was moving so slowly. A soft haze enveloped the entire world. It all seemed so unreal.

And then it wasn't beautiful.

And it wasn't unreal.

And he wasn't flying. He was falling.

He remembered suddenly. Just a flash of remembering. Someone in his apartment. Leading him outside. He remembered words. Just a few words . . .

I love you . . .

Things were moving faster now. There were no more glorious rooftops, only the drab sides of buildings with their pockmarked bricks and scarred concrete blocks. The wind cut into his eyes, blinding him so he could no longer see into people's secret worlds. His hands and feet were not outstretched, they were clawing, reaching upward, trying desperately and illogically to reverse what couldn't be reversed.

More words came into his head. Standing on the balcony. Looking out . . .

Why don't you love me?

Everything was even faster. And faster still. Out of control. Spinning. Faster and faster and faster.

Whose voice was it?

I love you . . .

Why don't you love me?

Sounds blared, overwhelming him: horns honking, tires screeching, dogs barking. People yelling. Someone screaming. A painful, terrible scream that filled the air, swept over the city. A siren of death.

It was *his* scream. Louder and more terrible as the pavement below swept up to greet him, as a passing couple scrambled to get out of the way, as a car swerved, knocking over metal garbage cans. As his flight ended and his teeth were jarred from his body and his nose flattened, then splattered on the cement. As his skull splintered and bones in his arms and legs and hip and back cracked and shattered.

The screaming stopped.

For a moment, there was quiet.

And then a new summer color was added, a bright and savage red, which spread over the dirty gray New York City sidewalk beneath him, then flowed into the gutter and streamed quickly onto the newly poured patches of ragged black tar on the street.

Latrell Sprewell scored his twelfth point of the fourth quarter, a beautiful spin move under the basket, followed by a soft little jumper from maybe five feet away, over the outstretched fingertips of Jalen Rose. The crowd went wild and Sprewell raised a fist, pumped it in excitement, and the Knicks took their biggest lead of the night, eight points.

Normally, there was no place Jack Keller would rather be than at Madison Square Garden during a Knicks play-off game. Especially in his second-row seats, in the corner, right under the home-team basket. He loved the crowd's electricity and the scoreboard's computerized graphics, the Knicks City Dancers, and most of all the game itself. Tonight, especially, Jack should have been in heaven. His beloved team was hounding and containing Reggie Miller, Sprewell was slashing to the basket as only he could *and* his outside shot was on, and while the game had been close the whole time, the Knicks led from the very beginning. They had that look to them: the look of winners. But when the final buzzer sounded and the game was over, 103–98 Knicks—now they were on their way to L.A. to meet the Lakers in the finals— Jack was not a part of the ecstasy and hysteria around him. He barely noticed Allan Houston running around the court, the ball held high over his head. He never saw Spree slapping five with the courtsiders and he barely heard his longtime cronies and fellow lunatic fans—season ticket holders, ushers, vendors—congratulating him or felt them pummeling him on the back. All around him, people were hugging and screaming but Jack was still staring at the empty seat beside him, the seat that had never been filled during the course of the game. So as the crowd stood and yelled for the players to come back and share the celebration, Jack rushed out of the arena, raced onto Eighth Avenue, yanked his cell phone out of his pocket, and, huddling against the deafening noise that was even spilling out into the street, dialed.

He was pissed.

Jack did not like irresponsibility. He did not like wasting a Knicks ticket. And he especially did not like being stood up.

He'd called twice during the game. Once after the first quarter, once at the half. Both times he'd heard the same recording; neither time did he leave a message. Now, his third call of the night, the phone picked up and the machine offered the same apology: "Hey, it's Kid. Sorry I'm not available right now but I'll be checking in, so if you leave your name and number I'll call you back as soon as I can. Bye-bye."

This time, Jack spoke: "It's Jack, Kid, and you are in deep shit. You'd better have a damn good excuse for not showing up. *Damn* good. I'll be home in a little while. Call me whenever you get in." He hesitated and then, out of spite, added, "Great celebration. Thanks." He pressed the "Okay" button, disconnecting the call. Then he shook his head, muttered a fierce "Shit" to himself, and didn't even hear the fan to his right taunt, "Hey, what's the matter? Indiana fan?"

Jack shoved his phone back into his front pants pocket and started walking briskly uptown. He walked about twenty blocks before his legs started feeling tired. By then he was far enough away from the Garden to hail a cab. Ten minutes later he was saying a curt, distracted hello to Ramon, the doorman, another Knicks fan. By then, Jack was too busy being angry and wondering what the hell could possibly have happened to notice that there was someone watching him.

The someone was across the street, standing in the shadow of the small birch tree on the corner. It was someone who had been waiting for him to come home. And was prepared to wait as long as necessary.

Someone who had been waiting a long, long time for what was about to happen.

TWENTY-NINE

Patience McCoy had had a lot of bad nights over the past twelve years.

There was the night that Carmen Maria Mendez, a perfectly harmless transvestite whose real name was Alonso Jorge Mendez, had managed to get her/his testicles sliced off and stuffed into her/his mouth. McCoy had responded to the call with her partner, a rookie named Johnny Johnson, a big tough white boy, and when they arrived under the highway at the scene of the crime, Johnny took one look at his first murder victim and puked all over the body.

That was bad.

It wasn't a great night either when she'd responded to a phone call from an executive at a small brokerage company down on Wall Street, Pettit and Bandier, who said that a dissatisfied client was in the office waving a gun, threatening to kill everyone who'd been involved in his latest trade, which had lost him $265,000. By the time McCoy got there, the client had become even more dissatisfied. He'd shot four brokers, killing three and wounding one seriously in the back of the right shoulder, before turning the gun on himself and blowing his brains out.

Oh, yeah. She couldn't forget the time they were shooting a TV series, a cop show, down on Hudson in front of the

Sporting Club. One of the lead actors was fooling around with a prop gun that an extra had given him. He'd put it in his mouth, laughing the whole time, and pulled the trigger. He wasn't laughing by the time McCoy got there. He was dead as could be, the blank cartridge having been strong enough to go in right where he'd fired it—the back of his throat—and come out on the other side of his head.

Well, this was right up there.

For one thing, she'd promised her husband a romantic dinner tonight, just the two of them. Elmore was in charge of grilling the steaks, she was in charge of the salad and dessert. She'd already made up her mind that dessert was going to be an apple pie—she made a major apple pie, a lot of cinnamon in the crust, and some crushed coffee beans; they really added flavor and no one ever recognized what they were—along with homemade chocolate ice cream. She'd just bought one of those fancy Italian ice cream makers; she decided she wanted it for the summer. It cost a fortune but what the hell, they didn't have a lot of expenses, they both made decent money, and they both really liked their ice cream. Well, no ice cream tonight. No pie or steak, for that matter, either. Elmore would not be happy, no, sir.

So there was that.

And, more to the point, there was the fact that at her feet was one big bloody fucking mess.

Sergeant Patience McCoy of the NYPD, Eighth Precinct, Tribeca, was standing on Greenwich Street, about fifteen feet south of Duane. She was in front of one of the few tall buildings in this part of town. An apartment building that had been converted about five years earlier. There were no doormen, but there was a live-in super. He hadn't seen a thing, naturally, just heard a noise. And then some more noises—people yelling, horns honking, things like that— so he'd come out to see what had happened. He told her the name of the person lying on the sidewalk, told her that he'd moved in pretty recently, a few months ago, maybe. Nice guy. Friendly. Young guy.

Young guy, McCoy thought. He wasn't a young guy anymore. He was as old as you could get.

She was staring up at the roof of the building. It wasn't for any particular reason, it was just a lot easier than looking down at the crushed and shattered body a foot away from her.

"I'm gonna go up to his apartment," she told her partner, another goddamn rookie. She always got stuck with the white rookies.

"What do you want me to do?" he asked.

"Wait for the ambulance. Should be here any minute." She couldn't help but notice that he looked a little green. "And try not to puke, will you."

The super took her up in the elevator to the penthouse apartment. She couldn't help herself, she whistled when she stepped inside. She was not a whistler, normally; usually she thought people whistled strictly for effect, but this was impressive. Quite a view, too. She stepped out onto the small balcony; room for maybe a tiny table and two midget chairs. The sliding door that led to it had been closed, she noticed. Well, that made sense. This boy hadn't planned on coming back in.

There was no sign of any disturbance. The apartment was neat and in order. A half-empty bottle of beer, Pete's Wicked Ale, on the kitchen counter. An empty Diet Coke can on the coffee table. She poked her head into the other rooms. The bed was unmade, sheets were rumpled. Other than that, neat as a pin.

On the round dining table was a cell phone. It was already on, so she pressed "Menu" and clicked the arrow button forward until the word "Messages," followed by a question mark, showed up in the display window. She pressed "Okay" and then saw a new line appear. It said: *One message. Jack Keller.* And it gave a phone number. After that, it said, *Play?*

Sergeant McCoy clicked the "okay" button one more time and held the phone up to her ear. She heard: "It's Jack, Kid, and you are in deep shit. You'd better have a damn good excuse for not showing up. *Damn* good. . . . Great celebration. Thanks."

Another line popped up on the screen. It said: *Save message?* Sergeant McCoy pressed "okay" again. She put the phone back on the table, then pulled out her own cell phone and dialed. When the person on the other end answered, Sergeant McCoy identified herself, gave her badge number, and said, "Yeah, you can help me. I need an address. Right away."

Exactly thirty-seven minutes later, McCoy was in another part of town completely, East Seventy-seventh Street between Madison and Fifth. She was in another penthouse apartment, sitting in a leather swivel chair in an impeccably decorated living room, staring at an original Edward Hopper that adorned the wall.

She was in the midst of having to perform her least favorite part of her job.

She was telling Jack Keller that his young friend George "Kid" Demeter had a very good reason for missing the basketball game that night. He was dead. He'd jumped off the roof of his eighteen-story apartment building.

A suicide.

t was 3 A.M. and the city was as dark as it can get. The moon was hidden behind mist and thick, swirling clouds and there was not a star to be seen in the sky. On the streets there were few cars; almost no illumination came from piercing headlights. Inside the buildings, inhabitants slept. Windows were covered with shades. Even the usual flickering light that came from televisions left on all night seemed nonexistent. The city was black. And quiet.

Jack slid open the glass door that led to his terrace. Naked save for a light blue-and-white cotton robe, a long-ago gift from Caroline, he hesitated before stepping outside. He knew that what he was about to do was crazy but he was compelled nonetheless to do it. The magnet was there and it was drawing him outside.

Sleep was impossible, and he felt he had to try to understand, to see for himself.

One foot inched out onto the terrace and, although this was usually no problem for him, this night—or morning—his stomach immediately drew itself into a tight knot and his throat went dry. Another step and then another and then he was maybe six feet from the end of the terrace. His legs were rapidly losing strength; they felt as if they would barely keep him erect. But two more steps and he was closer yet. He reached out for the wall, tried to force himself to touch it, and he thought, *yes, I can do this, I can do this*, but then he started to shake and he could feel the magnet draw him closer and closer. He could see the fall. He could see them all falling. His mother, her mouth twisted, her eyes pleading, disappearing. Caroline, limp and lifeless, dropping. Kid . . .

What did he see when he saw Kid fall? Anger. Desperation. Clawing and fighting and resistance against something that could not be resisted.

The terror swept over Jack and took his body, his mind, his soul, and as his fingers strained to touch the brick he stumbled. His body half turned and he could feel himself shivering uncontrollably. Disoriented now, he didn't know how close he was to the wall, then he felt his shoulder scrape against it and he screamed. The scream was strangled in his throat, it didn't last long, but now Jack felt himself going. His hand was on the top of the wall and he saw exactly what was going to happen. His other hand would touch there and he'd force himself closer, and then his leg would magically rise up, and then his other leg, and then he'd be gone. He'd be flying above the city. All-seeing and -powerful. But then he'd be falling, too. Just like all the others. It would come with no warning; his flight would just stop and there he'd be, out there—out *there*—with nothing to grab on to, nothing to save him. He'd be dropping. Faster. Faster still. And even faster. And there would be the city, rushing up to envelop him, swooping over him and through him. The blackness would take him and make him its own.

The pain. The noise. The roar and then the stillness.

And then it would be over. . . .

When Jack's eyes opened, he was on the floor of his terrace. His right hand was stretched above his head, his left was resting tight against his body. He didn't know how long he'd been unconscious, didn't know it had been less than a minute. He got his bearings, saw the table and his usual chair, saw the barbell and the stack of weights. He shifted his head to look back through the glass door into his living room. All was still dark and silent.

Jack never turned back to look at the wall. He crawled the several feet he needed until his hand could touch the solid glass of the sliding door. When his palm was pressed against it, could feel its coolness soak into his hot flesh, his dizziness began to subside. His stomach slowly settled and his robe, damp from his sweat, began to drop away from his body and loosen. He took a deep breath and stood, slowly, in stages, as if unfurling himself from inside a trunk. Or a coffin.

Jack put one foot inside his apartment. For a moment he straddled the doorway, one foot in, one foot out. Then his back foot slid forward and he was in his living room. Without turning around, he fumbled for the handle of the door, found it, and slid the glass shut.

He wiped the moisture from his forehead, ran his hand through his sopping-wet hair, went into his bedroom and sat on the bed. When he lay down, he pulled the light, summer quilt up to his shoulders and then over his chin. Soon, almost all that was visible were his eyes. They stayed open for several more hours, staring straight ahead, and then, close to seven in the morning, they finally closed and Jack slept a fitful but dreamless sleep.

BOOK FOUR

THE FINAL FALL

TWO DAYS LATER

E ven for a funeral, Kid's burial was an extraordinarily dreary and sobering event.

Dom accompanied Jack and the first thing he said when Jack's car came by to pick him up was "Christ, Jackie, we're goin' to too many fuckin' funerals." When Jack nodded grimly, Dom then added, "Do you remember the last time we been to this goddamn place?" There was no need for Jack to respond to the question. They both knew exactly when they'd last been there. It was eleven years earlier. The day they'd gone to Sal Demeter's funeral. Sal was not quite forty-five when he died. His son had not lived to see his twenty-sixth birthday.

The car dropped them off at the loading station for the Staten Island Ferry. Both men bought tickets and ambled onto the boat. Jack and Dom were the only ones in suits and ties. Most of the crowd wore shorts or jeans and T-shirts. Most were tourists or adventurous Manhattanites, happy to be escaping the island for a few hours, anxious to see new sights. Some of the men on the boat, Jack was sure, were policemen or firemen sitting through part of their normal commute. A lot of city workers lived on Staten Island. It had a comfortable blue-collar neighborhood: houses had yards, which was great for raising lots of kids and having pets. And because of those workers, living on Staten Island had its practical advantages. Snow was always shoveled off the streets first. Blackouts were attended to immediately. Garbage was always picked up on time.

During the short ride across the water, Dom stayed down below but Jack was feeling antsy and went up on top. He'd never been a smoker but now was one of the few times in his life he wished he had a cigarette. He just wanted something in his hand, something to keep himself busy. Instead of tobacco, he went to a vending machine and bought a Baby Ruth bar. It was enough of an activity that it relaxed him. Chewing on the too-sweet candy, he leaned against the railing, looking down at the churning waves. Even though the sun was shining and the air was warm, the water looked cold and forbidding.

As the salt spray splattered on deck, daubing his face and hair, Jack's thoughts drifted back to his conversation with Sergeant McCoy. Even now, three days later, he was still trying to piece the whole thing together, still trying to have it make sense and absorb the impact.

"No, it's not possible" is how he'd responded to McCoy's pronouncement, as she stepped out of the elevator, that Kid had committed suicide.

"I'm afraid it is," the sergeant had said. She seemed genuinely sad, Jack thought, as if she weren't just delivering bad news as part of her job. It was as if she cared. As if she too felt the loss. It was her sadness that convinced him she was telling him the truth.

Jack didn't speak after that for quite a while. Her words had rocked him and he felt wobbly, so without even asking

McCoy inside, he made his way to the living room and sat down on the couch. McCoy followed but not immediately. She gave him time to compose himself.

When she stepped slowly into the living room, she eased herself down onto one of the leather club chairs. Even then she didn't speak, until finally Jack was ready, saying, "Did he leave a note . . . uh . . . Officer . . . what do I call you?"

"My first name's Patience, maybe the worst-named person on the face of the earth, because that is something I normally do not have a lot of. You can call me that if you want. Or Sergeant's just fine. Most people are more comfortable with Sergeant."

"Okay . . . Sergeant. Did he leave a note?"

"If there was one, we didn't find it," she said. "But we've got people going through the apartment now." Sergeant McCoy hesitated, leaned forward, a rather urgent expression on her face, then she must have thought better of whatever was behind her motion, because she just as suddenly tilted back into her original position.

"What?" Jack asked.

"Hmmm?"

"You looked like you wanted to ask me something, then changed your mind. Please, go ahead. Anything you feel might be relevant."

Patience McCoy let out a hoarse little burst of laughter. "It ain't exactly what you call relevant," she said. "I was going to ask if you'd mind if I made myself a cup of coffee. Not very professional, I know, but if I don't get some caffeine in me, I'll be falling asleep in this very comfortable chair."

Jack nodded, told her to stay put. He was glad to have something to do. He left her in the living room and headed into the kitchen, where he ground the beans and turned on the DeLonghi ten-cup coffeemaker. He was glad to be alone for a few minutes, doing nothing more than listening to the hum of the appliance and the steady drip from the filter to the pot. When he went back into the living room, he was carrying her coffee, black, as asked for.

Sergeant McCoy took a sip, exhaled a satisfied sigh. "This is delicious. Jamaican Blue, or something thereabouts, with a touch of cinnamon, am I right?" And when Jack nodded, she couldn't help but give a pleased little smile. The jolt from the coffee seemed to bring her back to her purpose for being there. She crossed her legs, began asking him about Kid, and she listened attentively as he told her what he knew—how they'd met years before, how Kid had reentered his life, the physical therapy they'd been doing, that Kid had been working as a personal trainer, that he'd been dating various women.

"Did you notice any signs of depression? Frustration? Any hint that he was thinking of ending his life?"

Jack shuddered at the phrase. "No. Just the opposite." He hesitated—the image of Kid's angry outburst at the restaurant popped into his head, and then Kid's face as he talked about his new Destination and his secrets. But he shook those pictures away. They were aberrations. Normal ups and downs. He didn't know if Sergeant McCoy had noticed he'd skipped a beat, but to cover it he hurried his next sentences. "He was going to graduate soon, from business school. He was really looking forward to that, getting his master's."

"Ahhhh," she said.

Her little noise annoyed him, as if she'd just now gotten a clue to something he didn't understand. "What does that mean? 'Ahhh.' "

Sensing his hostility, she said, "Sorry. The problem with being a cop is we tend to see things as statistics. You knew the person, so you're seeing something different, as you should. All I meant is that now there's some sense to this. We typically have an upsurge in suicidal behavior from students during finals. The pressure, you know. They bottle it up and then they just let go."

"I don't think that's the case here. I never saw any—"

He was interrupted by the jarring ringing of her cell phone. She gave him an apologetic look, took the phone out of the clip on her belt and spoke into it. "McCoy, go." No one seemed to be on the other end because she said, "Hello?" and then said it again, followed by a "Shit," then she whacked at the phone with her free hand. "Damn budget cuts. Next thing they'll be giving us some Dixie Cups and a string. Probably didn't pay the goddamn phone bill this month." She shook her head, held both hands up to show him the distraction had passed. "Sorry. Do you have any idea how I can reach George's next of kin?"

For a moment, Jack stared at her, thought it was all a mistake, that she was talking about someone else, then realized that she was referring to Kid by his given name. He nodded.

"His mother," he told her. "LuAnn Demeter. She lives on Staten Island."

"I better go talk to her. Not the easiest part of this job."

As she stood up, Jack said, "Is that all?"

She squinted at him, not quite understanding the question. "What else?"

"Sergeant . . . I've known Kid for a long time. I know . . . I *knew* him extremely well. I don't think there's . . . I don't think it's possible . . . I mean . . ."

"You mean there's no way he could have killed himself."

"That's right," Jack said. "The person I knew could never have done what you say he did."

"Sometimes we think we know people a lot better than we really do, Mr. Keller."

"That's very true. But that's not the case here."

"I never talked to anyone who thought that *was* the case where they were concerned."

"I *knew* Kid."

"But I thought you said you hadn't seen him for several years before he showed up in your living room. A lot of things can change a person, especially at that age, don't you think?" When Jack said nothing in response, when she saw how her words had registered, McCoy softened her tone. "I understand you were close to the boy, Mr. Keller. That you talked a lot. Sometimes people talk to us but they don't *really* talk to us. You know what I'm saying? They talk *around* whatever their reality is. Sometimes they talk just so they don't have to tell us what their reality is. They don't tell us they're hurting—not until it's too late."

Jack nodded. "Well, it's sure too late now, isn't it?"

"I'm afraid that it is."

He walked her slowly to the elevator door, pushed the call button. They stood in silence until the elevator arrived, then Jack reached for the knob and pulled the door open, but McCoy didn't step inside immediately. She had stopped to look at the framed photos that hung on the wall of the entryway. Pictures of Jack and Caroline. Of the various restaurants. The *New York Magazine* profile. Their first rave review and rating in *Zagat*.

"I'm sorry about what happened," she told him. "And I don't just mean tonight, with the boy."

"Thank you," Jack said.

"For our fifteenth anniversary, Elmore, that's my husband, he took me to Jack's. You don't remember, but you and your wife both came over to our table, found out it was our anniversary, and sent over a bottle of wine. That was a very special evening."

"I'm glad."

"Best steak I ever had, too—and you're talking to a meat eater."

"Good night, Sergeant."

"Good night, sir. You be well. And thanks for the coffee."

It was the smell of coffee now that brought him back to his present surroundings: leaning on the railing of the Staten Island Ferry. They were just about to dock. A few feet from him, a young woman, small with dark wavy hair, was doing her best to drain the coffee from her paper cup while three small children were jumping up around her, all trying to grab her arm. When the boat pulled in, Jack was one of the first off. He waited until Dom emerged, then he pulled out the sheet with his own handwritten directions on it.

Less than ten minutes later they were at the small church.

There were maybe thirty people there. Most seemed to be relatives. Jack saw Bryan, who was sitting up close to Kid's mother. He looked distraught and pale, as if Kid's death had taken away a chunk of his own life. Jack searched the sparse crowd for the several beautiful women he thought would be there but there were none. Unless Kid had greatly exaggerated their physical attributes, something Jack thought highly unlikely, not one member of his "team" had come to say goodbye. Jack found this particularly sad, the final jarring note to a life too soon ended.

The priest was clearly not privy to the details of Kid's life. His eulogy was short and lacked specifics. It could have been about almost anyone. There was no mention of the way Kid had died. Jack thought by denying the reality of his death it somehow diminished the memory of his life. But he knew that was a thought he'd keep to himself or maybe discuss with Dom on the ferry ride back.

After the simple ceremony, Jack and Dom went to the graveyard for the burial. As near as Jack could tell, everyone from the church service went. Kid's mother began to break down as she tossed the first handful of dirt onto Kid's coffin. Jack stepped forward to help her—he thought she was going to faint—but Bryan beat him there. Kid's lifelong friend gently took her elbow and held her steady. He whispered something in her ear that almost made her smile and when some color came back to her cheeks, she stood on her toes and kissed Bryan gently on his cheek. He stayed by her side until Kid was buried, then Jack watched as he walked her to the waiting car. He was surprised to see that Bryan was limping slightly. Then he realized the boy had also been limping when he'd left the restaurant and gone to search for Kid. Jack nodded to himself, watching him move. He thought that Kid would be proud of the dignified way the Wall had behaved in his stead.

Back at the house—the house that did not seem to have changed an iota since their last visit there—Dom and Jack each accepted a bourbon and were happy to sip it. They milled around the drab living room and it didn't take long for Jack to begin to feel claustrophobic. Most of the mourners stood—those who found room sat on the flower-patterned couches and slightly tattered chairs—nibbling cake and sipping coffee or liquor. Jack and Dom hugged LuAnn, who was genuinely moved that they'd come. Their presence was a reminder of her earlier tragedy, though, and Jack and Dom were both aware that they were an unsettling link for her between past and present. Still, she didn't want to let them wander away; she kept grabbing Jack's hand and pulling him closer to her. At some point, Jack found himself standing with Dom and Bryan above LuAnn, who was resting in the one easy chair. She had put a video-tape on and they were watching it on the living room TV. The tape was of a vacation the Demeter family had taken, parents and son, at the Jersey shore when Kid was nine years old. Seeing the young boy and his father made Jack smile.

"Our first trip to Asbury Park," LuAnn said, narrating the tape. "Kid loved the beach." Someone tried to hand her a cup of coffee but she shook her head and asked for a shot of bourbon instead. When she was handed the glass, she downed her shot in one gulp. Then she nodded back toward the television. "A real little butterball, wasn't he? That's what I used to call him. Mr. Butterball. Until he and Bryan started lifting together. You boys were always down there lifting those weights, weren't you, Bryan?"

"We sure were, Mrs. Demeter. I bet I spent more time in your basement than I did at my own house."

"You were never no trouble, that's for sure. Kid, he was a lot more trouble than you ever were. You be sure to still come around, won't you? I mean, even if Kid's . . . even without him, you'll still come by, I hope."

"I'll still come by, Mrs. Demeter. You don't have to worry about that. I mean, hey, who's gonna make me pot roast as good as yours?"

LuAnn Demeter wasn't really listening to Bryan's answer, though. She was staring at the television, watching the ghosts of her family walking along the shore. "He swore he'd outlive Sal," she said quietly. "That's how he got started with the weights. And the running and all that other stuff. He promised me he'd outlive his father. He *promised* me."

"LuAnn," Jack said, taking her hand. But he realized he didn't really have anything to say to her. There was nothing *to* say. So he just held her hand and hoped that his touch was of some comfort.

"Awww, Jesus," she said, finally pulling her hand away. "Mr. Butterball . . ."

Jack and Dom stayed until only a few people were left. LuAnn's sister was there and she was clearly in charge. When she began tidying up, they felt they could now think about returning to Manhattan. Bryan saw that they were getting ready to leave and he asked if they wanted to see the basement.

"There's a lot of Kid down there," he told them, so they nodded and let him lead them down a narrow stairway. When Bryan flicked on the light, they found themselves next to the boiler, in a half-finished cement room with fake-wood paneling that ran two thirds of the way up to the ceiling and a green shag carpet on the floor. A primitive gym was still set up: scuffed weights, barbells, a bench, and a mat. There were two full-length mirrors, no frames around them, hung up on the wall, and various trophies—Kid's first-, second-, and third-place finishes at various weight-lifting tournaments. On the walls were old photos, some in cheap black frames, some just tacked or taped up. There were a lot of pictures of Arnold Schwarzenegger from his *Pumping Iron* days, and covers of out-of-date bodybuilding magazines. There was a large poster of Bo Derek from her *10* days and one of Kathy Ireland in a skimpy bikini, her legs strewn with sand. It looked like a shot from a ten-year-old *Sports Illustrated* swimsuit issue. There were also quite a few photos of Kid and Bryan together. Jack walked around the room, examining each picture, watching Kid's progress from a chubby teenager to a slightly older version with a few burgeoning muscles to posing with Bryan in their high school football uniforms. Their jerseys were cut off below their protective pads, revealing washboard stomachs. By this period in time, there was no trace of softness in either boy. Bryan was huge in the photo—he dwarfed Kid—but he, too, appeared to be all muscle. There was one fairly recent photo of Kid. Jack couldn't tell exactly when it was taken, maybe within the past year. Kid was wearing sweatpants and a T-shirt and he was smiling at the camera. The perfect physical specimen. The all-American boy . . .

"He always wanted you to see this," Bryan said. "The Playhouse, that's what he used to call it."

Jack turned away from the photos, turned to face Kid's sidekick. "About the gym, Bryan. My offer's still on the table. If you want to go ahead and do it, I'll back you with half the money."

Bryan stared at Jack, obviously surprised by his words, and quite moved. But he shook his head, a very slight gesture, from side to side, and looked sheepish. "Naahhh," he said. "I don't have the smarts. You'd be throwin' your money away. Kid, he was the one with the knack. People wanted to be around him. He coulda made it work. But me . . . I'm just a brick wall with a limp."

Dom's roar surprised them both. "Hey, don't crap on yourself," he growled. "I hate that feelin' sorry for yourself shit."

Bryan was instantly mortified that he'd said the wrong thing around Kid's great friends. He began stammering and apologizing, his face turned red with shame, and Dom immediately backed off.

"All I meant," Dom said, his voice still gruff but a lot softer, "is that you were a player. I remember. I know how fuckin' good you were. Sorry, I told myself I'd watch my mouth today."

"No, no," Bryan stammered. "That's okay. I just, you know, I didn't mean to say anything that—"

Jack mercifully cut him off. He spoke quietly and soothingly. He found Bryan's embarrassment painful. The kid was too nice for his own good and he wanted to put him out of his misery as quickly as possible. "Dom's right, Bryan. I mean, about you being a hell of a player. A sensational athlete. What happened? How come you didn't go on with it?"

Bryan calmed down a bit. The flush in his face was diminishing. "All sorts of things happened," he said. "You know, I went to St. John's with Kid. Got a football scholarship. I was big then, I mean much bigger physically, maybe you remember, or you can tell from some of the photos."

"I remember."

"Christ, yes," Dom added. "You were huge."

"Well, some of that was natural. You know, the weights and stuff, my diet. But when I was a sophomore in high school, Coach thought I had real potential, thought I could get a scholarship as an offensive lineman. But he said I was too little for a big-time college program. So he steered me toward the juice."

"You mean steroids," Jack said.

"Yeah. I knew they weren't good for me, and Kid was really against me takin' 'em; he kept tellin' me I was nuts to do it. I mean, he never put a bad thing in his body in his whole life, but, hey, what chance did I have to go to college, you know? I mean, I wasn't gonna get any academic scholarship. So, anyway, we both make the team"—Bryan suddenly stopped and again his face began to turn red. "Am I talkin' too much? About me, I mean?"

"No," Jack said. "Not at all."

"We want to hear it," Dom added. "Go ahead."

Bryan hesitated but Jack nodded, a prod, really, so he went on. "Well, Kid and me, it was funny, because in high school he was the one, you know, he was the star. But at St. J's, I don't think he had the desire. I mean, he was still a helluva quarterback but he wasn't gonna go pro or nothing. And somethin' kind of happened to him, I don't know what. He kinda lost interest, you know?"

"It was after that thing happened with that kid on the team, the halfback," Jack said.

"That was horrible," Bryan said, wincing at the memory.

"I remember how it affected Kid. He was devastated."

"My memory's a little hazy," Dom said. "The guy got in an accident or somethin'?"

"He got hurt in practice," Bryan said quietly. "Harvey Wiggins. We were scrimmaging and he got hit. Hard. You could hear it, it was like breakin' a piece of chalk. Everybody could hear it. But Kid was right next to him when it happened. He said he could hear it most of all."

"Harvey broke his neck, didn't he?"

"Yes, sir. Paralyzed."

"Jesus," Dom said. "I forgot about that."

"I guess that's what did it, 'cause after that the stuff we

were doin' didn't seem so important to Kid. He never played the same, you know? Still, on a team the quarterback's the one. Gotta protect him at all costs. So I used to block like crazy for him, maybe so nothin' like what happened to Harvey could happen to him. I wouldn't let *nobody* touch Kid. My job was to keep him safe, so that's what I did. After my freshman year, there was some talk I could be a third-, maybe even second-team All-American. Not bad for Division 1-AA. But in the last game of the season, I blew out my knee. ACL, really bad. And I don't think the surgeon did a great job. It just never rehabbed right. So, junior year, I didn't have a thing. I mean, I tried and all, but I couldn't move worth shit—sorry—I couldn't hardly move at all. So I got cut."

"What happened then?"

Bryan looked confused. "What do you mean?"

"I mean," Jack said, "with school."

"Oh, hell, without football, what was I gonna do at school? I mean, maybe you noticed, but I ain't the brainiest guy in the world. And Kid left, you know, kinda ran away, really, didn't he, and I didn't really know no one at St. J's anyway. So I dropped out, worked at a few gyms, trained people, that kind of stuff. That's what I been doing. Until Kid came back and we started talking up our whole gym thing again. And then . . . well . . . and then *this*." He waved his hand toward the room above them. "This" meant the funeral. Kid's suicide.

"Why did Kid leave St. John's?" Jack asked. "After that junior year?"

Bryan looked flustered. Jack thought he was not used to being asked questions. He seemed unsure of his ability to take the thoughts in his head and translate them for other people.

"I don't really know," Bryan said, but he looked uncomfortable and Jack thought he knew more than he was telling.

"Did it have anything to do with what happened to Harvey?"

Bryan looked even more uncomfortable. Jack suspected he was not used to analyzing other people's actions. "He was a restless guy," Bryan said finally. "The thing about Kid was, he was never satisfied with what he had. I mean, he had a cushy life at school. The star of the team, all the girls he wanted. But that wasn't enough. Hey, for me that woulda been *more* than enough. For almost anybody. But not him. I don't think he knew what he wanted . . . he just wanted more. So he left to go find it."

"I wonder if that accident had anything to do with Kid becoming a physical therapist. If he felt responsible in some way."

"I just don't know," Bryan said.

"Why do you think he killed himself?" Jack said very softly.

"I don't know," Bryan said miserably. "And I've thought about it a lot. A *lot*. Sometimes I feel like I haven't thought about nothin' else since it happened. But I don't have a single idea in my head. All I know is he wasn't the only one who died. I swear to God, sometimes I think he took me with him."

THIRTY-TWO

THE MORTICIAN

She'd seen it in the paper. The *Daily News*. Page fourteen. A small story in the lower right-hand corner.

She was not surprised, of course. Although she mourned and she grieved. Not as much as she needed to, though. She hadn't had the time to mourn properly. For one thing, Joe had been with her the whole time, almost since the moment she'd gotten home that evening. It wouldn't do to let on too much to Joe. For another, she had things to do. Calls to make. Loose ends to take care of and details that had to be kept quiet. Still, she could not pretend to be herself, and the next morning, she saw Joe watching her. She knew that scrutinizing gaze and she couldn't help but think: He knows. And then she almost laughed out loud because her next thought was: Of course he knows. Who was she kidding? He'd always known. The only question was how *much* he knew.

She would miss Kid. She would miss her wonderful and precious possession.

But already she was realizing she wouldn't miss him as much as she thought she would.

Because he never should have tried to leave her.

He should never have tried to think about or talk about or finally even *do* the unimaginable.

So, yes, she would miss him. But she was already wondering how long it would take her to find a replacement.

SAMSONITE

It's all they were fucking talking about. At the club. All night long. The bartender, the bouncer, the waitresses. Even some of the customers.

Mr. Wonderful was dead.

They all said he killed himself. But she knew differently, didn't she? She sure as hell knew fucking differently.

At least she thought she did.

No, no, she *definitely* did. There was no fucking question about it. It took her a while to remember but it always took her a while to remember stuff. So she wasn't concerned. She knew something was bothering her and then she remembered what it was. Then, when she did, something *else* started bothering her.

Because once she remembered, she remembered something else. Congratu-fucking-lations, she thought to herself. Two biggies in one day. And of all the fucking things she'd have to remember, it *would* be these two, wouldn't it? There was an old Russian proverb: The more you forget the longer you live. But, no, not her. She was American now, so she remembered.

The first thing she remembered was weird enough. But the second thing was even weirder.

The second thing was: Jesus fucking Christ. I think *I* fucking killed him.

THE ENTERTAINER

One of the dancers from the club had called to tell her. *Ex*-dancer, whose stage name was Torre but whose real name was Sue Ellen. Torre didn't work at the club anymore. She'd gotten a little too fat and had been fired. So she worked at a place out in Queens now that was really the pits. Real lowlifes and bad tippers. But she knew Kid, too, and she'd heard about it so she'd called.

That night at the club, she wondered if anyone would say anything to her but nobody did. She kind of felt like talking but she didn't really know who to talk to. At some point, while she was sitting with a client, she'd said, "Someone I know just died. Fell off a roof," and the guy had said, "Yeah? Tell me about it," but she knew he didn't really want to hear about it, he just thought that maybe she was vulnerable and could use it, so she shook her head and didn't say another word.

Around one or so, Kid's friend came in. The one she always saw around and even talked to sometimes and whose name she could never remember. Kid's shadow. She watched him while he stood at the bar and had a beer and she didn't think she'd ever seen anyone quite as sad. Somebody must have called him, too. He was like some poor, friendly puppy who'd gotten his leg run over by a car and all he could do was cry and wait for someone to come help him.

She thought that maybe she should be the one to help him, then thought, *What am I doing?* It was the last thing she needed. Really and truly the last thing.

She watched him over at the bar. She wondered if he knew about her and Kid. He'd seen them together but she never had a clue what Kid used to talk about. Maybe he didn't know. Maybe it was okay to talk to him. She knew that he was nice but she knew if she talked to him one thing would lead to another. He'd want to come over and he'd want to touch her and she'd probably let him. But then he'd start to think that maybe this was going to be a regular thing. And it couldn't even be a *sometime* thing. Okay, so he was nice and certainly good-looking and his body looked like it was amazing. But he didn't have any money, that was clear. Plus, he did have that look to him, that puppy look, and the last thing she wanted around her all the time was a puppy—a *poor* puppy—nipping at her heels and wanting her to take care of him.

He looked up and saw her looking at him and he smiled at her, a really sad smile, but she turned away as if she didn't recognize him.

She did not want a puppy under her feet. Especially a puppy who knew Kid.

She realized she'd hardly thought about Kid at all. It was strange. She wondered what her psychology professor would say about that. She thought maybe she would ask him, but then she realized she did not want to talk about Kid with her psych prof. That would be really and truly dumb. Although the more she thought about it, the more she liked the idea.

She could see herself telling him how she had known Kid and now he was dead and how he had died and that she wasn't thinking about him at all and wasn't that strange?

She didn't really believe in heaven, but she thought there was just a chance that Kid could somehow be up above, looking down and watching her talk about him to the middle-aged professor who she knew drooled over her and probably stayed awake at night thinking about what she looked like naked. Kid would look down and see that and hear about the way he'd died and how she didn't care.

She smiled at the image.

Really and truly smiled.

It would kill him all over again, she thought. *Es verdad.* It really and truly would.

THE MURDERESS

She didn't think that anyone had seen her.

Well, sure, people had seen her, it's not like she was invisible. But no one had really *seen* her. Noticed her. Paid attention to her, is what she really meant.

That was good. She did not need to be noticed. Not with all that was happening. And certainly not with all that had happened.

She knew she shouldn't have gone to meet him. Goddamn Kid, with his tousled hair and that crooked little grin. Why couldn't she have stayed away? She'd been doing so well. She'd been on her way. And she'd been so . . . so damn sophisticated. Damn him for coming to see her, for begging her to see him, for telling her all the things he told her.

Just because he knew about her, knew about her past, that didn't give him the right to do what he did. Nothing gave him that right.

She felt herself getting angry again.

Then she stopped. Maybe there was no need to get angry. Maybe there was no need to be afraid, either. Kid was dead now.

So maybe it was all over.

Maybe this was the end of it.

She hoped so.

And she thought so.

But then why was she still angry? And why was she still so afraid?

THE MISTAKE

How could he be dead? It was impossible. *Impossible!*

They were supposed to spend the rest of their lives together.

They were supposed to love each other and help each other and be together forever.

Kid was too good to live, that's what it was. Too good and too handsome and too pure. He wasn't perfect—oh, no, he made some mistakes. That night at the party, Kid had said *that* was a mistake. But it wasn't. No, no, no. It was anything but a mistake. It was perfect. Perfect and wonderful and . . . and . . .

Over.

It would never happen again. No more perfect moments. No more love.

That was always the way, wasn't it? People were jealous, weren't they? People were lonely and sad and wounded. People always wanted to destroy love, didn't they?

Yes, they did.

But this time they'd be sorry.

This time they'd be *really* sorry.

Just like Kid. Poor, poor Kid. He was dead. No more love for Kid, either. No more perfection.

No more mistakes.

THE DESTINATION

One was as good as dead to her and now the other *was* dead.

So why wasn't she more depressed?

Perhaps because there was something eminently fair about it all. Something so bloody symmetrical.

As you sow, so shall ye reap. There was something comforting in that, wasn't there? He who inflicts pain shall have pain inflicted upon him.

It was God's way, wasn't it?

Or perhaps it was the devil's.

Either way.

It worked for her.

J ack knew he should be working out, should be on the treadmill and lifting weights and stretching, but this was his sixth day without even venturing into the gym. He was beginning to feel stiff, his hip was aching just a tad, but he wasn't ready to go back to that ritual yet. It seemed disrespectful, somehow, to use the equipment without Kid. Maybe it was an excuse, he decided. Maybe he was just lazy or tired or maybe he didn't really care anymore. Either way, he didn't feel like pushing himself, so he didn't.

He hadn't left his apartment yet that day and it was nearly 3 P.M. That surprised him. He didn't know quite what had happened to the rest of the day, but he felt he should do *something*. So he rang for the elevator and went down to the lobby to get the mail. A perfectly good activity.

There was a new doorman. Jack thought his name was Micah, and Micah had clearly been told that Jack was a sports nut. So they exchanged comments on the Knicks (already down two–zip to the Lakers in the finals) and whether the Mets' six-game winning streak actually meant anything. Micah thought that it did. Jack was not so sure.

Jack grabbed his mail out of his box and started sifting through it on the way back up in the elevator. Nothing

spectacular. A brochure for a cruise ship. A couple of magazines. A few bills.

Back in his apartment, he flipped through the magazines,
noted an article he wanted to read in *The New Yorker*, didn't
find anything that interested him in *Vanity Fair*. Caroline
had been the magazine reader in the family but Jack had
renewed all her subscriptions. It was another tenuous way to
keep her presence in the apartment. He knew it didn't make
much sense but he couldn't bring himself to cancel them.

There was not much personal in the day's mail and nothing really interesting. Until Jack got to a small, square
envelope. It was addressed to him and it had the right
address but no zip code. The handwritten return address
said that the letter had come from Kid Demeter. It gave his
address, 487 Duane Street, and his zip code. Jack checked
the date on the front of the envelope. The small, faint red
circle said that it had been mailed the day that Kid had killed
himself. Six days earlier. It had obviously spent a few extra
days at the post office due to the incomplete mailing
address.

Jack used his finger to open the top of the envelope.
Inside was an invitation. Not a fancy one—it came from a
preprinted packet that said things like "You Are Invited To"
and then had a blank to be filled in by the sender. This invitation said that Jack was invited to Kid Demeter's
graduation ceremony from Hunter College. He was receiving his MBA. The ceremony was in two weeks. At the
bottom of the invitation, Kid had scrawled: "I know it's
inconceivable to you that I actually made it, so you better

come see for yourself." Then he signed his name and after that added a P.S. All it said was "Thanks," and the word was underlined three times, with three exclamation marks after it.

Jack put the invitation down on the coffee table, went into the kitchen, grabbed a medium-sized plastic bottle of Poland Spring water, and gulped down about a third of the bottle. Then he went back to the living room, picked the invitation back up. He stared at it for a good five minutes and finally he understood what it was that was churning inside him. He actually spoke aloud. He said, "Goddamn!" and swung his fist in the air, an involuntary action. He stuffed the invitation back into the envelope and, clutching it in his hand, stepped into the elevator, took it all the way down to the garage, and started up his black BMW.

On the way downtown, he used his cell phone to call the Eighth Precinct in Tribeca to get their exact address.

SERGEANT PATIENCE MCCOY didn't seem unhappy to see him. But, then again, she did not seem happy, either. She did offer him a cup of coffee, which he accepted.

"It's no Jamaican Blue," she alerted him, "but it'll give you a buzz."

"It's fine," Jack told her after he took his first sip and she seemed genuinely glad to hear that.

"Now, what can I do for you, Mr. Keller? Today's kind of a busy day."

"I understand, Sergeant. I . . . um . . . I feel a little awkward doing this but I didn't know how else to handle it."

"No need to feel awkward, believe me. Nothing you've got for me is gonna be anywhere near as weird as the usual shit that comes across my desk. You can trust me on that one."

Jack nodded, reached into his pants pocket, and pulled out the envelope that had come from Kid. He removed the invitation and dropped it on McCoy's desk.

"Okay," she said after examining it. "What's the story?"

"It's an invitation to Kid Demeter's graduation ceremony."

"I can see that."

"Don't you get it?"

"Mr. Keller, I don't even get what I'm supposed to get."

Jack tried to keep his voice down. He could feel the excitement building inside him. "He mailed an invitation to his graduation the same day he died."

"Ahhhh," McCoy said. "Now I get it. You think this is—"

"I don't think. It meant he was planning for two weeks ahead. No sane person does that, then jumps off a building."

"I agree with you. No sane person does do that. Would you like to know what *I* think it means?"

"Yes, I would," Jack said.

"It can mean several things. One possibility is that we are not talking about a sane person here."

Jack kept himself under control. "Sergeant, Kid didn't kill himself. I think this is proof."

McCoy nodded, chewed on her lip for a few seconds. Then she picked up the phone on her desk and stabbed her finger quickly at three numbers on the base, an inside extension. When someone answered on the other end, she said, "Do me a favor, honey, and bring me over the file on the George Demeter suicide. That's right . . . that's the one."

Jack flinched at the word "suicide" but said nothing. In a few moments, a young black woman, slight with very bad skin, walked over to McCoy's desk and dropped off a thin folder. McCoy mumbled a thanks, pulled the papers out—official-looking forms—and studied them for a few seconds.

"I'm gonna give you some other proof, Mr. Keller. Would you like to know what this report says?"

Jack nodded but she wasn't looking at him, so she had to shift her eyes up. He nodded again and said, "Yes."

"I'll start with the ME's findings. That's medical examiner, in case you haven't been watching your *NYPD Blue*." She squinted at the report and shook her head. "Your friend didn't just jump off that terrace—he *flew*. At least he had enough LSD in his system to make him *think* he could fly."

"That has to be a mistake."

"No mistake. We also found a dozen tabs in his medicine cabinet."

Jack was incredulous. And getting angry now. "Kid was a health nut. All he ate was goddamn vegetables! He was totally antidrugs. He didn't even drink beer."

"Wrong again. We found beer in his system, too. Not a lot, but some. Which brings me to the second possibility. Maybe he wanted to jump, didn't have the nerve, had to fortify himself, so to speak. Or maybe you're right, maybe he didn't kill himself. Maybe he just ate too many pills and thought he was taking a little stroll into some low-hanging cloud.

Accidental death due to drug intake. I'm willing to put that down on the official report if that'll make everyone feel better." She held her hand up so Jack would stay quiet and she glanced back down at the report. "I'll give you all the details now, Mr. Keller, if you just stay calm for a second." Jack forced himself to settle back in his chair. "He also had sex shortly before he died," she then went on. "In his apartment. The sheets showed traces of semen and vaginal secretions. That's a bad phrase, isn't it? Vaginal secretions. Anyway . . . if you'd like to know what we think happened, it's fairly simple. He's got a woman over and whoever she was, she gives him a goodbye taste. Maybe she breaks it to him that the affair's over. Whatever, she says something to him that doesn't sit well. She splits, he drowns his sorrows, has himself a serious bummer of a trip, and over the side he goes. Accidental or on purpose, it doesn't really matter all that much now, does it?"

Jack half raised his hand, as if he were in school, waiting to see if he could ask a question. When Sergeant McCoy nodded, Jack said, "Isn't it possible somebody pushed him?"

"Who?" she said. "A robber? We do our homework, you know. There was no sign of forced entry. The man's wallet was full, the stereo, TV, all intact. Or maybe you think it was the woman? Still a no go. There was no evidence of any kind of struggle. No scratches, no skin under his nails . . . besides which, take your choice, robber or sex partner, he looked like he could take care of himself."

"But he couldn't," Jack said. His words were not forceful now. They were quiet and urgent. "I can't tell you how many times I saved his goddamn ass when he was growing up. Sergeant, I *knew* him. I knew him as if he were my own son. You don't understand."

"Evidence, Jack. *That's* what I understand."

Jack picked up the invitation again but McCoy cut him off before he could get a word out.

"No, no, no. That's not evidence. That's a piece of paper." She tapped a notebook on top of her desk, picked it up, and started flipping through it. "This is my little casebook. You know what's in here? I got me a liquor store holdup gone bad. Know what my evidence is? A dead clerk and an empty cash register. *And* I've got it on videotape . . . I got a hooker knifed to death not two blocks from here. Found in a hallway. My evidence? I saw her intestines hanging out onto the floor from the slit in her belly. How's that?" She looked up at him now, couldn't read his face. Couldn't tell if that was stoic defeat or determination she was seeing. "Look," she went on. "Life doesn't always make sense. And neither does death—at least not the deaths I see. But sometimes it *is* simple. Your friend got high, your friend let it fly. End of story. Hey, isn't that from a movie? Some guy, a bad guy, I think, always ends his sentences with 'End of story!' Who was that?"

"I don't know," Jack said. "No idea."

She furrowed her brow, motioned for Jack to be quiet, then nodded suddenly and said, "*The Longest Yard.* That's what it was. That Burt Reynolds movie. And that guy from *Green Acres*, that's who said it. He played the warden. 'End of stor-ee!' "

She looked relieved that she'd thought of it. Jack realized she was not someone who liked to leave any small details unrecognized. And then she looked embarrassed that she'd gotten sidetracked by a piece of movie trivia. She looked at him for an awkward few moments in silence. And then shrugged. That was the end of her embarrassment. It was a signal that she had nothing else to say.

"So that's it?" Jack asked. "You're moving on?"

"Honey," Patience McCoy told him, a touch of sadness in her voice, tapping her casebook one more time, "I'm already gone."

"JACKIE, GIMME A break," Dom grumbled.

The meat market was Jack's next stop and he hoped this visit would prove to be more satisfying than the previous one. Based on the first twenty seconds of conversation, it wasn't going to be.

"I feel like I have to do something," Jack said.

"What? What the hell are you gonna be able to do? Find some mysterious killer? Who probably doesn't even exist?"

"I know it sounds a little crazy . . ."

"No. It doesn't just sound crazy. It sounds unbelievably fucking stupid!"

"I'm not asking you for permission."

"Then what the hell are you doin' here?"

"I just need to explain it. I need it to make *sense* to someone."

"Well, it don't make no sense to *me*."

"Then stop being such a stubborn cranky old bastard and let me *explain* it to you!"

"Nothin' but grief," Dom said. "Over thirty years, nothin' but grief from you . . ." But then he saw the expression on Jack's face, really saw what was in his eyes, and he said, "Okay. So explain."

Jack stood up. Paced once around the butcher-block table, picked up one of Dom's carving knives and clutched it tightly.

"When Caroline died," he began, "nobody knows what that was like for me. Believe me, not even you. I didn't just lose her, I felt that *I'd* lost her, that I was responsible." Before Dom could interrupt, he said, "Yeah, yeah, I know. I know all the shrink stuff. But I also know what I did and how I feel. No one else thinks that, that I somehow caused it, I get that; not her mother, not you, not the cops. But I do. If I hadn't gone charging up there, who the hell knows what would have happened? Maybe whoever that animal was would have just taken the necklace and gotten the hell out of there. And, Dom, it's not just her. It's . . ."

"It's Joanie. And I think I *might* understand, Jackie. Over thirty years later, I'm still wonderin' what would have happened if I'd gotten to the seventeenth floor one minute earlier."

There was a strange silence between them now, a silence of shared grief and loss and understanding.

"You'll never know, Jackie," Dom finally said softly. "You can't go around blaming yourself."

"No, you're right. *Neither* of us will ever know. But that doesn't make it any better. In some ways it makes it a lot worse. Because I don't just blame myself for what happened, I feel guilty that I'm the one who survived." Jack put the knife down now, jabbed it into the butcher block so it stood straight up. He took a deep breath. "At least with my mother, we know what happened. It was crazy, sure, but there was closure. With Caroline we never *found* the guy. He disappeared without a trace. I mean, no one could find him. How's that possible? Police, the private detectives I hired. They said it was random. Which means there was no logic to it. So there were no real connections, no clues. No real motive, no idea how he did what he did. That's what I have to live with. Never knowing what really happened or why. Or if anything could have been done to stop it. . . . And then this thing with Kid. Dom, you knew him, too. You saw him grow up. You *know* he couldn't have jumped off that building. I spent almost every day with him this past year. Working with him, talking to him, understanding him. And he did something extraordinary. He *healed* me. He took away my pain. In a lot of ways, he brought me back to life. And I think I owe him something. Something more than what he's getting from everybody else right now."

"And what?" Dom said in his low growl. "You think that findin' out what really happened to Kid is gonna bring Caroline back? Or give you peace of mind? What the fuck's gonna happen? Kid'll come back from that fuckin' hole in that cemetery to thank you?"

"No, I don't think I can bring Caroline back. Or Kid. And, no, I don't think there's any magic that'll change the past. But I think what I *can* do is try to understand it. And that's what

I want right now. I want the truth. I *need* the truth. I need to understand something that right now makes no sense to me. Once I find out, then I'll worry about what happens after that."

"Okay, Jackie. I give you all this. I don't know exactly what the hell you're talkin' about, but I'll give you that you're makin' some sense. *Some.* But what are you gonna do? You gonna suddenly turn into a middle-aged superhero and go around and find a killer? I mean, what the hell are you gonna *do?*"

"I've been giving this a lot of thought," Jack said. "Here's what I think happened. Kid had this 'team,' that's what he called it. Four or five women he was seeing. It was another side of him, one we never saw, and it was a strange side. It was a strange world he was straddling. He told me a lot about them. Some of them were into drugs and some had dark things in their past and he was afraid of some of them. He thought they were dangerous and from what he told me, it sounded like they were. It's what he liked about them."

"Jesus, Jackie . . ."

"McCoy told me that there was a woman with Kid right before he died. In his apartment. I think it was one of his team. And I think she killed him. All I want to do is see if I can find out who these women are. Find out which ones really are dangerous. And which ones might have killed him. Had the motive, had the opportunity. Then I'll go to McCoy, with some evidence, and turn it over to her. And if I'm wrong, if he really did kill himself, then even that's something. Then maybe I'll be able to understand *that.*" When

Dom stayed quiet, didn't seem to have any response, Jack said, "I'm starting to think that when you get older it all comes down to the same thing: endings. Everything ends, one way or the other. And I'm not even looking for a happy ending, because when you think about it, there's no such thing, really, as a happy ending. I'm just looking for an ending, Dom. That's all I'm doing."

"Will you promise me one thing?" Dom asked, frowning even more than usual. When Jack nodded, the one-armed man in front of him said, "I may be older than shit but I still know a thing or two about the streets. So let me help you if you get into any trouble."

"Trouble?" Doing his best Bogart, Jack winked and added, "Trouble's my middle name." Then, when he saw how serious Dom was, he touched the old man on the shoulder. "My whole life," Jack said slowly, "people I've loved have died around me. And I've never been able to understand why. They've died and I've survived. Just once, I want to find out why. If you want to help, you old bastard, it's more than okay with me."

As Jack Keller stood in front of the building at 487 Duane Street, the only thing he could think of was that he must have the wrong address. The late-afternoon sun was bright and the glare made him squint as he stared up. He was clutching the envelope that Kid had mailed to him and he looked back down at Kid's handwritten return address. He matched it up once again to the number on the twenty-story red-brick building for the third time and, for the third time, it was a match. He put his finger to the buzzer that had the word "Super" printed to its left and rang.

It took several minutes for the superintendent to make his way to the front of the building. He didn't come out the front door but from around the corner. He had a slight accent, Jack thought Russian, and he wore overalls that were covered with paint. Peeking out of one of the overall pockets was a tattered paperback copy of Beckett's *The Unnamable*. He seemed impatient and Jack wondered if it was to get back to work or to get back to his near impenetrable choice of reading material.

Jack had rehearsed his story in his mind several times, even once in front of his bathroom mirror, but now, translating it into real life, it sounded forced and hollow. He hoped that was just because he'd practiced it so many times.

"I know this is out of the ordinary," he told the super. "But I saw the story in the paper about the suicide."

"Yeah, it was horrible," the super said. The way he said "horrible" convinced Jack it really was a Russian accent. "I was here. You a reporter?"

Jack was tempted to say yes, to improvise a whole new tale, but then he decided to stick with his original plan and see what happened. "No," he said. "It's a little more ghoulish than that—I'm a New Yorker. I'm desperate to live down here and I figured the apartment's free now."

"You want me to show you the dead guy's apartment?" the super snorted.

"That's right," Jack told him.

The super shook his head, almost in admiration. "You gotta go through the agency," he told Jack. "I'd like to help you, but . . ."

"I've called them already." Jack was prepared for this. "But it's not available yet. I guess there are some legal entanglements." That was a lie, of course. He hadn't called any agency. In fact, the story he'd seen in the paper didn't even give the exact address of the building—a detail which he hoped the super wouldn't realize.

"Well, there you go."

"But that means nobody else has seen it either. I figure this'll give me a head start. If I like it, I can just call the office and make an offer. Sight unseen, so to speak."

"It's a good plan," the super said. "You're a sick fuck and I like that. But I can't help you."

"How about for twenty bucks?" Jack asked. "All I want is a few minutes to look around the apartment."

"Sorry."

"How about a hundred dollars?"

The super cocked his head to the side now. "A hundred bucks to see the apartment?"

"That's right."

"Hey," the super said, "who am I to stop you from getting the place of your dreams?"

THE SUPER TOOK Jack up in the elevator to the penthouse apartment. They stepped out of the elevator and the super steered Jack to the right.

"Two apartments on this floor," he said. "Most of the others have three or four. Some even have five."

He took out a large ring of keys, found a master, and inserted it into the lock. The door swung open and the super stepped aside. Jack stepped into the apartment, stopped cold the moment he crossed the threshold.

"There's got to be some mistake," he said.

"What kinda mistake?"

"The man who . . . who fell . . . did you know him?"

" 'Course I knew him. He lived here."

"Demeter. That was his name, right?"

"Yeah. Kid," the super said. "Everybody called him Kid."

"And he lived *here?*"

"Mister, you want to see the apartment or not? This is the place and I only got a few minutes."

The sun coming through the curtains played tricks with

the light. The room was covered in shifting shadows. But as Jack stared, one thing was very clear: he was standing in an extraordinary apartment. One that was way beyond Kid's financial means.

Jack stepped through the small entryway to find himself in an enormous living room. The floors were thick pine planks and they had been sanded and then pickled with an off-white paint so it felt as if you were walking on clouds. The furniture, too, was mostly white. Two enormous easy chairs that looked like they came from Shabby Chic. Two full-sized couches covered in a linen with a fine and elaborately stitched pattern. Arranged on built-in, handmade oak bookshelves stood colorful Chinese vases and small modern sculptures. The artwork on the walls was modern, too, several abstract nudes. A few boxes stood in one corner, packed up, some taped shut with industrial tape, some still open. Kid's belongings, Jack thought. Someone's packing up Kid's stuff.

But who?

"You gonna look at the rest of the apartment," the super said now, "or you just wanna take it after seeing the living room?"

Jack turned to him and very quietly said, "I'll give you another hundred dollars if you give me half an hour in the apartment."

"Hey," the man said, taken aback. "I don't know . . . what's the story here?"

"No story," Jack told him. "And I'll make it five hundred. Five hundred dollars cash if you let me have half an hour alone."

The super stepped away from Jack, scrutinizing him. "I don't know if I can do that. Lotta valuables in here. Lotta valuable shit."

"I'm not going to steal anything," Jack told him. "If you want, you can wait right outside the front door. You can search me when I come out. I'm not interested in taking anything."

"What exactly is it you're interested in?"

"Privacy. Half an hour. You want the money?"

This time the super didn't hesitate. "Pal, I *always* want the money." He put his hand out, Jack handed him five one-hundred-dollar bills, and the guy headed for the front door.

"Wait a second," Jack said. And when the super stopped, he asked, "What's the rent on this apartment?"

"It's not a rental, pal. We're co-op."

"You're saying Kid *owned* this place?"

"All I'm saying is that I'll be in the lobby while you're in here. And I will search you when you come out. If you're not down in thirty minutes, I'll come up and get you. I could get fired for this, you know."

Jack didn't even respond and the super let himself out, closing the door behind him.

Jack stared for another few moments, still stunned by the splendor of the living room before him, then realized he didn't have a lot of time to waste, so he began a tour of the apartment.

The next room he entered was the master bedroom. The only phrase that Jack could come up with that would do it justice was a rather crude one: he was standing in the middle of one giant fuck palace. There was a huge round bed, covered with large pillows, and even larger pillows were strewn all over the floor. There was thick, plush carpeting, a pale gold, but it was barely visible underneath all the pillows. To the right of the bed was a round glass table with a lamp on it. The lamp shade was thick and crenellated, also beige. Jack guessed that it was more to lend atmosphere than to provide usable light. Across the room from the bed was a big-screen TV mounted into a console with enormous speakers built into either side. To the left of the television, resting only on the carpet, no table, was a CD/stereo system. A very expensive one, in fact. The exact same system Jack had in his own apartment.

He started to leave the room, stopped, went over to the large closet to the right of the TV. It was stuffed with perfectly tailored Armani suits and dress shirts. The shirts were in five different colors—white, light blue, light gray, charcoal and black—and each color grouping had five identical shirts arranged together. There were also about twenty Banana Republic T-shirts, also in different colors, hung up and pressed. Six or seven pairs of Bruno Magli shoes lined the closet floor, along with three pairs of Nikes.

Jesus, Jack thought. Pat Riley could go shopping in this place.

And then his next thought: Who paid for all this?

He heard something then, a squeaky floorboard, and he quickly shut the closet door. He shook his head—what difference did it make if the closet was open or shut? He was in

this apartment on false pretenses, he was probably commit-
ting a crime just by being in here now—and listened. But
the sound was gone. He walked back into the living room,
glanced around. Nothing. No one had come in. Doesn't take
long to get paranoid, does it, he thought. How the hell do
burglars do this for a living? To be on the safe side, he
walked to the front door and peered through the peephole.
He *had* heard something. The young couple across the hall
were carrying groceries into their apartment and laughing.
He could hear the elevator door slide shut and the elevator
head back down to the lobby. He shrugged off his attack of
nerves and began to explore the rest of the apartment.

There was a second bedroom, set up as a miniature health
club. Almost all free wall space was mirrored, which gave the
room a slightly surreal appearance and also emphasized the
vanity that went into its design. The equipment was almost
identical to what Kid had installed in Jack's apartment, as
was the layout. There were three seats, one for benching,
one for incline presses, and a flat one that could be used for
almost any exercise. There was a slant board that attached to
pegs built into a wall. There was a row of dumbbells, resting
on custom-built holders that ran under and along the length
of the windows on one wall. There was a full-sized barbell
and a specialized one for bicep curls. There was a Universal
leg-lift machine as well as one for benching and incline
benching. There was a state-of-the-art StairMaster, a treadmill, and a VersaClimber, which Jack did not have at home.
There was nothing in the room other than the equipment.
Nothing that seemed personal or relevant to what Jack was

looking for—whatever the hell it was he was looking for—so he ran his hand lightly over some of the weights, trying to figure out how Kid could have afforded all this, then he moved on to check out the kitchen and dining room.

The dining room was small, little more than an alcove, really. The table was black marble and there were six black-and-white stuffed, straight-back chairs around it. There was an armoire that held wineglasses and a set of dishes. The dishes were not fine china but were plain and perfectly nice. They looked like they might have come from the Pottery Barn or Williams-Sonoma.

The kitchen was perhaps the strangest room in the apartment because it was outfitted for a gourmet cook. There was a six-burner Viking stove, along with a convection oven and chrome vent above it. All the equipment was stainless steel, black or chrome: a Cuisinart; a blender, also Cuisinart; a Kitchen Aid mixer with all the accoutrements; a regular electric drip coffeemaker as well as a restaurant-quality espresso/cappuccino maker. There was a circular chrome device that hung from the ceiling and dominated one corner—its hooks held expensive pots and pans, cast-iron skillets, and heavy stew pots. To the left of the stove was a small, fifty-bottle wine cooler. Jack couldn't help himself, he checked the labels to find it full of '93 Barolos and Amarones and several superb '85 Burgundies. There were also two bottles of '83 Yquem, which Jack figured at an easy $800 per bottle or more. Next he opened the Sub-Zero refrigerator and by now was not shocked to find one shelf filled with Dom Pérignon and bottles of white wine, all Chassagne-Montrachet. The rest of the shelves were largely empty, although there were a dozen brown eggs, several tins of beluga caviar, a large container of plain, non-fat yogurt, a covered dish—which Jack lifted to find several partially eaten soft cheeses—and several jars of Dijon mustard. There were also six bottles of mineral water, three sparkling, three non, and two cans of Bud Light. In the freezer was a bottle of Polish vodka, the kind with strands of buffalo grass flavoring it, and a bottle of an Italian liqueur called Lemoncello. When he went through the cupboards, he found similar fare. He thought of a line from one of his favorite movies, *Pat and Mike*, with Tracy and Hepburn. He and Caroline owned a tape and used to watch it together. At some point in the movie, Tracy says about Kate, in his Brooklyn accent, "Not much meat on her—but what's there is mighty *cherce*."

That's what Jack was thinking about this apartment. Not much there, but what there was was expensive and fine. Mighty cherce.

And very un-Kidlike.

Jack went back into the living room now. He still had about twenty minutes—and, if need be, he was sure he could bribe good old Alex for a bit more time. But he wanted to get out of this place; it was starting to give him the chills. The sun was fading now, disappearing behind some of the tall buildings farther downtown, and the swaying shadows made the entire apartment feel as if it were somehow alive.

He sat down on the floor, back to the front door, and began going through the packed boxes.

He began with the ones that were still unsealed.

The first box was fairly uninteresting. More T-shirts, a few pair of jeans and sweats. Some socks. A light jacket that Jack recognized. There were a few other bulky items: a leather football, a baseball glove, a Sony Discman, and about thirty CD's.

The second box was more interesting. It was filled with personal papers, a calendar, and an address book. The first thing Jack pulled out were bank records from Citibank. With a little sifting, Jack found the most recent statement. It was valid as of two weeks earlier. On the first page of the four-page statement, it said that George Demeter had a savings account worth $9,468.72. In his checking account he had $680.

Not the kind of numbers that gets you this apartment, Jack thought. That's not even two months' rent, never mind buying the place. This could go for a million and a half bucks, maybe more!

He began going through more papers, not sure what he was looking for, surprised at how compelling it was to search through another man's life.

He pulled out a black day-at-a-glance calendar and began leafing through it, starting in January. Early in the year, Kid had several notations per day. Some of them were names Jack hadn't heard of—Lydia, Becky, Michele. One notation said "Paul: movie." Nothing much of any interest. In mid-January, he saw a line that just read: "Entertainer." And as he began moving forward in time, there were more listings for Entertainer and regular notations for Samsonite and

Mortician. In February, there were several bookings for Rookie. Those seemed to stop in March. Also in early March, the notation "Murderess" started appearing regularly. And at the end of April one date was marked, at seven in the evening, with "Destination." The word "Destination" was followed by several question marks.

Jack realized there were quite a few notations that just said "Butcher." They were almost all early in the morning and it took Jack a few moments before he understood that this was his own nickname. Kid had dubbed him the Butcher.

Son of a bitch, he thought, a vague smile crossing his lips. The nicknames were carefully chosen—that's what Kid had said. Is that what Kid had thought of him? After all was said and done, underneath it all, he was still a butcher, back at Dom's, back in his youth? Back with Kid's father?

In a sudden inspiration, Jack turned quickly to the month of June and checked the page for the date of Kid's death, but it wasn't there.

The entire page had been torn out of the book.

Jack frowned, set the calendar aside, found similar date-books from the two years previous. For the prior year, the notations were fairly similar. A lot of appointments with the Butcher and with Mortician, Samsonite, and Entertainer. There were a few other nicknames that Jack hadn't heard of—Catwoman, Cayenne, and Ginger—and he realized these women had been part of the Team before Kid had shown up in his apartment or else he'd stopped seeing them before he'd begun discussing the situation with Jack.

He went back one more year and there were a few nicknames that showed up, but more real names, almost all
women. It made sense—Kid was not doing as much
personal training then so there was no need to assign nicknames. The name Charlotte appeared quite a few times. And
the nickname that came up most often was Destination.

Jack didn't know what to make of all this. It seemed interesting but there was no discernible pattern and nothing that
led him anywhere concrete. The fact that the last page in
Kid's book had been torn out certainly seemed ominous.
But what the hell did any of it mean?

In another box—he had to rip the tape off the top of this
one—he found Kid's frequent-flyer statement. At first he
tossed it off to the side but then, for some reason, went back
and picked it up. He knew that Kid hadn't traveled much,
but he was curious nonetheless. When he glanced at the
statement, his curiosity changed to amazement. Over the
past year—the period when he was working with Kid on an
almost daily basis, when he was sure he'd learned almost
everything there was to know about Kid—Jack saw that Kid
had accumulated thirty thousand miles. In the last two
months alone he'd been to Bermuda, Palm Beach, and St.
Bart's.

This is impossible, Jack decided. Something's way off
here. Way, way off.

Kid wouldn't have gone away for two days and not told
me. He told me everything he did. He'd *have* to have mentioned taking off for fucking St. Bart's, for God's sake!

He glanced at his watch and began rummaging more

quickly through this last box. In there he saw a travel agent's itinerary for two tickets to Bermuda. The date of the tickets was mid-April, six weeks earlier. There was a credit card receipt attached to the itinerary and the credit card seemed to belong to something called Grave Enterprises. There was no signature; it had been charged and accepted over the phone. Jack stuck the receipt in his pants pocket and looked at the final, unopened box.

He was trying to decide if he had time to open it or if he should go down and check with the super. That's when he heard another noise behind him. Similar to the one he thought he'd heard before. The apartment was darker now, the shadows had sunk deeper into the woodwork, and he couldn't help himself, he felt his mouth go dry.

He was being ridiculous, he knew. It was nothing. Once again it was nothing. Or it was the super. The guy had said he'd come back up and get him if Jack didn't go down in time.

So, feeling silly, still on his knees, he half turned toward the front door, knowing he'd see nothing. And as he turned he decided that he'd open the final box, let the super come and get him if he wanted to.

But the super didn't have to come get him. And Jack didn't get a chance to open the last cardboard box. Because as he turned, he saw two men standing not three feet away from him. They were standing very still. They wore business suits and ties. Drab outfits. Were they police? Had the super called the police? He was going to ask them who they were but he didn't get a chance. Before Jack could say or do anything, one of them moved.

It was a fast movement, sudden, mostly his arm, although there was some body in it, too. Jack didn't know what the guy was holding in his fist, a pipe, maybe. Or a blackjack. But it had to be more than just a fist because the pain was startling the way it exploded behind Jack's eyes.

Jack didn't have far to fall, he was already in a crouch. But the man was very fast because he had time to hit Jack again before he toppled onto the pickled white floor. He didn't need to hit him a third time because Jack was not moving now. His breathing was heavy and labored and very slow and he was not moving at all.

He didn't move for quite some time. Not until long after the two men were gone, having taken the boxes and calendars and papers and all other traces that Kid Demeter had ever been inside the building on 487 Duane Street.

When Jack's eyes opened, he had absolutely no idea where he was. At first he thought he was in bed, that he'd awakened in the middle of the night because it was so dark. He thought he must have fallen asleep on top of the covers since he felt an unpleasant shiver of cold. Then he realized he wasn't in bed. He was lying on something hard. He was on the floor. A light-colored floor . . .

He forced himself to sit up and heard himself groan. The pain in his head rocked him but he wasn't dizzy and he didn't feel nauseous. No concussion, he decided. But a hell of a headache. He put his right hand up to gingerly touch the sore spot and he could tell he'd been bleeding. He must have been out for quite a while because the blood was just damp and sticky now.

Jack stood up and, strangely enough, that made him feel better.

It didn't take him long to realize that the apartment had been cleaned out. All of Kid's boxes were gone and, when he went into the bedroom to check the closets, he saw that there were no traces of Kid's clothes.

He checked the gym; that seemed untouched. And in the kitchen all the food and drink had been left as it was. It was only Kid's things that were gone.

Jack walked into the bathroom, forced himself to look at the side of his head. Not nearly as bad as he thought—or felt. There was a small laceration, some blood, and a swelling that he knew would keep rising and hurting over the next few days. He splashed some cold water on his face, cleaned off his wound with a damp washcloth, stood there in the small white-tiled room wondering what the hell his next move was going to be and realized he had no other choice but to leave. And leave quietly. He thought about calling the police but realized what he'd have to say: *I bribed my way into the apartment under false pretenses. I broke into and was looking through private property and I got mugged.* He also realized that whoever mugged him could easily say they thought he was a burglar and that they were simply protecting themselves. For all he knew, whoever hit him might already have called the police.

But he seriously doubted it.

Jack went to the front door of the apartment, peered through the peephole, but no one was outside in the hallway. He opened the door cautiously, stepped out of the apartment, closed the door behind him. The elevator took a minute or so to come up to the top floor and Jack then rode it down to the lobby. He did not expect the super to be waiting for him and he was right. The lobby was empty.

Jack found his car exactly where he'd left it, parked on Reade Street, two blocks from Kid's apartment building. Jack reached into his left pants pocket for his car key, felt a piece of paper that, for just a second, he didn't recognize. And then it came to him. He pulled the paper out, unfolded it.

Kid's travel receipt.

With a name: Grave Enterprises.

And a credit card number.

Jack felt the excitement well up inside him as he got behind the wheel of the car. He had some information. He had some evidence. *Okay,* he thought. *Okay!*

And as he reached the West Side Highway and headed uptown, here was his next thought, not nearly as exciting:

Now what?

"MMMMM," THE VOICE on the other end of the phone mumbled. The next word sounded vaguely like "yeah." It might have been a question.

"Randy?"

"Yo." The voice sounded sleepy, as if he'd just been awakened. Jack looked at his watch and saw it was 8:30 P.M.

"This is Jack Keller."

"Mr. K! Whassup?"

"Did I wake you?"

"Well . . ." The voice hesitated. That kind of hesitation when someone's been awakened but doesn't want to admit it. "Kind of," he said. "What time is it?"

"Eight-thirty."

"Morning or night?"

"Night," Jack said. "Are you okay?"

"Yeah, yeah." The voice was waking up now, coming to life. "I've been working on a complicated job. A security system. Kind of working day and night, so I catch up on the *z*'s wherever I can get 'em. You know me, all work and no play."

"You should try to get out more, Randy."

"Out? What's that?"

"You want me to call you back? When you're more awake?"

"No, no. I'm fine. Gotta get up anyway and get back to work. What can I do for you?"

Randy Pelkington was a twenty-nine-year-old Australian who'd moved to New York when he was eleven years old but he'd never managed to lose his accent. Randy's parents were good, upstanding middle-class people—his mother was a book publisher who'd been hired by an American firm and relocated to New York and his father was an architect who, when he had trouble landing work in his new country, became a professor of architectural history at NYU. They were both extremely surprised when their son, at age fifteen, got into quite a bit of trouble with the local police. Randy, it seemed, had a skill. He was one of the earliest and best computer hackers and, just as a lark, he'd hacked into the NYPD system and did some, as he called it, rearranging. When he was caught, Randy had been prepared. He'd saved all the original information on disk and was easily able to re-rearrange things back to normal. Since Randy's actions seemed not to be malicious and purposeful but rather done out of curiosity, some clever person on the force decided that there was a better alternative than tossing the young genius into juvenile detention. His punishment was that he had to spend a year on probation helping the department with their computer programming. At the end of the year, Randy was promptly hired by the city as a consultant to continue his work. He also, at the same time he attended NYU, started his own business. Most of his computer work was fairly benign. He described it as "helping rich people get over their terror of the unknown electronic universe." What he mostly did was go to those people who tended to work out of their homes—writers, architects, artists, what have you— and set up computer systems for them. He taught them how to use Windows as well as non-Windows applications and came over to rescue them whenever they thought they'd lost something of value in the bowels of their computers or just generally got confused and screwed up. He also did several small office systems installations, which is how Jack happened to meet him. Caroline had hired Randy to set up the computer systems for Jack's restaurants nationwide.

"I need some help," Jack now told Randy.

"No problem. At the restaurant?"

"No, no. This is personal."

"Sounds intriguing. What is it you need?"

Jack told him and Randy said he'd call him back in fifteen minutes.

"NO PROBLEM," RANDY said when he called back. "I don't even have to come there. We can do this over the phone."

"Are you sure?"

"Piece o' cake. You still on the ThinkPad?"

Jack said that he was.

"This is gonna be easy," Randy told him. "Go to 'Search the Internet' and when you come to the search line, type in 'CylockHolmes.com.' and click on 'Search.' "

Jack did as he was told, waited, and suddenly a line appeared that said: *1 of 1 Web Site Matches.*

"Okay," Randy told him, "click on the Web site line. You want me to hang on while you start it up and download, Mr. K?"

"If you don't mind."

"My pleasure," the computer whiz said.

To Jack's amazement, cartoonish drawings of a Sherlock Holmes–like detective popped up on his computer screen, followed by hype for the site. According to that hype, he could use this program to find long-lost friends, license plate numbers, Social Security numbers, and unlisted phone numbers. He could also verify educational records, get dirt on his neighbors—in essence, according to the on-screen promises, discover anything about anyone. Once he typed in his credit card number and registered as a user, the following grid appeared:

CYLOCKHOLMES DETECTION KIT

[Background Information Reference]   [Information Source]   [Internet Source]

[Information Sources]   [ADDRESS RESULTS WILL DISPLAY HERE]

[Current Search Category]   [PHONE NUMBERS WILL DISPLAY HERE]

[Business Records]

[Driver Records]

[Vehicle   [ADDITIONAL INFORMATION WILL
  Ownership]   DISPLAY HERE]
[Vital Records]
[Voter
                    State: [Alabama]   [Retrieve]
  Registration]
[County
                    [Return Address]   [Print Envelopes]
  Courthouse]

[CD Interface Help] [Check for Update] [About]
[EXIT]
  [Cylock Holmes   [Report]
    Notebook]

"Jesus," Jack breathed. "Anyone can just do this?"

"As long as you got a credit card," Randy said. "Feeling paranoid?"

"A little."

"Wise man. No such thing as privacy anymore. You want me to lead you through this at the beginning?"

"Yes," Jack said.

"Okay, tell me what you're looking for."

"Something called Grave Enterprises."

"What about it?"

Jack exhaled. "Not sure," he said. "How about exactly what it is and who runs it."

"Okay. I'm looking at the screen, too. Go to the icon that says 'Investigative Tools.'"

Again, Jack clicked as per his instructions. He then typed in the information that Randy told him to type in at exactly the spots where Randy told him to type it. Within moments there was a long list of corporations and companies that had the word "grave" in them.

"You're gonna have to narrow it down, Jack. Or else you're going to have to check out each one of these. Looks like there's about a hundred and fifty—and that's just in New York. A lot of 'em you can get rid of immediately, I'm sure. This doesn't look like it's the world's greatest search engine, so I think you'll find words like 'gravy' and companies that have names that are just close; stuff like that'll clog up the list."

"Okay," Jack said. "You don't have to hang on while I do that. That could take a while."

"What else do you need?"

Jack told him that he had a credit card number that he wanted traced back to the owner.

"You don't have the owner's name?"

"No," Jack explained. "Just the number."

"That might take a little more time 'cause it's not the way the system's set up. I'll tell you what. Try finding what you want on this 'grave' list. Then, if you can narrow things down to a few names, we can track the credit cards for each person until you get what you're looking for. If that doesn't work, give me the number and I'll do a search. But I'll have to tap into a few things that might not be kosher."

"All right. Let me try it the kosher way first," Jack said. "Although I don't understand how this can really be legal."

"Trust me," Randy said.

"Believe me, I do. I also owe you. How much?"

"This? This was just a wake-up call. Consider this a free-bie."

Jack thanked the Australian profusely, assured him he'd call him back if he got stuck on his search, and hung up the phone.

Then he went to work on his new CylockHolmes program.

IT TOOK ONLY twenty minutes for Jack to narrow his list down to six companies he wanted to check out. It was easy to eliminate all the "gravy" and "gravel" and "engraving" business that had popped up. Within minutes after he'd done that he had descriptions for the six he was interested in. There was only one that matched up exactly to the name on Kid's travel receipt, so Jack focused on that one first. It was a company called Grave Enterprises. The other five had addresses that automatically appeared alongside their names but there was no address for the company Jack was focused on. That fact alone made him certain he was on the right track.

He began using the various tools that CylockHolmes offered. He found a large number of vehicles registered to the company, all in New York State and New Jersey. He went into courthouse records to check the ownership of Grave Enterprises and found that it was part of another corpora-tion, Migliarini Construction. The name rang a bell, although Jack couldn't initially come up with why. He then used his new computer program to run a search on Migliarini. It didn't take him long to understand why he knew the name. The more he searched, the more astonished he became. As he went along, he printed up anything that struck him as particularly relevant. An hour into his reading and research, CylockHolmes sent him to a list of newspaper and magazine articles as well as published books that had references to Migliarini Construction and its parent company, Joeva, Inc. At ten-thirty, he called the nearest Barnes & Noble. Whoever answered the phone told him they were open until eleven. Jack didn't even say thank you. He slammed the phone down, ran outside, and hailed a cab. He made it to the bookstore in fifteen minutes. By eleven-fifteen, he was back in his apartment, sitting in the leather living room chair under the Hopper painting, tearing through a book that had been published six months earlier called *Future Crime: The 20th Century Gangster in the 21st Century.*

By one-thirty in the morning, Jack knew he had what he was looking for. But to double-check he went to the computer and logged back on to CylockHolmes.

He made a few mistakes, wound up at a page that kept telling him to register again, but he finally got back on track. Under "Search," he typed in the name Eva Migliarini, a name he'd gotten from his reading. Information popped up immediately. He clicked on "Business Records," saw exactly what he expected to find. And then for his final cross-reference he tracked down two months' worth of her latest shopping sprees. There was nothing at all suspicious or seemingly illegal. But that didn't matter to Jack. All he needed was to match one particular item. And match it he did: he wouldn't have to call Raymond the computer whiz to get her Visa card number. He had her purchases. And on April 16, she'd bought two tickets for Bermuda. Jack looked at the receipt he'd taken from Kid's apartment. Same date. Same location.

Grave Enterprises, he thought.

Very fucking clever.

And you, too, Kid. Just as fucking clever. He could hear Kid's voice, as clear as if he were still standing in the room: *She's got some really nasty friends and I don't think I want to piss them off just yet.*

Nasty friends is right, he thought. But that didn't bother Jack, not now, because he was feeling even cleverer. Because when he finally closed his eyes and went to sleep at three in the morning, he knew he'd found what he was looking for: the first member of the Team.

He'd found the Mortician.

I t was 11 A.M. and already feeling like a midsummer instead of late-spring morning. The air was warm and starting to buckle with humidity.

Jack had had no more than five hours' sleep but he felt well rested and, unlike most of the New Yorkers who were already in a sweat-induced stupor, energetic. He was oblivious to the city's clamminess. He was oblivious to just about everything other than the fact that he was standing outside an elegant double town house on East Fifty-fourth Street, looking up at a tastefully engraved brass plaque on the front of the building that identified it as the Migliarini Funeral Home. Underneath that, in smaller engraved letters, it said: Joeva, Inc. The building blended in nicely with the rest of the ornate brownstones on the block. There were several foundations, one embassy, and a few private homes. This was a monied street and every penny showed on its surface.

Jack was wearing a suit and tie now and he smoothed down the tie, straightened the front of his jacket, then buttoned the middle button. He gathered himself, went up the three steps to the funeral parlor in a surprisingly jaunty manner, and opened the front door.

He found himself in a subdued lobby. It all looked very . . . well, funereal. A receptionist eyed him, a look that conveyed her immediate condolences, then in a sympathetic and hushed tone asked if she could help.

"Yes," Jack said, matching her semiwhisper. "I'd like to see Eva Migliarini, please."

"Do you have an appointment?"

"No," Jack said. "But tell her I'll only take up five minutes of her time and it's very important."

"May I have your name, please? And may I tell her what it's about?"

"Jack . . ." He stopped himself suddenly. "Sorry. Tell her that Kid Demeter is here to see her." He fingered the painful lump on the back of his head and said, "I think she'll know what it's in reference to."

The receptionist picked up the phone and pressed an intercom button. In the same whispered tones, she passed along Jack's message and then waited for a response. It took a little longer than she expected so she gave a perfunctory smile to Jack while she waited. It was the look of someone who was used to smiling vacantly at grieving people. In a few moments, she nodded and murmured, "Yeah, okay," and hung up the phone. "Ms. Migliarini said she can see you in about fifteen minutes. She'll buzz up when she's ready." He thanked her politely, then she pointed to several chairs off in a corner and said, "Please have a seat. I'll let you know when she calls."

Jack sat facing the receptionist and realized he was nervous. He was tapping his foot on the black-and-white marble floor and the index finger of his right hand on the arm of the dark wood chair. He forced his foot to stay still and, to occupy his hand, he reached into a small bowl filled with matchbooks and pulled one out. The matches had a black cover with plain white lettering that simply said, "Joeva, Inc." For no particular reason, he put the book in his pants pocket, then did his best to bide his time and study the lobby.

It was all quite properly somber. Marble floors, two overly elaborate Greek-style columns that looked as if they were holding up the ceiling but which, Jack was sure, were purely decorative rather than structural. There were five doors that led to other rooms. He assumed these were waiting rooms for groups of mourners. The walls were thick and sound-proof because judging from the hearses waiting outside—Hearses! Those were the registered vehicles he'd seen on CylockHolmes, he was sure of it—there was at least one funeral in progress but he could not hear a word being spoken nor a note of music being played. Jack nervously fingered the matchbook in his pocket with his left hand and began tapping with his right again. Finally, he heard the receptionist's now familiar husky whisper carry across the room.

"She can see you now, Mr. Demeter. Just take the elevator down one flight."

Jack nodded and rose. He sauntered across the room to the elevators—there were two—and walked into the one on the left when it arrived. He took it down one flight, pressing the button labeled "B," and when it stopped he stepped out.

The elevator door closed behind him and Jack found himself in a long, sterile hallway. The floor was covered in a cold-gray industrial carpet; the walls were almost the same dirty gray. There were no arrows pointing him in any particular direction and the two doors that he could see did not look as if they'd lead to any kind of executive office. He thought perhaps he'd misheard the receptionist, that she'd said go *up* one flight, then he figured he'd at least walk to one end of the hallway and check it out. He made a right and got about ten steps from the elevator. That's when he realized that the receptionist had not made a mistake. She'd sent him where they wanted him to be sent.

At the end of the hallway, appearing from around the corner, was a man in a gray business suit. The color of his suit, as well as his complexion, so matched the color of the hall that he almost faded into the background. Jack was fairly certain that this was the man who'd hit him when he was in Kid's apartment the day before.

He turned around to see what was behind him and he was not at all surprised to see a second man in a gray suit, probably the other man he'd seen in the apartment. This man was much shorter and had a little bit of a tan but looked just as unpleasant. Both men moved slowly and steadily toward him and Jack realized he did not have a hell of a lot of options.

"Fuck me," he thought and he wasn't aware he'd said the words aloud until the first man, the taller one, said, "That's right, pal. Fuck you."

The little one got there first and before Jack could turn around, he was rabbit-punched in the small of the back. He moaned and started to twist to the side but the tall man grabbed him and threw a compact right to Jack's stomach. All the air went out of him and before he could either speak or move, they were on either side of him, they'd grabbed both his arms and shoved him through the first doorway Jack had seen when he stepped out of the elevator.

The room was dark and Jack was hunched over, trying to get his breath back. It wasn't until the smaller man flicked on the light that Jack could see where they were.

They were in a morgue.

Several dead bodies were laid out on stainless-steel tables. One was half dressed—a man wearing a shirt and suit jacket but no pants. Another had clearly not been touched yet; it was an old woman and she was clothed in a simple cotton nightgown that was bunched up around her waist. There were probably twenty drawers built into the wall that had the look of big, heavy filing cabinets. Jack did not particularly relish finding out what was being filed in them.

He looked up to speak to the taller man but he was not in much of a listening mood. The man slashed down with his fist and hit Jack a hard blow over his left eye. Jack again started to go down, but the smaller man held him up and wouldn't let him go. Jack felt a trickle of blood on his forehead, sliding down onto his cheek.

"Listen, pal," the taller man was saying. "Let's get this straight. It'll be a lot easier for all of us if you pay serious attention to what I'm saying, okay?"

Jack nodded but that didn't seem to satisfy them. The smaller man rabbit-punched Jack again. The stabbing pain in his kidney was almost unbearable; the heat ran up and down his body and he had a flashback to the hospital bed in Virginia, when the pain had taken over and he hadn't wanted to live. He started to sweat and began to keel over again but this time it was the taller man's turn to hold him up and prevent him from falling.

"I asked you a question," the taller man said, "but I didn't hear an answer."

"Okay," Jack breathed and he thought he would explode from the pain that came with just speaking. But then he thought: *No. I won't give in to it. I can't give in.* And he remembered Kid saying, when the pain was bad in one of their early sessions: *It's not injury. It's just surprise.* So that's what Jack concentrated on. He wasn't hurt. He was just surprised as hell. It was pain, but it was pain that wouldn't last. "Paying serious attention," he said as the tall man waited. "Paying attention."

"Okay, good. So here's the deal. You stop fuckin' around with anything that has to do with your friend from the apartment. You stop fuckin' around with anything that has to do with the person you're bothering here. I don't think we even have to say her name, do we?"

Jack shook his head but when he saw the man's fist draw back, he gasped, "No. Don't have to say her name."

"So it's pretty simple. The bottom line is you go home and you stop fuckin' around."

As punctuation, he threw a quick right to Jack's stomach. It could have been worse—Jack thought the guy's heart was no longer in it—but it still did some damage. Jack doubled over and he felt a tiny dribble of vomit escape from his mouth and stream down his chin.

"Do we understand each other?" the tall guy asked.

"Yes," Jack said and when he spoke, he felt the little guy behind him let go of his arms. Slowly, very slowly and gingerly, Jack straightened up. He was standing on his own now, bent over slightly, one hand on his stomach, one hand using the nearest stainless-steel slab, the one holding the old woman, to prop himself up. And again Jack thought: *It's not injury. It's just surprise.*

It's just surprise . . .

"Can I ask one question?" Jack managed to say.

"Okay. One question," the taller guy agreed. "You seem like a nice guy, so why the hell not?"

"Isn't embalming fluid extremely flammable?" Jack gasped.

"What?" the tall guy said. "What the fuck does that have to do with anything?"

Jack struggled to get his breath back. "I'll show you," he breathed out. And whirling to his left—they couldn't stop him, they didn't have a chance—he grabbed a glass bottle of embalming fluid that was sitting on the steel table. In the same motion, never slowing down, Jack finished his turn and smashed the bottle across the neck of the smaller man. Jack felt glass cut into his palm but he didn't even feel the sting. He saw blood spurt from the man's neck, but that didn't hold his attention either. The fluid flowed from the shattered container, drenching the man's jacket and shirt, and Jack, still moving, never stopping, had his left hand in his pants pocket. The little man staggered back one step and

Jack used the extra room to raise his right elbow and jab it as hard as he could into the man's chin, which sent him back another foot. Then both of Jack's hands came together and as he finished his turn, he had a lit match in his hand.

"You motherfucker," the tall one said and took a step toward Jack. His eyes were incredulous but cold and Jack had no doubt that the man was absolutely capable of killing him without ever changing that expression.

"Don't move," Jack told him. He held the match out an inch closer to the little one. "Take one more step and I'll have no problem turning your friend into the biggest goddamn toasted marshmallow you ever saw."

The big man hesitated and Jack saw the liquid soaking into the smaller man's shirt now. He was drenched in the stuff.

"Ronnie, don't fuckin' move!" the little guy screamed. "I'm fuckin' covered in this shit!"

The match was almost out and Jack quickly lit another one before they could do a thing.

"Now," Jack said. "I want you to pay serious attention to what I'm saying, okay?" He moved the flame a fraction of an inch closer to the little man. "I didn't hear an answer to my question."

"You motherfucker," the tall guy said.

"Okay, close enough. You," he said to the big guy, "you're going to get Eva Migliarini and bring her to this room. If she's not here in five minutes, call the fuckin' fire department 'cause you're gonna need 'em to put out your friend's head."

The tall guy didn't say anything. He just narrowed his eyes, then nodded, turned, and left the room.

Jack turned to give his full attention to the smaller man, whose eyes were popping in terror.

"I think you cut my fuckin' artery," the smaller thug said. "Look at the fuckin' blood."

"Turn around," Jack told him.

"What?"

"Turn around."

The shorter man turned so his back was to Jack. Jack threw as hard a punch as he could into the man's kidney. The thug grunted and immediately dropped to his knees. Before he could make any kind of a movement, Jack had another lit match in his hand.

They stayed just like that for several more minutes. Jack heard the footsteps in the hallway before he saw anyone. Then the door to the morgue opened and a dark-haired woman wearing a short black dress and high heels strode in. She wore no jewelry except for a magnificent diamond wedding ring and an antique pink-gold woman's pocket watch, which she wore around her neck on a black silk string. Jack was startled by how attractive she was. When she walked into the room he could see the muscles in her legs ripple, just slightly, from the middle of her thighs all the way down to her calves. Her arms were tightly muscled, thin and elegant, her skin was deeply tanned but smooth and absolutely unlined. Her breasts were small but perfectly formed under the tight dress. Her eyes were almost coal black and they shimmered; there was a deep and compelling mystery to her eyes, as if they were their own separate universe. She looked to be in her late thirties but Jack knew from his reading she was almost a decade older than that. As he looked at her, he could hear Kid's words echoing in his head: *They're almost perfect physical specimens. It's not only their looks. They're hungry. They want things. I don't know how else to describe it . . . their want is just overpowering.*

He finally understood. She *was* overpowering. Five-foot-six, five-seven, tops. Her chest moving up and down just a little too rapidly, the only sign that she was anything but in absolute control. Her lips thin and a deep, mysterious red, her dark hair thick and tumbling down to her shoulders. Jack forced himself to look away, just for a moment, just to break the spell.

"Turn around again," he said to the hood who was still on his knees.

The guy swiveled around to face Jack, who lit one more match, touched it to the corner of the matchbook, and set the entire small packet on fire.

"Tell me something I'd like to hear," he said to Eva Migliarini, aka the Mortician. "And quickly."

She waited, just long enough so Jack thought, She wouldn't mind if I burned him. She might even like it. Then she smiled thinly and said, "May I buy you lunch, Mr. Keller?"

Jack nodded, looked at the cowering man on the floor, and blew out the small burst of flame that had just begun to warm the tips of his fingers.

"My pleasure," he said to the woman in the black dress.

THEY WENT TO Jo Jo's, a French bistro not too far away, but she had her driver take them. In the backseat of the limo, Eva Migliarini made no attempt at conversation. She sat—lounged, really—and looked out the window. Occasionally she would cross her legs, her dress shifting up past perfectly tanned midthigh. Once she leaned down to languorously scratch her ankle. As she did, the car hit a small bump and, off balance, she leaned against his shoulder for support. She did not look at him as their bodies touched and Jack felt suddenly claustrophobic. As if he were in too-close confines with a black widow spider, exquisitely beautiful but equally poisonous.

At the restaurant, the maitre d' was extremely solicitous. He knew Jack—the restaurant community is a small one and everyone in it knew Jack—but he also knew Eva and he treated her with great deference. Jack thought he treated her as if he knew who her husband was.

She waited until they were seated—she asked for upstairs, in a corner—and the waiter had come to take their order before she looked directly into Jack's eyes and said, "Before we discuss what it is you know, Mr. Keller, or what it is you *think* you know, may I ask you something on a more intimate level?" He nodded and she said, "May I call you Jack?"

He nodded again, thinking her voice was just as enticing as her appearance. And how she could indeed make such an innocent question uncomfortably intimate. "And do I call you Eva?"

"Eve. That's what my husband calls me. It's what Kid called me. He liked the sound of it. He thought it made me sound . . . tempting."

Sitting at the table with her, so close he could smell her—not just the faint trace of her not-too-sweet perfume but the odor of sexuality she exuded—Jack was even more aware of the extraordinary ferocity of this woman. There was something almost feral about her. Even sitting still she was like a wildcat, not quite caged but not quite free in the jungle either, and certainly always aware that people were watching her—and thinking about trying to capture her.

"So," she said. "Are you asking or telling?"

"Both, I think."

"Which comes first?"

"Telling."

She shifted slightly in her seat and her leg brushed up against Jack's. He did not think it was accidental. And he found the touch thrilling. It sent an electrical charge up and down his spine. This is insane, he thought. I've been around beautiful women before. Women who were more beautiful than this woman. Caroline was more beautiful than this woman. . . .

But there's something about her. Something I've not ever seen before.

Eve is a fitting name. She seems more than capable of bringing the Garden of Eden down around her in ruins.

"You're Joe Migliarini's wife," he began. He wanted to talk so he could stop thinking about the way she was making him feel.

" 'Joe,' is it?" Her lips had a slight smirk, although her voice was even. "Do you know him?"

"You can't run a restaurant in New York without knowing him," he said. "I wouldn't say we're close social acquaintances, but we've met."

"I'll send him your regards at dinner tonight."

"I didn't realize you were so involved in his businesses."

"Am I?" she said.

"Apparently. Not in the trucking or cement contracting, at least not that I could find. But you've got a hand in the linen supplies and you seem to run the mortuaries all by yourself. He turned them over to you about five years ago."

"Yes. They're quite profitable." Her lips moved just slightly now. The white of her teeth gleamed against the textured red. "I enjoy business. I'm good at it."

"I'd say *very* good. You're probably the most powerful woman in the history of organized crime."

"Oh, please," she said, but the protest, even the tone of annoyance, was by rote, there was no conviction behind it. "We're one hundred percent legitimate. I guarantee you my workday is a lot more boring than almost anyone's you know."

"Excuse me, I didn't mean to insult you. Those co-workers of yours I met today, what area are they in? Personnel? PR?"

Her legs moved again under the table. Again, they brushed against his and he had to catch his breath. "That was an aberration and I apologize for it. They tend to be a bit overprotective. But here's what I'll grant you, Jack, since you did get an unfortunate peek behind the scenes: I make a lot of money for my husband, and in areas that were previously overlooked. My business has an extraordinary cash flow, which is important for us. And with that kind of cash, I'm a bit more trustworthy than a lot of people my husband could have hired."

"Congratulations. You're the Martha Stewart of the burial biz."

"I do have to admit, there was also something about that particular business that appealed to me."

"Nice name. Grave Enterprises."

"Thank you. Most of the people in my husband's business don't have much of a sense of humor. I thought it was appropriate for the holding company."

"When Kid talked about you—"

"Kid told me he *didn't* talk about me."

"Not by name, exactly. He had a kind of code name. He referred to you as the Mortician."

"How charming." No surprise in those eyes. No emotion at all. "Are you here to tell me my own background, Jack, or is there something else?"

"There are a few other things. That I don't think your husband or anyone else would particularly appreciate hearing."

She said nothing, and the waiter returned then, put their food down in front of them. She had the good grace to take a bite and nod her approval before Jack continued.

"I know that you took Kid away on weekends. Palm Beach, Bermuda, a couple of times to St. Bart's. I'll bet if I look a little closer, I'll find out you have houses there. Or you own a hotel."

"We have a house in Palm Beach," she said. "It's hardly a secret. And we own a share of a golf club in Bermuda. Both Joe and I play. Are you a golfer?"

"No," Jack said.

"It's an excellent game. Unlike anything else because to be good you have to remove all tension. You can't allow any outside interference while you're on the course. It's best if you don't even let yourself think. It's wonderful discipline for off the course. Joe says it's very Zen-like. You should try it." She looked down at her plate as if she were going to take another bite, then changed her mind. "St. Bart's was just fun," she said. "A lark. He'd never been there. Joe was away. We went for two days and drank a lot of rum and got away from the miserable cold. I could sunbathe nude because the cottage I rented had a little private beach. You know what I remember most about those two days? The way Kid rubbed suntan lotion over my entire body. He was very gentle and methodical. It was incredibly sensual. What else do you have?"

Jack took a sip of mineral water and cleared his throat. "You bought the apartment on Duane three months ago," he continued, "and you gave it to Kid. Maybe not legally, but you had him move in. I don't know how many nights a week you stayed there; my guess is you mostly used it in the afternoons. I don't know if Joe knows about the apartment, maybe he does, but I'll bet he doesn't know what it was used for. Or at least he didn't until recently."

"Which means what?"

"Did he kill Kid when he found out?"

"That's a question. Are you through telling?"

"No. You moved Kid into the apartment—if I think about it, I'm sure I can even tell you the exact day. Then you started demanding more and more of his time. Why not, you were paying for it. But Kid didn't like it, so he told you he was ending the relationship. He told me he was going to. I think he told you the night he died."

"And then what? I lured him out to the balcony and, with my vanity crushed, I pushed him off?"

"Maybe."

"Which is it, Jack? Did *I* kill him or did my jealous husband?"

"I don't know. But I think one of you did."

She pulled a cigarette out of her purse, put it between her lips, and leaned over for Jack to light it. He could see her breasts rustle under her dress.

"Sorry," he said. "I used up all my matches."

She shrugged, reached into her purse, pulled out a lighter, and lit it herself. "Kid was my trainer," she said, after a deep inhale. "And in a lot of ways I was his. I know a lot about you. He told me what you did for him when he was younger. Well, I helped him when he was older. I cleaned him up, I dressed him, I showed him which fork to use. He was a very, very beautiful boy with extraordinary potential and he knew that what I could teach him was going to come in very handy. And I knew that what we had couldn't last forever. He was young and"—she made only the briefest hesitation—"I'm not as young."

"That's not quite the way he told the story."

"Men are vain. They always make themselves out to be the hero."

Jack wanted her to talk more now. He tried to remember what else Kid had told him about her. What he could use that might nettle and get under her skin. "I think you wanted to control him," he said. "And he wasn't someone you could control."

"Wasn't he?"

"No."

"There are very few things—or people—I can't control, Jack. It's one of my talents. In addition to being a good businesswoman."

"I saw another one of your talents," Jack said. "One I'm sure the police will be interested in."

"And what was that?"

"You're good with a knife. I saw the proof on Kid's arm."

Her eyes flashed angrily but the expression on her face didn't change. "I suspect you might not be so easy to control," she said.

"I think there are a lot of things you're not going to be able to control so easily now," he told her.

She put her cigarette down on her bread plate. Her lipstick ringed the end of it, soaking into the paper like traces of blood.

"Jack," she said. "I don't know what it is you're doing exactly. And I don't really care. But the police believe that Kid simply fell. Whether he jumped or it was an accident, it's a sad and tragic thing but it's what I believe, too. You'd be very smart to come around to the same belief."

"Or?"

"That wasn't a threat, Jack. Despite what you think you know, I'm not really all that threatening. All I meant was, or you'll be spending a lot of sleepless nights. You'll be trying to find something that has no answer. Don't forget," she said. "I'm in the death-and-dying business. I know a lot about it. I know that there's nothing quite so final or quite so still. And I know that death is a thing completely unto itself. It exists; that's its only importance and its only value. It comes, it comes for everybody, and it's not very concerned with why or how." She raised her hand, the subtlest of gestures, and the waiter scurried over with the check. Jack reached to take it but she waved him off. "On Grave Enterprises," she told him.

As they reached the street, she took his hand, shook it, and let her hand linger in his. Again he was both unnerved and aroused by her highly charged touch. "Maybe we can have dinner some night," she said. "And talk about less depressing things."

"I believe Kid was killed," he told her.

"So I understand. But I still don't understand why."

"Because of the plans he was making for his future. Because drugs were found in his system and I don't believe he'd take them willingly. Because I knew him and I know how important life was to him."

"And if you're right? Then what?"

"Then I'm going to find out what happened."

Her hand was still in his. He felt her fingers move against his palm. "Let me steer you away from two very serious mistakes you could make," Eva Migliarini said. "One would be to involve my husband in any of this. That would be a *very* big mistake. But the other one would be even bigger. That would be if you make me angry." She leaned over and kissed him on the cheek. Her lips lingered just a second longer than necessary. They were warm and they sent a jolt of electricity through his entire body. "*That's* a threat, Jack."

He watched her step up into her car, saw her leg snake inside and disappear. He watched as the driver pulled away and the car turned at the next corner, moving out of view. He reached up and touched the spot on his cheek where her lips had touched him. He felt as if his skin had been seared. As if he'd been branded.

He rubbed the spot with two fingers of his right hand, then brought his hand down in front of his face. He looked at the small red smudge that had been transferred to his fingertips, and Jack understood that he had taken his first and mystifying step into Kid's unknown world.

What he didn't understand was the way he felt.

It was much the same sensation as during his initial workouts with Kid. It was painful. It was often unbearable.

But he liked it.

THIRTY-SEVEN

This time Sergeant McCoy's reaction to his appearance at the Eighth Precinct was not nearly as neutral as on his first visit. This time she was clearly not a happy camper.

"This is my husband, Mr. Keller. We're on our way out to dinner. He just picked me up so I wouldn't have to ride uptown alone. Wasn't that nice?"

"Very nice."

"Elmore, this is Jack Keller."

"Nice to meet you," Jack said. "Or to see you again. I know we met at the restaurant."

Elmore McCoy looked astonished that Jack remembered but his wife immediately said, "Close your mouth, honey-bunch. I told him we were there when I first met him. He may be good but he's not *that* good." Elmore McCoy now looked disappointed but the good sergeant didn't seem to pay that much attention. "Would you give us two minutes," she said, "and then I'll be ready to go." Her husband nodded and left them alone by her desk.

"Sergeant—" Jack began but she cut him off immediately.

"I think I'll do the talking now," she announced, "because I meant it when I said I only had two minutes. But this won't take long 'cause I just want to make one thing clear: whatever you're doing, stop."

"How do you know what I've been doing?"

"How do you think? We already got a call from the lovely Mrs. Migliarini saying that you were harassing her. Believe me, Jack—and I'm gonna call you Jack because this is so fucking dumb I can't bring myself to call you Mr. Keller—you do not want to be harassing any member of the Migliarini family. It just is not something you want to do. She talked about pressing charges against you for breaking and entering and, believe me again, that would probably be the nicest thing she could do in this situation."

"Do you know that she owned the apartment that Kid fell from?"

"I'm a police officer, goddamnit, of *course* I know! What the hell do you think I do with my time? But did *you* know that she owns two other apartments in that same building? She bought 'em for investments and rents 'em out. It's a business arrangement and they're owned by her company." Her words came out in a rush now, and she seemed to be getting more agitated as she went along. "Now, if you want to go prying, I'll grant you your friend probably was not paying top dollar to live there—I've seen the lady and I know what she's like—but that ain't none of my business. And it ain't none of yours, either. We talked to her about the drugs we found there and we're satisfied she didn't know a goddamn thing about it. That *was* our business and we took care of it. She may have been even more surprised than you were! So, Jack, here's what I suggest. Stop pestering her and stop pestering me."

"Did you know she stabbed him?"

"No," McCoy said, a little bit of indignation taken away from her. "I didn't know that. When?"

"Four, six weeks ago. She went after him with a knife and slashed his arm."

"Well, it was never reported. And a minor case of domestic violence don't mean jack, Jack."

"One call from a mobster's wife—that's all it takes to stop you from investigating a case?"

"Don't go dissin' me now, when you don't know what you're talking about, 'cause that really pisses me off. There ain't no case, there ain't no damn investigation!" She was yelling now. Another police officer took a step in their direction but she waved him off, letting him know that everything was okay. Turning back to Jack, she said, a little quieter, "If you come here again, you should either be under arrest or make damn sure that somebody tried to kill you. Otherwise, I don't want to see your face! Now that's the end of our little conversation because I'm already late for dinner with my husband and you got me so goddamn mad I broke my New Year's resolution, which was not to swear so fucking much!" Sergeant McCoy took a deep breath. "I told you I did not have a lot of patience."

Jack met her stare and said, "Will you just do one thing? Find out where they both were on the night Kid died, Joe and Eva Migliarini. And two guys who work for her, real thugs, one tall, six-two or -three, with a sickly, pale complexion, one short, five-five, five-six, tan . . ." He thought for a second. "With a scar on the back of his neck. From a glass cut."

McCoy looked at him incredulously. "No," she said. "I will not. And neither will you. Now do we understand each other?"

Jack nodded. And without another word, Sergeant Patience McCoy turned and left the station house to go have dinner.

As soon as she was gone, Jack nodded again, this time to himself. *Yes*, he thought, *we understand each other.*

But she was wrong. As wrong as she could be. So he wasn't going to pay any attention to what she thought she understood.

AT HIS APARTMENT, Jack sat at his computer and began to make a list of everything he could remember that Kid had told him about the Team. The more he worked, the more the list began to take a slightly different form: it was every detail Jack had heard over the last year about Kid's life.

He put the title "Kid" on it and centered it at the top of the page. He wanted to be as organized and precise as possible and he was. It took him the better part of three hours—he was sure he'd keep coming back and adding—and when he pushed his chair away from his desk and looked at the screen, he realized he knew both an awful lot and almost nothing. Some of his information was intriguing, some was trivial and silly. All in all, it didn't add up to much.

But among the trivial details he wrote down was that Bryan Bishop had been wearing a T-shirt that said "Hanson

Fitness Center" on it when they'd had their lunch at Jack's. And Kid had mentioned once that he used a place called Hanson's to train clients.

It might not be much but it was a place to start.

The Hanson Fitness Center was in SoHo, on Greene Street between West Houston and Prince. It was the second floor of a large restored loft building. On the first floor was an art gallery whose large window onto the street was halfway filled with sand. As Jack walked up and peered in, he didn't know if he was looking at a work of art or if it simply meant that they were out of business.

The gym was the entire second floor and it was a classy setup. There were weight machines scattered around, many of the same ones Jack had in his own apartment and that he'd seen in Kid's. One wall was a climbing wall. And there was a heavy bag in one corner, hanging from the ceiling. A woman was at the bag, both punching and kicking it, while a trainer stood and held it still. There looked to be seven or eight trainers working simultaneously with clients, and another dozen or so clients working out on their own. As Jack was looking around, he heard Bryan's voice call out, "Mr. Keller," and he looked up to see Kid's friend across the room standing by a watercooler.

"I was pretty surprised to get your call," Bryan said as they shook hands. "I don't know how you can remember stuff like this. I mean, from a T-shirt. *I* can hardly remember I work here."

"I thought it was worth a shot. Kid used to train people here sometimes, didn't he?"

"Yeah. During the day when it's not so crowded, then he'd give 'em twenty-five percent of his take. It was a pretty good deal. It's a nice setup, don't you think?"

"It's impressive," Jack agreed. "What do you do here?"

"Me? I do a little bit of everything. I train people mostly. I got a few of my own clients, not like Kid, but a couple. But mostly I do whatever they need. The Hansons, the guys who own the place, they're real nice."

There was one small private office in the place and a man in sweatpants and a T-shirt—also bearing the name of the gym—stepped out of it and surveyed the room. "Hey, B.B.," he called in Bryan's direction. "Before you go, you wanna clean out the big bathroom? It's a mess."

Bryan colored slightly and said to Jack, "We all gotta do it. Take turns, you know. Gotta keep the place clean." Then, to his boss, still standing in front of the office, he called back, "Okay, Bruce. But then I'm outta here." To Jack he said, "It'll just take me a few minutes. Then we can go talk, okay?"

Jack nodded and watched as Bryan moved to one of what appeared to be three different bathrooms. As he walked down the hallway, a young man, a Wall Streeter if Jack had ever seen one, came out of one of the bathrooms, still toweling off his hair. As he passed Bryan, he dropped the towel on the floor. There was a bin for towels not six feet from where the guy stood, but he just dropped the wet cloth on the floor and kept walking. Bryan stooped and picked it up. He looked back to stare at the client in disbelief, but saw Jack watching him, so quickly averted his gaze and docilely dropped the towel in the proper basket. Then he disappeared into the bathroom.

Fifteen minutes later, they were on their way out. But as Bryan reached the front door, another client—and another Wall Streeter from the looks of it—strode in and waylaid him. Bryan glanced at Jack and said, "Just give me a second," and then they both headed toward the back of the gym. Jack watched as the client chatted with Bryan for a moment, as friendly as could be, but also dug his hand into his pocket and came out with money. He glanced down to make sure of the amount, then surreptitiously slipped it into Bryan's palm. Bryan slapped him on the back, nodded, and came back to Jack.

"Sorry about that," he said. "Now we're outta here for sure."

"A tip?" Jack asked as they headed for the stairwell.

Bryan looked surprised. "It'd be a pretty good tip," he said and opened up his hand to reveal a hundred-dollar bill. Then he looked embarrassed—a look Jack was beginning to recognize—and said, "I do a little booking, you know. I can use the money and a lot of guys here like to bet. Lotta the stock market guys. I don't actually book, I can't really afford it, but I know a guy, so I take stuff for him. He gives me like ten percent of what I bring in. I pass out those little yellow cards, too. For pro football, you know. You gotta win three out of three or four out of four or seven out of eight or whatever. If you ever wanna place a bet, Mr. Keller, I can do it for you. You won't even get charged the vig, I swear."

"Thanks," Jack said. "I'll keep it in mind."

They walked a block south to the SoHo Wine Bar, sat down in a booth off to the side. The waitress came immediately to take their order—Bryan had a light beer, Jack had a Sam Adams on draft—then Bryan looked up and, with as friendly a smile as Jack thought he'd seen in a long, long time, asked, "So what can I do for you, Mr. Keller?"

"The first thing is, call me Jack."

Again, that flash of embarrassment. Bryan nodded quickly and vigorously to cover it up.

"Second thing, and this isn't why I'm here, but I thought of it when we were in the gym—I need a new trainer. Kid got me hooked, although it's not just vanity. Or even just staying in shape. I've got some specific physical therapy that I've got to keep up. It's important. You interested?"

Bryan could hardly get the words out. The smile on his face went from ear to ear now. "Are you serious? *Yeah*, I'm interested. Yeah, of course."

"I like to work out early in the morning, but I can be flexible. I'm an early morning person, though, and it's easier—"

Bryan interrupted him excitedly. "Hey, Mr. Keller— I mean, Jack . . . sorry—whatever you want to do and whenever you want to do it is fine with me. I mean, this is like an honor for you to even ask me. And I know a lot of the therapy Kid was doing with you. I'm gonna be really good at this."

"I know you are, Bryan. That's why I asked you. I'll pay you the same thing I was paying Kid, which is pretty fair."

"Okay, but, I mean, I'm no Kid. You gotta understand that. He was the best, really. I'm good, though, I don't want you to think I'm not good. I can do this."

"So do we have a deal?"

"Yeah." Jack didn't think it was possible but Bryan's grin got even wider. "We definitely have a deal. And I wasn't kidding when I said that this was a real honor for me. I'm gonna take it very seriously, I just want you to know that."

Jack nodded, pleased. "I do know it."

Bryan stuck out his hand and they shook on it. Bryan was so excited he could hardly sit still.

"And now there's a third thing," Jack told him.

"Sure," Bryan said. "Anything."

"I don't think Kid killed himself. Or that he just fell from the balcony."

Bryan looked confused, not quite able to grasp Jack's train of thought. "But, then what do you—"

"I think somebody killed Kid."

"For real? Are you sure?"

"For real," Jack said. "And I'm pretty sure."

"Have you told the police?"

Jack nodded.

Bryan was excited. "And what'd they say?"

"They didn't believe me. Or care."

"Typical," Bryan said. "They're stupid. It's just easier for them that way."

"I've been doing some checking on my own. Some things just don't add up. You told me he hassled you when you were taking steroids."

"That's for sure. He *hated* drugs. Kid wouldn't even smoke a joint."

"Did you know they found LSD in his blood?"

Bryan practically exploded in the booth. "That's bullshit," he said. "That's gotta be *total* bullshit!"

"That's what I think, too. But there's more. The night he died, there was a woman in his apartment with him. Right before . . . right before it happened."

"Okay, well, *that* sounds like Kid, I gotta admit. He was pretty much of a hound."

"Did he ever talk to you about his team?"

"The women, you mean? His girlfriends?" When Jack nodded, Bryan shrugged. "Sometimes. Not all that much. You know, normal stuff."

"Did you meet any of them?"

"Why are you asking about his girls?"

"Because I think that one of the members of his team was with him the night he died. And I think whoever it was killed him."

"Holy shit!"

"Yeah," Jack said. "I agree. So do you know any of them?"

"I might have met one or two," Bryan said slowly. "Seen 'em at clubs or something. But—"

"Do you know any of their names?"

Now Bryan hesitated. Then he said, "He had these weird nicknames, you know. That's mostly what he called them."

"I know," Jack told him. And then he gave Bryan as complete a rundown as he could. He told him about the Mortician, how he'd found her, who she really was. Bryan's eyes widened when he learned her real identity. They widened even more when he found out she'd been paying for Kid's apartment.

"I knew somebody was footin' the bill," he said. "But Kid was pretty tight about that. He didn't talk about it much. I think he might've been a little ashamed, you know, letting a woman pay for him."

Jack ran down the other nicknames. At each mention— the Entertainer, Samsonite, the Murderess, the Mistake—Bryan shook his head.

"The Destination?" Jack asked. "Did he ever mention her?"

"Yeah." His eyebrows came together and his shoulders rose. "Her I heard of. The Destination. Yeah. She was like his dream girl or somethin', right?" His shoulders fell back down slightly. "That was Kid," he said sadly. "Always dreamin'."

"So you don't know any of the others?"

"I'm sorry, Mr. Keller. I might've heard about 'em but I just don't remember. I can't believe you found one. That's pretty amazing."

"How about Kim?" Jack asked. "I overheard him on the phone once; he said that he worked with someone named Kim, at the Saddle."

"Sure," Bryan nodded. "The Golden Saddle. In Chelsea. Kid used to fill in there sometimes when he really needed money."

"Do you know Kim?"

"No. But I think they went to school together. Hunter. For the MBA. You gonna go to the Saddle?" Bryan asked.

"I guess so. Are they open late?"

"Yeah. Probably till two or somethin' like that. Maybe even later."

"Pretty late for a gym."

"A gym?" Bryan laughed. "It's a club, Mr. Keller. Believe me, the Saddle ain't no gym. You know, if you wanna wait till tomorrow, I can go with you. I just can't do it tonight."

"It's all right. But I appreciate the offer. And I'll tell you what—why don't we start the workouts day after tomorrow? Since I'll be out clubbing tonight, give me a day's rest and then we'll get goin'."

"You got it," Bryan said.

Jack paid the check and they stood to leave. As Jack was just about to ease his way out from behind the table, Bryan put his hand on Jack's shoulder.

"Mr. Keller . . ." he said. "Kid knew some pretty strange people. You be careful, okay? And if you need anything, someone to watch your back, you call me." He hesitated, as if afraid to say something that might sound like bragging, but then he said, rather wistfully, "I blocked for him. I can block for you. It's what I'm good at."

Jack nodded and smiled his thanks. "Day after tomorrow," he said. "The new torture begins."

T he Golden Saddle was on Twenty-third Street and
Eleventh Avenue. It was easy to spot by the crowd of
leather-clad, body-pierced, tattooed customers streaming in.

It was nine-thirty later that night and Jack stood outside,
looking up at the small red neon sign that flashed the club's
name.

"Bryan was right," Dom growled. "This definitely ain't no
gym. And I'll tell you somethin' else, Jackie. The people are
so fuckin' weird, I'm gonna fit right in."

"Let's stop talking and do it," Jack said. "We'll find Kim,
talk to her for a few minutes, then we'll leave. I called and
they said she was working."

"You really think I'm goin' in there?" Dom asked.

"I bought you dinner, didn't I? A deal's a deal."

"Nothin' but grief," Dom said. Then they paid their ten-
dollar cover charge and went inside.

They found themselves in a rowdy country-western bar,
dimly lit, so loud it was almost impossible to talk. There
were tables scattered around and two bars, one at either end
of the room. One of the bars had a platform extending from
it, as if there would be some live entertainment. A waiter led
them to a table after Jack slipped him ten bucks and they sat

and ordered beer. It took a minute, Jack was waiting for it, and then Dom said, "You notice somethin' a little strange about this place?"

Jack nodded. Then he started to laugh.

"There's no fuckin' women in here," Dom said.

As strange as Jack found it, too, he couldn't help it, the laughter just burst out of him. He couldn't imagine what Kid had been doing in this place, there was something vaguely disturbing about it, and he was not all that comfortable, he had to admit, but in his entire life he had never seen an expression on anyone's face like the one on Dom's right now. Jack hadn't been expecting this, that's for sure. He was probably just as shocked as Dom, he just didn't show it, but here they were, so they might as well finish what they came to do. He tried to explain to Dom, to say the words "We're in a gay bar," but the music came up and it was too loud, there was no way to hear or to talk. And then, over a loudspeaker system, a DJ's voice boomed out:

"Ladies and gentlemen . . . and there *are* a few gentlemen here, aren't there? . . ."

The crowd whooped and hollered loudly in response.

". . . the Golden Saddle is proud to present, direct from Texas . . . where everything is *soooo biiiigggg . . .*"

The crowd screamed its delight now.

". . . the lovely, the sensuous, the provocative . . . Kim!!!!"

The lights went down in the room and the spotlight came up on the stage protruding from the bar. By now, Jack wasn't too surprised—he should have expected it, he realized that—but still just a little stunned at his surroundings.

There was no denying it. The sexy stripper dressed in full cowboy regalia—boots, chaps, vest, and gun belt with two pistols—was the person they were looking for. This was Kim.

And Kim was not a woman.

THE ACT LASTED about ten minutes. Kim pranced and kicked and ultimately stripped down to the gun belt to the pounding of loud rock and roll. Every so often, Jack would glance over at Dom, just to make sure the old man wasn't having a heart attack. When Kim was finished dancing, Jack stood up, stepped into the crowd to find their waiter, whispered something in his ear, and then a few minutes after that, Kim was sitting at their table, the Western outfit back in place.

Jack did his best to explain what they were doing there, what they were looking for. Kim seemed to accept their explanation without needing to know many more details. They learned that Kid and Kim were, in fact, in the same MBA graduate program and that Kim also did some personal training. He said he was less weight-oriented than Kid, that he specialized more in stretching and yoga. At some point, he glanced at Dom, then said to Jack, "Your friend looks like he's in kind of a state of shock." Kim's thick Brooklyn accent was a bit jarring, it didn't exactly go with the cowboy outfit, but Jack figured that his outfit—and his home state—probably changed every night, depending on the club manager's whim.

"Well," Jack told him, "Kid never told us that he did this."

"He hadn't done it for a while. And never all that often. Just when he really needed money. It ain't a bad little living. A hunnert a night plus tips and the tips add up. Especially with Kid. That boy had a body to die for and he could shake his ass." He smiled sweetly at Dom.

"I'm trying to find some of Kid's clients," Jack said now. "The people he used to train."

"Can't help you there. We don't share names in this business. Too cutthroat. You wouldn't believe how many so-called friends of mine try to steal my customers." His lips took on a quick pout. "Not to mention other things."

"How about some of the women he went out with? There was one he called the Entertainer. She's a dancer—" Jack stopped suddenly. "Wait a second—was that *you?*"

"Don't I wish," Kim said. "But that's a big no, no, no. Kid was as straight as they come. This was just a job for him. Lotta straight guys, the bodybuilders, do it 'cause it's safe— it's a lotta lookin' but no touching. But you know what? I think I know who youse mean. This Entertainer. Kid used to leave here and go to another club"—he looked at Dom again—"one your friend will appreciate a little bit more. It's called Lace. Over on the East Side. Kid used to hang out there a lot. I got the feeling he went through a lot of dancers, but there was one girl in particular he used to talk about. She sounded *amazing.* He almost had *me* interested."

"Did he tell you anything specific about her? Anything you remember that'll help me find her?"

Kim made a clicking noise with his tongue, trying to remember something. "Oh, God . . . what did he tell me about her? Something weird. She was from someplace totally outrageous. . . . Ohio! That's what it was. Can you imagine coming from *Ohio?* Anyway, I don't know her name but she's a dancer there. At Lace. And maybe she won't be so hard to find 'cause Kid always said she was to die for. Oh. Sorry. Maybe that's a bad choice of words."

"You think she'd be working tonight?"

"Friday? All the good ones work on the weekends, honey. She'll be there."

"Thanks," Jack said. "I really appreciate it." He pulled some money out of his pocket and tried to hand it to Kim.

"No, no," the stripper said. "You're friends of Kid. No money, please." He smiled. "Use it to buy the old guy some oxygen."

Before Dom could say anything, Kim stood and slithered away.

"Now can we go?" Dom asked, draining his second beer. It was the first thing he'd said in forty-five minutes.

"Yeah," Jack told him. "Now we can go."

"You know," Dom said as they were almost out the door. "I gotta admit that guy had a pretty fuckin' good ass. And that's the last thing I'm ever gonna say about it."

LACE WAS JUST a block north of the Golden Saddle, on Twenty-fourth Street, but it was all the way across town, between Park and Broadway. They took a cab.

There was a bouncer wearing an ill-fitting tuxedo outside the door, talking to a doorman who wore a similar tuxedo that had a slightly better fit. The front of the club was a bit more subdued than the Saddle. No neon. And the customers stepping inside as Jack and Dom's cab pulled up were wearing suits and ties. The cover charge this time was twenty dollars apiece, which Jack paid. Then they stepped through a curtain, into a kaleidoscope of flashing lights and bare flesh—and into a fantasy world that Jack did not have any idea existed.

They were in an enormous, elegant nightclub. There were four small stages in different corners of the room and chairs were set up around each of the stages. Chairs were also set up on either side of one long runway that crossed the length of the room. Poles came down from the ceiling every ten feet or so, reaching the runway floor. There were booths built into some of the walls and more chairs and small round tables in the center of the floor. Music was blaring, popular rock songs that all seemed slightly out of date—a Madonna hit that had come and gone, then something from the Stones' disco era. On each of the four stages, a different woman, nude except for a G-string, danced and gyrated and shook. The men who had seats on the edge of the stage would reach up and slip bills into the G-strings. In exchange for that, they would get a very large pair of tits or an incredibly firm ass waved very close to their faces.

At most of the tables and booths, women were table dancing. Their clothes would slip off and they would dance around their chosen transfixed customer. The men would sit very still and stiff; the women would straddle them in their chairs, run their hands slowly through their hair, thrust their perfect body parts close and then closer. Their lips would pout and their legs and hips would twitch back and forth. Sometimes, when the dance was over, they would sit on a customer's lap, their arms wrapped around his neck, their breasts poking against his shirt or jacket. Every so often, a man's hand would start to reach or caress and a muscle-bound, tuxedo-clad bouncer would instantly appear.

"Christ," Dom said. "There's enough silicone in this place to raise the *Titanic*. You're never gonna find her."

"I'm sure as hell going to try. You game?"

"What the hell, why not? I ain't done nothin' like this in years."

"Dom," Jack said. "You ain't done nothin' like this *ever*."

"Hey," Dom snapped. "Try to leave me with some dignity, will ya?"

They wandered around a bit, through the maze of stages and tables. There was a room marked "Private Club." Jack asked about it and a waitress said that it cost a hundred dollars to go in there. They served champagne and there was more privacy. There was also another room that they stepped into. This room had tables and chairs but no stages. More romantic music was playing in here, and here you were allowed to slow-dance. As Jack looked, there were five couples on the dance floor. Each man was clothed, each woman naked except for a G-string and high-heeled shoes.

They walked out into the main room and Jack looked around. There were at least fifty, maybe seventy-five dancers and three or four times that many customers. Most of the audience were businessmen, many in their thirties and forties. Some were older. There was a decent percentage who were younger, in their late twenties. Quite a few of the men were Japanese. Some blacks but not many. There weren't many women customers but there were a few. All were with dates. Jack saw two who looked extremely uncomfortable and three who were enjoying themselves immensely. One woman not far from where they were standing had two dancers spinning tantalizingly over and around her while her husband or boyfriend watched. The woman was ecstatic; she couldn't take her eyes off the dancers' bodies and because she was a woman, more touching was allowed. Jack saw one of the dancer's breasts brush against the woman's lips and, briefly, he saw the woman's tongue pop out of her mouth.

"So what's your choice?" Dom asked.

"Let's try this room for a while," Jack told him. "And we'll see what happens."

What happened was that a hostess—sexy by normal standards, plain-looking compared with the women who were dancing or strolling and looking for someone to dance for— led them to a table, where they were immediately descended upon. Jack was barely seated before a dancer with close-cropped dark hair, almost in a crew cut, did her best to crawl inside his shirt. Before he knew what to say, she was on his lap, her dress was yanked over her head, and she was grinding herself into his thighs and against his chest. The music blared as she pursed her lips and winked and smiled and teased and ran her nail down his cheek. Jack understood the frozen positions he had seen around the room because he'd assumed the same pose. He didn't know how to sit, didn't know what to do with his hands, so he stayed as motionless as possible and tried to figure out exactly where to look. When the music stopped for a moment, the dance was over—it had lasted maybe three minutes—and the dancer placed her perfect leg up on Jack's chair in her best Sally Bowles impersonation, nudging her toes under his thigh. She lifted up the garter belt and said, "The minimum's twenty."

Jack slid a bill onto her thigh and the belt snapped tightly down on it.

"Would you like another dance? I'm just warming up," she purred.

Jack, feeling a little idiotic, said, "You're not from Ohio, are you?"

The dark-haired beauty smiled as the music started back up and said, "I *can* be if you want me to."

He shook his head, so she shrugged and sauntered off to a nearby table. Within moments, her dress was off and she was wriggling on someone else's lap.

Jack turned and saw a blonde with enormous breast implants sidling up to Dom.

"I never saw *you* in here," she said, eyeing the stub of his arm.

"Never been here," Dom said, mesmerized by her breasts, which were so stiff they didn't even move when she walked. "Where you from?" he asked her.

"Me?" the blonde said. "Nowhere." She waved her hand around the club. "I was *born* here. Right in this little room."

At midnight, after countless questions and even more twenty-dollar bills being passed around, Dom announced that he was leaving.

"I'm tired," he said. "I don't think nothin's gonna come of this, and my dick's had just about all the excitement it can take for the night. I'm gonna go home, sit in a hot bath, and wonder what kind of fuckin' world we're livin' in."

"I'm staying," Jack said.

"I didn't expect nothin' different, Jackie." Dom started to say something else, changed his mind, and walked out the front door.

Jack turned back in the direction of the runway stage. A young black woman had her legs wrapped around one of the poles and was lifting herself off the ground without using her hands. Two Japanese gentlemen sitting nearby applauded as if the curtain had just come down on *Swan Lake*. Jack raised his hand, signaling for the waitress. He needed another beer.

The rest of the night dragged on in much the same manner. By 1 A.M. the flesh had become boring. Women who'd once seemed perfect and exciting now seemed only identical to others standing right next to them. Jack had been in the private room, where, the hostess was right, there *was* champagne, but it was more like ginger ale and it cost a hundred dollars a bottle. There was more privacy in there and perhaps a bit more physical contact, but the women were the same, they just rotated in and out of the various rooms. He'd also been in the slow-dance room again but declined several offers to hit the dance floor. By 1:30, Jack figured he'd spoken to forty women. He had passed out a small fortune in twenty-dollar bills and had asked the same questions over and over again: *Are you from Ohio? No. Do you know Kid Demeter? No. Do you know anyone who knows Kid Demeter?*

No.

He was leaning up against the bar, nursing one final beer. The music was still pounding, the dancers were as mechanical and energetic as when he'd first walked in the door. And the place was nearly as crowded as it had been three hours earlier. But he'd had it. He put his half-filled glass of beer down on the bar, turned to head out. There was a dancer blocking his way.

"You look bushed," she said.

He nodded and smiled. She was lovely, this one, vaguely Latin-looking. In a flimsy gold-lamé dress that barely came down to the tops of her thighs. The top of the dress was unbuttoned, revealing small but firm breasts—My God! he thought. Could they be real? A miracle in this place!—and her smile was a little bit crooked. It somehow seemed more genuine than most of the ones that had glistened at him all night long. She looked at him curiously, as if analyzing him, or just simply filing away his mental image for future use.

"You want a pick-me-up dance?" she asked. "Better than vitamins."

"You're not from Ohio by any chance, are you?" he asked wearily.

"Newark," she told him.

Jack rolled his eyes upward, not that he was expecting any divine intervention in this place, and then threw his hands up, a defeated gesture.

"Good night," he apologized to the dancer. "I'm outta here."

As he started to brush past her, she stuck her hip out, annoyed. "Hey! I thought you wanted a girl from Ohio. Aren't you the one who's been asking everybody?"

"You said Newark," Jack said.

"Yeah," the Entertainer said back. "Newark, Ohio."

HER NAME WAS Leslee, she told him. That was her real name. She wasn't going to bullshit a friend of Kid's. Leslee Cesar. Her club name was Gwyneth. They liked to have the girls use actressy names and she was a big fan of Gwyneth Paltrow's, thought she was really and truly classy. She was an actress, too, she said. Well, she hadn't been working much lately. It was so hard. And dancing here was so easy. She made so much money, on a good night fifteen hundred, maybe two thousand, sometimes it didn't seem worth it, the whole acting thing. . . .

He told her he was interested in talking to her about Kid's death and he saw her eyes narrow just a bit, then return to normal. She was happy to talk to him, she said. But she couldn't just stop work. She could sit with him, but he'd have to pay her. Otherwise the management would get on her case. She might have to sit on his lap every so often; it made her look like she was working harder to take his money.

They went to a table and the waitress came over. "Just bring me a mineral water," she said. And to Jack: "They rip you off totally if you buy liquor for the girls."

Jack said he'd also have mineral water and the waitress went scurrying away.

He didn't have to prod Leslee. She was anxious to talk, both about Kid and herself. He settled back into his chair, his eyes half closed, and she pulled her chair close to him so he could hear her easily over the music. Occasionally she would shift positions, swing her legs over his, wrapping herself around him as if they were longtime lovers sitting on a couch watching television. Once, in the middle of the conversation, with no prompting, she slid out of her dress, danced a few circles around him, her breasts brushing the top of his head, and then she sat back down. But she didn't put her dress back on for another ten minutes or so, content to sit there topless while she chattered. Periodically he would pass money over to her and she would smile, which made her whole face look off center, as if the two sides didn't quite match up, and he realized the pull this young girl had, knew she fit on Kid's team not because she was the best-looking dancer in the club or the flashiest—she looked disinterested almost, as if she didn't need to be there doing any of this—but Jack was willing to bet that she made more money than anyone else when she was working. She had the look. And the feel. It was the same sensation he'd had sitting in the backseat of the limo with the Mortician. This dancer was a different breed as well. A breed Jack didn't yet understand but found himself being inextricably drawn to.

"A lot of the dancers'll tell you a similar story," she was saying. "My ex-boyfriend got me into it. He used to go to a lot of lap-dancing places, this was in Philadelphia, and I used to get jealous 'cause I'd ask him why he'd go and he'd say 'cause all the girls were better-looking than I was. Deep down, I always thought I was ugly. Really and truly. And he used to tell me I was, so that didn't help any. Anyway, one night we're out at a club and it turns out to be amateur night. Anyone—any woman—who wants to can get up and take her clothes off and dance. He kept daring me, so I did it. I really did it to show him, I guess, that I could be as sexy as those girls he used to give money to, to dance for him. I mean, he had me for free so I never understood why he'd want to pay just for a dance. Anyway, I did pretty well. The crowd went wild, to tell you the truth. And I won the contest. Two hundred and fifty dollars. So a few days later, I went into the club he was always hanging out in and I auditioned. They gave me the job immediately, right on the spot." She turned to him now, studying him again. "You know," she said, "you don't look like a cop."

He was surprised; he hadn't realized that's what she'd thought, since she was being so open with him. "I'm not," he said. "I'm just a friend. I run a restaurant. Or used to."

Now she really scrutinized him. And that lopsided smile appeared. This time there was something behind it, though. He wasn't sure what. But there was a certain awareness there this time. And maybe even some kind of a plan. "Oh, wow," she said. "You're the Butcher."

"I'm the Butcher," he admitted.

"And you don't think Kid killed himself."

He shook his head.

"Well, I think you're right," she said. "People like Kid don't kill themselves." And there it was, the grin again. "People like me kill them."

SHE COULD TAKE off at three, she said. And she thought he should come back to her apartment so they could really talk. Jack almost said no, he was tired, another time, but he realized that his adrenaline had kicked in. He wasn't tired, not now. He wanted to keep going. He wanted to find out more about Kid. And, he realized, about her. He also wanted to go back to her apartment.

She told him she'd hop a cab right out front but he had to take a separate one. Management didn't like the girls going home with customers, she explained. And she couldn't make it so obvious, even though this was pretty innocent, "because nothing looks innocent to these assholes." So she gave him her address and told him to leave a few minutes before she did. "Wait outside my building and I'll be there right after you," she said.

In the cab ride back, he realized he was fascinated by her. He wanted to know how she'd become what she was. He remembered Kid's words. She could surprise you with her intelligence, he'd said, and Jack could see that was true. She was hiding her smarts to a certain degree. He felt that even her speech was slightly dumbed down. He wondered why. Maybe because that's what her customers wanted. He also remembered that Kid had defined her as a Slash. So what did she really want to be? Where did she really want to go? And what was she capable of doing to get there?

Jack wound up waiting fifteen minutes for her to arrive. He didn't mind. The night air was warm and he sat on the concrete stoop in front of her apartment. It was a charming brownstone in the East Thirties. A true brownstone, not just a town house. He peered through the glass window in the building's front door. He could see that the first-floor hallway was covered in a thick, wine-colored carpet. It looked like the carpet ran up the stairs. On the hallway wall was a print. He couldn't quite make out what it was but it looked like it was in an expensive frame. It was an expensive neighborhood, he realized.

A cab pulled up and Leslee emerged. She gave a little wave, almost as if she hadn't really expected him to be there. She was wearing jeans and a tank-top shirt now. And white sneakers. At first he thought, She doesn't look like a lap dancer now. She looks like a normal young girl coming from a late date. But as she got closer he realized that wasn't true. Even now there was something about her. There was a bursting sensuality that jeans and sneakers couldn't remotely disguise.

"Sorry it took me so long," she said. "A few guys I'd danced for wanted my phone number. Well, they wanted *Gwyneth's* phone number. It's a lot easier to talk to them than to just brush them off. This way they don't get angry."

"Do you give them your number?"

"Oh, sure. Well," she smiled. "I give them Gwyneth's number. It's the number of the movie theater on Second and Thirty-fourth."

On the short climb up, she explained that it was an owner-occupied building. The owner lived on the first floor, that's why the whole building was so well kept. Leslee's apartment was on the third floor. It *was* the third floor. And it was a beautiful place. The scale was small and intimate and there was nothing remotely flashy about it. The floors were dark and wide-planked. Where she needed carpeting, she'd found subdued Oriental rugs. There was not a lot of furniture but where he was expecting chrome and sleek, modern things, she had delicate antiques. Small wooden chairs with hand-stitched seats, two matching gray sofas facing each other in the living room. The living room walls were lined with bookshelves and the shelves were filled with books. There were two or three tiger-maple end tables, and small lamps, which gave off just enough light, sat on them.

"Look around," she said. "I've *got* to take a shower. I'll be right out."

She was already yanking off her shirt as she headed into the bathroom—he got a glimpse of her bare back and a side view of her breasts—then she was gone and the door was closed behind her. In seconds he heard the shower running and he even thought he heard a momentary sigh of satisfaction.

He began exploring the apartment. Her books were *books*. No Danielle Steel or John Gray for this dancer. She had a lot of Freud and Jung and various writers' studies and analyses of both. He was amazed at what she had on her shelves and he wondered if she'd read it all. There were several rows filled with English novels: Swift and Defoe and Jane Austen and the Brontës. She had all of D. H. Lawrence and John Fowles, two copies of *The Magus*. There were a lot of contemporary novels Jack had never heard of and a lot of female writers he had heard of but had never read: Doris Lessing, Margaret Atwood, Eudora Welty, Kaye Gibbons. There was a well-worn paperback of *Cold Mountain*. Balancing those were a lot of thrillers, some by women, Patricia Cornwell and Sara Paretsky, but mostly by men: Parker and Connelly and Bloch. She seemed to be fairly compulsive. If she read someone, she read *all* of someone.

He peeked into her bedroom. It was totally different from the rest of the apartment. While the entryway and living room were impeccably decorated, fairly sparse and subdued, her room looked as if it belonged to a little girl. It was all fluff and lace and there were stuffed animals everywhere. The colors were bright—yellows and pinks—and didn't go at all with the colors in the other rooms. On her unmade bed he noticed that there was a rumpled pair of pajamas, lying there as if she'd kicked them off when she awoke and left them where they fell. They did not look like the sleepwear of a hardened lap dancer. They looked like they were last worn by a twelve-year-old.

The second bedroom, quite small, space for just a twin bed and a desk and chair, was more like the rest of the apartment. Conservative. Adult. He noticed that there were stacks of books in this room, too.

The water was still running—she'd been in there for a long time now, close to fifteen minutes. He went into the kitchen, where there wasn't much to see. Her refrigerator had a few bottles of white wine, a jar of peanut butter, half a roasted chicken that she'd bought already cooked, and not much else. It did not look like she spent much time in the kitchen.

It was another five minutes before the shower stopped. And it was five minutes after that before she emerged. One long white towel was wrapped around her body, long enough to go from her chest to just above her knees. Another, smaller towel was wrapped, turban style, around the top of her head.

"I'm sorry I took so long," she said. "I just have to get that place off of me as soon as I get home. I'm compulsive about it and I'm sure there are fairly obvious psychological reasons for it, but I don't really care. I stay in there and just scald myself until the hot water starts to go. Sometimes if I take a bath, I can stay in there two or three hours. Now, I'll be with you in a minute. Really and truly a minute."

This time she was as good as her word. When she came out of her bedroom, she was wearing a black lightweight skirt and a black T-shirt. No shoes or socks. Her hair was brushed but still wet. He thought she looked exquisite. Very young and very fresh and very, very desirable.

"I know what you're thinking," she said as they sat in the living room sipping the white wine she'd brought out. And for a moment he felt guilty. But then she finished: "My apartment surprised you."

"A little."

"Well, most of the girls at the club really are what you think they are. Most of them are fairly shallow and not all that bright. They all tell you that they don't do drugs and that they don't sleep with the customers for money. But most of them do. Or if they don't yet, they will."

"But not you."

"For most of them, this is it. This is their career. They'll make a bunch of money and hopefully they'll meet a guy and then they'll quit. Or else they'll keep doing this until they're way too old. For me this is a means to an end."

"What's the end?"

"Money. Other than that I'm not so sure. I thought actress for a while. But I'm starting to think I don't have what it takes. But that's all right. I'm in school now. Hofstra. Psych major. I graduate in one year."

"So you're twenty-one?"

"Twenty."

"How old were you when you started dancing?"

"Sixteen. But I looked eighteen and they didn't check. Now I'm twenty and I look sixteen and everybody checks."

"Doesn't it worry you?" he asked, surprised that he wanted to talk about her personal life. "That you might start doing what the other girls do?"

"Sure," she said. "I'd be dumb not to worry about it. I can feel it happening, too. It's weird, but what can you do? I try to keep some perspective but it's hard."

"I can imagine."

"Can you?"

"No," he said. "Maybe not."

"You mind if I make myself a sandwich? I'm starving." She jumped up, disappeared back into the kitchen, and returned a minute later with a peanut butter and jelly sandwich on a small plate. "You want one?" she asked. "Sorry, I didn't mean to be rude."

"No. Go ahead."

He watched her eat and he could see his list, the list he'd made about Kid, in a vision right in front of his eyes. *The Entertainer*, it said. *Eats with her mouth open*. And there she was, chewing away, that lopsided mouth open just a crack too much while she ate.

"A few weeks ago, I was at a party," she said when she was two thirds of the way through her sandwich. "A real party. Kids. College friends. None of them has any idea what I do."

"None of them?"

"Nope," she said. "It's not the kind of thing you can just drop into a conversation. Anyway, it was very weird. I was having a perfectly good time. It was a little dull, you know, like they thought smoking dope and drinking was as cool as it gets, but it was fine. And a couple of the guys were really hitting on me. Talking to me, trying to get me to go out with them; one of them invited me to see Beck at the Meadowlands. And that night I got a little scared because the whole time they were talking to me I kept thinking, this isn't right, they should be *paying* me to talk to them. I get twenty bucks every five or ten minutes, minimum, just to talk. That's weird, huh, that I thought that?"

"Not so weird," he said. "But you're right. Scary."

"I'll tell you something else weird. Last year my mother had a stroke."

"I'm sorry."

"Well, it wasn't so terrible. I mean, it was a stroke but she was okay. She needed some rehab, though, really could have used a private nurse or something to help her, but she couldn't afford it. Well, *I* could afford it. Easy. Only I couldn't give her the money 'cause she doesn't know what I do, either. She thinks I'm a waitress, and how the hell would a college-girl waitress have an extra ten thousand dollars for a private nurse?"

"So what'd you do?"

"Nothing. I kept quiet. Let her fend for herself. And before you say, 'Oh, that's so sad,' and 'Why do you do it?' it really isn't so sad. My mom's a lunatic and a serious bitch, and I do it because I'm twenty years old and I can afford to rent this apartment and I've got over seventy-five thousand dollars in mutual funds and in five years I think I'll have ten times that." She finished the sandwich now, chomping down on the last sticky corner. "You can read the rest in my auto-biography. Which I'm going to write one of these days. What do you want to know about Kid?"

She had brought him back around to the reason he was here and suddenly he wasn't all that sure what he wanted to know. It was distracting, listening to her chatter away. He was tired. And now one of her bare legs was curled up under the other and he could barely turn away from looking at it.

"Just tell me about him," he said, trying to focus. "I thought I knew him like he was my own son. Now I'm not so sure."

"He could be a real son of a bitch sometimes. Did you know that?"

"I never really experienced it. But I suppose I could see it in him."

"Not at heart, though. At heart he wasn't a son of a bitch at all." She took a sip of wine and rubbed her tongue around her mouth. She still had bits of peanut butter stuck up in there somewhere. "I cared about him. Really and truly. In my own way. I knew he was seeing other women, too—he never lied, which I liked. But that was Kid. He was a taker. He took me, I have to say. I loaned the bastard five thousand dollars right before he died. Never paid me back a nickel."

"Did he tell you what the money was for?" Jack asked, surprised.

"He said it was for tuition. That they wouldn't let him graduate unless he paid up. But I didn't believe him. It just sounded like he really needed the money."

"Did he say how he was going to pay you back?"

"Sure." She grinned. "He said he was gonna get the money from you." She poured herself a bit more wine, still working her tongue around her gums. "You know what Kid liked best?" she asked now.

Jack shook his head. Her voice had changed just a little. It was subtle but seductive and he felt the small hairs on the back of his neck start to tingle.

"He liked me to dance for him. Here in this apartment. A private dance."

Jack knew he looked awkward. He wasn't comfortable suddenly and it showed. But Leslee grinned again, as if she was enjoying his discomfort.

"You're rich," she said. "You're really rich."

He didn't say anything. She was grinning like crazy now. She stood up and went to her CD player. Put on a CD, R.E.M., *Automatic For The People,* not too loud. Michael Stipe's melancholy voice seemed to echo through the apartment.

"You want me to dance for you?" she asked. He realized she was very close to him. She had managed to slide over on the couch so she was less than a foot away. "You want to have a little private dance, just you and me?"

Jack shook his head. "No. I don't think so."

"Are you shy?"

"No."

"Are you married?"

Jack closed his eyes. Left them shut for what felt like a long time. "I *feel* married," he said.

"Most men feel married," Leslee told him. "I make them feel *un*married."

She was right next to him now. One leg curled over his and she was on his lap, facing him, her mouth maybe an inch from his. She was barely moving but he could feel her grinding herself into his crotch. And he could see her nipples jutting toward him from under her shirt.

"I think I'd better go," he managed to say.

She didn't make any move to get off him. Just kept smiling and for the first time he noticed that the smile could also make her look unattractive. It wasn't just charming. There was something off-putting about it. Something even kind of crazy.

"I could *make* you stay," she whispered. "I really and truly could. If I wanted. Do you believe me?"

He didn't answer. Because he didn't know the answer. He didn't know *what* to believe at this exact moment.

"I know what you're thinking," she went on. "First you thought no, she can't make me do anything. Now you're thinking maybe. Maybe she can because she's so sexy I can hardly breathe. But there are no 'maybes' about it. Ain't no 'maybe,' baby." As she whispered to him, she reached over, not far, to her small beaded purse. She reached inside, pulled something out, and Jack heard a sudden click. Then he saw the long, thin blade that she held in her hand. He didn't move.

"If I wanted, I could cut your throat and when the police got here, I could just tell them you tried to rape me." As she spoke, he could feel her warm breath on his face, on his lips and his cheek. "I'd get away with it. Really. Really and truly."

He saw her take a deep breath, watched her chest heave. She reached down, put one hand on his thigh, the hand with the switchblade, and he could feel himself hold his own breath now, but then she pushed herself off him. Quickly, with a gymnast's agility, her legs were no longer wrapped around him, she was no longer touching him at all. When she was standing, she folded the blade up, put it back in her purse.

"Maybe you should go," she told him.

He nodded. Keeping his eyes on her, he backed up slowly until he reached her front door. His hand groped for the knob, found it and turned it. Then he was out in the carpeted hallway.

He didn't let himself think of anything until he was down on the street. And then life seemed to come streaming back into him.

And that made two, is what he thought.

Two women who could easily have pushed Kid off the balcony and ended his life.

Without ever thinking about it again.

WHY IN THE world did she do that, she wondered?

Why do I get this overpowering urge to hurt men?

Oh, you know why, she thought. Of course you know why. But it's no excuse. Everyone's had something bad happen to them. Everyone's been abused.

She liked him. He was nice.

Really and truly nice.

But she'd gone and done it again.

And now she'd never get her five thousand dollars back.

THIRTY-NINE

"I think it's time to call it off, Jackie."

"Call what off?"

"The whole thing," Dom said. "It's gettin' too weird. Mobsters' wives, guys dressed up as cowboys dancin' around on stage, naked women with knives. I think it's time to stop."

"Can I tell you something, Dom? I mean, something you're not going to want to hear."

The older man looked at his younger friend, the friend he thought of as a son, and said, "There's nothin' you could ever tell me, Jackie, that I don't wanna hear."

"I had one affair when I was married to Caroline. One. That's it. It was a long time ago, eight, ten years ago. When we were opening up the Jack's in London. I was spending a lot of time over there, a decent amount of time by myself. And . . . I was out one night with a bunch of restaurant people. We were trying a new hot place. Somebody, one of the chefs, brought a friend along. Emma. And Emma was extremely attractive, funny, young—very young—she was great, so we had a fling. Very intense. Incredibly passionate."

"One night?"

"Five. Five amazing nights. Three in a row, then not, then

neither one of us could stand it anymore so we saw each other the next night and the next. Then I never saw her again."

"Why not?"

"Dom, you can't imagine how exciting she was. There was something about her, she just sucked you right in. But I decided I couldn't get sucked in any further than I was. The thing is, I loved my wife. Not only that, we were happy. And still passionate. We weren't having any problems at all and I thought she was as perfect as a woman could be."

"But you still went ahead with this other woman."

"That's right."

"Did she know?"

Jack had to smile. Even now, even in death, Caroline was "she" to Dom. "I don't know," he said. "Yes, I think she did. I'm sure she did. Part of it was that she seemed to know everything about me. You ever see that *Taxi* where Latka sleeps with a woman to save his life, so he doesn't freeze to death, and he walks in the door and what's-her-name, Carol Kane, looks at him and just screams, 'You did it with another woman!' Caroline was like that. And part of it . . . When I came back from London, things were different. She'd lost a baby and . . ." Jack shook his head, trying to bring the memory back into focus. "But if she knew, she never said anything. Ultimately I think she knew why I did it and why I stopped it, and it was okay with her."

"So let's hear it. If everything was so perfect, why?"

"Because I couldn't stop it. Not without hating myself.

And maybe even hating Caroline a little. And if I couldn't stop it, it had to be right."

"And then you *could* stop it."

"That's right."

"And you can't stop this thing now, this thing you're doin', is that your whole point?"

"You're not so dumb, are you?"

"There's somethin' else you're not tellin' me, though. Somethin' else is going through that stubborn little brain o' yours."

"The other day I thought of Emma. I don't think she's even flashed through my brain in five years, maybe longer, not the way she did this time, anyway." Jack looked out through the large sliding doors of the meatpacking plant. Saw that the sun was starting to fade in the sky and realized he should get home. "The thing is, I haven't made love to anyone since Caroline died. Have hardly thought about it, to be perfectly honest."

"And now you're thinkin' about it."

"I need something to make me feel alive right now, Dom. Otherwise I'd be wasting the fact that I'm the one who survived. The more I move into Kid's world, the more alive I feel."

"One thing, Jackie. Then I'll let you go. I used to think I had kind of a rough deal in life. Never felt sorry for myself, not my style, but I wouldn't say I had it easy. But in a way I did. In a way I had it a lot easier than you. I found my ghosts. I found 'em and I fuckin' got rid of 'em. Not the way everybody else would've, maybe, but I got rid of 'em. You got your own ghosts now, son, but I don't know how the hell you're gonna find yours. And if you do, I don't think they're the kind you can get rid of so easily."

THE NEXT MORNING at 8 o'clock, Micah the doorman buzzed Jack to say that Bryan was in the lobby, could he come up? Jack said he most definitely could.

As Bryan stepped out of the elevator, his eyes bulged a little bit. "Wow," he said. "Not too shabby, Mr. Keller."

Jack had already given up on trying to get Bryan to call him Jack, so he just smiled and said, "Thanks." He ushered Bryan to the terrace, where the equipment was set up. "Wow" was all the trainer could manage again.

The workout was fine. Jack was stiff and sore—not unexpected since he hadn't really pushed himself since Kid's death. Bryan was firm but gentle and he knew what he was doing. It only took Jack a few minutes to relax and trust him. At the end of the session, Jack realized that Bryan had been right. He wasn't Kid, didn't have that special quality, that intangible inspirational skill that Kid had, but Bryan was good. Very good. Jack was more than satisfied and told him so.

As soon as he paid Bryan the compliment, Bryan got a slightly pained expression on his face. He did not do well with compliments and changed the subject immediately.

"How'd it go at the Saddle?" he asked. "You find Kim?"

"I found him," Jack said. "And I also found the Entertainer."

Bryan looked stunned. "Come on," he said. "How'd you do that?"

So Jack told him, even the part about going to her apartment and having her draw the knife, and Bryan shook his head admiringly. "You're like a regular Columbo," he said. "So what now?"

"I don't know, exactly," Jack admitted. "Try to find the next one, I guess. Or see if I can find out anything more about Leslee. The Entertainer."

"You think she might have killed Kid?"

"I don't know. I think she's certainly capable of it."

"Wow. I wonder if I know who she is," Bryan said. "I used to go to a couple of those clubs with Kid. And I think I know which one you mean. Goddamn, I just never figured out, when you said 'the Entertainer,' that it would be one of those girls." He looked at his watch and frowned. "I gotta go. Workin' at Hanson's today. But like I said before, Mr. Keller, I'd really like to help. So if you need me, just call." And as he waited for the elevator he looked at Jack again and again, shook his head, saying, "I think I'm gonna have to call you Columbo from now on."

AT FOUR IN the afternoon, Jack's phone rang. When he picked it up, after the third ring, he heard a woman's voice say, "Hi." He was surprised that he immediately recognized the voice, but he definitely did. He didn't respond. Just held the receiver up to his ear.

"It's Leslee," the voice said now. And with a little giggle: "The Entertainer."

"What do you want?" Jack asked.

"Look," she said, "I know what I did was incredibly

stupid. I don't know what happened and I'm really and truly sorry."

"How'd you get my number?" he asked.

"I'm a great detective, too," she said. "You're listed." And after a pause: "I know you're not going to want to do this, but I'd like you to come over to my apartment tonight. I don't have to work. I can make you dinner. Well, actually I can't, I'm the world's worst cook unless you like frijoles, but I can order in Chinese food. My treat."

"Why?" he said.

"Because after you left, I started thinking. I remembered a few things about Kid. Stuff I heard, stuff he said."

"Like what?"

"There's just some weird stuff that you might find helpful. I'm not sure what any of it means but I'd rather tell you in person." When he didn't say anything, she added, "I'll tell you what. I'll wear something really unsexy and won't play any music and won't drink. And I'll leave my little knife outside my door so you can see it when you come up. What more could you want?"

What more could I want? he thought. But what he said was "What time?" And when she told him eight o'clock he also said, "And *I'll* bring the Chinese food."

SHE DIDN'T ANSWER the buzzer at first and Jack's immediate reaction was to get annoyed as hell because he thought she wasn't home, that he was wasting his time. He gave a yank on the door to the building but, as expected, it was locked. Just for the hell of it, not hoping for much, he pressed the buzzer again, and this time she buzzed back, a very quick one, and Jack pushed the front door to the brownstone open and started up the wine-colored carpeted staircase.

When he got to the third-floor landing, he took two steps toward her front door and saw her switchblade. It was lying on the carpet, on top of a piece of lined yellow legal paper. He picked up the knife, fingered it, held the note a little closer so he could read it. He noticed that at the top right-hand corner the paper was wet. A few drops of water had wrinkled it and blurred one of the lines. All the note said, in very precise handwriting, was *It's open. Come in.*

Jack put one foot inside the apartment, called out, "Hello?" but didn't get a response. He took another step forward, closed the door behind him. "Leslee?" he said. She still didn't answer but then he heard the rush of running bathwater.

In the tub, he thought. She must have rushed out to leave the note and that's how the paper got wet. Then rushed back in. He saw a few drops of water leading back to the bathroom.

He went into the kitchen, put the Chinese food he was carrying on the counter. She had plates and silverware already laid out. And a round platter, a piece of rough-hewn, handmade pottery.

Jack went back out into the living room, walked over to the bathroom door, and knocked once. "I'm hungry," he said but didn't get a reply.

Now he went back into the kitchen, searched for a moment, found a large serving spoon, and began opening the white food containers. Everything was still hot so he began dishing it out onto the large platter. "Time to get out," he called. "It's hot and I'm starving."

He didn't know where she wanted to eat, there was no dining room, so he figured they'd eat in the living room, on the sofas. He carried the platter out and put it on a small, painted-pine trunk that appeared to serve as her coffee table. *Okay,* he thought, *enough's enough.*

Jack walked to the bathroom. Knocked on the door, hard this time, and said, "You're clean enough! Let's eat!" Again, no answer, and now he felt something, heard it, too, and he looked down at his shoes. A stream of water was coming out from under the bathroom door, moving faster even as he stared down at it. It swirled into the entryway, making its way toward the front door. "Leslee?" he said. And then he opened the bathroom door.

Water rushed out now, it was an inch deep on the bathroom floor. The throw rug on the floor was sopping wet. The shower curtain was closed but bunched together and being pulled where it was touching the water. The faucet was on and water was running into the tub, but the tub was full, and the water was pouring over the top, spilling onto the floor, running now along the length of the apartment.

Jack took a deep breath, pulled the shower curtain open.

Leslee was stretched out naked under the water. The back of her head was half in the water, half propped up on the tub's porcelain rim. Her hair was wet and stringy. Her left arm was folded over her stomach. Her right arm was floating by her side. A long syringe was still embedded in the front of her elbow joint. Jack could see the needle, shiny and silvery under the water.

Her mouth was open slightly, giving her face that familiar lopsided appearance. But there was no grin visible. Her eyes were wide open and he thought what he saw in them was pure terror.

He stepped gingerly out of the small bathroom, went into the living room, past the platter of spring rolls and garlic chicken and noodles with sesame sauce and spicy shrimp and scallions. He walked straight to the phone, asked the operator to connect him to the Eighth Precinct, spoke to the sergeant on desk duty, and then was put through to Sergeant Patience McCoy, who was just on her way out, once again, to meet her husband Elmore for dinner.

"I told you you'd better have a good reason for pestering me, Jack," she said.

He told her that he did.

He told her he thought that murder was a pretty good reason.

What was he doing?

Playing policeman? Looking for clues? Talking to Kid's friends? Finding the Team?

He was crazy, Jack Keller was. Trying to find a murderer. What sense did that make? What goddamn sense?

None.

It could have been over. It could have been all over!

Why was he doing this? Why wouldn't he leave it alone?

Why won't he let me be? Why does he still want to ruin my life?

Why why why why why why why?

Trying to prove that Kid was murdered. Trying to find the murderer.

Okay. Let him try. And maybe he won't have to try so hard.

Maybe the murderer will find him. . . .

The first thing Sergeant McCoy did was to tell Jack to call his lawyer. He didn't want to, didn't think it was necessary, but she told him it was and insisted before she hung up.

Jack stood off to the side as first a police team showed up, then McCoy, about half an hour later, then an ambulance, with medics to take Leslee's body away on a stretcher. Jack took them through what had happened step-by-step, told them all that the only thing he'd done since discovering the body was to turn the water off in the bathtub.

The cops took about two hours to go over the apartment. While they did, Jack sat in the living room on one of the couches. No one paid any attention to him. He didn't demand any attention be paid. He just sat quietly and watched them do their job until nine-thirty, when Herb Bloomfield, Jack's lawyer, showed up. He pulled Jack into the bedroom, asked him a few questions—what exactly had happened, what the *hell* was he doing there, what had the police said or not said to him—then the two of them went back into the living room and waited quietly.

It was ten-fifteen when Patience McCoy came over to the couch. She sat down next to Jack; he could feel the cushion sag as her weight was added to his. She didn't say anything to him or to Herb for several seconds. Then she turned to Jack, shook her head, and said, "Is there anything you want to tell me?"

Herb didn't let him speak. He immediately jumped in and started insisting that this could be done the next morning, but Sergeant McCoy just looked wearily at him and said, "I don't think your client is a suspect, Counselor. I think he's a damn fool but I sure as hell don't think he killed this girl. And I don't want to see him tomorrow morning because I don't want to have to think about this by tomorrow morning. I want it to be over now. So give me five minutes and then we can all go home."

That shut Herb up immediately. He nodded, first at McCoy, then at Jack, a signal for him to say whatever he wanted.

Jack met McCoy's glare head-on. "I don't know what you're looking for me to say," he told her.

"I want to know if you've got any reason to think this is anything but a drug overdose. Our take is that she's the sequel to Kid's death. Maybe both were accidental, maybe not, but they both took too many drugs and they both died."

"You're not serious."

"I'm as serious as anyone you're ever going to meet, Jack. We got nothing to show that anyone's been in here but that poor girl—and you."

"Somebody buzzed me into the apartment."

"So you said. But you also said the door to the building was locked."

"It is."

"Uh-uh. The lock's been broken. So you ain't got a lot of credibility right now. Maybe you rang the wrong buzzer; it's possible. We're checking everyone in the building; a few people aren't home right now. Before we go to all that trouble, do you want to change your story?"

Jack was stunned. He knew the door had been locked. He'd tried it. What the hell was happening? Could it have been broken after he'd come up the stairs? And why? What in God's name was going on?

"Why would I lie?" he said to McCoy.

"You tell me," was her response. "You tell me, Jack."

"Thank you very much, Sergeant." Herb stood up now, took Jack's hand, and yanked him to his feet. "My client's said all he's going to say."

McCoy shook her head, held her hands out as if to signal a truce. "I *said* he wasn't a suspect and he's *not* a suspect." Standing now and turning to face Jack, she said, "If you've got any legitimate reason to think this is a murder, tell me now because my boys didn't find a goddamn thing. Pending the lab report, it's going in the book as an accidental OD."

Jack tried to gather his thoughts. Once again, he realized he was stymied. What could he say? The girl was killed by the same person who killed Kid? She was killed by someone who wanted to stop her from talking? She was killed because she knew something that none of them knew and now might never know? No, he couldn't say any of that. Because he had no proof. He knew it was true but he didn't have one shred of logical, irrefutable evidence. All he had was his gut. And his faith in Kid Demeter. And the fact that he knew someone had buzzed him into the Entertainer's apartment . . .

"No," he said slowly. "I don't have any reason to think it was anything but an accident."

"You called it in as a murder."

"I guess I was mistaken."

Sergeant McCoy nodded grimly, clapped her notebook shut, and nodded at the team of cops that had gathered in the Entertainer's living room. As her team began to disperse, McCoy looked at Jack and said, "I'm not sure why you're here, Jack, although I have a pretty good idea. I'm not gonna ask you because I don't think you'll tell me the truth, so what's the point. But I am gonna tell you something. Which is, whatever you think you're doin', stop it now. Not tomorrow, not the day after, *now*. Right this minute. Stop pokin' around, stop goin' places you have no business bein' in."

"Sergeant," Herb interrupted, "I've got to object to your behavior and your statement. My client has every right to be visiting a woman in her apartment."

"I'm not saying he doesn't have the right. God knows I'm a big supporter of the Constitution of the United States, Counselor." She smiled her most accommodating smile at the lawyer. "I'm just telling him to stop exercising that right," she said.

HERB HAD USED a car service to come to Leslee's apartment and he'd told the driver to keep the Ford Explorer waiting. They rode back to Jack's apartment in silence. When the Explorer pulled up in front of the building, Herb asked the driver to wait for him again, then, turning to Jack, said, "You want me to come up for a drink?"

Jack shook his head. "I'm fine," he said and opened the car door.

Herb reached for him, touched him lightly on the arm, started to say something. But then he shook his head and gave a sour smile and said, "Damn, this is the first time in my life I don't have any fucking idea what to say." Jack started to step out but Herb tightened his grip. "But that's not gonna stop me from talking," he said. "I don't know what's going on, old buddy, and if you don't want to tell me, that's fine. But as your good pal I'm telling you to be careful. As your lawyer, I'm telling you to be extra careful. That cop said you weren't a suspect but I know cops and she left out a word. And she did it because you're rich and well known and I'm almost as rich and, if not so well known, at least fairly well respected. The word she left out is 'yet.' You're not a suspect *yet*."

With that, Herb released Jack's arm, watched as he got out of the car, and then nodded wearily to the driver.

In the elevator ride up to his apartment, Jack tried to piece things together. But the pieces all seemed so scattered, so disconnected. He arrived at Leslee's apartment, rang her buzzer. No answer. Someone was in there with her, though, had to be. But doing what? Putting the needle in her arm? Waiting for her to die? And then what? Jack had buzzed a second time, and this one was answered. A short buzz back, letting him into the building. A minute to climb the stairs? Two minutes? And now there was no one in the apartment. No one except the dead girl in the bathtub.

He tried to imagine what could have happened. Someone buzzes him in, leaves the apartment . . .

Jack realized he was picturing this someone as a woman. Someone Leslee would trust. One of Kid's team.

She had buzzed Leslee from downstairs. Identified herself as a friend of Kid's. Or maybe didn't even have to. Maybe Leslee was already in the tub, assumed that Jack had arrived early, hopped out to quickly press the buzzer, then dashed back to the bath. That made sense. He could picture that.

She got to the top of the stairs, saw the note—and the knife—that Leslee had left by the door. Went inside. Maybe she sat on the edge of the tub and talked to the girl, lulled her into a sense of ease. Was Leslee already shooting drugs? Maybe. Maybe this woman knew it. Maybe she knew it wouldn't be hard to get her going. All she had to do was up the dosage. Or maybe it was a struggle. Or maybe Leslee closed her eyes, relaxed in the warm water, and then here it came, a sudden jab, the syringe stuck in her arm, a quick thrashing and then . . .

Then what?

Then Jack buzzed. Leslee was already dead or certainly near death. The woman turned the water back on, a good distraction for when Jack arrived. She buzzed him in, stepping over Leslee's note—maybe dripping water on it, maybe that's how it got wet—and then she went up a flight of stairs, perhaps only half a flight. She might have watched him enter. When he closed the door, she went straight downstairs, out the front door to the street. She was gone. Safe.

Stopping first to jimmy the lock on the door? To break it after the fact?

Why? What purpose did that serve?

For one, it made him look like a liar. Or, worse, it made it seem as if he were the one who broke into the building.

It could make him look like the killer.

The elevator stopped now on Jack's floor. The door slid open and he stepped into his living room. His imagination was running away with him, he decided. Why would anyone want him to look like a murderer? For that matter, how would anyone even know he was involved?

Well, one person already knew. The Mortician. Eva Migliarini knew he was gathering information. She knew he was trying to find the other members of the Team. He could picture her talking to Leslee. She could easily have access to drugs. And he could see her pulling out the needle, sticking it into the naked girl, the girl who was compulsively cleansing off the world's stench in her bathwater.

Jack shook his head as if to clear away his overly dramatic ruminations. He went into the kitchen, took out a highball glass, then turned and went into the living room, straight for the bar, poured himself half a glassful of twelve-year-old single-malt scotch.

Forget all this, he told himself. You just had a shock. You saw a dead body. And not just a body, someone you knew, someone you'd heard so much about. It's natural to start imagining things. Christ! No wonder McCoy was looking at you like that. You must have sounded like an idiot. A paranoid idiot. So just forget it, drink your scotch and watch *SportsCenter* and forget about outsmarting the New York City Police Department.

Jack flicked on the TV, sat in his regular chair, got comfortable as he heard Dan Patrick say, "A slider to McGwire ... and a *whiffffff.*" As Jack sipped his drink, he glanced to his left, toward the Hopper painting, prepared to smile, as he always did when he saw it. Only this time he didn't smile. Because he didn't see it. The painting was gone.

Jack jumped up, the scotch swishing over the top of the glass and spilling onto his shirt. He took two steps over toward the bare wall, stopped suddenly, because he saw now that it was not gone. It had been taken off its hook on the wall. Someone had removed it, leaned it carefully against the baseboard. Jack ran to it, saw that it was unmarked and unharmed.

Someone had been in his apartment. But how? It was impossible to break into this building.

And even if someone could break in, why?

Why would anyone ...

And then he knew.

His eyes went to the space on the wall where the painting had hung. In its place, in very small letters, two words had been carefully written. It looked like crayon, Jack thought. No. As he peered closer, more like red Magic Marker.

Jack ran back into the kitchen. Checked the walls and the cabinets. Everything was undisturbed. Then into his office. Normal. Next, he ran into his bedroom and what he saw there stopped him cold. There were *three* words, also in red Magic Marker, scrawled on the wall above his bed. The writing was neat, the lettering precise.

Jack realized he was breathing hard. And he was trembling. He went back to the living room, where the words were now all he could see. They dominated the room.

Stop looking is what they said.

He didn't have to go back into the bedroom to check the words there. The message was similar. The first two words were the same. But there was a third word added. And it was the third word that made Jack shiver and wonder what the hell he'd gotten himself into. And how he'd possibly get out of it.

He closed his eyes and could perfectly picture the message above his bed. In thick, precise, bloodred letters.

Stop looking now.

THE FIRST THING Jack did was call down to the doorman on duty.

"Carlos," he said into the phone that connected directly to the front door of the building, "did anyone come up to my apartment tonight?"

"No. Who?"

"I don't know. Anyone."

"No, sir."

"*Can* someone get into the apartment?"

"Not unless Frankie or I let 'em up."

"Tell me how you do that."

"What do you mean?"

"I know it sounds crazy, but tell me exactly how someone gets into my apartment."

"Are you kiddin'? You know how."

"Just humor me. How does someone get up here?"

"They come into the building, give their name, we call up for your okay, and whoever's at the door releases the elevator for your floor."

"There's a device at the door."

"Yeah, sure. Right under the stand, you know, when you come in."

"What if I'm not home?"

"If you're not here, we don't let anybody up. Unless you give us a written note with a name on it. Otherwise, ain't no way."

"Is someone always at the door? Could anyone get by you and release the elevator on his own?"

"Did someone get into your apartment, Mr. Keller? You want me to call—"

"No. Do me a favor and just answer the question."

"There's always two of us. Three or four shifts, always two at a time. Pretty hard to get by. I'd say impossible. And they'd have to know exactly how to release—"

"How about if you don't release it? Can someone get by you and just use the elevator?"

"No, sir. Well, they could, but they'd have to have a key."

"Like the one I use to come in through the garage?"

"Yes, sir. Same, exact key. You just insert it in the lock next to the button for your floor."

"And it only works for my floor?"

"Your key works for your floor, Mr. Babbitch's key works for the fifth floor, every tenant's got a key that works for them and them only."

"So my key won't work for Mr. Babbitch's floor?"

"That's right. What's goin' on, Mr. K?"

"How about the stairs?"

"To get up to you? Long climb."

"I know. But how do you do it?"

"Ain't you never climbed the stairs to your apartment?"

"No," Jack said, and he realized that after all these years he didn't even know exactly where the stairway entry was in the lobby. "How do you do it?"

"Gotta have a key for that, too. A key to get into the stairway from the lobby and a key to let you out when you get to your floor. Each floor has a different lock."

Jack hesitated. He didn't know what else to ask.

"You sure everything's okay, Mr. Keller?"

"Yeah, thanks, Carlos. Everything's fine."

He hung up and immediately called down to the garage. He went through a similar routine. No one there had seen anyone come in and use the elevator. No one who didn't belong, anyway. Pablo, the main guy at the garage, wouldn't swear that no one could get in without being seen but it was unlikely. And anyway, he said, nobody could get up to the apartments without having a key. It was impossible.

Jack tried to think who had keys to get into the place. He had one, of course, plus a duplicate set. As a reflex, he stuck his hand in his pocket to feel the key. It was right where it should be. He then went into the kitchen, to the small hook that hung by the refrigerator where the spare was kept. It was there, too. In fact, two spares were there, which puzzled him for a moment, then he realized he had a third set. Caroline's keys had been returned to him, along with her other possessions from Virginia.

Who else? Dom had one and his name had also been left downstairs as someone who could be let in anytime. If anyone was above suspicion, it was Dom. Mattie had had a key and her name had also been left downstairs. But poor Mattie was dead and, even if she were alive, could never have done anything remotely like—

Jack realized now that there was some kind of commotion out on the street. Strange. Usually you couldn't hear the traffic up this high, but there was frantic honking. *Must be some kind of an accident.* Jack instinctively turned toward the balcony, at the same time felt a small blast of hot, summer air, and that's when he realized the sliding door was open. No, not just open . . .

Someone had broken it.

A small section of the large glass pane had been shattered. Right by the handle. And the door had been left open. Maybe six inches.

Jack walked slowly over to it. He stared down at the

shards that were gleaming in the carpet. Looked back up at the jagged hole. Then he looked out across the balcony, at the wall that stretched over to the next building.

No one had needed a key to get into his apartment.

Someone had walked across the wall. The ten-foot-long, one-foot-wide wall. Eighteen stories above the street.

Jack remembered Kid, not long before his death, leaping up onto the retaining wall and walking.

Hey, do you know you could actually walk to the next building from here?

Jack remembered his stomach tightening.

Seriously. The buildings are connected.

He remembered his mouth going dry. He remembered getting dizzy . . .

Someone could walk along this ledge and get to that rooftop. You'd have to be kind of nuts but . . .

Jack slid the balcony door shut, hard enough so more glass cracked and showered to the floor. He stood there, sagging a bit, holding on to the handle for support, still staring out at the nearby rooftop. No longer just wondering who had killed Kid. No longer wondering who had killed Leslee.

Now wondering if that same person was going to try to kill him.

Jack took one step toward the phone. He was going to call McCoy. Get her over here, let her see this, make her understand what was going on and let her protect him. Then he thought: No. She still won't understand. And cops don't protect, they react. She'll tell me to get a new door. And an alarm. She'll ask me if I did all this myself just to make her think I was right.

Fuck McCoy, he thought.

And fuck whoever did this.

I'm not going to stop looking. I'm going to find her. And I'm going to find her *now*.

By three o'clock the next afternoon, the glass door had been replaced, an alarm system installed—the installer muttering, over and over again, "Who'd be crazy enough to try to break in from here?"—and a painter was at work on the living room and bedroom wall.

And Jack had spent just over three hours sitting in front of his computer, trying to find the Rookie.

She was the logical one to go after, partly because Jack suspected she had, over time, metamorphosed into the Destination, and partly because he had remembered back to winter, about two weeks into January. He remembered so specifically because it was the first day Kid had seen the Hopper painting. After checking the day he'd gotten the painting, then using his calendar to pinpoint his first session with Kid after that, it was not difficult to specify the exact day—January 17.

Jack could recall the conversation as if it were yesterday.

I regard Edward Hopper as the depressive's Norman Rockwell.

What!

Jack, I don't know shit about art. I'm just quoting.

A member of your fucking team?

The Rookie. She has very strong feelings about art.

Do me a favor and tell her to go fuck herself.

You don't want to mess with her, Jack. Not with what I've learned about her.

Your goddamn team. I don't think they even exist.

They exist, all right. Hey, the Rookie was even written up in yesterday's Times. *She's famous.*

He was annoyed as hell at the time, even hurt, but the words had still been mere banter then. Now they seemed so much more. *The Rookie has very strong feelings about art.* And clearly did not like Hopper. If the Rookie had been the one to break into his apartment the night before, was that why the Hopper had been removed from the wall? *You don't want to mess with her, Jack. Not with what I've learned about her.* Because she was so dangerous? Because she was capable of killing? And best of all: *The Rookie was even written up in yesterday's* Times. *She's famous.*

A starting point.

Using AOL, he went to nytimes.com. At the web site, he registered, typed in a password—"jacks"—and as various choices came up, he elected to go back into their selected archives. He typed in "January 16" and, suddenly, there was that day's newspaper of record up on the screen. He decided there was only one way to do this and that was thoroughly, so he began reading the paper from cover to cover. As he read, he took notes, keeping track of any woman being written about who conceivably could have had a connection to Kid or who could, in any stretch of the imagination, have been on the Team. After a few minutes of reading, he realized he should keep track of every single woman mentioned, just in case he needed to backtrack. So on a yellow legal pad, as he went through each section—front page, Metro, The Arts, Sports, Business Day and Dining In—he started dividing the names into three columns labeled Likely, Less Likely, and Unlikely. With each name, he jotted down any relevant information—a brief description, a job title, a company name or the name of an agent, anything that might help him locate her.

The first story he came to where the woman seemed "Likely" was about a young, dynamic assistant DA who was prosecuting the killer of a high school principal. The next was a hotshot Wall Street executive who was handling a large merger. He put a star by the name of a young professional tennis player who lost in the quarterfinals of a tournament. Others on that list were a policewoman who had been fired for posing nude in a magazine and the daughter of a real estate developer who was now in Paris modeling. Margaret Thatcher, who was lecturing on global economics at Harvard, was placed in the Unlikely column, as was a fifty-two-year-old lesbian colonel in the air force, a very overweight black woman who was the voice of a service that gave movie times, and Kathie Lee Gifford. Tipper Gore also went into Unlikely, although Jack's pen lingered over Less Likely for just a moment.

By midafternoon, he had twenty-two Likelys, twenty-seven Less Likelys, and a long string of Unlikelys. As he ran his finger over the final list, staring at the information he'd written down, one line popped out at him. It was when he came to the name of an up-and-coming young art dealer.

She was getting attention for an avant-garde show she had put together at a gallery in SoHo. But it was the address of the gallery that got his attention: 137 Greene Street. It seemed familiar. He recognized it from somewhere. His mind drifted, trying to picture the street, imagining the last time he'd been in that neighborhood . . .

Bingo. One-three-seven Greene—the address of the Hanson Fitness Center, where he'd met Bryan and where Kid had worked. On the ground floor was an art gallery, the one with tons of sand in the window. It wasn't out of business, Jack thought. That *was* art.

The coincidence was too great. It had to be. He glanced down at her name again. Grace Childress. Yes, Grace had to be the third member of the Team.

She was the Rookie.

THE WINDOW OF the Waggoner Gallery was still filled with sand. Jack spent a moment studying it, realized he could stand there the rest of his life without figuring out what it was meant to say, so opened the gallery's front door and stepped inside.

The artist being displayed was named Pinkney Wallace. Jack learned from browsing through the catalog that his medium was the earth: sand, dirt, mud, grass. His artwork was scattered throughout the spacious ground floor. There were perhaps twenty large glass boxes that looked like fish tanks. Inside each box was a wave of sand or a mountain of mud. One was divided perfectly in half; one half of the box was completely empty, the other was jammed full of cut grass. He was staring at the grass when he heard a woman's voice from behind.

"Like it?"

He turned and Jack knew he had come to the right place. The woman who spoke to him was absolutely stunning. She was not tall, maybe five-foot-four, but somehow she *seemed* tall; her perfect posture and angular body seemed to add inches to her height. Her hair was hennaed a sparkly copper color, which was the only color on her entire body except for her bright blue eyes and thick, coppery-red glasses surrounding them. Everything else was black: a black tank-top T-shirt, covered by a sheer black blouse, a short black skirt, black tights, and mid-calf-high black boots. Her lips were thin and the tight smile they formed managed to convey an air of both confidence and vulnerability. Jack was dazzled.

"I don't understand it," he said, gesturing toward the glass box and the grass.

"It's postmodern," the woman said. "There is no understanding. Only confusion."

"Ah. Now *that's* something I'm familiar with." Jack stuck his hand out. "You're Grace Childress, aren't you?"

She nodded, put her hand in his, and they shook. Her grip was hard and firm and Jack felt the same electric shock he'd felt when he'd met the Mortician and the Entertainer. Although this woman was much more appealing. She had the sensual aura that the others had but she did not radiate the same air of danger, of walking too close to the edge.

"I'm Jack Keller," he continued. The name obviously

meant nothing to her so he took a shot in the dark. "The Butcher," he said, and this obviously registered, he could see it in her eyes, as they narrowed, and in the curious cock of her head.

"What can I do for you?" she asked.

"I'm a friend of Kid Demeter's. I'm trying to find out what happened to him."

"He's dead."

"Yes, I know," Jack said. "I mean, I'm trying to find out how. And why."

"We know how, don't we?"

"Do we?"

"Yes," she said. "Somebody killed him."

Jack stared at her a moment, startled, then he couldn't help himself. A smile of relief spread over his face.

"Would you mind saying that again?"

"Somebody killed him. I think that's pretty obvious, don't you?"

"Yes," he said, "I do."

THEY WERE EATING in Jerry's, a casual place specializing in simple grilled food on Prince Street.

"The Rookie, huh?" Grace was saying. "Certainly not very descriptive."

"I think it changed. I think you got another nickname as time went on."

"Well, whatever it is, it's got to be better than the Rookie."

"It is," Jack said. "It's possible he started calling you the Destination."

Grace's eyes flickered, and she tilted her head down. "No," she told him. "That wasn't me. Kid told me about the Destination. It was someone from his past. Someone . . . well, let's just say he told me about her. I don't really feel comfortable sharing his secrets. Even now."

"He told me about her, too," Jack said. "But he also told me that he'd met someone he thought could be a second Destination. I think that could be you."

"Why do you think that?" Grace asked.

"Just a hunch. He told me a few things . . . and you seem to fit the description." Jack raised his hand and when the waiter came over, he ordered a second beer. He looked at Grace, who shook her head. She was still working on her first. "Do you know why he came up with the nickname 'Destination'?" Jack asked her.

"No."

"Topeka's a place, Cleveland's a town . . . Rome is a destination."

She smiled, a sad smile, and shook her head. "I don't know if that's me or not," she told him. "But he did always have this idealized, dewy-eyed fantasy about me."

"Maybe it was more accurate than you give him credit for."

"No. Believe me. I throw things, I bite my nails, I've done my share of things I shouldn't have done. Hell, I still do. I make a *lot* of mistakes."

"Maybe he just didn't care about them."

"No, he didn't see them. He didn't *want* to see them."

"How'd you get to know him?"

"He picked me up on the street. I was going into the gallery, he was heading up to the gym. I brushed him off—I'm not big on street pickups—but Kid was extremely persistent. He started coming into the gallery, we talked, and then one night I was out at a club with a girlfriend and he was there. He was by himself, it was late, maybe two or three in the morning, and he looked kind of rattled. I asked him what the matter was and he said he'd just had a fight with someone, an argument. He wouldn't tell me what it was about, not then, but he looked so vulnerable he was hard to resist. We wound up talking almost all night. And then . . . you know how these things happen."

"Did he ever tell you what the argument was about? Or who it was with?"

She hesitated. "I told you. I'm not completely comfortable sharing his secrets."

"Are there a lot of secrets to know about him?"

"There are a lot of secrets to know about everybody, aren't there?"

"Yes," Jack said, "I suppose there are." He took a long swig of his beer. "Were you still seeing him when he died?"

"No," she said. Again, she hesitated, seemed as if she were going to say more, but stopped.

"Who broke it off?" he asked.

"I did. It wasn't right. I mean, Kid was interesting and great-looking and I liked him a lot, but it wasn't going to go anywhere, not for me. He wasn't what I needed or what I wanted."

"How did he accept that?"

"He didn't accept it at all. I told you, Kid was persistent." She pursed her lips together. A memory. "Did you ever see him lift a really heavy weight? Well, that's what I was to him. He thought if he pushed himself harder, worked himself more, eventually it would happen between us. There was no quit in him. That's why I know he'd choose life—if he had a choice." She drained her beer. "Is there anything else you'd like to ask me?"

"Where were you when Kid fell?"

"Am I on your suspect list?" When Jack shrugged, she didn't seem offended, just said, "I had an opening at my gallery that night. *Tons* of witnesses." Grace waved her hand in the air, almost apologetically. "Listen," she said then, "Kid was a club guy. He knew every druggie and pervert below Fourteenth Street. It comes with the territory. Whoever did it, you'll never find him."

"I'm pretty sure that him is a her. There was a woman with him in his apartment the night he died."

That seemed to surprise her. "How do you know that?"

"The police."

"I thought you said the police weren't involved."

"They're not. But they were involved enough to know that."

She stuttered a bit over her next few words. The news had clearly thrown her. "But just being with him, that doesn't mean she killed him, does it? Even if you find her, it doesn't prove anything."

"Maybe not. But I won't know till I find her."

Jack didn't say anything after that. The waiter came and broke the silence and Jack paid the check. As Grace started to stand, Jack spoke. "Kid told me he spoke to the Destination. The *new* Destination. She told him a secret that bothered him a lot. And he told her things about himself. Some of the things were disturbing. Was that you?"

"It might have been." She sank back into her chair, closed her eyes briefly, and nodded. "I've got a secret or two. And he told me things. And they scared me."

"What things?"

"Things that still scare me."

"Tell me." But she shook her head. When he realized he would get no more information about that conversation, he asked, "Do you know the other women he was seeing? Did he ever mention their nicknames?"

"Like who?"

"Samsonite?"

"No."

"She fits with what you were saying. He said she works in a club, she wants to be a singer. In the meantime she deals."

"There are a lot of those. Who else?"

"The Murderess?"

She picked her head up, her blue eyes flashing. But the spark was immediately extinguished and she shook her head yet again. A brief pause, then, "Did he tell you why he called her the Murderess?"

"No. But Kid's nicknames were fairly pointed."

"I guess it would be too obvious if it was her, wouldn't it?"

"I don't think anything is too obvious right now."

Another silence settled in. It was broken when Grace
reached across the table, touched his arm, and said, "You're
going to go looking for them, aren't you?" The briefest of
smiles. "I mean, once you check out my alibi." Jack nodded
and she went on. "I know the club scene. Almost as well as
Kid did. Let me help you find Samsonite."

"Why would you do that?"

Grace Childress stood now and ran a hand through her
short, coppery hair. "That'll be one of *my* secrets," she
said.

THE NEXT MORNING was a workout with Bryan. They
were out on the balcony and Jack felt strong as he was put
through his paces. He updated Bryan on his quest, told him
about finding Leslee, the Entertainer, in her apartment, and
Bryan was astounded by that. He told Jack he'd never seen
a dead body before and he seemed genuinely troubled that
Jack had had to experience it. Jack then told him about
tracking down Grace, who turned out to be the Destination
as well as the Rookie. He told him that they were going to
hit a few clubs that night, searching for Samsonite and possibly even the Murderess. Again, Bryan apologized as he
realized he must have known who she was from the gallery
below the gym, just had never made the proper connection. As always, Bryan seemed interested but slightly
confused. Jack was never sure how much information he
was actually absorbing. He asked a few questions, said he
was amazed at Jack's ability to track these people down,
gave Jack the names of a few clubs Kid used to frequent,

hoping that might be helpful. As the end of the hour approached, Jack was sweating and he felt invigorated, more than satisfied. But he noticed that Bryan seemed sad. Or sadder than usual.

"That's good," he said, as Jack started his second set of squats. He counted off with each one, as if he'd lose count unless he said the number out loud. "Six . . . seven . . . very good . . . Fuckin' A. You are Hercules Unchained, man."

"I've heard that one before." Jack finished his final squat, leaned against one of the weight machines to catch his breath.

"Yeah. Me and Kid, we used to tell each other that, down in the cellar, you know, to pump ourselves up." Bryan paused. He started to speak, stumbled over the first two words. Jack looked up and saw how nervous he was. "I-I s-saw him last night," Bryan managed to say. "Kid."

"*What?*"

"Yo, it wasn't him or nothin'. Just a guy who reminded me of him. And for a second, I kinda forgot he was dead." The sadness hit him full force now. "I miss him," he said. "Kid was the only person I could talk to."

"Dom."

"Huh?"

"For me, that's Dom. He was my father's best friend, now he's mine. I've been telling him things since I was twelve. Anything I've ever thought, Dom knows."

"Yeah, that was me and Kid. I didn't have to speak, even. He could always tell what I was thinkin'. Ever since we were little."

"You're lucky. Not many people ever have friends like that."

"Yeah, I'm gonna miss that. I really am."

JACK PICKED GRACE up at twelve-thirty that night. He couldn't help but notice that she was wearing a short white silk dress and white lace stockings that left very little to the imagination. And she couldn't help but notice that he was noticing.

"I'm not used to starting this late," he told her as she hopped into the cab and gave the driver an address in Tribeca.

"Hope you drank a lot of coffee because all we're going to catch right now is the early crowd. For the real players, you're going to have to stay up a little later."

On the way downtown, he gave her all the information he had on Samsonite. She didn't seem surprised at what she heard. She was more surprised when he'd finished the run-down and she looked up to find him staring at her.

"What?" she said. And then before he could answer, "Ohhh. I get it. You feel like you know me. You know all about me because of what Kid's said." When he nodded, she said, "Well, I know a lot about you, too."

"Do you?"

"All the key things, courtesy of Kid. I didn't know it was you at the time . . . but it was definitely you. You're disgustingly rich . . ."

"Oh, yes. Disgustingly."

"You went from twenty-four-percent body fat down to fourteen . . ."

"Twelve."

"Sick, insane Knicks fanatic . . ."

"Guilty."

"You've been pretty much a celibate shut-in since your wife was killed . . ."

Jack jerked his head up sharply. His eyes widened as he stared at her.

"Whoops," she said, when she saw his expression. "That was a fairly tasteless thing to say, wasn't it? I'm sorry."

"Is that what he said?"

"Is it true?"

Jack nodded, slowly and grimly.

"I am sorry," she said, and reached over to touch the top of his shoulder. Then: "Was it that terrible, what happened down there? Do you want to talk about it?"

"No," Jack said. "I don't. And I can't."

"Kid talked about it all the time. He was obsessed with it."

"Was he?"

"He talked about you all the time, too. You were his idol."

"What I was, maybe. Not what I am now."

"I don't think so, Jack. I think he wanted to be you in any of your incarnations." She grinned, moved one finger to touch his lips to gently change his solemn expression into a smile. "Kind of spooky, isn't it?"

"What?"

"You and me. You're his idol, and if I'm the Destination, I'm his perfect woman. His two ultimate fantasies coming face-to-face, colliding in space . . . Didn't they do a *Star Trek* about that once?" The cab pulled to a stop in the middle of the block. "We're here," she said.

Jack looked out the window at the empty and silent Tribeca Street. There were a few warehouses that had not yet been converted into apartments, a few small loft buildings, one four-story office building, and that was it. No sign of activity. No hint whatsoever of any kind of club. "Here *where?*" he asked.

"Welcome to downtown," she told him. "Follow me."

SHE WENT STRAIGHT up to a heavy steel door, its old red paint barely peeking through the rust, in the middle of the block. As she rang an unmarked buzzer, Jack looked up to see a dark building with no indication of life.

"Are you sure you know where you're going?"

Grace nodded.

"There's no sign."

Grace nodded again. "They don't want to be found."

"Then how do you know it's here?"

"You just know."

The buzzer sounded and Grace struggled to push the heavy door open. Jack put one hand on the door and pushed along with her. They found themselves in a dingy hallway, with a wide stairway leading up to the first floor. They climbed and when they got to the equally dingy landing, there was another door. Jack looked questioningly at Grace, who waved her hand toward it with a flourish. He rang the buzzer to the right of the hinges, the door opened, and they were greeted by a huge bouncer, one of the largest men Jack had ever seen. His eyes ran up and down Jack's body, studying him, then he glanced at Grace and nodded.

"Let's go," she said. "You passed inspection." And with a quick raised eyebrow: "Barely."

From that moment on, Jack felt as if he'd stepped onto another planet.

Everything in the after-hours club was sleek, modern, and steel. The people were just as sleek and just as steely. The place was a winding maze, filled with smoke and pounding music, packed with extraordinarily beautiful models, male and female, lounging, sitting, dancing, drinking. Flamboyant transvestites paraded back and forth. Hard bodies were everywhere and almost every body part was exposed. The lights were low and sporadic; everything and everybody looked to be hidden in shadow. Grace took his hand and led him through the maze to a back room where there were sofas and chairs, a few tables, and a long bar. Jack brushed against two women, embracing and kissing passionately, backed against a steel column. One of the women turned and glared at him, then turned back to her partner and began licking her neck.

They found two seats on a sofa near the bar, wedged in next to two men, one shirtless, both busy fondling the other. Grace leaned over and said something into Jack's ear. He waved his hand, indicating that he couldn't hear a word she was saying.

"I said, 'Having a good time?' " she yelled as loud as she could.

He shrugged and yelled, "Come here often?" and Grace nodded happily.

They stayed for two hours, each nursing two drinks, sizing

up the patrons, waiting to see if anything sparked any kind of connection to Kid, keeping in mind the description of Samsonite as a singer/bartender/dealer. There were two female bartenders, both attractive, and Grace asked them both about Kid. Neither of them had ever heard of him. One of them responded, "No, but Bruce Willis was in here last week."

When Jack finally signaled that he thought they'd had enough, Grace led him back through the throng and down to the street. The neighborhood was eerily silent after the explosion of noise they'd just been immersed in, and as Jack looked back at the building, the whole experience seemed as if it were a dream, a heavy-metal Brigadoon.

"Ready for more?" Grace asked, and when he nodded, they hailed a cab on Hudson Street and headed into the West Village.

She asked the cab to stop off at an all-night deli, and when he did, she hopped out of the cab, dashed in, and returned a few moments later with a six-pack of beer. Before Jack could say anything, she said, "Just wait. You'll see," then directed the cab toward Eleventh Street, right off Tenth Avenue. There, two buildings in from the corner, was a tiny music club called B Sharp. Jack paid the ten-dollar cover charge, then they stepped into a stripped-down basement. There were maybe ten small tables, each with two or three cheap folding chairs around them and no decorations other than a few black-and-white photos of jazz musicians on the walls. To the left of the room was a long bar. But there was no bartender and no liquor bottles. Spread across the bar was an array of plastic cups. At the front of the room was a small stage, a flimsy plywood platform that could fit four or five musicians. A trio, two black guys in dark suits and ties and one white guy with a buzz cut and a Hawaiian shirt, was playing as they entered—guitar, bass, and piano. Grace grabbed two plastic cups off the bar and they settled into a table.

"No bartender here," Jack asked. "How are we—"

"Just be cool," Grace said. "Have a beer and wait awhile. It's early."

They listened to the music, which was excellent—rhythmic, subtle, and just harsh enough to fit the room and the late hour—and drank some of their beer. By three-thirty, the place was packed with people. By then, Jack had noticed several people, perhaps ten in all, had surreptitiously slipped off behind the stage and disappeared through a curtain shielding the wall at the front of the room. He looked at Grace, nodded his head questioningly toward that wall, and she glanced at her watch. She looked over at a young black man with beaded dreadlocks who was now standing behind the bar. She quickly pointed with two fingers toward the curtain and the man nodded.

"How much money do you have on you?" she asked Jack. "Why?"

"You have five hundred dollars?"

"Probably."

"Then let's go look for Samsonite."

She stood, walked to the front of the room, and he followed. As they passed the stage, Grace held her hands in front of her and applauded and the musicians eyed her gratefully. Then she was behind the stage, slipping into the folds of the curtain, Jack right behind her.

The curtain was not directly up against a wall, as Jack had thought. There were perhaps three feet between it and the wall at that end of the room. The thin walkway smelled faintly of urine. There was one door to the right that said "Toilet." Grace went to the other door, tried to turn the knob. It didn't turn, but she waited patiently, then Jack heard a faint buzz and she tried again. This time it worked and suddenly, they were in a back room, twice as large as the music room they'd just left. There was no live music here, just quiet jazz playing on a CD. This room was even darker and it took Jack a moment for his eyes to adjust. When they did, he saw perhaps twenty people seated in small, comfortable chairs or love seats. Most of them were smoking, both tobacco and marijuana. There was a small bar, this one reasonably well stocked with alcohol. Two women were behind the bar, one blonde, one brunette, both wearing tight jeans and tighter black T-shirts. The blonde was pouring from a bottle of bourbon. The brunette was using a paring knife to divide a small, flat plate of glimmering white cocaine.

"Come on," Jack murmured. "These places don't really exist."

Grace didn't answer. She just walked over to the bar and took a seat. He stood behind her.

"How much?" she asked the brunette.

The woman glanced up quickly, then turned her eyes back to her work. "Three hundred," she said.

Grace looked at Jack, gave him a quick nod. He reached into his pocket, pulled out three hundred-dollar bills, and handed them to her.

"To go or to stay?"

"To go. And two beers, please."

She pulled two bottles of New Amsterdam from beneath the bar. Both bottles were cold and dripping wet. The bartender twisted them open, set them down. Then she wiped her hands on a bar towel and again started separating the coke. Jack watched as she made small piles, about a gram each. When she was satisfied, she took out a baggie, scraped one of the piles cleanly into it, smoothed the powder into the bottom of the bag, folded the plastic neatly into a small square, and handed it to Grace. She then licked the tip of her finger, rubbed it down on the plate where the mound of coke had been. She held the finger out to Grace, who shook her head. The bartender shrugged, rubbed the finger across her own gums, and smiled contentedly.

"Haven't seen you for a while," she said to Grace.

Jack thought Grace squirmed a bit, but she just said, "Been traveling."

The woman said nothing in response to that, simply picked up her plate, turned, and disappeared into another room behind the bar.

"Surprised?" Grace said to Jack, without looking at him. When he didn't respond, she said, "I told you. Everyone's got secrets. This used to be one of mine."

"Used to be?"

"Mmm-mmm. I'm a working stiff now. We fast-trackers can't do this kind of thing anymore."

"I feel like I walked into some twisted version of the sixties. Or a bad Sammy Davis movie."

"Hey, drugs are big again. Coke, heroin, they're back. Even speed. You can't keep a good thing down."

"Kid used to come here?"

"I know he was here once. I brought him. I don't know if he came back, but he liked it, so he might've. I thought it was worth a try." She indicated the bartenders. "They seem like his type."

"Did he do this stuff?"

She shook her head. "The drugs? Are you kidding? Mr. Healthy Body? But he liked being around this kind of place. He thought it was exciting."

Yes, Jack thought. Christ Almighty, it *was* exciting. It felt sordid and wrong but it stank of danger and eroticism and Jack could already feel the atmosphere and the music seep inside his blood. He could feel his heart pumping faster and his head start to throb. It was light-years away from the confines of his restaurant, even farther from the isolation of his apartment, and it frightened him. But it was exhilarating. The same way the flash of thigh from the Mortician had been exhilarating. And the moment when the Entertainer had straddled him in her apartment. And . . .

He looked over at the Destination. At Grace Childress. She was watching him.

"I guess you and Kid have more in common than you thought," was all she said.

They stayed an hour, gradually drawing both bartenders into conversations. Neither of them were would-be singers. Neither of them knew Kid. And this time, when Jack took Grace's hand to lift her off the barstool and head her back to the street, that hand dug into his while her other hand lightly touched his back, and he felt his breath come hard now and heavy.

They went to two more clubs, the last one a place called Meyer's, down on the Lower East Side. It was the one Bryan had told Jack about, saying it was one of Kid's main hangouts. Both spots were dark and dominated by pulsating music, both filled with hard bodies and a sense of sexual urgency. But in neither could they find any substantive connection to Kid nor any indication that they might find the next Slash on Kid's team, Samsonite.

It was five-thirty in the morning when Jack brought Grace back to her apartment. She stepped out of the taxi, and by her lack of hesitation it was clear she expected him to get out as well. She sat down on the top step of the three-step landing that led to her building and said, "I'm sorry this didn't lead anywhere."

"It takes time. It's not a TV show where everything comes easy and works out perfectly first time around."

"Jack," she said. "Are you sure you want to do this?"

"Is there some reason I shouldn't?"

"Do you trust me?" she asked.

"Not entirely," he answered. "But mostly, yes."

"I was about to ask you up to my apartment. I was hoping for something a bit more positive."

"Do you trust me?" Jack asked.

"Yes," she said. "I do."

"Then tell me what Kid told you. Tell me the things that frightened you."

"God, I wish I still smoked. Or still did coke. What are you going to do with your purchase, by the way?"

Jack felt in his pocket, surprised, and pulled out the small packet of cocaine he'd purchased. He took several strides to a wire trash basket on the corner and tossed it in. Then he came back to stand inches away from Grace. She was staring at the trash can longingly.

"It's hard for me to describe. Yes, what he told me did frighten me. But partly because *he* was frightened. For himself and, I think, for you, too."

"Why would he be frightened for me?"

"I don't know. He was vague, he couldn't really explain. This might sound crazy but I had the feeling he wanted me to know certain things in case . . . in case you found me. I don't know how else to explain it. I got the feeling that there was something going on that had been going on a long time. For years. And I think he felt responsible for certain things, people getting hurt." She hesitated. "Maybe even getting killed."

"What people?" Jack asked very quietly.

"I don't know. I just know he seemed to feel some special connection to you. And it had something to do with the fact that bad things had happened to people around him. People he loved."

"I know what he means," Jack said.

"He didn't mention you by name, I didn't even know your name, remember, but now I'm sure it was you he was talking about. And he seemed to think he was putting you in some kind of danger."

"Why didn't you tell me this before?"

"Because I wasn't sure. I'm still not sure. But from talking to you, I just get a sense . . . it's a feeling I have, that's all. I can't be more specific."

There was an awkward silence, not broken until Grace's awkward laugh. "So now that I've put us both in the mood, do you want to come up to my apartment?"

"Yes," he said.

She got up, walked toward the door of her building. She turned, realized he hadn't moved from the sidewalk. "*Are* you coming up to my apartment?"

"No," he said. And then: "I'm not ready. I'd still feel like I'm cheating on my wife."

She slowly walked back down to where he was standing. She put her hands on his shoulders, lifted herself up, and kissed him gently on the lips. When the kiss ended, Jack slowly put his hand up and caressed her cheek. Then he turned and started his walk home.

When he was not quite half a block away, she said, "Be careful," and, as the first rays of dawn began to lighten the sky, watched until he crossed the nearly deserted street and turned the corner.

WHY DIDN'T HE *stop?*
Why was he still looking?

He'd been warned but he was still asking questions and getting closer and . . .

What difference did it make, why he was doing it? Reasons weren't important. Kid had his reasons and they were lies. Reasons were always lies. What mattered most was the heart.

The last words that Kid had heard were I love you.

What would be the last words Jack Keller would hear?

It was time to find out.

JACK WAS ASLEEP fifteen minutes after he walked into his apartment. And he'd been asleep all of ten minutes when the phone rang.

"Jack," the voice on the other end said urgently, "it's Grace. I figured it out. I can't believe I was so stupid. It was right in front of us the whole time."

"What was?" Jack managed to say, his words thick with exhaustion.

"Can you meet me again tonight?" she asked.

"What are you talking about?" Jack said. "What did you figure out?"

"Samsonite," Grace gushed. "I know how to find her."

FORTY-THREE

They met at 1 A.M., as per Grace Childress's instructions. She would not tell him why she thought she'd found Samsonite, she would not elaborate on anything. She just told him to pick her up in a taxi and when he did, she directed the driver to head downtown on the FDR Drive.

Jack had spent much of the day sleeping. He had a steam shower in his bathroom and in the interval, when he was awake, he took three long steams. The heat and sweat were cathartic; by the time he was due to dress, his body had made a reasonable recovery. He ached, but he was used to aches. And he was stiff, but he had long ago overcome stiffness. This was something he had learned both from Kid and from the life he had led: it was possible to get used to pain. And once you got used to it, it was rendered fairly harmless.

The taxi dropped them off in the East Village, on a small, shabby side street near Rivington and Essex. Grace took Jack by the hand and led him up to the fifth floor of an unmarked tenement building. Once again, nothing was visible from the outside. Inside, after climbing the five flights of stairs, they were met by a bouncer, a black man with a shaved head, dressed all in black except for bright-red suspenders. He opened Grace's purse, checked it out, and patted Jack down. When he found no weapon, he let them pass.

"What was that about?" Jack whispered as they headed down the hallway.

"There's a lot of money inside," she told him. "They don't want guns in there."

"You do know the most interesting places," he said.

When they walked through the door of the club, Jack was amazed to find that they'd entered an enormous room that, from its size, he guessed had been three, maybe even four apartments at one time. But they were apartments no more. Now it was a very serious casino. Jack felt as if he'd been beamed up into a Las Vegas starship.

The action was palpable. Two crap tables dominated the front of the room and a roar went up from the crowd around one of them as the shooter hit his number. Jack counted five blackjack tables. Four of them were filled and one of them was marked "reserved." At that one sat a bulked-up black man, an NFL Hall of Famer and onetime linebacker for the New York Giants. He was betting five-hundred-dollar chips and the only other people at his table were two women, one white, one black, who were availing themselves of his stack to place their own bets. As Jack looked around the room, he saw several other athletes he recognized—one basketball player, a star on the Philadelphia 76ers who was a regular at the restaurant whenever he was in town—and two rap stars, one of whom Jack had read had been arrested the week before on an assault charge.

The decor was not particularly elegant. There were couches and upholstered chairs scattered around, most of which looked comfortable but well worn. The various tables were wicker and glass, cheap and functional. There were two long bars that had been built on either side of the room. There were also four or five larger rooms leading off the main one. As he wandered, Jack caught a glimpse of a roulette table and one small room in which six men were puffing on cigars and playing poker.

Jack and Grace finally found two chairs in the main room. She motioned for him to sit, which he did, while she went to the bar, returning a few moments later with two bottles of beer. She clinked the neck of her bottle against his and said, "So here we are again."

She smiled at him but Jack was not in a smiling mood.

"It's time to tell me what's going on," he said. "What's the revelation about Samsonite?"

"It'll hit you," she said. "I don't know for sure if I'm right, but I think I am. It might be a little early but if I *am* right, she'll be here. And you'll know when she is."

"I'm not much for games right now," he told her.

"It's not a game," she said. "Just wait and see. If I'm right, you'll understand soon."

They sat for over an hour, not speaking much. Jack was too restless to make small talk, too intent on absorbing the scenes around him. At 2:45, Grace, who had barely moved, leaned forward and said, "I think she's here."

Jack swiveled, glanced around the room, saw nothing that jumped out at him. He turned back to Grace, who simply said, "Just look. Pay attention and you'll see it."

He stayed in his seat, stared at the people sitting around him, at the crowds around the gaming tables. Nothing came to him. He stood, then began walking. In and out of the various rooms, back to the main room, slowly strolling and studying. At one of the crap tables was an extraordinarily sexy woman, her arm around a short Arabic-looking man. The woman had to be six feet tall without the three-inch heels she was wearing. Her legs were long and muscular and she emitted the smoldering sexuality that Jack had come to expect from anyone on Kid's team. He watched her gamble, thought, *Yes, she's the one,* but how could Grace be so sure she'd be here? How could she know that a particular customer would . . .

Not a customer.

Samsonite *worked* in a club.

A singer/bartender/dealer.

It wasn't the woman at the crap table. It was someone who worked there.

He went to the built-in bar to the left of the room. Two bartenders, both male. At the bar on the right, also two bartenders. One man, one woman. The woman had thick red hair cascading down almost to her waist. She wore tight black pants and a blue work shirt, unbuttoned halfway down to reveal a tan neck and chest and a provocative glimpse of firm, white breasts. She was sexy enough, no question about it. Was she the one? Was she as crazy as Kid had described Samsonite? Was she dangerous?

Was she a potential killer?

Jack turned away, trying to figure out how best to approach her. Ask her about Kid? Try to buy drugs? Strike up an innocuous conversation?

He tried to drown out the sounds coming from the rest of the casino but was unsuccessful. He heard another roar come from one of the crap tables and a shooter yell out, "Ee-yo, baby, ee-yo," and then another roar as the eleven hit. He heard the spin of the roulette wheel, that distinct *clackety-clack* of the steel ball wending its way around and in and out of the numbers. He heard a groan from one of the blackjack tables and then a woman's voice, from the same table:

"That's thirteen . . . fifteen . . ."

A man's voice: "Hit me."

The woman's voice: "Twenty-two. Sorry." Then, the same voice, raspy from too many cigarettes and raw from too much whisky: "And twenty for the dealer."

Jack turned now, watched as the woman he'd just heard shuffled the new deck of cards. Her shuffling was mechanical and expert but not clean or sharp. When she dealt, her movements were a little off, slightly dulled. He heard her say, "Two aces . . . wanna split 'em?"

Now Jack was moving toward the table. He'd forgotten about the bartender, was standing a foot behind the seated blackjack players, staring at the woman as she handed out cards, tapped and collected the hands of the losers, and paid the winners.

A singer/bartender/dealer.

He heard Kid's voice: *Samsonite wants to be Courtney Love but for now she's a singer-slash-bartender-slash-dealer.*

A *dealer*.

A *blackjack* dealer.

He turned back toward Grace, who was nodding and

smiling. Then he turned back to the woman behind the table. She wore a flimsy black skirt slit up both sides; the slits revealed thighs that were both ripe and sinewy. Her shoulders were bare and in her sleeveless black-and-blue top she looked angular and hard and spectacularly, dangerously sexy. Her nipples jutted out from under the fabric of her tight shirt. Her arms didn't just ripple with muscles, the left one was covered with tattoos running from shoulder to wrist, the right one had a tattoo chain drawn around her taut bicep. Her hair was very short, almost mannish, and as dark as could be. Her face was white and thin, her cheekbones spectacularly high; her skin tightly drawn and flawless.

She looked up now, saw him staring at her. She smiled and he was reminded of nothing as much as a vampire. It was a blood-sucking smile that both aroused and chilled. But he didn't move or back away or stop watching her until, twenty minutes later, she was replaced at the table and stepped away to take a short break. Jack was next to her in a flash, holding on to her thin, steely arm and asking, "Do you know Kid Demeter?"

She looked at him blankly, he could see her trying to focus, and suddenly he thought, *I'm wrong. She doesn't have a clue who he is,* but then she smiled again, baring those sharp teeth, and Samsonite said, "Hey, baby, kneel and cross yourself when you say that name. Kid was a fucking saint."

IT WASN'T EASY convincing Grace to let him go off with Samsonite. But after a few heated moments, his logic won out. If she talked at all, he was certain she would talk more freely one-on-one, particularly to a man. And if she was indeed dangerous, they shouldn't go together. Using the only analogy he could think of, he said that one of them had to stay down underneath their own basket and play defense. It made much more sense for Grace to be that defensive player. He told her that if he didn't call her within two hours after he left, she should call Sergeant Patience McCoy at the Eighth Precinct. Reluctantly, Grace agreed. At 4:30 A.M., the fourth member of Kid's team said she could leave work and she and Jack headed for her apartment, where she said she could drink and smoke and he could talk about whatever the fuck he wanted.

Samsonite—her real name, she said, was Rita; no last name, just Rita, but Jack couldn't stop thinking of her as Samsonite, it fit her too perfectly—lived on a run-down street in the East Village, one that had not yet been made aware of the booming economy and the renovations going on in the neighborhood. The entire block was little more than a row of burned-out tenements and rubble. One of the tenements was Samsonite's apartment building.

"You live here?" Jack asked, surprised. He thought it looked as if it had long ago been abandoned.

"I've lived in worse, believe me."

She fumbled for the key to the front door, couldn't find it in her purse. After several minutes, she mumbled a curse and reached into the right pocket of her skirt to fish out the key. When she opened the door, she motioned for Jack to go ahead of her.

Inside was even worse. The hallway was squalid and filthy and smelled as if it hadn't been cleaned in years. She headed up a flight of stairs and Jack hesitantly followed. One of his feet grazed a pile of rags on the first landing—and the pile moved angrily.

"A crackhead," Samsonite said. "Don't mind him."

She also told Jack not to mind the rat that scurried past them on the way downstairs. He considered grabbing her, dragging her the hell out of there and taking her back to his place, then he thought: No. I'm too close. I'll know what's going on soon. Don't spook her. Just let it go.

They reached her apartment, which was on the third floor. The soiled green door was protected by four interior locks and one outside padlock. As Samsonite began her unlocking process, she said, "It's not like I'm paranoid. I know you're thinkin' I'm paranoid. It's the Russian mentality. You always think someone's trying to take whatever you've got."

By now she had managed to open her door. She stepped into the apartment, flicked on the light, and recoiled at the brightness. She immediately flicked it off and, as Jack stepped in behind her, she began scurrying around lighting candles. Not three or four candles. Fifty, sixty candles, maybe even a hundred that were scattered all over the place. And there was not all that much place in which to scatter.

Samsonite lived in two rooms plus a kitchen. Although it could barely be called a kitchen now. It was a room with a dirt-streaked white refrigerator and countertops that were covered with food-encrusted plates and bowls and ancient cardboard cartons of Chinese food. When she lit the four candles that sat by the sink—which was filled to the brim with dirty plates and silverware—Jack saw what looked like a herd of cockroaches scuttle into the cracks in the wall.

The living room had rags and towels thumbtacked up as window curtains. There was one sofa that looked as if it would collapse if anyone sat on it, and a small orange crate that Jack guessed was a makeshift coffee table. That was it. Through the open bedroom door, he could see mounds of clothes scattered on the floor and an iron, four-poster bed.

"You know, when I first came here, I thought I'd be a model. That's what everyone said, beautiful girls come here from Russia, they become models."

"What happened?"

"Maybe I'm not beautiful enough."

"I don't think that's it."

She smiled a bitter smile and continued lighting the candles scattered around the room. As she reached over to light two on the floor, in the corner, she picked up a small hypodermic needle and held it up for inspection. "Maybe I found something else I like better," she said. When she was done lighting the candles, she seemed exhausted by her effort and flopped down on the ruin of a sofa. "Have a seat."

"Where?" he asked.

Without answering—he wasn't certain she'd even heard him—she popped back up off the couch and went to the kitchen. He heard the fridge open and the rustling of various implements in her cabinets, then saw her, her back to him, pouring wine into two paper cups. On her return trip to the sofa, she handed him one of the cups, filled nearly to the brim. She flopped again, this time stretching out so her head rested on one arm of the couch and her black boots on the other.

"Oh, God," she sighed. "Will you take my boots off?"

Jack hesitated, then set his wine down on the scuffed hardwood floor. He moved to the couch and she gingerly lifted one leg. He took her left foot in his hand, worked his fingers around the black heel, and pulled. It took three yanks, then it came free. He saw the look of pleasure on her face as she wriggled her toes. Without a word, she lifted her other leg and held her foot out to him. He grabbed this boot and pulled. When it was off, he set it down on the floor in front of her. Her head back, her feet flexing, she closed her eyes and Jack wasn't certain that she hadn't fallen asleep on him. But before he could even check, her eyes flew open and she said, "You know what Kid's biggest problem was? He was trying to reform me. I mean, shit, reform me from *what?*"

She took a long sip of her wine. A tiny bit of it slid from her lips and down her chin. She caught it with a finger and, with a look of great contentment, stuck that finger in her mouth and sucked it. Jack went back to where he'd been standing, picked up his own wine, and took a long swallow. It was cheap stuff, too cold and vinegary-tasting, but he didn't really care. He drank again.

"Someone was with him that night, just before he died. Did you know that?"

"Who?"

"I don't know. I was hoping you would. It was a woman."

"Oh." She was drifting now. He wondered if she'd taken something when she went to get the wine. "Kid." She seemed to be lost in her own thoughts. "Besides," she said, "who wants to be reformed?"

"Were you with him?"

"I was with him a lot," she said dreamily.

"That night. The night he fell, were you with him then?"

"How the fuck would *I* know?" she said. "I don't even know where I am *now*. Where *are* we? I mean, *Jesus*."

She reached down under the couch without looking, felt around, pulled out a pack of cigarettes and a book of matches, and lit one.

"Kid was tripping when he fell," Jack said.

"Yeah?"

"Are you surprised?"

"You wanna know the truth? I'm beyond surprise. That particular, whaddyacallit, that thing in my brain, it's like some kind of electrical thing, well, it's gone. The fuse is blown or whatever. I don't know the exact medical terminology."

Jack sipped his wine again. He was surprised to find that it was tasting better.

"Goddamn, I miss him, you know? I mean, he saved my ass. Did I tell you that already? Yeah, I guess I did. Sorry. Sometimes I don't remember what I said and what I didn't say."

"No," Jack told her. "You didn't tell me."

"Really?"

"What happened?"

"Oh, man, I did somethin' so fucking stupid. I mean, it was so fucking stupid it was even stupid for me. But all that money, you know, it's just right there in front of you."

Jack watched her sit up. Her movements were almost snakelike. She seemed to slither when she moved. She looked at him and bared her teeth. As she did, she took her right hand and began rubbing her left breast. She twisted the shirt fabric over her nipple and squeezed and massaged it. Her head lolled back and her mouth opened just a bit. He saw her eyes lose their focus and he thought she was about to begin masturbating. But then, as suddenly as she'd started, she stopped. She was just sitting on the edge of the couch now, leaning forward intently, staring at him.

"You're talking about when you're dealing?" he asked, trying to get her back on the subject. He glanced at his watch. He'd left Grace exactly half an hour ago. "Where all that money is?"

"Yeah," Samsonite said. "When I'm dealing. It's not like we're in Vegas, you know. I figured, with those bozos, I mean, you slip a coupla chips into your panties, who the fuck is gonna know?"

Jack realized he was sweating heavily. He wiped his forehead as perspiration dripped down into his eye. "Can I open a window?" he asked. "It's very hot in here."

"Open whatever you want," she told him.

But when Jack went to the living room window, he was surprised to find it was already open. The air was cool and blowing and he realized that now he was shivering slightly.

"Somebody caught you?" he asked.

"You got *that* fucking right. They were gonna cut my fuckin' hands off if I didn't make good on it in twenty-four hours. Yeah, like it wasn't already up my fuckin' nose."

"Five thousand dollars," he said suddenly.

"What?"

"How much did you steal?"

"Hey, it wasn't stealing. I mean, it didn't really belong to anyone, it was, like, gambling money, you know?"

"You took five thousand dollars, right?"

"Yeah. How'd you know?"

Half to himself he said, "The Entertainer's money."

"You're really weird, you know that?" Samsonite announced.

Jack felt as if one minor key had been unlocked. "That's why he needed the money. Kid gave *you* the five thousand dollars."

Samsonite sat up now, excited. "In a flash. I mean, that *day*. It was, like, amazing. Like he was some kind of angel, you know? I paid those assholes back ASAP and it was, like, totally cool."

Jack was sweating again. He realized that his shirt collar was sopping wet and his hands were moist. He felt like he had a fever. He was suddenly dizzy.

"But . . . you're still working there," he said. His voice sounded strange to him, as if he were in an echo chamber.

"Yeah?"

"Why didn't they fire you?"

"Hey, good people are hard to find."

He felt himself rocking from side to side. He thought he should sit down but he suddenly didn't think he could make it to the couch. Talk to her, he thought. Keep talking. Focus. You'll snap out of this.

"His other women . . . Did Kid ever talk to you . . . about . . . his other women?"

She was standing now. Walking around the room. Circling him, he thought. Like a vulture.

"Oh, he talked," she said. "He was a good talker. There was the rich old lady in the 'burbs. She was hot, he said. Wild. And there was a stripper; I remember that 'cause I wanted him to bring her up here, do a little threesome thing. I always wanted to be a stripper, you know. I think it'd be cool. . . ."

Jack felt himself go down on one knee. He wasn't aware of his body touching the floor, though. It was as if he were in some kind of dream. Disconnected from his body. Looking down, seeing himself sag and fall.

"Then there was this Miss I'm So Perfect Downtown SoHo Art Bitch. He used to go on and on about her. Oh, man, it used to make me puke. And it takes a lot to make me puke."

She was standing in front of him now, staring down at him. She didn't look concerned. Just predatory. He felt his hands start to tingle. The left one went numb. He reached out to her, wrapped both arms around her hard thighs, fell forward.

"He used to talk about *you* a lot," she said.

She seemed so far away . . . so out of focus . . .

"Christ, what I don't know about you. Your stupid red-meat crematorium. Your fantasy apartment. The whaddyacallit, the balcony that you're terrified of. Your big affair in London. How you tried to have a baby but your wife had an abortion. Kid told me *everything* about you. Stuff he didn't even know he was telling me . . ."

It sounded like she was speaking in slow motion. *Everything* was in slow motion. His hands slid slowly down her legs. Her skin felt so smooth, so warm. His legs fell out, ever so slowly, from beneath him. He was stretched out on the floor now, his chin resting on the top of her bare foot. With her other foot, she nudged his chin and he felt himself roll over. Twisting, turning, on the wood floor . . .

"I know why you're here," she was saying now. Her voice was even slower, and deep, like a record being played at the wrong speed. "I know what you want me to say. I figured it out, too. But when he came to buy the fucking acid, I didn't know who it was for. I didn't know what he was going to do with it. . . ."

The rest made no sense to Jack. It was too slow. Too deep. He was drifting. He was almost gone. His last thought was *Goddamn you, what did you put in the drink . . . ?*

Then he was still, not moving at all. He was lying on his back and Samsonite was kneeling over him, straddling his chest.

"This is going to be way cool," she said. "*Way* fucking cool."

He never knew what he dreamed or what was real. Not while it was happening, not after it was all over.

It was all so distorted and twisting. Twisted. Sometimes delicious. And funny. Sooooo funny. He couldn't stop laughing, it was impossible to stop the laughter. Nothing ever felt so good. Until it felt bad. And then *nothing* was funny. He couldn't stop crying. It was excruciating. Terrifying. Unbearable.

Sometimes he was naked. Once he was on the bed like that and he couldn't move, he didn't know why but he couldn't, and Caroline, sweet Caroline, lovelier than ever, was on top of him, riding him, her eyes rolled back in ecstasy, saying over and over again, *I love you, Jack . . . I love you, Jack . . . I love you . . .*

Then suddenly it wasn't Caroline. She was gone and instead it was Samsonite. Laughing and moaning. And dripping something. What was it? Dripping all over. It was red. Wine. Blood. Red red red everywhere . . .

How did Grace get there? She was naked, too, spreading her legs, climbing over him. She was delectable. Petite. He wanted her more than he'd ever wanted anyone. She was saying something, yes, she was saying, *The Destination.* She drew it out, *Dessssstinaaaaashunnnnnn,* so it sounded like a train, chugging far away, around a bend and gone forever. He was inside her. She was on top of him and he could feel himself inside her. She was leaning forward, bending down low, her breasts grazing his bare chest, and she was very beautiful. *So* beeeaaaauuutifullll. Her lips were soft and moist and he kissed her. Her tongue was inside his mouth, exploring his teeth and the hollows of his cheeks. Her breath was sweet, like wisteria brushing up against his face. But then her tongue got too big to keep in his mouth. It was so long, like a snake. It *was* a snake. It hissed and licked him but it kept going, slithering out past the bed, along the floor. So thick and getting thicker. Growing. Expanding like a balloon being pumped up with air. It was filling up the room. And getting longer. Going out the window . . .

The window . . . out the window . . . *he* was going out the window . . .

No, not the window. The balcony. Kid's balcony. He was going over, he was falling. Plunging! Going faster and faster and faster and faster. He was going to hit!

He heard the screaming. Was *he* screaming? Yes, yes, it was him, because the red was everywhere now, covering him, flooding the room in a rushing wave, filling it up to the ceiling. Everywhere he looked, there was red and more red. More red everywhere.

And he was fucking them all now, one at a time. And yet all together. How could that be? But it was. Steady, hard, rhythmic fucking. The Rookie. So beautiful, so gentle. The Entertainer. Grinning at him, a knife in one hand, a long needle sticking out of her arm. The Mortician, her long nails scratching his back, ripping his flesh. Samsonite. Her sharp teeth biting his neck, then his shoulder, before she exploded in a burst of red and he began screaming again. And even Emma! Sexy, delicious Emma from long ago. But then Caroline was back . . . perfect Caroline. Calming him down. Loving him. Making him safe . . .

He wanted to say to her, *I can't be safe. I've almost done it, I think I've found them all, but there's one missing. No one's safe until we find her! They were missing the Murderess. Where was the Murderess? Why couldn't he find the Murderess?*

More red. Oh, God, it was impossible, how could there be more red? But there was. Caroline disappeared, submerged in a river of red. A red rolling river . . .

And Kid's voice. How could it be Kid's voice? Saying: *Say when it hurts . . . Say when it hurts . . .*

Even more red . . . Even more pain . . .

Naked.

Fucking.

All of them.

Alone. Together.

Red red red red.

Say when it hurts.

When . . . Jack screamed . . . *When when when when when when when! Please, God, it hurts . . . Oh . . . my . . . God . . . It huuuuuurrrrrrrttttttsssssss. . . .*

t took him several seconds to realize that he was awake. His mouth was dry and nasty. It felt as if he had eaten a bucket of sand. His tongue was coated with a hard, rough crust and when he tried to clear his throat it came out like a croak, like he hadn't spoken in years and years and his throat had stopped working.

Jack was disoriented. He had no idea how long he'd been dreaming or what time it was now and instinctively he went to look at his watch. But he couldn't. His left hand was handcuffed to the bedpost at the top left of the bed. Not yet comprehending where he was or what had happened, he yanked his hand but he couldn't get free. He yanked again, harder, and the pain of the cuff cutting into his wrist brought reality back to him in small drips: finding Samsonite, going to her apartment, talking, drinking, the hallucinogenic drug that had been slipped into his wine. He didn't know exactly what had happened after that, but flashes of it slipped in and out of his brain, and with them came anger and confusion and humiliation and, he couldn't deny it, excitement.

He yanked his hand again; it did no good. But his hard pull twisted his body over and Jack suddenly realized he was not in bed alone. He twisted his head to look to his right. Samsonite was next to him. Naked and still sleeping. Enraged, he shoved her with his right hand, pushed her hard in the back, but she didn't wake. He went to push her again, overcome by anger, but as his hand touched her spine, he saw that on the sheet by her lower back was a red stain. He could see her legs now, and they, too, were splashed with red. Jack looked down at his own naked body and realized that he, too, was stained. His chest, one arm, a thigh was splotched with thick, red blood.

He wanted to yell at her, to scream, "Wake up, you crazy bitch!" but there was no point because when he grabbed her shoulder and turned her body toward him he saw the river of blood covering her neck and breasts. He saw the slash marks, the deep stab wounds. Saw that she'd been gutted, her stomach slit wide open.

He yanked his arm as hard as he could and the bed rattled noisily, but Jack couldn't free himself. The handcuff cut into his wrist as he pulled again, grunting. He was starting to panic, in bed with a corpse, covered in her blood, but he forced himself to be calm. He could not afford to lose it, not now, so he told himself he'd been around many dead bodies before. Not human bodies but he'd seen a lot of blood and torn flesh, that's all this was, and there was nothing to be done about it now, and he made himself close his eyes and take a deep breath and think. *Think* . . .

Jack examined the bedpost. He stopped pulling and turned so he could put both hands on the knob at the top. He gripped it tightly and yanked upward. Straining, he felt something give. He took another deep breath, got another grip on the post, and pulled again. And again. He thought maybe the give had been his imagination but he shook that thought away and forced himself up onto his knees now, using them to dig into the mattress and give him more leverage. He forced himself to lift up as hard as he could. His jaw clenched and his entire body was as taut as it could be and this time, yes, definitely, he felt something move. One more tug, it moved again, and then a frantic pull and he was free, the metal post flying out of its socket. Jack tumbled out of the bed and, still scrambling on the floor, slid the cuff down and off the bottom part of the post. It dangled from his wrist as he ran to the phone. . . .

Dead. No, not dead. *Cut.* The phone line had been cut, he could see the splayed cord sticking out of the baseboard.

Shaking, his breath coming in short, emphatic bursts, he spotted his pants lying crumpled in the middle of the floor, pulled them on, searched the pockets for his cell phone but, no, he realized he'd left it at home, he'd forgotten to take it when he went to pick up Grace. He saw his shirt, torn, ripped down the front, but he put it on and, not bothering with his shoes or socks, he ran to the front door, out into the hallway, down the steps, practically leaping from landing to landing, and out the front door. He was on the street now, still running. Ahead at the corner he saw a telephone.

He ran past a parked car and, as he did, he saw the front windshield explode. He stumbled and then there was a second explosion. Behind him, a storefront window had shattered into thousands of pieces. Jack's first thought was that the apocalypse had come. The world was blowing itself up. Madness had won out and destruction was complete. And then he realized it was nothing so overwhelming. It was much more banal and much, much more dangerous.

Someone was shooting at him.

What the hell was happening!

What the hell was going on!

Another window burst behind him and Jack dove for safety behind a parked car. An alarm went off, the noise echoing up and down the street. He heard footsteps. Running. And then the only sound was the blare of the alarm. Jack stayed on the ground, panting. When he finally raised his head, he saw a cop car pulling up and jerking to a stop. Two uniformed policemen ran out, their guns drawn. One took off down the street in the direction of the footsteps. The other stood over Jack, pointing the pistol straight down at him. The cop was telling him not to move, not to move one fucking inch or he'd get a bullet in his head.

Jack was only too glad not to move anymore.

He glanced down, saw the blood that still covered his body, stared back up at the cop and hoped that his eyes conveyed his fear and his innocence, and then Jack didn't move again until the second cop returned, panting, shaking his head to show he'd found nothing. By that time another cop car had pulled up and Sergeant Patience McCoy hopped out, mad as hell, Jack presumed, because she was probably missing breakfast with her husband.

THEY WERE STANDING in the shabby, puke-green hallway outside Samsonite's apartment. A locksmith was busy working to get Jack out of the handcuffs that still dangled from his wrist. Cops were going through the bedroom, examining the body and going over every inch of the place. It did not take long to establish that Samsonite had been stabbed fourteen times or that the murder weapon was not in the apartment or anywhere in the vicinity on the street. They had people going through garbage cans and searching in alleys but no one seemed particularly hopeful that anything would turn up.

McCoy had retrieved Jack's socks and shoes, which he'd put on, and in the trunk of her car she'd found a blanket, which, although it was quite warm outside, she'd put around his shoulders. The sergeant didn't say a word, just waited until the cuffs were off and the locksmith was heading downstairs. Then she nodded and said, "Let's start at the very beginning, and you tell me everything, only this time I'll believe you. And then we'll see if we can catch this crazy motherfucker."

Jack nodded and forced himself to remember every single detail he could. McCoy had also managed to get some hot coffee, which he sipped gratefully as he talked. He went through it all, from the first moment Kid showed up in his living room, through all the conversations about his team, every detail Jack could dredge up. He told McCoy all of it: about Kid's funeral and how, after that, he'd tracked down the Mortician. He explained what happened in Kid's apartment, and later at the Migliarinis' funeral home. He told her about talking to Bryan, which led him to Kim. How he'd found the Entertainer, and exactly what had happened the night of her murder, and how next he found the Rookie. At that point, he said, "I guess you know about her, though, she's the one who called you." When McCoy looked confused, he said, "She called you, right? When I didn't show up. In fact, if I wanted to be picky I'd ask what the hell took you so long." When McCoy finally told him she didn't have any idea what he was talking about, Jack shook his head, as if he were talking to somebody who didn't understand English, and said, "Grace Childress. The Rookie. She was with me at the gambling club. I told her to call you if I didn't check in with her in two hours. That was, what, four, five hours ago now, and you just got here, so—"

"Nobody called in for you," McCoy said.

"Of course she did," Jack told the sergeant. "She had to."

"I'm here because while somebody was shooting at you on the street, the guy in that apartment there"—McCoy jerked her head across the hallway—"came outside to go to work and saw this shit in here." Now her head nodded at Samsonite's blood-soaked apartment. "Somebody else reported the shots and we had a car in the vicinity."

"She *had* to have called you," Jack said. "I don't understand."

"I don't understand either," McCoy told him. "But I think you'd better give me her address and phone number."

"There's a reason she didn't call," Jack insisted. "She didn't do this. It's not possible."

"There's a lot of things I didn't think were possible just a few days ago," McCoy said, shaking her head. "So just give me the info. I want to find her immediately. Because if she's *not* the killer then there's a pretty good chance whoever *is* is gonna try to turn her into another corpse."

Jack nodded, solemnly repeated Grace's name, and gave McCoy the address. He couldn't remember her phone number but she told him not to worry about that, they could find it. She excused herself, disappeared for a moment into the apartment, and Jack could hear her give the information to one of the cops. Moments later, they both emerged. McCoy stopped to stay with Jack; the other cop kept going down the stairs.

"He'll find her," McCoy said. "One way or the other." She saw him stare after the cop who'd just left and she knew Jack wanted to go, too, to check on the woman he called the Rookie, but she told him to keep talking, to tell the rest of his story. "It's the only way we're going to finish this," she urged. "The most helpful thing you can do now is talk."

So Jack kept talking. He backtracked, told her everything he could remember about the Team. About Kid's world and his Slashes. She asked to hear more about Grace and he said that he thought she'd become the new Destination and he told her about Kid's romantic notion that Rome was a destination. He told her about the Mistake, a woman from Kid's past who'd appeared again, and how Kid had seemed shaken by both the past relationship and the current one. He told her about the break-in at his apartment, then worked his way back to Samsonite, told McCoy about finding her at the after-hours club and recounted how he went to her apartment, the things he'd learned about her—her stealing money from the club, Kid loaning her the five thousand dollars he'd borrowed from the Entertainer. It was a jumble of information to him now, hard to sort through, especially as new flashes began to come back to him: the things Samsonite told him she'd learned from Kid.

I know all about you, she'd said to Jack. *Your stupid red-meat crematorium. Your fantasy apartment . . .*

He told McCoy how he began to feel dizzy. At first he'd thought it was exhaustion, then the stifling atmosphere of the tenement apartment. Only as he stumbled did he begin to realize that he'd been drugged.

. . . The whaddyacallit, the balcony that you're terrified of . . .

He told McCoy what she'd said about the drugs: *I know why you're here. I know what you want me to say. I figured it out, too. But when he came to buy the fucking acid, I didn't know what it was for. I didn't know what he was going to do with it. . . .*

"What did she figure out?" McCoy asked.

"I don't know. I think she meant she figured out who killed Kid."

"How come everyone seems to have figured it out except *us,* goddamnit? And who came to buy the acid? Kid?"

"That's what it sounded like," Jack said. "But I don't know for sure. I don't know *anything* for sure."

There was more but Jack couldn't dredge it out of his memory. His body was giving out now and his brain was not far behind. McCoy saw him fade and she told him he'd done more than enough, that she'd give him a ride home.

I'm missing something, Jack thought. What the hell am I missing?

In the ride uptown, McCoy tried to make sense of what he'd told her but she wasn't having much better luck than he was. "We'll check into Kid's background," she told him. "See if we can dig up anything from his past that might help. Get his college records, even high school. I'll go talk to Ms. Migliarini again, too."

"I think she's the one," Jack said.

"No. I don't think so," McCoy told him. "I'm certainly going to discuss that possibility with her. But there's one thing that doesn't fit."

"What's that?"

"Why would she let you live? If there's one thing your Mortician knows, it's not to be careless or sentimental. If it's her or somebody who works for her, it doesn't add up. You're the one who confronted her in the first place. You're the only one who's put the various pieces together. You're the one who tracked down all the other women—and let's assume that whoever it is we're looking for killed those women because they knew something, because they could've led us to where we want to go. Well, the person who's got the best chance of leading—you—was right there for the taking. Doesn't make sense. Especially for someone like little Eva. Why kill Samsonite and leave you there to keep hunting?"

Jack didn't have an answer to that. But McCoy did.

"You *know* something, Jack. You know something you don't even know you know. You're the point man, there's some kind of connection between you and whoever's doing this."

"No," Jack said, shaking his head. "I don't know *any* of these women. I never heard of them until Kid told me about them. I never met them until I started finding them."

"You don't know that."

"I do. I've met—"

"You've met them all except two, possibly three."

"The Murderess and maybe the Destination. And the Mistake."

"You don't know who they are," McCoy said. "You never saw them, you don't know their names, so how the hell do you know there's no connection?"

"I think if we find the Murderess we'll have the killer."

"We got good news and bad news on that one: most of the others have been eliminated. Your instincts have been pretty good so far, Jack. Mine have pretty much sucked but you're in my territory now and I'm telling you that Kid is the key. And you knew Kid. You knew him well enough to know he didn't kill himself, didn't you?"

Jack nodded.

"Then you know something else, too," McCoy said. "Your job is to try to figure out what the fuck it is."

THE FIRST THING Jack did when he got home was to call Grace. There was no answer, just a message on her machine saying she wasn't available. "It's Jack," he said after the recording instructed him to talk. "Call me so I know you're all right."

He took a steam, made it as hot as he could stand. Didn't press the off switch until he couldn't take it any longer. Then he turned the shower on and let icy-cold water run down over him. Toweled himself off and got dressed. He was dreading what he was going to do next. He didn't know why, exactly, except something inside of him knew that it was leading him somewhere he didn't want to go. But he knew he had to go there. If he wanted the horror to end, if he wanted the killing to stop, he understood that McCoy was right—he knew something and now it was time to dig it out of himself.

You're the point man, McCoy had said. *There's a connection.*

But what the hell was it?

What did he know? What was the secret?

And how far back did it go?

That's what scared him, Jack realized. He didn't know why, but he did know it was what was holding him back, what was blocking his mind.

How far back did it go?

Jack went to his computer, called up the file he'd made on Kid.

He studied the information he'd put in. As he studied, his mind flew to anything relevant he'd picked up from the women on Kid's team or from Bryan. What he had learned since he'd typed in these notes.

Kid had spent three years at St. John's quarterbacking the football team. He'd left after his junior year and he and Caroline had never gotten to the bottom of it. There seemed to be some connection to his teammate who had been injured on the practice field, had been hit hard enough to paralyze him, but what was it? And what else had happened that made him leave?

Question number one: The football accident was tragic, yes, but what was it that affected Kid so greatly? Why would a teammate's injury drive him to leave school and run off to another state? And what, if anything, did it have to do with what was happening now?

All right. What next? *Think!*

Kid bummed around for a while. Eventually went back to school, to Maryland State, where he got his degree. Why there? And what else could have happened there? It was where he met his first Destination. Who was she? Why did that end? Kid said it was because she chose another man. Who was it? Did any of that matter?

Why did Kid come back to New York? What was he into that would lead to his death?

It kept coming back to the same thing: the women.

The Entertainer: He'd found her, she was just as Kid had described. Beautiful and smart and sad. She'd given Kid five thousand dollars that he'd never returned. Kid had told her it was for his tuition but he'd lied. He'd given the money to Samsonite. Why did he lie? Because he was giving it to another woman? Because the Entertainer would have been jealous? Jack thought that the money was irrelevant. But what had the Entertainer known? Why was she killed? She said she'd heard things, noticed things, but what? Did her killer take anything from the apartment?

The Rookie. Grace. Jack checked his notes and saw that Kid had told him that the Rookie was dangerous. He couldn't believe that Grace was capable of violence, though. Jack realized that he was attracted to her, that he liked her; it was hard to be objective. But why hadn't she called McCoy? Why hadn't she called *him?* Where was she now?

Where was she when Samsonite had been murdered and Jack had been shot at?

The Destination #1: She seemed unlikely. Out of the picture for a long time. But the Destination #2—Who was she? Grace? Jack was fairly certain that's what she'd evolved into, but he couldn't be positive. Was there someone else out there? Someone else with a secret? Someone who knew Kid's secret?

The Mistake. Kid hadn't talked much about her. He'd seemed particularly evasive. They hadn't had sex, he'd said. But the relationship was sexual. Was the Mistake in love with Kid? Had she been in love with him all these years? Did she kill him because that love was unrequited?

Finally, the Murderess. Jack didn't have much to go on. She'd been scarred by an accident in her youth. That was pretty much it. McCoy had said she could be anyone. Who? Someone he knew? Some link between him and Kid?

Who?

Jack got up from his chair and began pacing. He was getting nowhere. The more information he had, the more confused he was becoming.

What was he missing?

All right, he thought. Dig into the specifics. Go back to Samsonite. A sick girl, no question about that. But she didn't deserve to die like that. No one deserved to die like that. He knew he'd never get the image and the fear that came with it out of his mind.

Stop it, he told himself. Don't think about that now. Think about what you learned. What you can still learn. What had she said?

Christ, what I don't know about you. Your stupid red-meat crematorium. Your fantasy apartment. The whaddyacallit, the balcony you're terrified of . . .

Jack felt violated, thinking about the things Kid had shared. Things he had told these women about the man they knew only as the Butcher.

Your big affair in London . . .

Jesus Christ! How could she have known about that? How could *Kid* have known about that? It wasn't possible. Had she really said it? Or was it part of his own psychedelic fantasy?

How you tried to have a baby but your wife had an abortion . . .

No, it was impossible! She couldn't have known that! He'd tried to forget it himself. It was too painful; he'd shut down the memory. He had never even been able to tell Dom. They had wanted a child so desperately. Caroline had been pregnant when he'd gone off to England. When he'd had the affair with Emma. And when he returned, right after he got back, Caroline aborted the baby. She told him she'd done it, that she no longer wanted the child and, although neither of them had ever acknowledged it, they both knew it was because of what had happened in London. How she'd known what had occurred there, he never discovered. He had his suspicions but they didn't matter. What mattered was that he had hurt her and this was the only way she knew to respond. They had created the child out of love and she had destroyed it out of pain.

They'd recovered from it, though, individually and as a couple. He had wounded her, the scar had healed. Ultimately, she had understood and that understanding had made them closer. It was something that had been so private, so personal; the healing process had drawn them together—

Jack straightened up and stopped his pacing. There was something gnawing at him now, he didn't know exactly what. But something didn't compute.

It had been so private.

So how did Samsonite know about it? And about the affair? *How?*

His stream of consciousness took him to the front of Grace's apartment building. He remembered standing with her, asking her what Kid had told her that had frightened her.

This might sound crazy, she'd said, *but I had the feeling he wanted me to know certain things in case . . . in case you found me. . . . I got the feeling there was something going on that had been going on a long time. For years. I think he felt responsible for certain things, people getting hurt. Maybe even getting killed.*

What people? Jack had asked. But she didn't know.

Then he flashed on Samsonite again: *How you tried to have a baby but your wife had an abortion . . .*

What was *wrong* with that?

There was something going on for a long time. For years.

How many years? What had been going on for years?

He felt responsible for people getting hurt. Maybe even getting killed.

What people?

But your wife had an abortion . . .

How did she know?

Maybe even getting killed.

Who? What people?

Your affair . . .

An abortion . . .

"Oh my God."

Jack said it out loud; the sound of his own voice made him jump. He knew now what had frightened him about searching the past. Somehow he must have known all along. He knew what the connection was. He didn't understand it, didn't *want* to understand it, but he knew.

Kid had told Samsonite about Caroline's abortion.

But Jack had never told Kid.

Jack had never told anyone. Not a soul. Which meant only one person could have told Kid.

Only one person . . .

But how was that possible? How? Why? And when?

Jack, forcing himself to move slowly, refusing to bow to the urgency that was kicking at his midsection, sat back down at his computer, immediately logged on to the CylockHolmes program. He knew what he was looking for and he scrolled down until he found it.

FIND: License Plate Numbers
Social Security Numbers
Business Records
Unlisted Phone Numbers
Unknown Addresses

And then:

LOCATE Long-Lost Friends
DISCOVER Dirty Secrets Your In-Laws Don't Want You To Know
Criminal Search Background Check * Find Out About Your Daughter's Boyfriend
NEIGHBORS! Find Out What They Have To Hide!
Education Verification! Did He Really Graduate From College! Find Out!

Education Verification.

Jack double-clicked on it. At the prompt, he typed in Kid's real name, George Demeter. Typed in his home address on Staten Island. Listed St. John's and Maryland State College, then clicked on the "Verify" button and waited. It didn't take long.

Kid's name popped up on-screen. So did his date of birth. So did verification that he attended St. John's University in

New York City for three years. The program listed the exact dates he was enrolled as well as his official extracurricular activities. In this case it was singular: SJU football team, freshman through junior.

Jack scrolled down. He knew what he was going to find, there was no doubt about it. And find it he did.

Kid had lied to him. He did not receive his degree from Maryland State. He did not attend, at any time, Maryland State or any other school in Maryland.

As he realized what had happened, the thoughts and images came into Jack's head as if driven there by a tornado. They whirled through him, rocking him back in his chair.

Kid's datebook. The one Jack found in the Mortician's apartment. It listed the Destination over and over again. And one name: Charlotte. Not a name, he realized. Not a name of a person. A place. An abbreviation for a place!

Grace: *Bad things had happened to people around him. People he loved.*

Samsonite: *You tried to have a baby but your wife had an abortion.*

Grace: *He felt responsible for certain things, people getting hurt. Maybe even getting killed.*

No, it was impossible. It was fucking impossible!

McCoy: *You're the point man. There has to be some connection.*

But it's not impossible, Jack realized. It was all too possible. There *is* a connection. And it's from one horror to another. From one nightmare to the next.

And now he remembered something. Something Caroline had told him several months before the Charlottesville opening. He had thought it was about the restaurant. Now he thought differently. *That's the way I feel down in Virginia*, she'd said. *I have something down there that's beautiful. That's mine.*

Jack forced himself to look at the computer screen. He saw the name of the second college that Kid had attended. Saw the location. Saw the dates he was there.

Virginia State University.

Thirty minutes from Charlottesville.

There the entire year Caroline was opening up the restaurant.

Caroline was the one who had told Kid about her abortion. It's the only way he could have known.

He felt responsible for people getting hurt. Maybe even getting killed.

Kid had lied when he stood in Jack's living room that first time. He had known about Caroline's death and Jack's injuries before he'd come back to New York, before he'd gone to see Dom. He had come back to New York specifically to heal him; Jack knew that now. To save him. Because somehow, some way, Kid had been unable to save the woman he loved. His Destination.

Caroline.

JACK KELLER HAD not been back to Charlottesville since the robbery and murder. He had told himself he would never go there again. But now he decided to return. He had to. Everything led back there. Everything seemed to start there. He *had* to go. And as soon as he'd made the decision, he knew he would have to leave immediately. Well, not quite immediately. He had one other thing to do first.

First, he wept.

I t was much easier than expected.

Easier than Charlottesville, which was surprisingly easy.

Easier than that black woman in the park.

Easier than the stripper in her bathtub and even easier than that whacked-out junkie, tripping and helpless and moaning in her bed.

This one was waiting, waiting for her own death. She was smiling, welcoming, reaching out with open arms. How could it be any easier than that?

It couldn't.

Her skin ripped right open and she didn't make a sound. She was supposed to be so ferocious, so strong, but she tore as easily as a piece of cheap paper. Her throat and then her chest, open and exposed, sliced and severed. She crumpled and fell like a rag doll and lay still on the floor of her bedroom.

Easy, easy, easy.

The surprise was the man, when he came charging in. She had said they were alone, so it was confusing when the door opened and that angry roar filled the room. It was a surprise, all right, but it didn't change anything. The man was strong but flabby. Old and out of shape. He was easy, too. He died as quickly as all the others.

That was the thing about death, wasn't it?
For something that lasted forever, it happened so quickly.
Life was long and hard. So, so hard.
But death was quick. And so, so easy.

Sergeant Patience McCoy spread the photographs across her desk.

She knew this wasn't the only place she was going to see them, either. By tomorrow morning, they'd be plastered all over the tabs, from the *Enquirer* to the *New York Post*. She didn't know how the hell those papers got crime-scene photos but they always seemed to manage. And this was definitely worthy of the front page.

Joe and Eva Migliarini stabbed to death in their own home.

In their own bedroom.

Christ. How does the head of one of New York's mob families get suckered in his own suburban bedroom?

She could feel the headache coming on. Double Christ. Just what she needed was a migraine.

McCoy had spent the day trying to find Grace Childress. No luck. The woman had disappeared. She didn't like the fact that, when she and her latest partner went to the woman's apartment, it had turned out to be a sublet. It indicated rootlessness, never a good sign. They'd gotten a judge to immediately give them a warrant to enter the apartment but McCoy's search turned up little except that it appeared that a good deal of Grace's clothes were gone. It looked like

Kid's Rookie/Destination had packed up and flown the coop. McCoy had a lot of people out looking for her but they didn't have a hell of a lot to go on. Her neighbors barely knew her. The sublet had been arranged through an agency; the apartment owner had met her for all of thirty seconds. The doormen didn't know her well, she hadn't been there that long.

McCoy picked up the phone, dialed a two-digit extension. "Lewis," she said, picturing the pasty-faced nerdy cop at the other end. Lewis looked like he'd never seen fresh air before. Like he lived in the precinct, which he easily could have done because the only things he liked to do were go through files and study statistics. "I just had an idea for once in my damn life. I want you to look up any records we've got on Jack Keller."

"That's the one, his wife was killed, right?"

"That's the one," she said.

"What kind of records you looking for?"

"Break-ins, burglaries, harassment, arrests, anything. Go back as far as you can go. There's a connection here somewhere and I'm gonna find it if it's the last goddamn thing I do." She hung up, harder than she intended to.

McCoy didn't like what was happening. She didn't like what they'd found in the computer about Grace Childress, either.

What she didn't like the most, however, was that Jack Keller had disappeared, too.

The Entertainer dead. Samsonite dead. Now the Mortician. Dead.

The Murderess—invisible. Nonexistent.

Grace Childress gone. Whether she was the Rookie or the Destination or both, she was gone. And Jack Keller was just as gone.

The sergeant had ordered a DNA test on the vaginal secretions found in Kid Demeter's bed and wondered why the hell it wasn't back already. She wanted to compare it with Grace Childress's DNA, which was already on record.

Patience McCoy wondered if Jack knew what she now knew about Kid's favorite team member. She wondered if Jack knew that Grace Childress had, once upon a time, committed murder.

She sure as hell hoped so.

JACK NEEDED THE entire three-and-a-half-hour drive to compose himself. And by the time he saw the first sign announcing he'd reached Charlottesville, he had succeeded. Or, at least, he now knew exactly what he needed to do. He decided he'd settle for that.

He was hungry, wanted a quick lunch, but decided to skirt the center of town. He was not so composed that he was ready to go anywhere near Jack's yet. He knew that he might have to face that soon, but not yet. Not first. So he kept driving, went straight to the university, parked, and, after wandering a bit, found someone who could direct him to the athletic department. When he asked for Coach Kampman, he was then directed across the campus to the football stadium. The security guard at the door checked his list to see if Jack's name was there—it was—then let him pass. He walked through the arena's maze of concrete tunnels before emerging on the field, coming through the entrance behind one end zone. He stood for a moment, watching the team practice in the summer heat and humidity, then moved up the sideline, stood as patiently as he could until one of the coaches whistled for a break. That same coach, with tousled white-blond hair and a boyish face that was craggy and lined by the sun, now turned and spotted Jack. He walked over, extended his hand, and said, "Bobby Kampman." Jack introduced himself and thanked the coach for seeing him. He said he didn't realize that practice began so early in the year, wasn't it still summer vacation, but the coach told him that football at VSU was a year-round game. Then Kampman, perfectly polite but obviously anxious to get back on schedule, skipped any further pleasantries and got right to business.

"I got the photo you scanned," he told Jack. "Or, rather, my secretary did. I couldn't have pulled it out of the computer if I had a hundred years to work on it. But I got it. And I distributed it to all my boys before we started the workout this morning. A lot of the kids were on the team two years ago, maybe twenty. A lot of them knew Haywood and Neufield, those were the two who fought in your restaurant. A lot of my boys were their friends. But none of them knew anyone named Kid Demeter."

"Maybe under a different name—is that possible?"

"I don't think so. They didn't recognize the photo. Not one of them." When Jack didn't respond, the coach said,

"We can try to reach the rest of the kids who were on the team at that time, we can probably find most of them, but I don't think it'll do you any good, Mr. Keller. If these kids don't recognize him, I don't think the others will either."

"Maybe they were afraid to come forward. Maybe—"

"Not my kids." Kampman shook his head vigorously. "Believe me. They know how important this is and I guarantee none of them are holding anything back."

Jack was speechless. He was positive he'd find a connection between Kid and the two players who'd fought in the restaurant and later been shot to death. It had seemed so right. The failure was a little bit like walking headfirst into a brick wall. He was stunned and he wasn't sure in which direction he should now step.

"I'm sorry, sir," the coach was saying now. "We all felt for your tragedy. And I wish there was some way we could help. If you can think of anything else . . ."

Jack couldn't. He thanked the coach, shook his head, and left the stadium. Still rattled by his lack of success, he stood in the parking lot and used his cell phone to make a call and confirm the next stop on his agenda. He got in the car and drove for thirty minutes. When he stepped out, he found himself in a familiar pebbled driveway, staring up at Caroline's childhood home.

"I BEEN WORKING for the Hales for thirty-eight years," Louise Trotty was saying.

"And for me, thirty-three," her husband added.

"I know that," Jack told them.

"I loved that girl since she was seven years old," Louise said.

"I've loved her since she was twenty. Nothing you tell me is going to change what any of us felt for her. *Feel* for her. And I promise you," Jack said, "nothing you say can hurt her. Not now."

The black couple stayed silent and unmoving as Jack slid the photograph of Kid in front of them on the brightly tiled kitchen counter.

"Did you ever see him?" Jack asked.

No movement at all from the Trottys. Then John C. Trotty nodded, the barest of nods, at his wife.

"Yes," she said. "He been here at the house."

Jack had known it, had known it as absolutely as it could be known, but when his knowledge was verified, he felt as if all the air in his body had been released. But along with the blow to his gut also came a strange kind of relief. As painful as it might now be, there was a breakthrough. The connection was made. He didn't know where it would lead, but the unraveling had, at long last, begun.

"Tell me," he said to them.

And they told. Kid had indeed been to this house. Many times. He had first appeared about a month into Caroline's start-up of the restaurant. The Trottys remembered Caroline bringing him there—he hadn't appeared on his own, so she had met him somewhere else; Jack guessed that he had heard about the restaurant and probably surprised her there. They seemed intimate, Louise Trotty said. Very close. He doted on her, complimented her, did everything he could to please her. He spent the night there, they said, slept in the house quite often. Not in the same room as Caroline, Louise was quick to point out. In one of the guest rooms.

"Were they lovers?" Jack asked, keeping his voice as calm as he could.

Louise took a long time before answering. So long that Jack didn't need to hear the answer. He already knew it.

Keeping his voice steady, he asked about conversations they might have overheard. Louise did not have much more information to offer. John recalled one thing very clearly.

"It was two days before the opening. Two days before she was . . ." John stopped himself, didn't finish that sentence. There was no need to. "He was here. That boy. I served them coffee out on the porch. Reason I remember is that Miss Susanna was here. We was all a bit surprised 'cause she don't come around much. But I remember that she and Miss Caroline had a big fight. I don't know exactly why. Something to do with that boy, though, I believe. Miss Susanna left and Miss Caroline was very upset. She and . . . her young man friend, they went into the den, that room right off the dining room there. And she closed the door, talked for quite a long time. When they came out, he was very upset. So was Miss Caroline. They sat on the porch a long while after that"—he hesitated, then plunged ahead—"holding hands, I remember that, too. And Mr. Jack, what I remember is that she said she would take care of him. She would make sure he had a place to live and a job. I remember she said he would have a good job. She told him not to be afraid, that nothing would happen, and that she would make sure he was all right."

"Do you remember what he was afraid would happen?" Jack asked quietly.

"No, sir, I don't," John said. "But it was something bad, because that boy was scared to death."

They all heard the noise of a car pulling up in the driveway now. Louise went to look out the window and, with a catch in her throat, said, "That's Miss Susanna's car."

"Yes," Jack told them. "I asked her to come over."

"Mr. Jack," Louise said. "I don't like to say nothin' bad about nobody. But you watch out. Miss Susanna, she's a mean one."

"Yes, I know," Jack said. "That's why I want to see her."

"I NEVER LIKED my sister," Susanna Rae Hale said to Jack Keller.

"You made that fairly clear over the years," Jack told her.

"I don't much believe in hiding my feelings."

Jack nodded. "That was pretty clear, too. Your feelings were not very well hidden."

"That whole 'blood is thicker than water' thing . . ." Susanna Rae shook her head disapprovingly. "I just don't cotton to that."

"Tell me about your sister," Jack said. "Tell me about my wife."

"What is it you want me to tell you?" she asked.

"The truth."

"About what, in particular? Her childhood? Her popularity? Her perfect skin and her perfect legs and all about how she was the absolutely perfect person?"

"Tell me about Kid Demeter," Jack said. "Tell me what you two fought about a few days before she died."

Susanna Rae lit up a cigarette. "I'm not gonna ask if it's all right for me to smoke," she said. " 'Cause I don't give a damn."

Jack waited for her to inhale deeply. He watched her blow a perfect smoke ring into the air. Then she said, "What we fought about is going to surprise you." Her Southern drawl was becoming slightly thicker as the smoke relaxed her. "We fought about you."

She was right. He *was* surprised. "What about me?"

"You know, it's not just one-sided, it's not just me who doesn't like the family. The family doesn't care for me too much, either. In our family, everybody has somebody. Or *had*. Caroline and Llewellyn, they were close as can be when they were little. Then Caroline had you. Llewellyn has her boring-as-shit husband and her even-more-boring-as-shit children. Even Momma and Daddy, they were just a little world unto themselves. Always were. But me, well, I had my own self and that was pretty much it. But that doesn't mean I ever liked it that way. I know what it's like to be alone. And I don't think anyone should throw her life away and risk *being* alone."

"Is that what you thought Caroline was doing?"

"That's what I believe happens when you have an affair, yes."

"Was she having an affair with Kid?" he asked, closing his eyes.

"That is my belief, yes."

"How do you know that?"

"I have lived here my entire life, Jack, and even though we are now a very sophisticated town, we are still a small town. And in a small town, people talk and gossip. I am one of those talkers and gossipers, so I hear more than my fair share."

"So you came up here to tell her what?"

"To tell her that she was not going to hurt her beloved husband and ruin her own life and bring shame to this family. I may not be loved but I still know the meaning of a family name."

"How did she take it?"

"As we say in our neck of the woods, we had a little quarrel."

"Tell me."

"Not much to tell. She said I didn't understand, that it wasn't what I thought, and that I should mind my own business. I said I agreed it was none of my business, but that I understood extremely well."

"And then?"

"And then I left. I left her to do what she wanted to do with your friend and hers."

They faced each other in silence, the pain etched in Jack's face, Susanna's unmoved and uninvolved. "Yes," she said, as if he'd asked her a question. "I am indeed an unfeeling and sharp-tongued bitch. And I was not being so unselfish when I came to see her; I enjoyed the pain I was bringing. I was jealous of my little sister and I wished her nothing but ill will. But I didn't wish her what she got and I don't wish you what you have." Her tone softened, just a tad, and for a moment Jack heard a trace of Caroline's voice—that slight drawl, the surprising hoarseness—as Susanna said, "You haven't been down here since she was buried, have you?"

"No," Jack said.

"Do you want to see her grave? If you do, I will show it to you and I will be quiet and say I'm sorry for you and mean it."

IT WASN'T AS bad as he'd imagined.

Partly because it didn't seem real. This wasn't her. This was just a stone. It was not the woman he'd loved and been married to and spent his whole life with. It was a slab of stone and a small patch of earth.

It was a beautiful spot, where Caroline was buried. It was, he knew, her favorite spot on the property. Near the barn, under a magnificent magnolia tree that threw off hundreds and hundreds of large white blooms. He could picture her leading her horse out of the stable, gracefully swinging her leg over his back and gently touching him with her heels. He could see the horse take off like the wind and Caroline laughing, sitting in the saddle so easily, as if they were one creature. He could see her lounging under the tree, her back curled up against the trunk, her eyes closed, her lovely face tilted toward the sunlight.

"In some ways you're the lucky one," he said to the stone in front of him. "You don't have to feel anymore."

THE RESTAURANT WAS as bad as he'd thought it would be.

It hadn't changed very much and he thought he'd prepared himself for it but as he walked in he was overwhelmed by the horrific images that would always stain its memory. Standing in the main room, he could hear the voices, the argument at the far table in the corner as if it were happening this very moment. He could see, looking back toward the bar, the masked figure forcing Caroline up the steps. He could remember his panic and his rush to rescue her.

Jack forced himself to go up to the office. He moved slowly as he ascended, not like that night when he'd bounded up, two and three stairs at a time. He could feel himself barging into the room, getting hit, going down. As he stepped back into the tiny room now, he could see and hear it as if it were happening right in front of him: the fear on Caroline's face, the unintelligible phrases, the jumble of words that cascaded through his fractured thoughts.

Tear down the wool.

What the hell had it meant?

Wooly here . . . the will is strong . . . wool candy broken . . .

It was one of the things that had torn at him all these months. It tore at him still. If he could only make sense of what he'd heard. He'd been right there! He had been so close! But he hadn't been able to fight through his pain, through the fog, through his terror, to understand what he was hearing.

He was right next to her and he couldn't save her.

He was right next to the killer and couldn't identify him.

Wooly . . . candy . . . forever . . .

Gibberish. Meaningless, insane gibberish.

What if . . .

Bella, the restaurant's manager, was asking him something.

"Do you want a drink, Jack? This has got to be hard for you."

Jack shook his head. He realized he was back downstairs, sitting at the bar. He didn't even remember leaving the upstairs office. "I just want to talk and get the hell out of here, if you want to know the truth."

"I don't know what to tell you. I told everything to the police."

"Just go over the invitations. For the two football players, Haywood and Neufield."

"Caroline was in charge of the final invitations. A few of us had some input, she discussed it with me. We eliminated a few people, didn't have room for a couple of local businesspeople—nothing strange or out of the ordinary. A day or two before we sent them out, I saw the final list and Caroline had written in 'Raymond Kutchler and friend.' They turned out to be the football players and it was a fake name but that was how they were listed. I asked her about it, who they were, and she said they were nobody, it was a favor for a friend. She also said she'd deliver them herself, no need to mail them."

"Was it a favor for Kid Demeter?"

Bella looked uncomfortable. "I don't know, Jack. She never told me that."

"You were close to Caroline. I know that. She talked about you all the time, said you'd become good friends when she was down here."

"We were. But she was still my boss. She was the soul of discretion, especially around employees. But here's everything I know about Kid and this is it, I swear. Caroline told me he was like a little puppy around her. He was just madly in love with her, had been since he was a boy, and you could see it, the way he looked at her."

"Like she was perfect."

"Like she was beyond perfect. I don't think she took it all that seriously but it kind of thrilled her, if that makes sense. I mean, here was this gorgeous young hunk who couldn't take his eyes off her."

"Do—"

"Do I think she was having an affair with him? Yes. I hate saying it to you but yes. He was the wonderful young thing she'd always wanted. But I also know that whatever their relationship was, she ended it before you came down here. She was very upset. But not sad. Kind of relieved and weirdly happy. You know, the way you are when you make a hard decision it took you forever to make, but then when you make it, it all seems so easy, like it was the only thing you could ever have decided."

"Thank you for saying that."

"I'm just telling you what I saw. And what I knew. Whatever was going on was over."

"Except she was going to give him a job."

Bella looked surprised. Jack heard her draw in some air through her teeth. It made a faint whistling sound. "Yes," she said. "She didn't want anyone to know, but she told me that she was going to get him a job with one of the restaurants.

She said he wanted to get away, to start something new. Not here and not New York. She was going to set him up as an assistant manager at one of the restaurants. Maybe London, that's what I remember. She'd told me you never went to the London restaurant anymore, so I figured that's why she'd picked it."

"She was going to send Kid to London?"

"That's what she told me, Jack. And really—now you know everything I know."

Jack kissed Bella on the cheek and left the restaurant.

Yes, he knew everything she knew. And everything the Trottys knew and everything Susanna Rae Hale knew.

But it wasn't enough. Not yet.

He was getting closer. For the first time he felt like he was getting close.

But he still didn't know nearly enough.

It was getting to the end.

This was almost the last one. Hardly anyone was left.

That was good, it was definitely good, because suddenly it was all very, very tiring.

There was nobody else around, just the old man, and he was right where he was supposed to be. That's what was amazing about people. They were almost always right where they were supposed to be. They were so predictable. And "predictable" was another word for soft.

That was a good one, wasn't it? Who said that? Why was it so hard to remember stuff like that? Stuff like who said "predictable" was another word for soft.

Oh, well. It didn't matter. Nothing mattered except what had to be done here and now. And fast. There would be more people soon. There wasn't much time.

It had to be now.

The old man's back was turned. And he had something in his arms. Oh, that was just too perfect. . . .

Go!

Three silent footsteps. Pick the knife up, the long, beautiful knife on the butcher-block table. Three more steps. He heard something. He's turning . . .

Slash down. Now! He's surprised. Oh, yes, he is. And he's staggering. This won't be hard, he's too old to fight you. . . .

He's bleeding. He can't believe what he's seeing. He can't believe you're here and you're so strong. He can't believe he's going to die. None of them ever believed they were going to die.

Use the knife again. Stick him. Slice him. Slash him open and make sure he can never feel or think or ever, ever, ever tell anything he knows. . . .

But the old man is strong, too. God, how can he be this strong? And why is he still struggling? Doesn't he know it's pointless to fight? It's pointless to struggle against death. Death always wins—

Stop fighting me!

Is he really this strong? Are you weakening? Is that possible? Are you getting weaker? No. No, no, no, no, no! You're just tired. You just need some sleep.

But no time to sleep.

No time.

You have to run. People are coming. They'll be here soon.

Sleep when it's all done. Sleep when you're safe. Sleep when it's over.

And it's almost over.

The old man wasn't fighting anymore. He wasn't moving anymore. He was perfectly still.

It's almost over. . . .

Patience McCoy decided that she was, in fact, an idiot. How much simpler could this have been? The answer: *no* simpler. This was Basic Police Investigation 101. They would have done this on *Law and Order* before the first commercial. So why the hell hadn't she thought of it earlier?

Lewis, the records nerd, hadn't just called her back, he'd actually come to her desk. He'd left his beloved records to give her the news.

"What you got for me, File Boy?" she said.

"Absolutely nothing on Jack Keller except for a liquor license application for his restaurant, which was granted. Long time ago."

"Shit," McCoy said.

"But," Lewis said, "there *is* something on Caroline Keller."

"What?"

"She called in a complaint. Over ten years ago. She was being harassed."

"Don't drag it out, I don't got the time. Just give it to me."

"Her husband was in England and she was being harassed by a woman. Emma Rhowam. English. She was here visiting." He tapped his file. "It says Ms. Rhowam repeatedly made threatening and obscene phone calls to Mrs. Keller, once assaulted her on the street. Keller got a restraining order, which seems to have worked. Calls stopped, no more assaults. Anything else?"

But McCoy had stopped listening. This didn't have to mean anything, she told herself. Ten or more years was a long time. And there didn't have to be a connection. Could be something simple. The Kellers made fun of this lady's dog. The Kellers served her a bad steak in the restaurant. The Kellers—

It hit her like a lightning bolt.

Don't think *Kellers*, she told herself. Think *Kid*.

What was it Jack had told her about the Destination? Kid's romantic description? *Topeka's a town, Cleveland's a city, but Rome is a destination.*

Rome is a destination.

But how about *Rhowam*?

You bet your fucking ass she's a destination. She's *the* Destination. Gotta be. And nine years ago Emma Rhowam attacked Caroline Keller. McCoy had no idea why but right now, the whys were unimportant. All that mattered was finding her.

If she were involved with Kid, that meant she was probably in New York. McCoy reached for the Manhattan phone book. Could it possibly be this easy? Yes, it damn well could. Emma Rhowam, 627 West Ninth Street.

Son of a bitch.

She called the listed phone number and had to admit she was surprised as hell when a woman's voice said, "Hello?"

"Is this Emma Rhowam?"

"Yes. Yes, it is. Who's calling?"

"Sergeant Patience McCoy, NYPD. Do you know a Kid Demeter, Ms. Rhowam?"

"Yes. Yes, I do. I *did*."

"How about Jack and Caroline Keller. Do you know them, too?"

A pause. "What is this about, may I ask?"

"I'd like to discuss that in person. I can be there in twenty minutes."

"I'm afraid I'm on my way to the airport, Sergeant. I'm off to London. I was on my way out the door when the phone rang."

"Well, I'll tell you what, Ms. Rhowam. How about you change your flight?"

"I'm sorry, but—"

"You'll be sorrier if you don't. Because what I'm gonna do is find out what flight you're on. I can do that with a couple of phone calls; it's easy for us big-shot police types, takes a lot less time than it'll take you to get to the airport. And what'll happen is that if you don't talk to me in person now, you'll get out there to that airport, you'll go to get on board, and two big, scary security guards are gonna grab you, arrest you, put your hands behind your back and cuff you. Then they're gonna bring you here to me. And I'll be *angry* by that time. So what I suggest is you reschedule your flight and go to England another time. And right now, you wait there in your apartment and I'll be there just as soon as I can. Okay?"

There was a long pause and she heard the woman on the other end of the phone mumble "Okay" and Sergeant McCoy slammed the phone down. She stood up from her desk and almost collided with Lewis, who was standing over her, hanging on her every word.

"Can you really do that?" he asked breathlessly. "Can you really find out what flight she's on just like that and get those security guards to arrest her?"

"Lewis," she said, "I'm lucky if I can get the damn elevator to stop on this floor. But *she* don't know that, does she?" And when his eyes widened in appreciative awe, she said, "Now check that file one more time and tell me what lawyer Caroline used when she got her restraining order."

"It was Herb Bloomfield," Lewis said. "I already checked."

"Good boy," she said. "You just might make a policeman yet."

She then arranged for two policemen to get to 627 West Ninth Street as fast as they could and make damn sure that Emma Rhowam, suspected in the murder of at least four people, was waiting for her when she arrived.

MCCOY RECOGNIZED BLOOMFIELD from the Entertainer's apartment. But she also knew him by reputation. He was a rich man's lawyer and everything about his Park Avenue office looked the part. All the furniture, except for the glass coffee table, was brown leather. The blotter on the partner's desk was sheathed in brown leather. Most of the books on his bookshelves were bound in brown leather. His pen-and-pencil set was brown leather. She felt blessed that Herb Bloomfield was fifty pounds overweight or she was fairly sure that he'd be wearing a brown leather suit instead of his conservative pinstripe with white shirt and red tie.

"Sergeant, as I told you, I—"

"Yeah, yeah, yeah," McCoy said. "I know, we did all this on the phone. But let me lay this on you one more time, Herb. Your first client, Caroline, is dead. Your second client, Jack, is missing in action and I am worried as hell about him. You want me to start counting up again how many people have been killed so far? If you don't, why don't you just tell me what I want to know so I can try to stop anybody else from dying."

The lawyer tapped his brown leather cigar case on the desk. The taps started out quick and rhythmic and ended with one decisive slam.

"He was having an affair with her."

"What?"

"Jack. With this Emma Rhowam. About ten years ago. Well, no, I'm sorry, he wasn't having an affair with her. He'd *had* an affair with her. And he'd ended it."

"So how did—"

"She was kind of a nut. What else can I tell you? Obsessive, I guess. Jack was a catch. Still is. Apparently, for him it was a fling, for her it wasn't. And she didn't like being dumped. So while he was still in London, she came over here, started harassing Caroline. Called her, told her about the affair, tried to give her intimate details. I suppose trying to break up the marriage."

"And what did Caroline do?"

"She didn't want any part of it. At first she didn't believe it. But this Emma gave her enough information so Caroline knew it was true. She was devastated, of course. Furious. But then she calmed down and just wanted the whole thing to go away. So she came to me and I made it go away."

"And what did Jack do when he found out?"

"He never did."

"Come again?"

"She never told him. And swore me to secrecy. To this day I've never told Jack what happened."

"Why would she do that?"

"I can't say for sure. Humiliation, maybe. Strength, just as likely. I think that Caroline wanted to handle it in her own way. And it's fairly safe to say that she was right. Their marriage certainly survived and flourished. And maybe it wouldn't have if this had all come out in the open."

"And what about Kid Demeter?"

"What about him?"

"Do you know anything about the connection between Emma Rhowam and Kid?"

Now the lawyer looked surprised. "I didn't know there *was* a connection."

"Oh, yeah. There was quite a connection."

McCoy didn't say anything for quite a while.

"Is there anything else I can help you with, Sergeant?"

"Yeah," she said. "Can you explain to me why it is that people do what they do to other people?"

"I'm afraid you're on your own with that one," Herb said. "That's out of my league."

"Mine, too," McCoy said. Then she headed downtown.

SHE DIDN'T EVEN have to talk to the cops on the street to know what had happened. She'd had too much experience and knew the moment she stepped out of her car.

She went up the three flights of stairs two steps at a time. When she got to Emma's apartment, the door was ajar and McCoy said, "Shit."

She stepped inside and saw the ME, already hard at work. When she saw the woman on the floor, the first thing she noticed was that she was extremely attractive. Short dark hair. Superb body. Early thirties.

Her damn throat spoiled her looks, though.

It was cut right in two.

Ruins the whole effect, McCoy thought.

And that's when her cell phone rang. She answered it, listened as the cop on the other end told her what had happened at Dominick Bertolini's Meat Mart on Gansevoort and Greenwich streets.

"Nobody saw anything?" she asked.

"Not a soul. And the old guy sure can't tell us what happened."

"Can we get any prints?"

"They're probably all over the weapon," the cop said. "Only problem is it ain't here."

"Do what you can," she said, then immediately called Jack Keller's apartment and left her third message on his phone machine. "This is McCoy," she announced. "We got a full-fledged lunatic on a rampage now, Jack. Don't let anybody into your apartment without checking with me first. Anybody. Particularly Grace Childress. She ain't the Destination, Jack. The Destination's dead. She's the Murderess and my guess is she's doin' her best to live up to her nickname. I don't know where the hell you are but call me as soon as you get this. Bad has gotten worse and you need to know about it."

She didn't hang up immediately, felt she should say more, but didn't know what else to leave on the tape. So she tapped the phone against her arm, realized she was still recording, and pressed the "End Call" button.

And when she hung up the phone it was the first time in her professional life she'd ever felt a sense of pure and utter panic.

SURPRISES CAME IN *threes.*

Somebody said that, too, but there was no time to remember who. Whoever it was had definitely been right, though. First was the angry guy at the Mortician's—the paper said he was her husband—barging in through the bedroom door. Then there was the way the old guy, Dom, had fought back at the meat market. Damn, he was ferocious. It was still impossible to believe. How could somebody that old be so strong? Then the Destination, she was expecting a cop, opened the door without even needing to hear a story. None of the surprises mattered, of course, not in the end. Everything had happened the way it was supposed to happen.

Everything was turning out beautifully. . . .

BACK OUT ON West Ninth Street, McCoy sucked in some fresh air, hot and humid and not very refreshing. She decided she had to do something. She needed to move. She took the unmarked car—not a bad one this time; a little rust on the passenger door but, all in all, perfectly acceptable—and drove all the way up to East Seventy-seventh Street. To make everything seem a little more urgent, but mostly just to give herself a little needed pleasure, she put the rotating light on the roof and turned the siren on.

When she arrived at Jack's apartment building, McCoy flashed her badge at the doorman, but he'd had a lot of experience working the ritzy part of town. He couldn't just let her up, he said. A lot of tenants would have him fired if he let anyone into their apartments, even a cop. Mr. Keller wasn't like that, the doorman said, he was a nice guy, but still . . .

McCoy didn't argue. She just told him that it was a matter of life or death and that if he didn't let her go up, she'd make *sure* he was fired. Guaranteed, today would be his last day on the job. When he still wavered, she said, steely as she could be, which was pretty damn steely, "Congratulations, you're outta here." Then she started back out to the street, but he grabbed her by the arm and said, "Okay, look, you gotta make it clear that you said it was life or death." McCoy didn't bother to respond, just headed for the elevator as he called after her, "Press 'Penthouse.' I'll release it."

She made a quick search of the apartment. When she was

done, she realized she'd been holding her breath in. She had thought she might find another body and when she didn't, she felt herself able to breathe again.

McCoy knew that she should just sit quietly and wait. If she got impatient, she could leave. But as she'd discovered, by the age of three, she was not the patient type, so what the hell, as long as she was here, she decided, she might as well poke around. She wasn't really violating any laws. Jack Keller wasn't a suspect and she wasn't looking for anything incriminating. She was just hoping that something might jar a thought. An action. Any kind of clue as to what was happening . . . and how to stop it.

She was there maybe forty-five minutes, sifting through papers, opening drawers, finding nothing of any import and feeling kind of silly, actually, knowing she was being a snoop, not a cop, when she heard the elevator.

It's about time, McCoy thought. Then she steeled herself to deliver the bad news.

SO MUCH FOR *surprises coming in threes.*

Here was surprise number four. Unbelievable. But not a real problem, not yet anyway.

Surprise number four would be dealt with, too.

This had to be the cop, the woman sergeant. That's the only thing that made sense. But what was she doing here? By the way she looked so startled, she was probably alone. That was good. But she also looked suspicious, and that was bad. She wouldn't have her guard down long. She would know what was happening before too long. So better to move now. Better to strike immediately and ask questions later. That way, maybe there wouldn't be any more surprises.

She was smart, this cop, that was obvious. The way her eyes narrowed, she sensed something was wrong. And she was quick, because as soon as their eyes met, she didn't even ask any questions, she just reached for her gun. Oh, yes, she was smart and quick.

But not smart and quick enough.

MCCOY KNEW SHE'D make it.

"Can I help you?" she asked. And when the answer came and all it was was "No," she knew. She'd been trained to know and to act simultaneously and that's what she did. So she wasn't even particularly worried because it all seemed so right: her coming to the apartment, sticking around on little more than a whim, being there now with the opportunity to end it all. So when she moved, she was nothing but confident.

But going for her gun, she missed. Not a big miss, but she didn't grab it cleanly; her fingers grazed the handle and she had to fumble for it. She understood immediately that those extra few seconds were fatal but she didn't stop trying.

She leaped back, hoping that would give her the time she needed, but like everything else in this goddamn case, nothing went as planned.

She realized that the knife that was slashing at her was the one that had been taken from Dominick Bertolini's market. She realized she was looking at the Entertainer's murderer. And Samsonite's and the Mortician's and the Destination's. And hers. She realized that, too, now.

Her final realization was that she could forget about retiring in Bucks County with her beloved Elmore. She was going to die right here in New York City.

THE COP WAS moving. Couldn't let her move.

No more surprises. That was even a better motto than better safe than sorry.

The blade ripped through the air one more time and once was all it took.

The red blood rushed out and spread thickly down chocolate-brown skin. She grabbed for her throat, dropping her gun, and for the first time there was someone who didn't look as if she couldn't believe she was going to die. She looked like she expected to die. But she sure was angry about it.

Even after the cop was dead, she looked really, really angry.

Hard to blame her, really. But not much to be done about it.

Except clean up.

Why did death have to be so messy?

The traffic was heavy and every driver on the road seemed to be driving for the very first time, inching slowly when they could have gone normal speed, weaving unsteadily when they should have been stable. It took Jack over five and a half hours to get back to the Lincoln Tunnel, where, of course, things were bumper-to-bumper and he was stuck even in the EZ Pass lane.

Fidgety, he picked up his cell phone and dialed his home number to collect his phone messages. He was hoping that Grace had called. He needed to talk to someone, to try to put the pieces of the puzzle together, and not just the disparate pieces connecting the murders but the complicated thoughts and emotions that were charging through him. He was surprised that he wanted that someone to be her.

As he punched the "Okay" button, the car in front of him lurched forward and miraculously the traffic was momentarily clear. Just as he heard his phone machine connect, he found himself in the tunnel and the connection was severed. He clicked off the power, shrugged, and figured he could wait twenty more minutes until he was home.

Driving uptown, he wondered if he should stop off at Dom's. Dom would sit and drink with him, would let him talk until he was all talked out. But suddenly he was too tired to even think about sitting or drinking or talking. All he wanted to do was go straight home and fall into bed. He wanted to sleep for the next twelve hours and, if possible, not think or even dream about everything that had happened.

He parked the car in his garage, put the key in the slot for the penthouse, then changed his mind and went to the lobby to pick up his mail. There had to be a magazine in there, there was always a magazine in his mail, and he decided all he'd do is read whatever dumb story he could find on whatever dumb star or starlet they were writing about, and then he'd pass out.

It's a plan, he thought.

But it was a plan interrupted. As he stepped out to walk through the lobby to the mailboxes, he saw someone waiting for him. Raoul, the doorman on duty, looked fidgety and the expression on his face said that the person had been waiting a long time.

"What are you doing here?" he asked.

"Waiting to see you."

"I've been calling up every fifteen minutes, Mr. Keller," Raoul said. "In case you came in through the garage. Also, Frankie said a cop was here to see you; he let her into—"

"How long have you been here?" Jack asked, interrupting the doorman. He was focused only on his visitor.

"Two hours. Maybe more. I don't know. Do you want me to leave?"

"No, no." Jack realized he was flustered. But pleased. As tired and drained as he was, he was very pleased. There was no one he wanted to see more.

"Come on up," he said to Grace Childress. "We have a lot to talk about."

HE USHERED HER out of the elevator and as he did he cocked his head slightly to the left.

"What?" she asked.

"Ever since the break-in," he said. "I'm just skittish. I keep feeling like someone's here. Or has *been* here." He listened intently—she stayed absolutely quiet—and glanced around the entryway and living room. Then he shrugged. "Nothing out of the ordinary," he told her. "Just you and me."

"Could I get a drink?" she asked.

"Anything you want is in the bar in the living room. I'm just going to check my messages."

He walked to the den, unable to shake the feeling that something was different, but he couldn't pinpoint it. Nothing seemed out of place. Nothing was broken. There was a strange odor, he thought, but he couldn't put his finger on it. And it was so faint, it could be coming from anywhere. Still . . .

He told himself he was being ridiculous. He saw the green light flashing on the phone machine, saw that he had three messages. He wondered if any were from McCoy. He'd been so consumed with his own search he hadn't even thought about the fact that she might have uncovered something new.

Jack went to press the "Play" button but as he did, he heard a noise from behind him. Grace was standing in the doorway, her hands empty, her shoulders hunched down.

"What happened to your drink?" he asked. But she didn't answer. And when she looked up, there were tears in her eyes. "Do you want to talk?" he said.

"No," she told him. "I don't want a drink and I don't want to talk."

"What do you want?" Jack Keller asked.

"I don't want you to ask me any questions till the morning. And I want to make love to you until then," Grace Childress said. And, as the tears slowly rolled down her cheeks, she said, "Please."

SHE INSISTED ON turning out the light. She didn't want him to see her.

"But you're so beautiful," he told her.

She kissed him then and held his hand tight, as if her strength alone could keep him from shining a light on her body. He broke away from her kiss, said nothing, didn't move for what seemed to him like hours, but he was only a second or two away from her as he thought of Caroline, felt longing for all that was past. Then he grabbed her and pulled her toward him, hugged her so it seemed their bodies might merge, and he kissed her again, a quick kiss, then another, and another, this one long and sweet and deep.

Their lovemaking was both tender and brutal. There were demons to exorcise. He knew what his were, and he was happy to unleash them. He did not know what was behind her passion but, as their bodies grazed, caressed, and rammed against each other, as he kissed her shoulder, licked her muscular back, heard her moan and even scream, felt her take him inside her and her legs squeeze around him, trapping him, draining him, exhilarating him, he did not care.

They lay quiet together in the dark. He could feel her soft, consistent breaths. He was aware now of his nakedness, and felt awkward until her hand brushed against his arm and all self-consciousness disappeared. He tried to talk once, to ask her why she was crying, but she held a finger up to his lips and hushed him. Then they fell asleep, her head buried in his chest, his arms covering her gently like a soft summer blanket.

JACK WOKE, THE sharp, wonderful odor of sex on his bed and in his skin, and he reached over to turn off the alarm. But the alarm was not set, he realized. Hadn't been set in quite some time. He was not getting up to go to work. There *was* no work. He did not have to worry about disturbing his wife. His wife could no longer be disturbed. Someone else had shared his bed last night, was about to share his morning. This was something new and while the world around him seemed to be collapsing, exploding, he couldn't help but allow a quick, contented sigh here in the world that was his bedroom.

He lifted his head, turned to see if Grace was beside him, but she was not. He heard a noise from the kitchen and luxuriated in the sudden, pungent smell of coffee that floated in. Jack swung himself out of bed, went into the bathroom, brushed his teeth, and took a quick, hot shower. When he emerged, he put on a pair of jeans and a T-shirt, then heard Grace calling to him: "I know you're up. Get out here."

She was on the terrace, relaxed and comfortable in one of the two chairs around the cast-iron table. It was a glorious early morn; the chill had already disappeared. Jack saw that on the table was a wooden tray, set with two mugs of coffee and a plate that held a hunk of bread and a sharp, white Cheddar cheese. It was a scene he had lived many times with Caroline and he couldn't help but feel a tug at his heart. But the softness and vulnerability in Grace's eyes forced him into the present. And the sight of his blue-and-white silk robe, loose on her body, open to reveal one thigh and the curve of her breasts, made him smile and long for her yet again.

"I'm starving," she told him. "So I just foraged in the fridge."

He went to her and kissed her. She shifted in her seat and the robe loosened further; her right leg was bared almost to her hip now. He couldn't help but glance down. She quickly went to cover her leg but the silk billowed and, again, he saw a glimpse of what she'd been trying to hide.

"What is that?" he asked.

Grace flushed. He could see her biting her lower lip. She shook her head tightly.

"What happened to your leg?" Jack asked again.

Grace stood up from the table. She turned her back on him, walked to the edge of the terrace, put both hands on the brick retaining wall, and looked out over the park.

He felt his stomach tighten. She was too close to the edge. When he spoke, he could hear the words come out thickly. "It's morning," he told her. "I'm allowed to ask questions now."

She turned around to face him, said, "Yes," and nothing more, then started crying again, silent tears that ran down her face like rain streaking down a windowpane. Jack took a step toward her, felt his legs weaken as he got too close to the balcony's edge. He reached for her arm, touched her, but as he did, she jerked away from him, stepped back. He was left alone then, by the wall, and he found himself looking out, looking down. He was horrified to find that his stomach was in his throat and his legs were like iron anchors rooting him to the spot. He felt the dizziness coming on and couldn't move. He wanted to speak, to tell her to take his arm and lead him back to safety, but he couldn't. His throat was closing and the panic was setting in.

"I didn't call the police," she was saying. "When you went to Samsonite's apartment and didn't call me when you were supposed to, I didn't call the police. You must know that by now."

Jack tried to nod. Maybe he did. He couldn't tell.

"That's partly why I came here last night," she was saying. "I was worried about you. I thought maybe you were . . . I didn't know what happened and I was worried about you."

He tried to concentrate. *Yes, concentrate on what she's saying,* he told himself. *Answer her. Distract yourself. Look at her, look away from the edge and think. Concentrate.* "Why?" he managed to say now. "Why didn't you call?"

Grace was trembling. "I know he told you, Jack."

And now, here it came, like an unavoidable sledgehammer. It was upon him: the vision. His legs felt like they were nailed to the floor, but he could feel his body drifting toward the edge, could feel the inexorable force lifting him, throwing him over. He could feel that he was toppling over. He was Icarus, unable to fly, falling to his death . . . *Concentrate. Talk to her.* The sweat was pouring off him. Couldn't she see what was happening to him? Couldn't she help him?

"You figured everything else out, you should have figured this one out, too. I *couldn't* call the police."

What was she saying? Couldn't? Why not? He could feel the wall, as if it had hands that were reaching out and grabbing him, pulling him closer and closer. *What was she talking about?*

"It's stupid, I know, and if you'd gotten hurt I never would have forgiven myself, but I couldn't . . . I'm terrified of them. Terrified of going through all that again."

And suddenly, as the robe blew open again, fluttered in the slight breeze, even as his worst fear was gripping him and squeezing, cutting off his air and his clarity, he understood. "An accident," he breathed. "When you were young."

She nodded and he could see her entire face tighten and her eyes go hard.

He could hear Kid, right here on the terrace, saying: *There was an accident when she was a kid. That's all it was. At least that's all I'm gonna tell you.*

Jack staggered forward, one small step, forcing his feet away from the pull of the edge. He forced himself to look down, decided to focus on the table. It was important to focus on something, important to concentrate on something safe, so he stared at the tray. First he took in all the accoutrements, then made himself take in the specifics. The deep-blue color of the plates. The roughness of the bread. The pale waxiness of the cheese. And then the knife. The beautiful knife with the finely honed blade and thick dark wood handle. The butcher knife that he knew so well.

Dom's knife.

"Where . . ." he whispered. "Where did you get that?"

She looked down at the knife. Said: "In the kitchen." She picked it up by the handle, held it in front of her, the blade catching a streak of sunlight and glistening. "It was sitting on the counter."

"No." Jack's breath came quickly and hard. He focused on her bare leg now, lifting his head so he could see the long, jagged scar that ran from the middle of Grace's right thigh up to her hip.

Kid's voice: *An accident . . . that's all it was . . . But she's definitely still scarred by it.* Sexily *scarred.*

"The Murderess."

"Let me explain."

"You're the Murderess," he said. Staring at his friend's knife, still fighting the fear, the wind that was whistling only in his head, and the image of his body, leaping, falling, dying, he screamed at her: "Who else did you kill!"

"You have to believe me," she said. "It was an accident. It has nothing to do with today, with what's happening."

"I have to get off the balcony," he said.

"No," she told him. "I know you're frightened. But if you stay here you'll listen. I don't care if I have to force you to listen, but you have to listen."

His voice came out raspy. "Have to go in."

But she barred the door. He didn't have the strength to push her aside. When the vision came, when the fear took over, there was never any strength left. "I was fourteen," she was saying. "Fourteen years old. Just a little girl, wanting to be a cheerleader. And my best friend, Kara, she was trying out, too. And you know how important that is to a little girl. Well, it came down to me and Kara. We heard that only one of us would make it, and we made a pact that no matter who won, we'd always be best friends. And . . ."

Jack was trying to focus on what she was saying. Fighting the edge, struggling against the pull and trying to understand. Grace took a deep breath. "And," she continued, "on a Saturday, two days before we were going to find out which one of us made it, we were on Long Island, where we lived. . . ." The words were painful to her. They were coming very slowly. "We snuck out. Told our parents we were biking to the library. But we biked to the train station and we were sneaking into the city. A last celebration before one of us didn't get what we'd both worked so hard to get."

What was she talking about? What did this have to do with the knife in her hand and the bloody body of Samsonite lying on the bed next to him and the girl in the bathtub with the needle in her arm?

"Only . . . before the train came," she was saying now, "we started talking. Kidding around. Pretending we would do anything to win. People were listening and they heard what we were saying, and it sounded awful but we were only joking, we were really only joking. And she pushed me and I pushed her back. And we started wrestling . . ." Grace was crying now. Not silent tears but slow and difficult sobs. She was trying to hold them back so her words came out in bursts and gasps. "And," she said. "Oh, God, and I gave her a shove but we were too close to the tracks . . ."

I remember this, Jack thought. Why do I remember? Why is this familiar?

"She fell right in front of the train as it was pulling in. I tried to save her, people saw me, I jumped down after her and tried to pull her up. But I couldn't and then the train was too close and I panicked. I pulled myself up, I gave her up and let her die. I didn't make it all the way, the train caught my leg, almost severed it. But it was saved. And that's what this scar is. My reminder, every single day, of what happened."

He could see it all now: The newspaper headlines from fifteen years ago. The local tabs leaping on the story and blaring it as their lead: GIRL KILLS FRIEND TO MAKE CHEERLEADING SQUAD. It was a scandal and everyone was talking about it, writing about it: How could this happen? Is there too much pressure in schools? What's happening to children today? But the name was wrong. The name was so famous for those weeks, it was like the Amy Fisher thing, people made horrible jokes, but the name was wrong. . . .

"Remember," he breathed. "The name . . . not your name . . ."

"I changed my name," Grace said. The crying had stopped and she was calm. The sobs seemed to have exhausted her. "After she died, you can't imagine what it was like. The police *cleared* me, I was *innocent*, they understood what happened, that it was an accident, but everyone else—the kids in my school, Kara's parents; oh, God, Kara's parents, they lived on the block and it was so horrible. . . . It was in all the papers, on TV . . . People thought I killed my best friend so I could be a goddamn cheerleader. My parents had to move, my father quit his job, I left school . . . You can't imagine. So I changed my name."

Grace Lerner. That was the name. He remembered: Grace Lerner!

"No one ever knew. When I moved into the city, I was Grace Childress; that was my mother's maiden name. No one knew who I was and I could go back to being a normal person. I never told anyone. Until Kid. We used to talk about everything and I trusted him, and you can't imagine the burden of carrying it around with me, no one knowing, so it just came out one day. I told him the whole story. I guess that's when he changed my nickname from the Rookie," she said. "That prick."

He could see her clenching the knife. As she talked, her grip got tighter and tighter.

"Afterward, I hated that I told him. Sometimes I couldn't sleep, knowing that someone knew."

Jack looked up. Saw a movement behind her. He couldn't believe what he was seeing, thought maybe he was hallucinating. But it was real, all right. It was amazingly, blessedly real. Keep her talking, he thought. Keep her talking now, just a few seconds more . . .

"That's why you killed him," he said.

She looked stunned. Shocked that he had said it out loud. "No." She shook her head violently. "Is that what you think?"

When he nodded, she said, "No! It just meant *he* could talk to *me*. It's why he came and told me what he told me. How afraid he was. He trusted me because he knew I'd trusted him. The way I'm trusting you now. I just want you to understand why I didn't call the police. I was with him the night he died. I left my party to go there. I'm the woman you've been looking for. But I left before anything happened. I did, Jack, you've got to believe me. I left, but later I came back to tell him I'd made a mistake, that it was all over, for real this time, but when I got there he was dead. I saw him on the street and . . . I couldn't tell you. I knew you were looking for me but I couldn't tell you. Or that sergeant. I couldn't face more publicity, I couldn't imagine living through that again. But I didn't kill anyone."

"Dom's knife," Jack said.

"I *told* you. I found it in the kitchen! I don't understand what—"

But Jack didn't wait to find out what she didn't understand. He looked behind her and said, "Get Dom's knife."

She whirled and Bryan was right behind her now, he'd crept up on her, so light on his feet, and he grabbed her wrist. Jack heard the crack and Grace's quick scream, and Bryan had the knife. He'd taken it away from her. Held it in front of him, an expression of wonder on his face.

"She killed him," Jack said. "She killed Kid and the others."

"No!" Grace screamed. "You can't think that! Jack, after last night, you can't think that!"

Jack stumbled forward, away from the wall. He grabbed

hold of the table and the world stopped spinning around him. He felt the pull of the wall recede and Grace's story began to echo now inside him. He saw the look of pain deep in her eyes as she held her broken wrist. He saw the look of fear as she stared at Bryan behind her. Jack started to take a step toward Bryan, to thank him, but he stopped short. Looked up and said to Kid's friend, in a voice that was low and terrible, "How did you get in here?"

"It's time for our session," Bryan said. "Did you forget?"

"I didn't ask that," Jack said. "I asked how you got into my apartment."

Bryan didn't answer at first. Then slowly, oh so slowly, he said, "I let myself in."

It was as if ice water were running through Jack's veins. He could feel the chill devour his entire body. "And how did you do that?" he asked.

Bryan answered as if he were talking to a simpleton. "With my key."

"What key?"

"The one I took," Bryan said. "The one I took off the black lady."

"Mattie," Jack said.

"That's right," Bryan nodded. "I used it before, you know. Came in from the garage. That time I tried to warn you, when I wrote on the wall. You didn't know I used it, though. I was smart that day. I broke the glass so you'd think I came in from the balcony."

Grace moaned, a low, barely audible expression of pain. All of the color had drained from her face.

"Give me the knife, Bryan," Jack said calmly. "Why don't you just hand me the knife."

"Oh, no," Bryan said. "It's mine. It belongs to me now. I just left it here by mistake. When I was cleaning up."

Jack didn't understand what Bryan meant. What he did understand, what was very, very clear, was that he was talking to a madman. And he knew he had to stay calm if he wanted to stay alive.

"When were you cleaning up?" he asked gently.

"This morning. Very early this morning. It was very messy. After I was gone I realized I left it on the kitchen counter."

"Can we go in the living room and talk about this?" Jack took a step toward the sliding glass door but Bryan raised the knife, jabbed it menacingly at Jack.

"No," Bryan said. There was no anger in his voice. No tone at all. No emotion. "I'm sorry, Mr. Keller, but you're going to have to stay out here."

Jack tried to keep his tone as even as Bryan's. "I think Grace needs to get to a doctor. Why don't you let me call a doctor and then you and I can stay out here and talk."

Bryan's brow furrowed just a bit. He didn't seem confused, though. He looked slightly offended. "Everyone thinks I'm an idiot," he said. "But I can't be such an idiot, can I? I outsmarted everybody, even you." He looked over at Grace and shook his head. "You think I'm going to let you call somebody?" he said to Jack. "Come on, Mr. Keller, you can do better than that." And as he said those words, Bryan's face lost that blank look. Now he looked deeply angry. Although his voice never wavered, got no louder, his cheeks turned red. The rage in his eyes made them shine like a beacon of hate. "That's what you told *him*—'you can do better.' "

"What?" Jack asked. "What are you talking about?"

" 'You can do better,' that's what you said. I remember. In the restaurant."

Jack remembered, too. Kid and Bryan around the table at Jack's. Jack telling them their plan wouldn't work. Bryan gently asking questions, Kid urgently telling Bryan that it didn't matter, that Jack was giving them the money.

I think it's a shitty idea for now. For you, Jack had said to Kid. *And partly because you can do so much better.*

Kid saying: *Jack, don't say that,* please. The "please" was so urgent, as if he were trying to tell him something crucial.

He was. He was telling Jack not to issue a death sentence.

"It was all about the gym, wasn't it?" Jack said. "It was all about the fucking gym."

"Everyone was always trying to take him away from me," Bryan said, standing on the terrace, the knife held loosely but still pointing straight at Jack. He sounded so sad now, like a petulant child who couldn't comprehend why he was being made to stand in the corner. "But we were gonna be *partners*. Our whole lives we said we'd be partners. The gym was going to be our place. Why would you wanna split us up?"

"No," Jack said. "That was never the idea. He wasn't going to leave you behind."

"Yes, he was. He was always trying to leave me behind. Even in school. Even in St. John's. I was his best friend. I *loved* him. I *protected* him. But he liked somebody better than me. He got another best friend. . . ."

"Jesus," Jack said softly. "The boy on the team. The boy who broke his neck."

"Harvey Wiggins," Bryan said, nodding. "I'm nicer than him, I'm as smart as him. Why wouldn't he like me as much as Harvey?"

"You're the one who hit him. In practice. You broke his neck."

"I had to make Kid understand, didn't I? He thought he liked Harvey *better* than me."

"That's why he went away. It's why he went to Virginia. He wanted to get away from you."

"He thought I wouldn't find him. But I did. I found him, all right. He was very surprised when I showed up but I think he was happy. I think he was glad to see me."

"Did you go to school there, Bryan? To Virginia State?" Jack could barely get the words out. "Were you on the football team?"

"For half a year. Then my knee got real bad. The coach wouldn't let me play anymore."

"You knew the players, the ones who came to my restaurant."

"They were nice guys," Bryan said. "They were real nice guys."

"You killed them."

"I felt bad about it, Mr. Keller, honest. But I had to. They didn't understand. I made the plan; it was a smart plan, wasn't it? But I only told them half of it. They thought I was just gonna rob the place and they'd make some money. And they were really excited when they heard I got this." Bryan opened the top two buttons of his polo shirt to show Jack what was underneath. Jack moaned when he saw it, closed his eyes, and felt a nauseating bile rise from his stomach up through his throat.

Around Bryan's thick neck was the diamond necklace Jack had bought for Caroline.

"It's beautiful, Mr. Keller," Bryan said. "It's the most beautiful thing I ever saw."

Jack's head rolled back and he heard it plain as day now. The words in the office that terrible night. The crazy words that made no sense. The last words Caroline ever heard: *Wooly here . . . the will is strong . . . wool candy broken . . .*

"Kid's nickname for you, when you played football," Jack said to Bryan. "He told me what it was. He called you something."

"The Wall," Bryan told him. "I blocked for him. I saved him over and over again. Since we were little boys. So he called me the Wall."

Wooly here . . . the will is strong . . . wool candy broken . . .

He understood now. He was hearing it all for the first time. With no concussion, with no pain distorting the sounds. Oh, God, he could hear it as plain as day.

The Wall is here . . . The Wall is strong . . . The Wall can't be broken.

Jack could barely get his next words out.

"You killed my wife," he whispered. "You shot me and you killed my wife."

"I didn't want to hurt you," Bryan said mournfully. "I really like you. But she was trying to take him away, too."

"No," Jack said. "It's not possible."

"He saw her. It was an accident, he wasn't looking for her, but he saw her down there. Right after I found him." Bryan's voice was high-pitched now, the sound of a puppy locked up in a room and left alone for too long. "He *told* her, Mr. Keller. All about Harvey Wiggins. He said he didn't, but I could tell."

"She didn't do anything," Jack said. "She was just trying to help him. She didn't have to die."

"Yes, she did. She was going to send him away. Far away."

Jack sagged. "To London."

"How was I gonna get to London, Mr. Keller? How was I gonna find him when he was so far away?"

"He knew? Kid *knew* that you . . . that you killed her?"

"No. Not then, anyway. But back here, back in New York, he was starting to understand how smart I really was. He was starting to figure it out. I didn't ever want him to know because I wanted him to love me. I was so afraid he might . . . he might hate me if he found out."

"What was there to figure out, Bryan?"

"That I got the invitations. To your opening. I told Kid I'd leave him alone, let him go where he wanted. I told him I was leaving Virginia 'cause he didn't want me. 'Cause he didn't love me anymore. But I didn't leave. I figured out a better plan. So he couldn't love anyone else, only me."

"You went to my wife."

"She knew about me and she was scared. I told her I'd leave him alone, I'd leave *them* alone, but she had to help. She couldn't say anything to anyone, 'specially not to Kid. She just had to get me two invitations to your opening. At first she didn't want to do it but I convinced her it was okay. She thought she was being so smart, I could tell. She thought I was gonna rob the place. But that's what I wanted her to think, 'cause I knew she didn't care about money. But I didn't care about money, either, Mr. Keller, I just wanted what was mine. I just wanted Kid to stay with me."

"Bryan," Jack said very slowly and very softly. "Kid had another nickname for you, too, didn't he?"

Bryan nodded. And began pacing. Small fidgety steps that belied the deadly calm of his voice. "I didn't like it, though. It made me angry."

"The Mistake. That's what he called you."

"He told it to me when we were in college. The first time I told him I loved him. He told me that I didn't understand what had happened, I didn't understand anything at all about that night when he cried and I hugged him and I kissed him. He said that everything I knew was just one big mistake. But it wasn't, Mr. Keller. And I proved it wasn't. Over and over again, I proved it."

"When did he know? When did he find out about Caroline?"

"The night he died. He finally asked me."

"And you told him?"

"Oh, no. I told him that no matter what he thought, he couldn't prove it. And I told him he'd better not say anything, either. I said that if he told you, you'd never see him again. I said you'd blame him. And he knew I was right. It's why he couldn't tell you about the woman, either, the English one. He knew you'd hate him."

"What English woman?" Jack asked. "What—"

"That's why he was so wrong," Bryan said, not hearing Jack. Bryan's pacing had brought the two men nearly face-to-face. "I would *never* hate him. No matter what he did, I couldn't hate him. I loved him. I loved him so, so much. The only people I hated were the ones who tried to take him away from me."

At the far end of the terrace, Jack saw Grace move. She looked like she was going to faint—her wrist was dangling at a terrible angle—but he saw her gather herself and silently move toward the terrace wall. Jack realized what she was going to try to do and he felt it again. The dizziness started to take him over and he thought to himself: No, you can't let it. You have to fight it. You have to beat it this time. You *have* to beat it.

"What happened when you came back here, to New York, after Virginia?" Jack forced himself to ask.

"He said he'd do the gym with me," Bryan answered. "So we started making plans. And then he started helping you; he thought he could fix you, fix what I done to you. He felt guilty, you know, what happened with him and your wife. He felt guilty but I thought, hey, you're rich. So I told him to get the money from you."

Don't watch her, Jack thought. Don't watch her crawl out on the ledge, crawl onto the wall. Don't even flick your eyes that way because Bryan will see and then it'll be all over. Don't even think of Kid, out on the terrace, saying, Hey, do you know you could actually walk to the next building from here? You'd have to be kind of nuts but . . .

Grace was on the wall now. The Rookie/Murderess took her first timid step onto the ledge that would lead her to the rooftop next door and to safety.

"But you tried to take him, too." Bryan was talking again. "You tried it years ago, tried to steal him from me, and you were gonna take him again."

"Bryan, I wasn't stealing him. I—"

"Yes, you were! And he was gonna go! That's what he said to me that night, up in that apartment of his. He begged me to let it happen, said he'd set me up if I'd only let him go work with you. And you know what I couldn't believe? He was *afraid* of me, Mr. Keller. All I ever did was save and protect him and he was afraid of me! As if I'd ever hurt him."

"You killed him, you stupid son of a bitch. Don't you understand that you *killed* him?"

"But I didn't *hurt* him! I'd *never* hurt him!" And now Bryan was angry. His voice grew loud as he took a step closer to Jack. "And don't you call me stupid. I'm not stupid. I'm smarter than you or any of them!"

Don't look at Grace. Don't think *about Grace.* She was crawling now, on her hands and knees eighteen stories high and she was almost a quarter of the way there. *Don't think about her and don't be afraid of Bryan. Stand up to him and give her time to get away.*

"I'm sorry," Jack said. "I'm really sorry. I was just angry. I know you're not stupid. I can't even figure out how you did all the things you did." That seemed to calm Bryan down so Jack went with it. "What happened that night? With Kid."

"I couldn't believe he was afraid of me. It made me feel so sad. And then so angry. So I told him, sure. I told him, okay, I'd let him go with you. Only he had to talk to me for a while. Let's have a beer and talk, I said. I told him I always wanted to see him drink a beer. So we did."

"Only you drugged it," Jack said, and remembered going to meet Bryan at Hanson's, Bryan handing something to a client, getting money in return. "The guy in the gym, the guy you said was betting. That wasn't a bet, it was a drug deal."

"I do a little dealing sometimes, to make ends meet. Kid told me about that crazy Russian girl. The blackjack dealer. I got to meet her and talk to her and she got me stuff sometimes."

I know what you want me to say, Samsonite said. *I figured it out, too. But when he came to buy the fucking acid, I didn't know who it was for. I didn't know what he was going to do with it. . . .*

Jack had thought she meant Kid. So had McCoy. But it wasn't Kid. It was Bryan.

"Samsonite got you the acid. You got it from her and you put it in the beer."

"I told you I'd never hurt him. I knew if he took it, he'd be okay when he fell. I knew, when I threw him over the side, he'd be happy right up until he died."

Grace was almost halfway. *Move faster,* he thought. *Move goddamn faster!*

"What about the women?" Jack asked. "What about the Team?"

"That was all your fault. It was over. No one was gonna steal Kid from me anymore, everything was fine. Then you had to start looking. You coulda gotten me in trouble."

"Why did you have to kill them, Bryan?"

"Different reasons. The dancer, you know, the stripper . . ."

"The Entertainer."

"Yeah. Her. I'd seen her. I knew her. I went up to see if, you know, with Kid gone, maybe she'd be nice to me, do the kinds of things she used to do to him. So I went up to ask her. But she laughed at me, told me I was a loser." Incredulously, he said, "A loser, Mr. Keller. Can you imagine that? She was dancing all that dirty stuff and taking drugs and she called *me* a loser." He shook his head and looked at Jack as if they were conspirators, the two of them against a crazy world. "I was there, you know. When you buzzed. I let you in, went up a flight. I saw you go in, then I went down and nobody suspected nothing."

"You *are* smart, Bryan. You even broke the lock so they'd think I did it."

Bryan smiled, pleased at the compliment. But the smile disappeared immediately when he heard the noise behind him—the little fluttering of wings and the gasp that followed—and saw the look in Jack's eyes, the look of absolute and total despair.

GRACE KNEW SHE could do this.

She had never been so terrified in her entire life but still she could do it. Just don't look down, she kept telling herself. Don't look down, stay quiet, and keep going. Julia Roberts could do this, she thought. So just pretend you're Julia Roberts and this is a movie and when you get to the other side, Richard Gere's going to be waiting for you.

The lunatic hadn't heard a thing. Jack was doing a good job keeping him talking. So all she had to do was concentrate on crawling. She was on her stomach, her arms out in front of her, keeping her steady, holding on to the side of the wall. Her legs were out behind her and she used her thighs to grip and balance as she propelled herself forward. She thought about nothing but inching toward the next building and making sure she didn't fall. She wouldn't look up, either, she decided, until she made it to the other side. She wouldn't let anything distract her. Anything. And she didn't.

Which is why she didn't notice the pigeon.

It had flown down, landed on the ledge a foot ahead of her. When she reached it, her arm grazed its soft feathers. She felt the wings flap, heard the bird coo its annoyance, and it did the one thing she couldn't afford, couldn't let happen. . . .

She gasped in surprise and she drew her hand back. And when the pigeon flew up, hovered by her hair, she waved it away, panicky, and as she moved she lost her balance. She knew the madman would hear her now but she didn't care. That was the least of her problems. Here she was, walking a tightrope a million miles above Manhattan, and she panicked, she was going to fall off a goddamn roof because she touched a goddamn pigeon. The thought that came into her head now was a saying she'd seen on a coffee mug at the gallery: *Life's a bitch and then you die.* Pretty damn apt, she thought, because she was rolling over to her left now, she had lost her balance, she was falling. Then she wasn't falling any longer.

She fell.

JACK WATCHED GRACE disappear and he wanted to scream, he thought he would jump out of his skin, but he knew it was his only chance and he had to take advantage of it. He couldn't think about her, refused to let himself think, and as Bryan turned, as his eyes followed the path of the frightened pigeon soaring up into the sky, Jack swooped down, grabbed a ten-pound dumbbell that was sitting on the terrace carpeting a few feet away, and swung it as hard as he could at the back of Bryan's head. As Bryan sensed the attack and tried to dodge it, the weight crashed into the side of his neck. It was not a crippling blow but it was good enough. Bryan, stunned, fell down hard and Jack threw himself through the open door and into the living room. He knew he wouldn't have enough time to get the elevator or even to get to the stairway. Bryan had not stayed stunned for long. He was up immediately, he was already on his feet and coming after him. . . .

Jack knew exactly where he was heading: to the guest coat closet in the foyer. It's where Caroline kept her hunting rifle. He was supposed to have brought it to her in Virginia but he'd forgotten. It had to still be there. It had to be. So he sprinted; all he needed was time to throw the door open and reach into the corner of the closet and grab it. He didn't have a clue if the gun was loaded but he didn't care. It was his only hope and all he could think about was that he could yank it out, aim it at Bryan and pull the trigger, and hope that he blew the crazy fucker all the way to hell.

Jack stumbled on the living room carpet, slipped; his knee grazed the floor for a moment and a stab of pain went through his hip, but he was up immediately and moving. Bryan was through the door now, but Jack had enough time, he was sure of it. If the gun was there, he could reach it. He was close now. Bryan stumbled, too, on the carpet, was up fast, was moving again. . . .

Jack was there now. He was at the closet. He grabbed the door handle and pulled. Without waiting, he practically leapt inside, reaching frantically to push past the coats to find the gun standing in the corner. Please, let it be there . . . please, let it be there and be loaded . . .

But something was wrong. Something was falling out of the closet, falling onto him. Something big and clumsy, knocking him back and getting in his way. He couldn't reach the gun. It was impossible. He couldn't even reach the coats. This thing was on top of him and Jack was going down, he was on the floor, the thing wrapped around him and pulling him down.

No. No, no, no, no! Not a *thing*. Jack realized it was not a fucking thing at all.

A person. A *dead* person.

Patience McCoy.

Her head was practically severed from her body, her beige suit was stained a deep, pervasive red. A foul smell enveloped him as surely as her rigid limbs.

Oh, God. She was on top of him. Jack was on the floor, fighting off the policewoman's dead body, her skin cold to the touch, his stomach heaving as he looked into her still eyes, felt her blood as it stuck to his shirt and face. He was trying to scramble to his feet, nearly blind with fury and the realization that it was over. No one could save him now. No one. Bryan was standing over him. Jack had lost.

Bryan kicked him in the ribs. Jack could feel the first thud and his side was rocked with pain. He felt another and another until he realized he'd been kicked against the wall, he was propped up against the hallway wall. He was hurt pretty bad but it no longer mattered. The frenzy of movement was over. McCoy sprawled, lifeless, in front of the open closet. Bryan was calm now, staring at him. His eyes had become vacant again, empty of rage. In his hand was Dom's knife, the tip pointed at Jack's heart. The room was absolutely silent except for the ticking of the grandfather clock that faced the elevator door.

"I guess I shoulda told you," Bryan said, nodding at McCoy. "She can't help you anymore."

"You killed Dom, too, didn't you?" Jack managed to get out. He saw blood drip down from his chin onto his shirt.

He didn't know if it was his own or McCoy's. He didn't really care.

"No, Mr. Keller. *You* killed him. You said you told him everything you knew. So I had to find out what he knew, didn't I? He was a tough old fuck, I'll say that. He pulled a meat cleaver on me. Can you believe it?"

"Yeah." Jack thought of Dom. Remembered his strength and his stubbornness. "I can believe it." Bryan was slowly moving toward him now, with short, deliberate steps. "When you killed Samsonite," Jack said, "you had *me* there. Why didn't you just kill me then?"

Bryan looked at him incredulously. "I *like* you, Mr. Keller. You're my friend. I don't just go around and kill everybody, do I?"

"But on the street . . . the shots. You shot at me."

"They were warnings. I couldn't let you *tell* on me, could I? What kind of friend *are* you, that you'd go tell on me?"

Oh, my God, Jack thought. Oh, my God, oh, my God.

"All those others, they *made* me kill them," Bryan said, and took another step toward Jack. "I never wanted to hurt any of them. They made me. The one in the tub, she laughed at me. The one in the bed with you, she could've connected me to the drugs. The one in the house, the one with the husband, she asked me to be her trainer. She came to Hanson's just like you, then she was starting to ask questions. The English one. He told her. He told her what was happening and she was going to go back with him to London. Everyone was trying to take him away from me! Your wife most of all; she wouldn't listen when I had her up in that room. She kept thinking I wante[...] want money, Mr. Keller, I wanted Kid." Brya[...] grabbed Jack by his shirt collar, and effortless[...] to his feet. "I've never murdered anybody, M[...] eyes were absolutely cold and dead and his vo[...] into a whisper. "You're the first."

Bryan cuffed Jack across the face, knocking him[...] ward. Immediately grabbed him, held him upright, hi[...] again. He spun Jack around, slapped him a third time, a[...] Jack went down. He was on the floor, on his knees, and h[...] saw Bryan jab at him with the knife. He scrambled away but he felt the blade puncture his skin, and warm blood began to ooze down his side. Bryan jabbed again and again as Jack frantically dodged the thrusts, backing away each time, and Jack realized they were back on the terrace. His eyes bulged and he made a desperate attempt to lunge back into the apartment but Bryan jabbed him again, in the shoulder, and when Jack grabbed at the wound, Bryan hit him again, knocking Jack backward until he was up against the retaining wall. He was at the edge of the terrace. There was nowhere else to go now.

"I feel really bad about this, Mr. Keller. But it's like I told you—there's some really weird people out there."

Holding the knife against Jack's neck, he bent him backward. Jack felt his feet leave the ground, his waist leveraging the top of the wall. The upper half of his body was leaning over into space.

"You're going over, too, Mr. Keller. You can go over easy or you can go over hard—but you're going over."

was coming true. The wall was finally winning their
e. The edge was calling to him and drawing him near.
n he would know what it was like to heed its call. Soon
would be falling. Flying. He would be Icarus. Out of con-
ol. Screaming . . .

When he heard the voice, he thought he had to be hallucinating. But he realized that Bryan had heard it, too,
because Bryan relaxed his grip on Jack's neck and cocked his
head.

It's not possible, Jack thought. It's just not possible.

But it was. There was no question. It was Grace's voice
they heard, her quivering, frightened voice saying, "Help
me." And then again: "Please, help me."

Bryan grabbed hold of Jack's shirt and dragged him to the
corner of the terrace, toward the spot from which Grace
had fallen. Bryan leaned over, holding Jack close to him.
Jack tried not to look but he had to. What he saw was worse
than any blow he'd taken from Bryan.

It was Grace. She had not plunged to her death. She was
clinging desperately to one of the gray stone gargoyles protruding from the building. Her hands and legs were
wrapped around the gargoyle's neck. Her broken wrist pre-
vented her from pulling herself up but her will was not
allowing her to let go and plummet.

"Help me, Jack. Please help me," she cried.

Jack saw a tiny smile cross Bryan's lips. "That's a good
idea, don't you think, Mr. Keller?" And when Jack looked at
him questioningly through his swollen eyes, Bryan said,
"Let's go help her."

The next thing Jack knew, he was lifted up and he was somewhere he went only in his deepest and darkest nightmares: standing on top of the retaining wall. Eighteen stories below him was Madison Avenue. With no net.

It was worse than any hallucinogen. He could not stop the images from sweeping over him. And he could not stop the fear from paralyzing him. He was ten years old again; his mother had fallen. He was hanging on to Reggie Ivers's leg, dangling from the seventeenth floor. The noise from below was suddenly all around him: cars thundering by, horns honking wildly, vendors hawking their wares with harsh and angry screams. The street rushed up to meet him, bending and folding like a concrete flying carpet. Traffic lights were blinking furiously; the sky was filled with glittery explosions of red, yellow, and green. Jack's head snapped back. He was looking straight up into the broiling glare of the sun and he knew he was going over, that this was the end. The images and cacophony of noise all merged into one stultifying and choking blackness and Jack began to lose consciousness until a hand appeared magically in the small of his back, holding him up and pushing him back to an upright position on the ledge.

"Go get her," Jack heard.

For a moment he thought he must be waking up from a dream, but Bryan's face came back into focus and Jack knew this was no dream.

"Jack, please," he heard Grace call again. "I can't hold on much longer."

As Bryan jabbed at his leg with Dom's knife, prodding him

to move, Jack turned his head so he could see Grace. She was sweating and petrified, trying desperately to keep her grip on the grotesque sculpture. She saw him now, said nothing, but their eyes locked and Jack nodded once. He was coming.

As the knife nicked his calf, Jack's right foot slid tentatively forward. Then his left foot slid after it. His first step. He was six inches farther along the ledge. He slowed his breath, commanded himself to stop trembling. The right foot slid again, then the left.

Twelve inches.

"Jack," Grace said. Her voice was calm and soft; it did not betray the urgency of her words. "You've got to move faster. I'm slipping."

Slide. And again. Eighteen inches. And yet again. Twenty-four.

He could no longer hear the traffic below or Grace's raspy breaths. There was no sound at all anymore but the steady pounding of his heart.

Thirty inches.

Thirty-six.

Three feet away from the terrace. The knife no longer cut into his legs. He was far enough away to be just out of Bryan's reach.

Jack's right foot slid again. His left started to follow . . . and then stopped. Long seconds passed and Jack didn't move. He was frozen.

"Jack," Grace said. That's all she said. There was nothing else she *could* say.

"Keep going, Mr. Keller."

Nothing from Jack. No response to Bryan's words. No more movement. His body was rigid. The only sign that he was alive was the slow rise and fall of his chest.

"Mr. Keller, I said don't stop. I don't have much time. You don't want me to come get you."

Still nothing. He looked catatonic.

"I'm coming now," Bryan said. "And you're going to be very sorry."

Bryan put his hand on the top of the wall, pushed off, and slowly lifted himself up to step onto the ledge. He did not seem at all afraid or tentative.

Jack turned his head, the first movement he'd made in over a minute. He watched Bryan take one firm step toward him.

And he thought: *Got you, you fucker. I've got you now.*

BRYAN'S NEW PLAN was simple. Let Jack Keller get out as far as he could and just watch. He knew the man's fear would overtake him. He knew he'd fall and that would be that. The girl couldn't hang on much longer. By the time anyone else figured out where the bodies had come from, he'd be long gone. And besides, they would fall on their own. He wouldn't even have to push them. So it wouldn't even be murder. He could just walk away.

And then, once and for all, it would be over.

Bryan never figured that the fear would screw up the plan. Frozen as he was, Jack looked like he could stand there forever. And the longer this took, the more chance of failure. The key to success was always speed. Who'd said that? His coach, he thought. But which one? That guy in Virginia. He was a jerk but sometimes he was right. And he was right about speed. It was essential now. Someone could show up looking for the cop. Maybe another cleaning woman was coming. Bryan couldn't risk it. This had to stop now.

He wasn't afraid, standing on the one-foot-thick wall. Heights didn't bother him. He wasn't going to fall, no way. This was going to be easy. Just walk out and give one little shove. Then wave bye-bye. If he had to, he could do it to the girl, too. She'd be easy. All he had to do was walk out a little farther and down she'd go.

He took his first step and was surprised when Jack finally moved. The guy had been like a fucking rock. But now he turned to face Bryan and Bryan thought it was a strange movement. Not confused like it should have been. It was weirdly confident and deliberate. He didn't look so paralyzed all of a sudden. And he could even speak. How weird was that? What was he saying? What the hell did he say?

It sounded like: "Hold on, Grace. Just hold on."

And now he was saying something else. What was going on? This time it sounded like he said, "How's your knee, Bryan?"

What? His knee? His bad knee? It was like it always was. He looked down to see what the hell this guy was talking about. . . .

JACK REMEMBERED BRYAN limping out of the restaurant after their lunch with Kid. He remembered Bryan saying, after the funeral service, that he'd blown his knee out at St. John's and lost his scholarship. And just a few minutes ago he'd said the coach at Virginia State had told him he couldn't play anymore because of his knee. Bryan Bishop had a weak spot. It was time to find out just how weak.

He waited until Bryan looked down. Jack had thought the bad knee was the left one and that's where Bryan's eyes went. He didn't wait any longer.

Jack took a deep breath and dropped down. He'd spent his rigid moments trying to figure out how best to keep his balance when he let himself fall and he'd figured right. He was going down on his right side, used both hands to grab whatever brick he could and keep himself from toppling over, and he lashed out with his right foot as hard as he could. His heel connected solidly with Bryan's left knee and he could see the pain shatter Bryan's dulled expression. As Bryan bent over, Jack was already on his way up.

Don't think, don't look down, all you've got to do is make it two feet and you're back on the balcony. Two feet and you've won.

Bryan was struggling to keep his balance. He was on his side and grabbing wildly to try to keep from turning over and rolling off. Jack jumped, hurdling Bryan's thrashing body. His hands made it—his chest banged down hard on the brick but his head was over—all he had to do was pull the rest of himself over and he was on solid ground.

Bryan kicked wildly. His knee slammed into Jack's thigh and Jack could feel his lower body going over the side, but his fingers dug into the brick. His legs were dangling, Bryan had hold of his ankle, was trying to twist him over, and Jack felt his own grip weakening. He was starting to get pulled back out. He was losing. And if he lost he was dead.

You only fall if you want to fall, Jack.

You only fall if you want to fall.

I don't want to fall, Jack thought. I don't want to fall. And he realized he was not just thinking it. He was screaming it, yelling at the top of his lungs: *"I don't want to fall! I'm not going to fall! I am not going to fall!"*

He could feel the strain in his forearms as he pulled. He kicked his leg free, still screaming. He felt pain rip through his right leg—it was the knife again; he was sure Bryan had just slashed him because his leg felt as if it were on fire—but then he was over, slamming down onto the terrace floor, rolling all the way until he flipped into the cast-iron table. Without hesitating, he was up on his feet.

Bryan had regained his balance. He was on his knees, still two feet from the ledge. He was moving slowly, careful not to make a misstep. He was on his feet now, and as he faced Jack, his expression was one of murderous rage. Jack knew that Bryan thought he was running, that he was expecting Jack to head for the front door and the stairway, anything to get out of the apartment. But that wasn't Jack's intention. He wasn't running. He wasn't going to leave Grace. There would be no what-if this time. There would be no more deaths.

No. Jack knew that wasn't true. There would be one more.

Their eyes met and now Bryan seemed to be the one paralyzed. Standing on the wall, he watched, transfixed, as Jack made no move to turn and run, simply stood his ground and stared back at him. Bryan smiled because Jack was waiting for him, was going to take him on, was going to meet him man-to-man, and, making sure the knife was tightly in his grip, he took one more step forward. . . .

Jack took one step, too. He went to the barbell that sat on the terrace in the middle of the workout equipment.

This is a clean, Kid had said. *The hardest lift there is.*

Jack bent down.

The only thing holding you back is fear. He could hear Kid urging him on. *You're strong enough to get rid of the fear. You're strong enough now.* Right *now.*

Jack started to look at the weights on the end of the barbell.

Don't ask how heavy it is, Jack. It doesn't matter.

He gripped the bar, his hands shoulder-width apart.

You're strong enough now. Right *now.*

He lifted the weight up to his waist.

You are fucking Arnold.

He bent his knees, breathed in, made a sudden shift, and then the weight was above his head.

You are Hercules Unchained.

His legs wobbled but stayed firm. His arms were crooked at the elbow.

He remembered all the pain. Lying in the hospital and feeling broken. Realizing that Caroline was no longer with him, that he'd never see or touch her again. He remembered sitting in the wheelchair, crippled, and the agony and the fear that came with his struggle to once again become whole. He remembered Kid telling him he didn't just want him to be back to normal, he wanted him to be better than normal. He remembered the glory of taking off his brace and being pain-free. He remembered the Entertainer's lifeless body floating in the tub and the expression of pure horror on Samsonite's lips, her throat slashed inches away from him. He could feel McCoy's body tumbling out of the closet onto him and he envisioned Dom, his beloved Dom, being hacked to death by a lunatic who didn't know the difference between love and hate or life and death. He heard the explosions in the office in Charlottesville. Felt his life slipping away. Heard the doctor telling him that Caroline would not be coming to see him. Caroline was dead. And now he was looking at her murderer! Jack remembered running his hand over Grace's body and making love to her in the dark.

Jack Keller looked straight into the eyes of the madman who was standing on the wall, looking confused, waiting to see what he was going to do.

You're strong enough now, he told himself.

Right now.

"Bryan," Jack said. "Catch."

His knees bent, giving him the leverage he needed, then they snapped straight up. As they did Jack tossed the two hundred pounds of weight into the air, straight at Bryan Bishop. Bryan's hands reached out and his fingers curled around the barbell before it could reach him. He caught it, brought it to his body, and stood facing Jack, a thin smile lighting up his face, waiting for Jack to acknowledge his amazing act of strength. Then he realized what Jack had done. He realized that his amazing strength had just killed him.

The momentum of the barbell staggered Bryan. He bent back, way back, first his head, then his neck and shoulders, then his legs.

He couldn't keep his balance. He couldn't stop moving backward. He was shaking his head in disbelief. It didn't seem right. He was so close. He'd been so smart. It had been such a good plan.

Bryan's bad knee buckled now and he could no longer stay on his feet.

Jack saw one foot step backward, find nothing but air. Bryan's eyes widened. Then his other foot went back. He opened his mouth to speak but nothing came out.

And then he disappeared.

JACK WASTED NO time jumping up onto the ledge of the wall but he did not look to see Bryan's fall.

He moved carefully but quickly. One step then another. He made it almost all the way to the next rooftop, stopped, and bent down. He straddled the ledge with his legs, put his hand down and said, "Take my hand." When Grace didn't move, *couldn't* move, he just repeated it, very quietly, "Take my hand," he said. "Now. I won't let you fall."

He saw her close her eyes, saw her broken hand raise up toward him. When he grabbed it, he heard her gasp, but he had her and didn't let go. She reached her other hand up in the air and he grabbed that, too, slowly pulled her up, straining, fighting to keep his balance, but nothing bad was going to happen now, that he knew, this was the easy part, and then they were both on the ledge. He did not care about the street below. His head was clear and he realized the edge had lost its ability to call out to him, to grab him and pull him over. He was stronger than that. He was stronger than anything.

Still holding Grace's hand, he stood her up and they slowly walked back to his terrace.

Jack felt the heat of the sun now. And he once again heard the noise of the traffic from so far down below.

He watched as she stepped onto the terrace floor. Then he followed. They were hugging, her face buried in his chest, and he stroked her hair and told her she was safe. Told her they had won.

Jack Keller held her tight and told her that, at last, there was nothing more to fear.

BOOK FIVE

AFTER THE FALL

When he was through with the police and the extraordinary crush of media that swarmed all over him, turning him into their hero of the moment—front-page stories in every paper, television cameras outside the entrance to his apartment building, a blind offer of a book deal from three publishers, and calls from two agents and a network seeing if he was interested in a television movie about his life—Jack took a taxi down to the lower tip of Manhattan, boarded the Staten Island ferry, and took the boat over to go to Kid's grave.

Grace had asked if she could go with him and he agreed. They didn't talk on the ride over; both stood on the top deck watching the waves and letting the cool spray of the water wet their faces. At some point, their fingers touched and intertwined and they held hands until they landed on the other side.

Jack didn't know exactly what this trip was meant to accomplish but he felt it was necessary. As he stared down at the simple headstone that said "George 'Kid' Demeter," he thought of Dom saying they'd been to too many funerals. And he thought of Kid saying that, in his world, everyone was a Slash. Everyone wanted to be someone else. Everyone pretended to be what they weren't. Everybody angry and trying to escape their own skins, reaching for some elusive goal that was meant to provide a simple answer and hand over the greatest prize of all: happiness.

His head down, Jack thought about Caroline. He would never know what had truly happened between her and Kid. And he realized he didn't really care. He knew all he needed to. Whatever she had done, he forgave her. Ultimately, she had tried to help Kid; she had been kind enough and strong enough so that Kid was able to trust her, to tell her the truth, or at least the truth as he had suspected it. That truth had killed her, Jack knew, and he thought: That's what truth often does. It's why everyone's pretending. It's why everyone becomes a Slash. To try to avoid what will eventually and unfailingly destroy them.

He knew one other thing, too, and it was important to him. Caroline had chosen him. The affair had ended in Virginia and she was coming home to him. There was one truth that did not kill and one emotion that did not have to be avoided and that was love. Caroline had loved him and he had loved her and that was the only truth he needed to know. It was the only thing in the past that ultimately mattered.

He had learned about Emma, after his battle with Bryan on the terrace. She had kept a diary, it turned out, discovered after her murder, and the police allowed him to read what was relevant. It had filled in some gaps that would otherwise have remained elusive. He'd had no idea of her obsession with him; it had continued all these years. He hadn't known about her assaults on Caroline, either, and that knowledge pained him. Emma and Kid—that had been an unlikely and horrible twist of fate. Emma had moved to New York, transferred by her company, and she had seen Jack in the street, near his apartment. Strictly a coincidence. Kid had been with him. Then Kid and Emma had met at a club, one of Kid's regular haunts. She recognized him and, all these years later, the obsession resurfaced. She decided to see him, and seduce him, and then she had her connection back to Jack. Gradually, Kid had fallen for her, hard, which Jack understood. And she had, over the same period of time, gotten more and more information. In her diary, Jack read how the memory of her unfulfilled relationship with him had caused her much conflict. She was enjoying her life with Kid but she couldn't make the past go away. She, too, couldn't shake the ghosts. Finally, she had told Kid of her past with Jack and it had stunned him. She wrote in her diary: *He wanted to be Jack Keller, had fallen in love with his wife and now his mistress and so, in a sense, he'd succeeded.*

Jack could not imagine the depths of Kid's turmoil. The knowledge that he had inflicted Bryan on the world. The awareness of what he'd set in motion. But Jack did understand one thing absolutely.

It was time to leave Kid's world.

Maybe that's why he'd come out here. To say goodbye.

Jack looked up and Grace nodded. They walked out of the cemetery and, still holding hands, strolled slowly back to the ferry.

"I survived the publicity," she said as they walked.

"I knew you would," he told her.

"The *Daily News* said I redeemed myself. I was the Murderess who'd become the Heroine."

"It's over, Grace. It's all over and it doesn't matter anymore."

"You know what I think?" Grace said.

"What?"

"I don't think you *can* redeem yourself. I don't know if there's even anything to be redeemed. I think you just do what you do and you are what you are."

They walked in silence until the ferry dock came into view. "What about us?" Grace asked him. "Are we over, too?"

Jack stopped. He said, "I don't know. I think . . ." He smiled. "I don't know what the hell to think except that everything's different and I just have to see what life is like now."

"Me, too," she said. "But I'd like to see you."

"I'd like to see you, too," Jack said.

"Well, that's something, isn't it?" Grace asked.

He took her hand and they started walking again. Ahead of them, the ferry was pulling into the dock. "Yes," he told her, "that's definitely something."

THE LAST TIME Jack had been in Italy, he'd been with Caroline. He'd been young and the future held nothing but greatness.

He was back now and the future was a bit cloudier. But one thing had not changed.

"I'm starting to like this fucking thing," Dom said, tapping the side of his wheelchair as Jack wheeled him down a small side street in Milan.

"Don't get used to it. You're already supposed to be walking around."

"I'm supposed to be *dead*."

"If there's one thing we've learned about you," Jack told him, "it's that you don't die so easy."

"Twenty-seven goddamn stab wounds," Dom muttered. "*You* walk around with twenty-seven goddamn stab wounds."

"I never knew you were such a whiner," Jack said. And, after a quick, calculated pause: "Old man."

"Nothin' but grief," Dominick Bertolini said. "You never gave me nothin' but grief."

Jack found the restaurant he was looking for and settled the two of them into a table on the outdoor patio. The owner came over, introduced himself to Jack, brought over a bottle of '97 Barollo that he said was magnificent.

When Jack and Dom were alone again, they raised their glasses in a toast.

"What do you want to drink to?" Dom asked.

"You first," Jack said.

"I'd like to drink to your mother," Dom said quietly. "I think she would have liked it here."

They clinked glasses and Dom said, "Now you."

"What time is it?"

Dom glanced at his watch, a confused look on his face. "Quarter to one," he told Jack.

"Then let's drink to that," Jack Keller said. "A quarter to one." And now their glasses touched a second time, then Jack turned his face to catch the full flush of the hot afternoon sun. "I always like to see another one of those roll around."

Aphrodite

Whenever the word Aphrodite is whispered somebody dies. The victims never know what it meant: is it a person, a product, a code word – what? And why is keeping its meaning secret, so important?

Justin Westwood has retreated from reality by taking a menial post with the police department in Long Island. Mindless traffic duty and a lot of booze stop him reliving the past, but his dormant professionalism is reluctantly awakened when he realises that the death of a young journalist is deliberate, not accidental.

Retreating the woman's movements in the hours before her death, Justin learns she's been in trouble for quoting some erroneous facts in an obituary of a man who had been living in the local old people's home. Not the sort of mistake which normally brings a duo of professional hitmen to the door of a fallible reporter, and certainly not one which brings the FBI into town.

As Justin attempts to unravel the puzzle, he finds someone is a step ahead of him, disposing of witnesses and setting him up for the rap. Realising he has to face real life at its starkest if he is to survive, he goes solo – and finds himself at the centre of one of the greatest conspiracies of his time.

Hades

Police Chief Justin Westwood was content to escape his big-city past in sleepy East End Harbour. But the brutal murder of a Wall Street shark is about to change everything . . .

While Justin is in bed with his married lover, her husband is murdered. He can provide a solid alibi for her, but his own position isn't so clear cut – after all, it's he who has the contacts to arrange for his rival's removal.

At least that is what his bosses think, so Justin is on his own – it's up to him to solve the crime. A trail of dead bodies draws him back home to Providence, RI, where he must deal with the demons of his past. Here, Justin will discover a complex corporate scam with unimaginable murky depths and, at the heart of it all, a deadly individual whose greatest joy lies in human suffering and death.